THE GARDEN WHERE THE BRASS BAND PLAYED

S. VESTDIJK

THE GARDEN WHERE THE BRASS BAND PLAYED

NEW AMSTERDAM
New York

New Amsterdam edition published in the United States of America in 1989.

NEW AMSTERDAM BOOKS
171 Madison Avenue
New York, NY 10016

Originally published in Dutch as *De Koperen tuin*.

978-1-56131-037-1

This book is printed on acid-free paper.

Printed in the United States of America.

[1]

The first thing I can remember of W..., where my father was appointed a judge soon after I turned five, is that warm spring afternoon when the ball my brother and his friends were playing with came sailing over the ornate iron railings of the balcony and fell into the stillness of the drawing-room. I was sitting on the floor, near the balcony, reading a book of fairy tales. It was wonderful, just like a scene from a fairy tale, the way the ball bounced across the room. Every time I thought it had finished bouncing and was going to roll in one or other direction until it reached that mysterious point where a rolling ball comes to rest, it rose up in the air again. I can still see it falling right beside the water carafe on the table. Somehow it missed the carafe and soared on towards a forest landscape in a gilt frame. The first sound had startled me, but the movements of the ball, so clever and so careful, so young and resilient, reassured me, as if an invisible juggler was taking care that no harm would come to me or the breakable things in the room.

When the yelling in front of the house reached a menacing crescendo: 'Nol, get the ball, Nol, get the ball'—they couldn't see me, but my brother knew I was there—I scrambled to my feet and fetched the ball to throw it down to them. What else could I think of doing, jolted like that out of a book of fairy tales, meek from a surfeit of wonders. Holding the ball in my hand, I stood on the slate step of the balcony door, and below me they were stamping and shouting, and I saw them, their hair flying, jumping up trying to catch sight of me. Every time they jumped they seemed to be struck blind. I could see them, they couldn't see me. They shrieked and kept yelling: 'Nol, get the ball', and while I watched them I listened to the elms rustling in the warmth and the ptt-ptt sound of a boat in the canal at the end of our street. They were jumping higher and higher and still they couldn't see me; it was so strange and fascinating. A sudden silence was broken by my brother's piercing voice: 'What the hell are you doing, Nol? Give us the ball and be quick about it.' (My father always said 'and be quick about it.' He would say it even when there was no need to.) I knew I ought to throw the ball back but I wasn't going to take any notice of Chris. Even at that age I was beginning to find him a little ridiculous, and I understood what 'making a fuss about nothing' meant. I knew that he irritated my mother and that my father spoilt him, but I was sure all that couldn't last too long because, sooner or later, my mother would notice that at mealtimes he used to kick my shins under the table. I knew that one of these days Chris would be toppled off his high horse.

A couple of them had run farther back from the house shouting triumphantly to the others that they could see me. The spell was broken. Almost smugly, my stomach stuck out a little, I walked with slow mincing steps across the balcony, stretched my arm over the iron railings and opened my hand, languidly, like a young girl letting a scented handkerchief float down to a group of clamouring admirers. With the comic inanity of parrots foolishly repeating a name, they went on jeering for a while: 'Rotten Nol.' Chris didn't join in the chorus, he was satisfied with what he thought was a prompt reaction to his command. From a house or so further on there came the elastic smack of the ball against the wall, then they were gone, and when I could still hear 'Nol', it might have been 'ball'. Away to the right there was a big open square where the space would swallow their noise.

The longer I stood there with my hands empty, the more I regretted that I had given in to them. It was all Chris's fault. None of the others would have dared to throw the ball so that it would fall in the drawing-room and maybe cost my parents a good hundred guilders. Instead of dropping the ball to them, I should have gone and told my mother. That was telling tales, but I had been sitting there reading a fairy tale, and dwarfs and elves and mermaids didn't 'tell tales', they took their complaints to higher beings of their own kind and it nearly always turned out

6

that they were in the right. But besides, I felt that any trick at all was good enough to get even with Chris. I could have pretended I'd had a fright, maybe I could even have cried. As I went and sat down again to finish reading my story I was hoping that the ball would come flying through the window again.

The warm street with the elm trees was wrapped in a mysterious silence. Beyond the silence there was the ptt-ptt of the boats, and once or twice a bell tinkled to warn the bridge-keeper. That tinkling always used to make me think that the strangest things happened with the boats on the canal, especially late in the evening, when there were so many green and red lights. Once my mother had explained to me that when the bell rang the bridge-keeper came running out of his house over to the bridge (later I found out that he didn't have a house at all and that he was there at the bridge all the time) and, with his face all tense, started turning, or pushing rather, and the bridge opened. But I didn't believe this explanation. For me the tinkling of the bell was a sign, a prelude to something unimaginable, a shipwreck maybe, or a procession of boats hung with flags, with music playing and lanterns between the masts. I was sure it was the bridge-keeper who rang the bell, and that the boats did what he wanted them to do, at least, nearly always. All day he carried this wonderful toy around with him—and I, I had let an ordinary brown ball fall out of my hand for those others to run off with. Now it was desecrated, unclean. All at once I was frightened that I might be hit on the head by the ball thrown unexpectedly from the noisy square over there, and I went away.

A few years later something happened that made me feel I was getting the better of Chris. Halfway through that period, when I was still at the elementary school, I'd been nicknamed 'the judge's son', and I liked to hear this, because it was my tactic in my undeclared war against Chris, who was three years older than me, to use the most indirect weapons and manoeuvres, with an occasional unexpected gesture. 'The judge's son', so full of his own importance, excelled in unprovoked attacks on weaker school-mates, hoping that Chris, who hardly ever got into a fight, would be watching from a distance. I acted with a faultless intuition and an innate self-control. If I'd been asked why I hit the other boys, I wouldn't have been able to answer, I wouldn't have been able to reason it out, I would only have felt vaguely that it was because they were smaller than I was.

Chris had no intuition. It was all temperament with him, super-ficial, pseudo-brilliant. He was excitable, he tried to make an impression by talking, boasting, jeering, he had a dash of youthful presumption that would soon be used up, then there'd be nothing left, he'd be finished, completely finished. As far as I know he was never called 'the judge's son', probably because he had started school quite a while before my father's appointment, or maybe because he was always trying to play the little judge, with those shining glasses of his and his feverish, but always cold and calcu-lating, bombast. In our daily 'Rotten Nol-Rotten Chris' duel I always let him come off best, it gave me a feeling of inward calm. Once he said: ' "Rotten Nol", everyone understands that, but "Rotten Chris" doesn't count, it's different.' 'Why?' I asked naïvely. 'The Javanese say "rotten kris", you fool.' These puzzling words were accompanied by a clumsy stabbing movement aimed at my chest. It never entered his head that he could have humiliated me far more easily by pointing out that 'Rotten Nol' was at least original and 'Rotten Chris' was only a childish imitation. Later I was sure that it was one of his friends who had been the first to say 'Rotten Nol.' Mostly I'd say, 'Names'll never hurt me.' This was more tactful than 'You hit me, and I'll hit you back', because Chris was still stronger than I was then.

The certainty of my triumph over Chris was hinted at most of all in our contrasting complexions. I took after my mother, healthy and ruddy-cheeked, while Chris, worn-out with his noisy, restless squabbling, got paler and paler, and once he was taken to the doctor to be examined, a disgrace he always tried to cover up.

Not long afterwards, at supper one evening, he said that he'd heard me coughing all night long. It was a lie, but when he said it he believed it. Admittedly, I got all the commonplace childhood illnesses first—measles, mumps, and chicken-pox too, I think—and he'd caught them from me. That wasn't anything unusual, but then he got bronchitis, whooping cough, nephritis, and everything else that drives parents to despair just when they think all the trouble is over. All the same, he was far noisier than I was when he had to stay in bed sick.

At mealtimes, too, he always had a lot to say, but he knew he was safe because my father was on his side. My mother, I was sure, was watching all the time, with that gentle smile of hers, for a chance to come down on him, but no one could really object to talking at table when it was mostly telling about something that had happened, or asking questions. It all seemed so reasonable, so grown-up, so intelligent. There was the afternoon when he showed he knew more about the local town council—the names of the councillors, anyway—than my father, who listened benignly and then explained to him in well-chosen phrases the right of the specialist to restrict himself to his own particular subject. A judge only needed to know who was guilty and the reasons for a verdict. My mother burst out laughing and said softly, as if she was speaking to herself, that a guilty councillor was treated differently from a rag-and-bone man, whether he was guilty or innocent—but I'm not sure any more if she said this last bit as well.

My father's name is Rieske. His grandfather was, as they say, 'of German origin', though he was in fact German, neither rich nor distinguished, but he did manage to send his son to the university. That side of my family excelled in determination and diligence, and the women were given to a heavy sentimentality. Despite three generations of mixed stock my father was the most German of them all in manner and appearance, thoughtful and serious, peering through those watchful spectacles, a mannerism Chris had inherited from him. He was formal, even for a judge, but in lighter moments, in the company of friends, he was not without a certain sharp-witted joviality, which he had stopped indulging in, however, by the time I was seven or eight.

Both sides of the family are musical, but my father could not listen with his eyes ecstatically closed to anything later than Brahms and Schumann, both of whom my mother played badly and without interest. She used to sing. She preferred Wolf and Duparc, and soon after we came to live in W ... she began taking lessons from the mercilessly strict Mijnheer Talsma, who was too shy to stand on a platform and conduct a choir. He left the choir-leading to a lively young fellow, I can't remember his name, who wasn't there long before he was off to somewhere else more promising. Chris had lessons from Mijnheer Talsma, but music wasn't his strong point, and I hated the sound of Chris playing because I hated Chris. He kept time by stamping his foot. He made noises as well. He played every piece over and over and he could never get it right. There are sonatinas by Clementi that I still can't hear without a sick feeling in the pit of my stomach. The tunes used to linger in my head even after I was asleep, and then get mixed with the clanging of bells from barges that probably weren't there.

Even if Chris didn't have any musical talent I couldn't imagine that he didn't get some pleasure from playing or that he mightn't later develop an appreciative ear. My father had told us about Mozart as a little boy—much younger than Chris was—and how his father had to take a stick to him to make him practise the piano or harpsichord, and his sister too, and afterwards Mozart was always mad about music. Maybe there are people who hate what they are good at, like office clerks, for example, or teachers, but with Mozart it wasn't like that, no, you could tell at once from the music he'd composed.

As for myself, when I was very young I was like Mozart had been, I didn't want to go near a piano, though I secretly enjoyed listening to my mother singing, especially when the little stuttering

Court Recorder, Mijnheer van Son, played the accompaniment for her, jerkily but without mistakes. When my mother accompanied herself, and he turned the pages for her, he lapsed into a sort of artistic abandon, which was expressed in the almost violent grab he would make at the sheet as my mother reached the last notes, his arm brushing past her right shoulder. With knees slightly bent and leaning forward he propelled himself quickly over the carpet like a timid aesthete scurrying away from some milling throng. He always stood at least a yard behind my mother, probably so he wouldn't distract her with an all too attentive shadow on the edge of her field of vision. Chris, even though he had no sense of humour, could imitate him perfectly (I think my mother must have started it in an unguarded moment), and his 'A-a-are you r-r-ready, M-M-Mevrouw?' repeated ten times over, was amusing for anyone who knew the little Court Recorder. My father usually stopped Chris, looking disapprovingly over the table: 'Now, that's quite enough,' and then Chris kicked me in the shins as if he was passing the order on. I got used to this Prussian mannerism, but I still wondered why he did it. At that age it upset me far more that he took up so much of my mother's time, running to her with his complaints, his questions, his confessions, the latest news and football rules, and the depths of rivers. It was worse once I had started going to school: every time I wanted to be alone with my mother after I came home in the afternoon I'd find Chris there.

Late one afternoon I heard him practising the piano. I ran into the sitting-room to get as far away from the noise as I could. At every false note—and there were a lot that afternoon, it wasn't Clementi this time but a piece by Dussek, I knew by heart every mistake he made in it—something welled up inside me, hate, gloating, rebellion, aversion to all music, perhaps a longing for a different kind of music. All of a sudden he stopped playing and banged the piano shut. He slammed it with a mad force, the crash must have echoed out into the street, leaving a vacuum that could only be filled, it seemed, by the sound of frightened whimpering. There was a long silence. But at last I heard his voice in the distance, and, much more softly, my mother's voice. Then, for the first time in his life as far as I can remember, he burst out crying, wailing with drawn-out groans, and gulping for breath. There was nothing put-on about this crying. It was a long pent-up resentment breaking loose. It was like the whining howl of a solitary wolf in the night, beyond all sympathy or consolation. As I tiptoed along a passage and across a room to get as near as I could, my heart pounded with a painful, fear-laden happiness that I had never experienced before. I didn't know then what it was, but I do now. It was sympathy, what the grown-ups called sympathy. This new, unknown feeling gave me a boundless pleasure, and if I hadn't wanted to hear what was going on in the next room I would have sunk into a chair and leaned back with my eyes closed like my father did when he was listening to music composed before 1860... 'I just won't, I won't. I won't go near that bully anymore, I can't do my schoolwork if I've got to learn music from that pig... Let him play his own piano himself...' While my mother reasoned with him, he kept banging the piano open and shut, sniffing and snivelling all the time. Something tinkled near my ear. The crying started all over again and I heard my mother promise him something. I scurried off. In a minute or so Chris was quiet, and I sat in a corner of another room, sobbing because of the shock and the sympathy I felt.

Both of us came to supper with red-rimmed eyes, looking dazed, like geese after a storm. It had already been decided that Chris didn't have to go to piano lessons any more. After the soup he had just as much to say as ever, but during the dessert, when my father told him to keep quiet, he didn't kick me, which was just as well for him, because, despite the sympathy that gave me a glow of pleasure for days afterwards, I had my answer ready. I wasn't going to say: 'He kicked me, the beast', as I had done once and been sent to the kitchen by my father. I'd just make a sign, a movement of my hand, tracing the course of a tear down my own cheek with a finger.

The events of that day brought us a little closer to each other. After all, we had both cried in chorus, and besides, Chris wanted to be sure that no one else heard about the scene he'd made, and though he had never caught me telling tales, he didn't know what I might say at school. We felt bound together by a new hate we shared, and from then on we united to avoid those impromptu musical gatherings that might be organized at any hour of the day. Not only Mijnheer van Son, but other young men, some not so young, as well as local ladies with whom my mother had become friendly during the couple of years we had been living there, would drop in. They were all musical, some more, some less than the others. The judge's two sons formed a temporary alliance against the screeching and bellowing and tittering and cups of tea, and we spoke about Dijkhuizen, Caspers and young Tjallingii with just as much contempt as we bestowed on the stuttering Court Recorder. Occasionally we heard some talk of a lawyer called Vellinga, but in that period we never saw him. It was Chris's tactic to impress me by preserving a mysterious silence about this Mijnheer Vellinga, while implying that he knew quite a lot about him. But Chris knew so much, and his knowledge seemed to me to be only a trick to confuse a younger brother.

2

The first time my mother took me to the Garden it was one of those hot summer afternoons. My father was away, and Chris was off for the day on a school outing. If I'm not mistaken, this visit to the most elegant of the pleasure spots in W... occurred after our annual family holiday, when Chris's boredom always ended in summer diarrhoea, and my parents would say nothing for half-days at a time, not that they weren't speaking to each other. We always went to some quiet and dusty place, and stayed in a hotel or boarding-house where it was possible to purchase, for a fancy price, the illusion of being superior to the other guests—a room each for my brother and myself, private service for the whole family, disdainful nods or vague smiles to people with whom my mother would be expected to exchange no more than a few casual remarks in the course of the day, and the righteousness and olympian determination of my father as he emerged from behind a barrier of pleated newspapers for our morning stroll which was performed in double file.

Yes, it must have been after one of those weeks of imprisonment in the open air that my mother unexpectedly took me with her. She had a carriage come and fetch us, and on the way she collected three of her friends—she called for five of them but two weren't at home—so that I had to sit up beside the driver and ride through the town to the accompaniment of female voices half muffled by colourful parasols. My mother had to catch up on the gossip, it was like medicine for her, the words, the exclamations, the bursts of laughter about nothing at all. The day was hot. The clatter of the wheels made me sleepy, and the flies on the horses' backs posed sombre riddles. After watching the coachman, I concluded that he was aiming at the flies with his whip, but every time the whip cracked, or coiled and twisted from a skilful flick of his wrist, there was never more than one fly out of a group of thirty or so that moved. The coachman didn't speak. That performance of his, that pointless twirling of his whip, so far away and safe from all the animals in the world, wasn't enough to evoke my admiration. I sat with my arms folded, and I noticed that none of the houses threw a shadow that reached our heads. Sometimes a shadow fell very near, an expanse of coolness floated towards us, and my sweat-soaked skin experienced a soothing shock, as if I had plunged into an underground cave, or a Moorish courtyard, or a leafy valley in Luxemburg where, to judge by the numerous picture postcards, my father was staying. But because the houses were never high enough, or because the streets weren't narrow enough, we were always just out of range. The parasols too—I was watching them particularly—glistened and drooped in the heat, and under those parasols, away below me like figures on a tiny grass lawn in summer, the ladies sat chattering.

We clattered over a wide, arched bridge and I tried to listen to what they were saying: 'A change, but I always say the music is in the notes.' 'And what sort of music,' another one said sarcastically. Then a few minutes later: 'I'm going to have a glass of milk, everything is rubbish there...' 'Except the éclairs,' my mother said, and they all burst out laughing loudly, rolling from side to side, to the delight of an old man with a beard who raised his cap to them. A little further on a coolness glided over us. A real coolness this time, welling out of the shadow together with a grimy statue, and stone posts with chain railings, and a gothic building —my mother had once told me it was gothic—and at least three gentlemen who greeted our arrival. While the ladies giggled behind their languidly drooping parasols, I thought I recognized young Mijnheer Tjallingii. I looked round stealthily, and there he was, a smiling cynosure, skinny as a stick, his back slightly hunched. His straw hat absorbed all the light in that austere, half-historic square, for in those days the young Tjallingiis didn't wear light summer suits.

Once more the sun wrenched the rows of houses apart, and then we were at the Garden. Holding on to the coachman, I climbed down from the seat and gazed at the silent water in the moat from which the Garden rose up like an abandoned castle covered with green vegetation. It rose higher and higher. Under the treetops the bold curving outlines stretched into the distance through the shrubbery. Against that background, the gate at which the coach had stopped, where visitors were buying entrance tickets, looked grotesquely low and voracious, like the fanged jaws of a sea monster on the surface of the water. On either side of the gate was a weather-beaten pillar. While my mother paid the coachman and bought the tickets—they'd been fussing about this all the time—the ladies surrounded me as if I was their prisoner and I marched through the gate under a canopy of colourful parasols. My mother soon caught us up. Her face was red and perspiring, her small blue eyes glittered as if she had just played a trick on someone.

We went on up the path. It divided and came together, again and again, every time forking to the left and right of a sturdy beech trunk or a chestnut tree that had finished flowering. There were other groups walking in front of us and behind us. The ladies were silent, gathering their strength for more conversation. All of a sudden my mother tapped me on the cheek fairly hard and said I could run off now and go for a walk or play on my own, it was still early, if I came back to the restaurant in half an hour (I was to ask if I couldn't find it) I'd get a glass of milk and an éclair, yes, an éclair. I could have all I wanted, one of her friends called out, and I laughed obediently with them. It couldn't have been more than a minute before they were out of sight. I still don't know whether they went off and left me, or if it was the other way round, or if we were separated by the crowd. I stepped out boldly, and suddenly I didn't notice the heat any more. I was wearing a sailor suit with brass anchors.

There couldn't have been a shadier garden than this one that spread over the slope where the old wall around the town had stood. Under the trees it was cool and green, here and there black.

It would be cold there, I thought to myself, and where arm-thick creepers twined round the trunks of fenced-off beech trees it would be damp as well. Then there were the elms, as big as the elms that stretched their branches over our street, dozens of them along the sides of the pathways and on the open lawns where you could walk or sit. The path I had taken went up and up, and everyone in the crowd I was following walked bent forward. Farther on, in clouds of dust, well-dressed children were playing, and higher up still, a covered walk led to a ridge half hidden behind a barrier of wild bushes. That would be the top of the steep slope, but how could I reach it, which group of grown-ups should I follow to get as far as that? I heard a nanny saying: 'It's still far too early.' A group of children rushed over to a row of small cages. They came scampering from every direction, running towards two other nannies who were beckoning and making explanatory gestures. As I recognized at least three of them from my school, I felt myself more than ever 'the judge's son', and so, solemn and gravely self-confident, I went over to them and stood with them, watching a troop of brown or gold-tinted birds they were all calling pheasants. There were some friendly birds I didn't know the names of strutting up and down, there was a little peacock with trailing tail, there were sparrows twittering round a feed-bowl in one of the cages and the bird in this cage kept out of sight in the hutch in a corner at the back. After the cages with hordes of white mice there was a white goose that made musical whistling noises, it had a kindly glow in its black, red-ringed, little eyes, even when it hissed absurdly at a dog in front of its cage and stuck out its hard and sharp tongue. Then more gold and brown, the glittering vanity of other 'pheasants' pecking at seeds. All the birds looked tame. Listless in the heat, the children did nothing more than kick up dust and stick fingers through the wire netting that was rusty here and there. The nannies were silent.

That was the end of the row of cages, and a little later I was playing with some still younger children, whose nanny, or mother, or cousin, had intimated with a stroke of the hand over my sailor suit that she had no objection to letting me take over an irksome responsibility. These children followed me as their acknowledged leader, they followed me even when I ran as hard as I could past rows of trees and across grassy patches, going up higher and then down again, but never going down too far. Perhaps I ran like that to shake them off, but I would have been disappointed if they hadn't kept following me. Every now and then I jumped up and down waving my arms round to frighten them or maybe to encourage them. Little girls with sweaty faces screeched: 'Nol, there's Nol!' (I'd crept out of sight behind a tree.) I was a little annoyed at my mother because it was really her fault that I'd got mixed up with these silly little kids. Still, I felt happy, and I kept thinking that if Chris was here too I wouldn't let him see me. But would Chris ever come here? The park was too beautiful, it would all be spoilt if he came. With these babies, who all seemed to know my name, trailing behind me, I raced past bright coloured flowers and deep green shade, past tumbledown summer houses and ever so many benches where, besides men and women, old ladies and gentlemen were sitting, and the newest nannies as well, their prams, symbol of their tiresome task, with white teddy bears sleeping inside, nearby on the path. The nicest thing of all was that the whole garden lay on a slant. Here and there right down the slope grass lawns surged up like mountain lakes, the patches of light-green broken by the figures of playing children or a man sitting with his black knees drawn right up to his chin.

After passing a row of blue fir trees with my yelling convoy I reached the highest point, the ridge I hadn't lost sight of all the time, which, though it looked jagged from a distance, was fairly level. Away below us a nanny clapped her hands and called out something. I pushed straight on through the bushes right to the edge, which was built up with big stones, and I clamped my arms round one of them before I dared look down. The nanny must have been clapping again because now the children behind me were asking me if I was coming back with them, and when I didn't answer one of the little girls said: 'Silly Nol!' and gave me a push in the back. There was a crackling of branches behind me. The nanny stopped clapping. Entranced with wonder I stood looking down over the edge.

My eyes feasted on the most unexpected, the most inviting, the most exotic valley imaginable. This wide round crater couldn't have been more than thirty feet deep and the height of the rock wall directly beneath me not more than half that, but it all looked to me as immense as the chasms in the photos of the Bavarian Alps my father had hanging in his study. Over on the other side the garden started again. In the bottom of this miniature valley there was a pond surrounded by a border of red flowers and ornamental metalwork. A rustic bridge of beech branches, the upper section rotten in parts, and so long that it seemed to have been built to meet the contingency of heavy floods, led to a huge, enormously high wooden structure with a rounded rear wall, that I could only see part of from where I was. Three men were sitting there holding brass instruments in their hands. One of the three was waving across the pond to where a baby, held up by its mother, was waving back.

On the other side of the pond there were people sitting on endless rows of chairs, with tables here and there in between. There were glasses of milk on nearly all the tables. At the other end of the bridge, to the left, opposite the bandstand where the three men were, stood another building that must be the restaurant. This was also of wood, but painted bright yellow, while the bandstand was a warm brown with a black, rather dirty dome. The bright-painted building was as big as a large house, but not as high. A waiter came out of the door carrying a tray piled with sandwiches, no, they were éclairs, the éclairs that seemed to be so amusing. As well as the waiters, there were girls in white aprons serving the tables. A few people were strolling along the path round the pond to the bandstand, and some children too, but I couldn't see a single pram or any nannies. Far away on the left was a row of tables on a raised pathway sheltered by lime trees and right next to a low wall with little round openings like the windows in old stables. This wall reached out from the restaurant like a protecting arm that didn't end anywhere, as if the fingers had seized and blended invisibly with the shrubbery.

From the path a lawn sloped downwards, too steep for chairs or tables. Treetops rose up above the bandstand roof, moving majestically in the fierce sunlight, nodding and bowing, and now and then exposing a white, scaly streak where lightning had struck years and years ago.

I was wondering if my mother would be sitting at one of the tables away down there, or at one of the tables by the lime trees on the pathway over the old city wall, nearly as high up as I was, when I noticed a short thick-set man in a morning coat who had appeared on the steps of the restaurant. He stood there all alone and wiped his forehead with a white handkerchief. His face looked red, he had a black moustache, he looked like someone who was going to conquer the world. He wasn't alone for long: three or four others came out and joined him and there was a lot of handshaking. Maybe he was the manager of the restaurant, or even manager of the whole Garden, or perhaps he was a rich foreigner who was finding the heat too much for him. When he was by himself on the steps again, I saw that the waitresses dodged out of his way, laughing, so I supposed he pinched these girls (and perhaps the waiters, too) in the arm as they went past, and they could do nothing to stop him. This was good fun, I thought, and while I was planning how I could climb down the rock wall so as to be as close as possible to him he strode towards the rustic bridge, his head held high. Resolutely I put my leg over the top of the ridge, lowering myself on to a steep pathway, a narrow but not really dangerous goat-track between rough, unruly rocks that I gently stroked with my hand and held on to tightly at every turn.

Sliding more than I ran, I reached a sloping stretch of grass and when I crossed this lawn I found myself looking into the eyes of an old park attendant who shook his finger at me reprovingly. Far behind him, the man in the morning coat went up the steps of the bandstand as bursts of applause echoed from every side. The old park attendant apparently hadn't noticed that I had come from the ridge up above, or maybe there was an aura of distinction about the 'judge's son'. In any case, after a bit of mumbling he let me step over the curved white-painted railings. I made my way furtively towards the restaurant. There was hardly a sound. Then all of a sudden the thunder of the music broke loose.

From where I was standing I had a view right into the back of the bandstand, the taut faces behind the glinting brass instruments, the red necks that blew out the music, the big round bass-drum, the sheepish figures holding the flutes and clarinets, and all this guided and roused to a frenzy by the vigorous movements of the man in the morning coat. He stood and rocked back and forward and swung from side to side on an upturned box draped with a dark-green cloth. He waved and twirled his baton, proud and sure of himself, yet there were gentler qualities in him. If he wished, that baton could suddenly evoke pain and sorrow. I couldn't look away from the bandstand, the music was quivering in my bones, in my head, in my spine.

It wasn't till a long while later that I learnt what they were playing. It was Sousa's 'Stars and Stripes', a stirring march by a long forgotten composer that was sweeping Holland just as it had swept America. What a blaring flourish the composer used to announce a jaunty, yet dignified ramble. After the opening flourish, a passage as ruthless as a hangman, ringing with truculent unconcern for man and god and the American flag, then a placid calm, a cunning reticence, a discreet whispering. The trio began

21

with a sly, swaggering step. It had the lilt of a bright, catchy song, but cautious, tactfully subdued, filled with hints of violence, of hard blows and the crash and clatter of fighting, all suddenly heightened to a thunderous volume that made me tremble. The acoustics of the crater could hardly cope with this whirlwind of sound, every tree, every stone, every bit of ground seemed to be roaring in chorus with it. The biggest brass instruments were shaking like drenched poodles. The drums joined in the jungle clamour, there was a piercing clash of cymbals, next a slower pace with all the band playing, the conductor shrinking himself up by some fantastic contortion to control this massive ritardando, a new tone, a new pattern, no, it wasn't the logical sequence of an even more nerve-shattering outburst, no, it was only the re-emergence of the half forgotten trio, enlivened this time by the raving of a high-pitched piccolo, an interlude of feverish twittering that sent wonderful shivers over my back, making me want to whistle and shout and laugh and cry, ending abruptly when the last tremulous notes gave way to an enraged blast, a signal for the march to resume, to unfold itself again like an entrancing, amazing vision. Now I had some idea of what sort of man the conductor was, I could see what a tyrant he must be. He would stop at nothing. He was surely the greatest man in W...

While my hero, the conductor, acknowledged the irregular patter of lukewarm applause, not so much bowing as gesturing towards the orchestra as if he was presenting the musicians one by one to the audience, I made my way to the entrance of the restaurant. He'd have to pass through that door sooner or later. A few young men were standing there together, and a group of gentlemen wandered back and forward in the entrance, not wearing morning coats, but disclosing their higher status by the way they turned round quickly when the music began, by their patronizing glances at the audience and by their familiarity with each other. They blew clouds of cigar smoke in each other's faces and, laughing mockingly, went inside, still keeping an eye on everything, then they were standing in the entrance again, or at least some of them.

All through the next piece, a selection from some opera or operetta, I kept my eyes glued on the conductor. There was an intimidating strength in him, but he was a comedian as well— that was obvious from the jokes he made with the musicians, little exchanges that didn't affect the flow of music. The man behind the drum, who was pounding out a deafening rumble after a soft mellow passage from the flute, was shaking with laughter just because the conductor had looked at him. But then my hero, his white handkerchief pushed inside his collar, turned the frivolity into earnestness again, and, in the quiet of the sweltering afternoon under the rainbow arch of a new, too sweet melody, he made a pleading bow to the left, his right arm coaxing more and more wood pigeons out of the four upraised flutes.

There was a lot of whispering and talking and lighting of cigarettes going on around me. This would have annoyed me if the music hadn't made me dead-tired. I suppose the others were tired too and were only trying to keep themselves awake. While the orchestra was playing the third piece I noticed a tall, pale girl in front of the restaurant, a little way from the restless, cigar-smoking gentlemen. She was standing there by herself, watching the band. The waiters and waitresses streamed past her with milk and éclairs and lemonade and blackberries in gin, but her eyes never moved, and I sensed in her the same excitement I felt at the miracle that was taking place on the other side of the pond.

When the last piece before the interval was almost finished a waiter hurried over the bridge with a sheet of note-paper in his hand. From somewhere high up behind me there was a sound of yelling and cheering. It could have been students jumping up and down around the first table on the tree-lined pathway beside the low wall, swaying and waving their arms. The stone stairway going up past the restaurant was crowded with people, so it was hard to see them clearly. The conductor bent down, almost losing his balance for a moment, to take the paper from the waiter, then facing the audience, he read it through without a trace of embarrassment. He had a broad, smooth forehead, and jet-black, curly hair. He stroked his moustache with a mechanical movement of his fingers. He swung round suddenly and said something to the musicians, they moved, some listlessly, some nervously, putting a new sheet of music over the one they had just played. He tapped his magic baton on the stand in front of him, the baton went up, his left arm lifted and the march boomed out, the 'Stars and Stripes'.

I was filled with such a warm surge of gratitude, such a tingling elation, that I looked around expecting to see a glow of excitement in every face. But there wasn't a sign of it. I felt disappointed, I felt that I had something like a sacred duty to protect the march from unresponsiveness and indifference. After all, I had already formed an attachment to this march. I had a responsibility to see it wasn't neglected, and there were other things I could do to attract attention besides writing notes. For a while I stamped my feet in time with the music. I wasn't the only one doing this but I kicked up much more dust, and the space that cleared around me was an irresistible invitation to do something more than stamp, to march up and down, to skip and jump in march tempo. I took no notice of the tittering I heard. It was cooler now, so I could throw my arms and legs about without being bathed in sweat. If I'd known how to I would have stood on my head to make them understand. Even though I was hardly listening to the music any more, it was only the rhythm that pounded inside me, in my legs, in my clownishly wobbling head. Still, I was an embodiment of the march, I was Sousa's slave and defender, I was the majestic expression of his music. I heard snatches of laughter. Oh yes, some of them were laughing, but hadn't they all seen the waiter handing the note to the conductor, couldn't they hear the music, hadn't they come to enjoy good music...?

Just then two cool, slender hands clasped mine. I looked up and, at the end of the loosely forged chain our arms had formed, the tall, pale girl I had seen near the entrance was swaying gracefully with me in time with the band. She was a head taller than I was. Sometimes it seemed that she pulled me closer to her, but I knew that she would never let me put my arm round her as in an ordinary dance. No matter how tightly she held on to me we danced opposite each other rather than with each other. Two light-blue, moist, almost liquid, but mischievously laughing eyes held mine hypnotically, as we moved slowly, circling round and round. When the trio started she said: 'Haven't you got red cheeks!' As the piccolo whirled its blustering, saucy impertinence across the park her eyes lit up, she tossed back her ash-blond hair, and a soft blush spread over the almost transparent white of her cheeks. After this, a short, fast whirl, that I was barely able to keep up with, then she let my hands go and flew back to her place near the doorway where I saw her, through clouds of dust and the throbbing mist in my eyes, standing just as motionless as before. Her face was turned toward the bandstand, she didn't give me another glance, and I felt a fool. It wasn't nice of her. But there could be another reason. She was older than me, she was grown-up, I told myself, and it was always like that with grown-ups, they would play with children, then suddenly go off without a word of explanation. I wanted to say to her: 'We danced together' by way of confirmation in case she thought it was only a childish game, but I didn't dare go over to her, especially as the gentlemen had come out on to the steps again.

I could hear more snatches of laughter. I turned round and looked up into my mother's laughing face. She was standing behind one of the tables under the lime trees, like the students or whatever they were, but much farther to the left. She hadn't waved, she hadn't clapped, she looked and laughed, and I had a feeling that when she looked it had nothing to do with her laughter, and I thought she might be worried about me. I stayed where I was, limp with tiredness waiting for the end of Sousa's march, when the crowd would thin out again.

Before the applause had died down the red-faced, sweating musicians came walking over the bridge, their brass instruments gleamed forlornly under the high arch of the light-brown bandstand. It puzzled me that the conductor didn't exercise his right to walk in front, but as soon as they had all got over to the other side of the pond he pushed his way energetically forward, a broad smile under his marvellous black moustache. His forehead was red and shiny, and under the forehead were two jet-black eyes with a fierce, bold gleam. The pale girl rushed towards him and flung her arms round his neck, hugging him tighter than I could have hugged my mother. She was wearing a blue dress, and one of her black-stockinged knees was raised as if she was going to climb up on to his shoulders that weren't so much higher than hers. During the few seconds that his arm was round her waist he looked past her towards the entrance to the restaurant, where those gentlemen were standing. I couldn't hear what he called out to them, but he looked pleased, and a little expectant too, and his voice was deep, strong and penetrating, as if the sound wasn't absorbed by the space around him. He gave the girl a last squeeze, then let her go and followed them inside.

When I reached the path by the row of lime trees, I wasn't welcomed as a Don Juan—though one of the ladies stroked my dust-grimed sailor's collar—nor as a naughty show-off, but just as a little boy wanting a glass of milk. The milk was ordered, and then came the joke about the éclairs all over again. If the waiter knew why it was that the éclairs sometimes tasted like cardboard and at other times really tasted as they should, he didn't tell anyone, he walked through the barrage of scornful questions with an expression of self-assured innocence, carrying a tray heaped with fifteen big éclairs—they had smaller ones too—that I couldn't notice anything special about except a lot of air inside them. They were smooth and soft, one bite and that was all, and soon there wasn't much left of the heap on the tray. But the ladies, bursting with laughter or making sarcastic remarks, hadn't done with the éclairs, and whenever the waiter who had served us came past they teased him about the restaurant pastries, while he raised his eyebrows, tilted his head to one side, politely nodded and laughed with them. I thought one of them would throw an éclair at his head. A long while afterwards I heard that the éclairs in the Garden restaurant were always stale and tasteless, except at weekends.

One of my mother's friends said that the programme after the interval was boring and they might just as well go, but they all stayed till the end. Pressed against my mother's knee, a half-eaten éclair in my hand and my stomach full of milk, I watched the uneven shadows of the trees near the pond stretching nearer and nearer to the bandstand, where the miracle of sound went on too long, too overwhelmingly. I couldn't see the girl anywhere, I didn't care. I couldn't make up my mind whether it was an indelible disgrace or a heroic feat to have danced with her. I wasn't sure what my mother and her friends thought about it. I can still remember how the conductor lost his balance in the middle of a breathless polka, with the big drum banging loud enough to burst, and how an agile flautist caught him just in time and pushed him up straight again on his draped dais. I felt empty and disillusioned. After all, it was him I had danced for and he had only taken notice of that pale girl. She was only a few years older than me, maybe less.

I interrupted the whispering ladies by asking my mother fretfully: 'How old is that girl I was dancing with?' and she made out she didn't understand: 'Were you dancing with a girl?' 'You don't even know how to dance,' one of her friends said. She had scrawny, pale yellow cheeks and spectacles, and when she said this she looked sideways past me as if I had already taken up too much of their time. I looked at her for as long as I could, annoyed at the way she ignored me. But the grown-ups could wait, I had to settle with Chris first and that might take years and years.

3

It was weeks before I got to know anything more about my conductor because I didn't ask straight out. His name was Cuperus, the tall girl was his daughter Trix, and she was twelve, four years older than I was. *Henri* Cuperus, the gallic touch of the Christian name gave lustre to a reputation not, in our town at least, particularly distinguished. It was from my mother, who enjoyed a musical Sunday afternoon with a few of her friends and sometimes one or two gentlemen as well, Mijnheer van Son, Mijnheer Caspers or young Tjallingii, with their jokes about the marches and the waltzes, that I gathered he had only recently come to live in W . . ., he came from a very ordinary family, but he had studied a year or so at the conservatoire, everyone found him impossible, though he wasn't really disliked, not even in the clannish little villages where he had been an organist before he came here. I wasn't able to follow most of this talk. But the word 'impossible' was vaguely familiar, and when I asked what it meant, I got an answer like 'he thinks he's an artist', an explanation my mother didn't seem to find very convincing herself. It sounded, despite the undertone of derision in her voice, too glib and commonplace. According to Chris, Cuperus drank like a fish, and this almost caused our first fight.

In September she had a lot more to tell about him, a long tale my father listened to with no other reaction but a sarcastic gleaming of his spectacles, though his comments at the end of it were more reasonable than anything else that was said. Apparently Cuperus had suffered a crushing blow. It wasn't the tuberculosis his wife suffered from that had crushed him, and it was nothing to do with his daughter, who was 'too much of a handful' for him. He stood humiliated before his Muse, the public and the gentlemen of the Management Committee. The Committee, my mother disclosed, had noticed long ago that the man . . . well . . . (at this pause, Chris emptied several imaginary glasses, but my mother ignored this pantomime although she had actually provoked it) well, anyway, this... little habit of his didn't seem to affect his musical talents, and if he could have conducted a Liszt rhapsody without falling into the pond no one would have minded the difference in his complexion before and after the interval, even if that didn't come from too much milk or too many éclairs. My mother lowered her eyes and gave me a furtive glance. Most of what she had been saying was too involved for me, but now I listened carefully. 'Do you mean he got drunk?' I asked sharply. My mother didn't answer. She sat saying nothing for five or six long seconds. Then she shook her head. Chris looked at her open-mouthed. That precocious, but always erratic, intelligence of his just couldn't fathom these contradictions.

It wasn't a Liszt rhapsody that Cuperus had come a cropper over, but the *Tannhäuser* overture. That fateful afternoon he had marched up to the bandstand like a messenger of the gods, his face heavily flushed, his black, curly hair falling over his forehead. Every few paces he pulled hard at the handrail of the bridge, trying to rip away the branches, but up on the draped box he gave an even fiercer demonstration with an impromptu speech to the fairly large audience. They'd messed about enough now, there'd been more than enough rubbish played, a lot of noise shattering the quiet of this lovely park. The orchestra was itching to play some real Music, and so he had chosen a piece by Richard Wagner, one of the greatest composers of all time—not that Liszt wasn't a great musician, but that rhapsody they played two Sundays ago, that wasn't the work of a genius, no, that was nothing but cat-and-dog wailing... and so on. In my mother's version, the first clarinettist, an odd-looking fellow with a big family, a painter and decorator in his spare time, had to remind him with a warning finger and disapprovingly pursed lips that the minutes were ticking relentlessly by. The shadows were long, sharp and menacing when Henri Cuperus raised his baton for the first chords of the famous Pilgrim's Chorus.

29

He must have been at loggerheads with his orchestra for weeks about this piece. Not because it was difficult (there were excellent instrumentalists in W...), but because he wanted to make them think as he did. In the opening passage the only mistake they could manage was to start on the wrong beat, but once on the Venusberg Music they unleashed a riot of discord, the tremolos were all off-key, the lusty march was drowned by the pounding of the bass drum, and with the hysterical screech of the flutes and piccolos—in the original orchestration violins, if I'm not mistaken —the reprise of the Pilgrim's Chorus was no longer recognizable. *Tannhäuser* was *not* redeemed, my mother said, and the orchestra was making sure of it. Usually they laughed and joked with each other, this time they sat with set faces like a lot of dangerous criminals cooped up in a prison-yard. Just before the end Cuperus rapped on his music stand, he broke his baton in two and stamped back to the restaurant. There must have been a fine row, and then something of a reconciliation so he could finish the season—young Tjallingii, who never missed a chance of barging in on such occasions, and with every right to, for he was a member of so many other Committees, had heard everything—but the result was a flowerily worded termination of the engagement and the appointment of another conductor (from some other town) for the next year's summer concerts. Cuperus didn't come off so badly, for, besides a sort of compensation payment, he still had his two choirs and the church as well, and then his lessons. Chris piped up: 'So he can still go on the booze.' I said: 'Little Chris imagines things', and my father closed the debate with the observation that someone like that could always do useful work on a modest scale. Conducting those summer concerts seemed to have gone to his head, but he was devoted to his music, and that showed he had a high mind. 'So high he couldn't stay on his feet,' my mother murmured, trying to stop giggling.

I don't imagine I gave much thought in the next few months to the pale girl I had danced with. I didn't see her anywhere and I

30

didn't look for her. From what I heard she didn't go to school any more but just had music lessons from her father, and in my eyes this made her even more grown-up than before. I was only a little boy waiting for the autumn so I could start playing football, which I felt would bring me nearer to being grown-up too. Chris, who was an authority on the rules, hardly ever played, because of his glasses, he said. So I was determined to be good at it.

One Saturday afternoon my mother took me with her to her dressmaker, who lived out on the edge of the town where the open fields started. It was a grey, rainy day and I hadn't been able to find anyone to play football with. These fields were criss-crossed with unexpected pathways with the most unexpected names—one of them was called Little Pig Dike, though there was never a pig in sight—leading to a big new dairy factory. In the other direction, running towards the town, each of these pathways doubled back along a parallel course about twenty yards away, still lined with wire fencing and straddled at odd intervals with loosely hanging gates, finally, after careful twists and turns through grass studded with blobs of cow dung, leading to quite another neighbourhood. Both the football pitches were on this vaguely defined edge of the town too. In those days I never knew which one was which and I was never sure of the way.

So that we wouldn't have to stay long, my mother and I didn't sit down. There was an old woman in the chair behind the table. The thin, overworked dressmaker rushed in and out of the room loaded with sample pieces of cloth, there was no measuring this time. She was silent and subdued, the old woman was voluble. I could sense that my mother was struggling with the temptation to stay and talk till late in the evening, and perhaps even to sing a song or two accompanied by the old harmonium that was covered with family photographs. That was why she hadn't sat down. She was fond of poor people, though charity was never her strongest point. She liked to hear their talk and their tales, so different from the talk and tales she heard from my father and from Chris.

I stood looking out of the window, past the wind-blown gardens and clusters of fruit trees to the inescapable green fields. The horizon seemed to belong to another land, with the dairy factories put along the border as a protection. From nowhere a disc went soaring over one of the fields. The disc fell and flew up again, each time tracing an immense curve. I couldn't see where it came down. Sometimes it seemed as if it would disappear into the low-hanging clouds. When I pointed to let my mother see it too, the old woman, who had been watching all the time, said: 'That's Vellinga at it again. He's as good as the best of them.'

'Mijnheer Vellinga, the lawyer?' my mother asked, just as the dressmaker came back into the room, and then for more than ten minutes she was busy picking out dress materials to hold pressed against her shoulders or at arm's length in the light. Now I knew what sort of disc it was.

'Is he playing football on his own, kicking the ball so high all the time? There must be some others with him too?'

The old woman didn't answer. 'Every Saturday he's at it. I'm always frightened the ball will fall in our garden.'

'Then you can throw it back to him,' my mother said, looking at me with a stern glint in her eye and giving an almost imperceptible shake of her head. It was a silver-grey piece of material that she had draped around her. For a moment I thought she meant I shouldn't look at her.

'He's as good as the best of them. He's always at it, kicking that ball and always ever so high. He can kick high but he's not the sort that go far.'

My mother coughed. As it happened, I knew what 'go far' meant. I had heard my father say this when he was talking about Chris, and I asked: 'Isn't he clever?'

'He's been to the university,'—for the first time the old woman put her sewing down—'and being as he is a lawyer, you wouldn't say he was stupid, young man. But a cousin of mine, his son it was, a peat dealer, and quite a bit he earns with it too, well, he had a

32

law case with him, I mean he had him for his lawyer, and what happened? Lost the case, he did, and 450 guilders he had to pay Vellinga. And he shouldn't have lost the case at all. No more of that Vellinga, he said. He could crack a joke and all that, he was always making everyone in the court laugh, but my cousin says he didn't know what he was talking about, he looked up everything in a law book afterwards and there it was, just the opposite, he says, and his son says, that's no man to do business with, a nice fellow he may be, but if I ever have any bother again he's the last lawyer I'll go to. And there you are, every Saturday I see him out there with his football.'

'He's not a lawyer any more,' my mother said coldly, and from the rebuff in the over-friendly way she put her hands on the dressmaker's shoulders I could see that the visit was over. Years later, when she recalled this incident, she told me she couldn't stand it if people like that discussed anyone she or my father knew personally. Not that she minded what they said, but she just didn't know what to say herself, or whether she should smile or look offended.

The same evening I managed to get out of Chris that Vellinga had recently left the legal fraternity (I wasn't sure of the meaning of this word that Chris used so off-handedly, I mixed it up with maternity) and that he was now editor of the local newspaper, which we didn't read but we would read it now. He must have visited our house sometimes, but as Chris and I were still boycotting those musical evenings he was no more to me than a shadow just as ridiculous as Mijnheer van Son or young Tjallingii, who sang in a quavering tenor and was allowed to turn the pages if van Son was tired. I was sure I had never even seen Vellinga. Now here he was revealed as a footballer, and Chris informed me that besides making a 'career' for himself, he was goalkeeper for the local first-division team, and he was always ready to play left-back or right-back, it was all the same to him, or as stand-in for the centre-forward.

Seeing that I only played football with boys smaller than

myself on the big square near where we lived that everyone called Zaailand, I would never have come into contact with Mijnheer Vellinga, the goalkeeper, if I hadn't made friends with two older boys, who took me one Sunday afternoon to watch a match at the biggest of the two pitches. I called these two friends of mine 'Brown' and 'Blue' and while the friendship lasted, for three or four weeks, I lived in a wonderful haze of self-importance, tingling with almost painful feelings of gratitude and loyalty. 'Brown' was fifteen, he went to a technical school, he was lean-built but slow in his movements, his face was thin and sallow, and he always wore an old brown suit. 'Blue' was solidly built, his age was never mentioned because he was going to leave school soon, he had a broad face with grey, intelligent and trustworthy eyes, and his hair and his eyebrows looked grey too, a tint of grey, faintly speckled like the cocoons of a certain type of brightly coloured, striped caterpillar.

He used to wear a blue sailor suit that had got too small for him. They both swayed as they walked—like tramps who had been dead drunk only a little while before and were now sobering up.

It was probably at the Zaailand, where the only time no footballs were being kicked around was at night, that they had mooked on to me, maybe because I was the 'judge's son'. Whether they liked me for my company or regarded me as a prize protégé, or whether they were snobs or good-natured and well-meaning, I never found out, but in any case they certainly did not expect me to play the role of an admirer. They didn't speak much, and they thought for a long while before they said anything. Vanity and ambition seemed to be completely foreign to them. They were too indolent to play football, though 'Brown' could twist and turn like an eel between two heaps of pullovers used for goalposts. They could slouch round, wandering aimlessly for hours on end, and when I went with them in the evening I discovered narrow alleys that I could hardly ever find again on my own. In the long street where all the shops were—it was so long that as it curved it seemed to be turning back to where it started—I learnt from them how to look at girls. I thought the girls we looked at were insulted by these brazen stares, and that the reason they didn't look back was that if they did they would have had to box my ears. But 'Brown' and 'Blue' rarely talked about girls. They preferred to instruct by demonstration, and whatever there was to learn could be learned by watching. When 'Brown' suddenly turned and glided into a pitch dark alley he was like a master-housebreaker who had once been a seaman. These alleys always turned out to be short-cuts to somewhere, and the light from the paraffin lamps shining through the yellow blinds pulled down over the windows on each side, only an arm's length apart, was somehow more reassuring than the endless procession of strollers strung out every evening unvaryingly along the same streets and congealing on the wide, arched bridge where our coach had gone rattling past young Tjallingii that Sunday afternoon. That bridge was as wide as a square. 'Brown' and 'Blue' never stayed there long. They had a restlessness in them even though they were slow in their movements.

We must have walked a long way the afternoon we went to the football match. They had called for me fairly late, my two bodyguards, and their first meeting with Chris was as irritating as I could have expected. First, he tried to appropriate them to himself, and later when he spoke about them he said they were 'rowdies' and 'riff-raff'. When I came running down the hall Chris punched me on the shoulder, but I didn't stop. A quarter of an hour later I was standing with 'Brown' and 'Blue' on the edge of a muddy football field where the match had just started between the W . . . first-division team and a visiting team from Liverpool. Up in the grandstand a local band was playing feverish march tunes that half the time were blown away by the wind. The visitors were playing against the wind, but even so they penetrated Mijnheer Vellinga's stronghold again and again, and they scored six goals by half-time. I wanted to stay near Mijnheer

Vellinga too, so 'Brown' and 'Blue', who wanted to see the English keeper doing his stuff, went off and left me on my own when the second half began.

Mijnheer Wubbo Vellinga was fairly tall and well built and at twenty-seven he was already developing a paunch. His mischievous, pleasantly featured, bulldog face extended into a studious lawyer's skull, slightly bald at the crown. In appearance he was of a blond and ruddy patrician type which, in W . . . suggested something of the caveman, and he had every possible qualification for leadership of the local *jeunesse dorée*, member of the skating-rink committee, the life and soul of every party, and trouble-shooting journalist who would, in a few years, be the only one to be depended on if the town, apart from the slum districts, was to be saved from ruin. A long time later he confessed to me that he felt himself married to W . . . Somehow or other I knew quite a lot about him—that he wasn't interested in music and he must have foisted himself on my parents for other reasons than van Son or young Tjallingii had, that he wasn't genuinely good-natured like Henri Cuperus must be, that he would never have a daughter who threw her arms around his neck, and that he played football for the popularity it brought him and not for the sake of playing. Why were those leather hands so big against the thick, bare thighs? There he was in a yellow raincoat and a pink woollen cap with a tassel so everyone would notice him whenever the ball was at the other end of the slush-covered field. What was the sense of embracing someone who had just kicked a ball past him into a roughly-knotted net? He had a way with him, and I was under the spell as much as anyone else. He could bellow like a wounded bull, but there was a refined lilt and a cultivated whine in his bellowing when he wanted to encourage his sliding, mud-spattered team. Standing in front of the goal in the rain and wind, covered with mud and sweat, his pince-nez loose, not even held with a cord, dancing up and down, the lenses all splashed and dirty, shouting jovially and commandingly

'Keep at it, boys' when the score was 9-1, jumping up, kneeling, holding his hands on his thighs, he was an imposing figure, someone not to pick a quarrel with. Still, something inside me resisted the attraction of this man.

But my resistance did break just for a moment. That was when he was walking off the field after the match was over and he had to stop by the gate to the dressing-room. I had followed him. Amongst the crowd standing in his way were three or four admiring young boys about the same age as myself and, as he couldn't walk over them or kill them, he put his big, wet hand on the head of one of them, looked down with a smile, baring his teeth like a bulldog, pushed the little chap gently aside, and went striding on, carelessly jerking his powerful body. The little boy swayed unsteadily, and I felt my heart beat quicker. Ach, but he was only a lawyer anyway, this Vellinga, far less important than my father, one of those fellows always splitting hairs and finding fault, though they nearly always know beforehand whether or not they will convince anyone (this is what I had heard from Chris) so they never really get what they want. A lawyer who wasn't a lawyer any more. Who did he think he could fool with that unexpected touching and tender gesture: 'I've lost, it's my fault. I let the ball into the goal thirteen times, and in front of my fellow citizens whom I hope to rule with plenty of noise and fun and news. If anyone deserves sympathy, I do. But look at what I've done, I've given all that consolation, all that attention, all that sympathy to that scruffy little kid standing in my way. I let my hand, warm from being cased in leather gloves, rest on that insignificant little head with the red barbed-wire hair of the disinherited, and no one can say that I'm a brute, a scoundrel, a braggart, a fat slob. No one can say that about me.'

On one of the last evenings I spent with 'Brown' and 'Blue' I talked to them about Chris. They'd seen for themselves what he was like, I said, and I wanted to punch him on the nose, but how could I do this and when? I didn't hate him really, but he had too

37

much to say for himself, and I'd made up my mind years ago that I'd do it, and now I was as strong as he was. For a long while 'Brown' and 'Blue' considered my problem, kicking at stones or looking vaguely at the lighted shop windows that we passed. But it was only 'Blue' who gave any sign of having been thinking. I was walking between them, completely protected. I felt that I had a right to some solid advice.

'What you have to do,' 'Blue' said, 'is to pick the right time, when you're sure everyone will be on your side. We had a cousin of ours staying with us, and he was always going to the kitchen grabbing something to eat. He was a nasty piece of work, but the way he was always eating gave me a chance to knock a couple of his teeth out. All my brothers and sisters backed me up, and my mother too, because she'd sized him up long before. We hadn't gone telling tales about him, you mustn't ever tell tales.'

'No,' I said uncertainly. 'Brown' just grinned.

'You have to be in a strong position,' 'Blue' went on thoughtfully. 'You have to be sure the whole family knows you're doing it for them. My father was the only one who got angry when he saw him bleeding so much. We had a fight after I hit him, and the blood was all over my sailor suit, it was new then. But my mother said to my father. . .'

'Brown' broke in: 'So you did tell her why you hit him?'

'Yes, we had to tell her,' 'Blue' said in a tone of surprised indignation.

Without having solved the problem of whether or not this was telling tales, we turned in single file into another alley, narrow as a crack in the wall, completely dark except for a feeble light in a basement where we could hear a sound of softly clapping hands but we couldn't see anyone. We soon reached the canal with the wide bridge across it, where the brightest lit shops were and a few big houses and one or two offices. It was a quarter to eight. My two friends stopped in front of a barber's shop. There was a display in the window advertising a hair lotion called

'Koko', pyramids of big and little bottles of 'Koko', and jars and hair brushes and gilt-edged cards inscribed with the slogan, in English, 'Koko for the hair', and diplomas with medals, and photos of busy hairdressers' saloons, and in the middle a doll with long, gleaming tresses, sitting in a revolving leather chair that was mounted on a round pedestal. It was some time before I realized that the doll in the chair was a live girl. There were others besides us standing there watching this spectacle, and it was amazing how the girl managed not to laugh or wink or catch anyone's eye as she turned round and round, in her white bath-robe that left her arms uncovered. It must have been the first evening that she was on show. 'Brown' and 'Blue' always heard if there was something new to see. They watched with serious faces, and the other spectators, most of them men, adapted themselves admirably to this impersonal exhibition of a perhaps quite respectable young lady. She gazed far into the distance, seeing nothing, except perhaps—though it was difficult to be sure—when her face was reflected in the mirror fixed across the back of the display. Her big calm eyes seemed to narrow into focus, but I might have imagined this.

As we walked away 'Blue' mumbled: 'Koko for the hair-r-r. Not much of a job, but she only has to sit there in the evening.'

'In the afternoon, too,' 'Brown' corrected him. 'I didn't see it, but this afternoon she had to scratch her head. She must have thought no one was watching, but the barber, that Taconis, he saw it, and he came and tapped on the board at the back of the window.'

'No one'd want to look at Taconis twice,' 'Blue' said with a knowing laugh, 'but maybe you could start something with her.' 'Brown' grinned and kept his eyes fixed on the expensive pastry-cook's shop four or five doors farther on, and the last-minute stream of well-dressed women and servant girls going in and out.

'What do you mean, "start something"?' I asked.

Obviously this was a subject 'Blue' didn't feel like enlarging on. He said 'Koko for the hair-r-r' a couple of times cheerfully derisive, then he said, 'Of course, it wasn't her own hair,' and after that he was mute again. Both of them had talked much more than they usually did. Suddenly 'Blue' raised his hand and called out fairly loudly: 'Hullo, Trix.'

On the steps by the door of the bakery Trix Cuperus, tall, pale and arrogant, stood looking down at us. She was bareheaded just as she had been that day at the Garden, but if 'Blue' hadn't called out I would never have recognized her. There were two small bags in the basket she carried on her arm. She looked so proud and aloof that I turned away at once and let my eyes wander over the houses and the street lights opposite. With my back to her I felt more at ease. She was grown-up, something between my mother and the girl who came every day to do the housework. I just happened to be with 'Blue' and 'Brown', but I certainly didn't want her to think I was bad-mannered. This shouting out at someone at eight o'clock in the evening wasn't polite. So I wasn't surprised that the greeting was ignored and there was no exchange of conversation. When I turned round again she had disappeared, and 'Brown' and 'Blue', who had taken two or three steps in the direction of the bakery, stopped with their hands in their pockets and looked back at me indolently and expectantly in that slouching stance of theirs, the back slightly hunched, the neck bent watchfully forward.

'You could start something there, too,' 'Brown' grunted.

'Oh, I don't know,' 'Blue' said, putting his arm protectively round my shoulders. I was walking in the middle again. One by one the shop lights were going out, and the procession of strollers was turning into a parade with masks of evening shadows. 'Blue' said that at the beginning of the summer Trix used to play with his sisters, but she was no good to play with, she was so touchy. After that came a quarter of an hour of silence. Every time I saw a tall girl in front of us I thought it was her, and I would feel a tingling in my legs, that same tingling I had felt the first time I had listened to Sousa's march.

There isn't much more to tell about my friendship with 'Brown' and 'Blue'. They drifted out of my life like a slow, kindly puff of wind sucked away through one of those narrow cobbled passages that I gave up exploring in my later boyhood years. I never saw them again, and as I didn't know their names I could never ask about them. I liked to think that they had more natural refinement in them than all the pupils at the lyceum put together, that they moved away to another town to start their wanderer's existence all over again, and that they took leave of each other by turning into different alleyways, without saying a word, their backs hunched a little more than usual.

[4]

One Friday evening when the snow had already started melting, I was walking alone along a narrow street. Perhaps, without realizing it, I was looking for 'Brown' and 'Blue', who had gone away, or were dead, as I had imagined to myself for a while. I didn't know that there was a dressmaking school in that neighbourhood, and, when a door suddenly swung open to let loose a crowd of girls carrying satchels, and I recognized amongst that noisy crowd the girl who had been my friend so briefly one summer afternoon, my first thought was that I was the victim of a conspiracy. I jumped behind a flight of steps a couple of houses farther on to hide myself. The light from the school threw a sharp brightness over the smooth, slushy snow and on the girls who sauntered off scuffing their feet over the slippery road surface, or stopped talking by the door. The noise of their chatter was like a chorus of spring-fevered birds. In twos and threes they went past me arm-in-arm. Then there was a scream, and I saw Trix slapping a smaller girl, about the same age as herself, and after that she lashed out with her satchel at a fat girl with black plaits. The smaller girl ran off, the other one hit back, lost her balance and fell backwards. Then I heard Trix's voice for the first time, it sounded so shrill, so common, 'If you say that again, you cheeky bitch. . .' Another girl who answered back got a kick in the stomach. The circle of light was all at once empty, and Trix was striding off in the other direction defiantly swinging her satchel. One of the frightened, excited girls hurrying past where I stood hidden was saying, in an awestricken voice: 'She said that her father was drunk, she shouldn't have said a thing like that. . .'

They went past and I was alone again. It was snowing, more sleet than snow, the door of the school was still open, letting the light shine through, like a church after evening service. I shook myself loose from the stone steps I had pressed myself against. My hands were ice-cold, but my cheeks were warm and flushed, and I felt that strange tingling in my legs again. It made me limp, as if there was something pushing me down to make me crawl on my knees across that enigmatic circle of light, through the snow that had just fallen and through the little puddles. After the door was closed by unseen hands, I remained where I was gazing up at the sky, and I sniffed the smoke of burning wood. A man walked past, then turned to look at me, and the street lights flickered behind a curtain of watery snowflakes. But couldn't she fight, that girl. I kept thinking about her all the time I was doing my homework, until ten o'clock that night.

We did our homework in separate rooms upstairs. We slept upstairs too. The year before Chris started at the lyceum it had been decided that we shouldn't go on sharing the same room to study in. At that time he was nervous and quick-tempered, his glasses glittered like a mirror in the sunlight, and he seemed to walk around all the time with clenched fists. Every mealtime he started an uproar at the table. My father found this just as unbearable as my mother did, but he rarely showed it because he always made allowances for Chris. Visitors, most of them at least, were usually inclined, just from what they saw of us, to prefer Chris to me. I knew that, for all his jeering about those musical evenings, more than once he had sneaked downstairs without telling me and seen my father sitting there with his head in his hands and Mijnheer van Son and young Tjallingii, who always brought his trained poodle with him, rushing at the piano like savages to turn over the sheets of music for my dear mother, and often tearing the pages as they grabbed at them.

Chris was unbearably noisy, but he could be still as a mouse when he wanted to, and that was even worse. When I was about seven, he had the habit of shutting one eye and staring at me across the table with the other, never moving a muscle. It was quite a feat, and if he kept it up for more than a couple of minutes, with the light flashing on his glasses so that no one else noticed, I couldn't swallow another mouthful. He kept his other trick, of

43

making his head swell up as if he was going to explode with rage, for when we were upstairs. With these feats he had achieved an ascendancy over his friends—not that they were particularly impressed by a swollen-up head, but they did admire the calm self-assurance that he performed with. It's very likely that this head-swelling damaged his brain in some way or another. Anyway, his egoism and ambition soon landed him in a mess. He was determined to be taken notice of, and in his constant fever of excitement it was difficult for him to distinguish between reality and fantasy. I was both more of a dreamer and more of a realist than he was. If I lied I knew I was lying, while Chris's whole existence was one big lie, a fiction of his own making, which the world around him gave a certain measure of approval to. He collected everything, even dried frogs, and he would talk about being 'scientific', but, whatever it was, as soon as anyone else started collecting the same thing he gave it up, then it was 'stupid' or 'useless'. He knew everything about everything. He told everyone what he heard or made up, he would forget it almost at once, and then avoid the boys who remembered what he had told them.

At the lyceum it was hard going for him, but he kept this to himself. Big mouth that he was, he had to endure his misery in silence. I think my father had promised him money if he was top of the class. At the primary school he had never managed that, though everyone thought he was 'clever', which, in a certain sense, he was—some weeks more than others. So he worked like a horse. I could understand his reasons well enough, and I appreciated his diligence as an example never to be followed. As evidence of his good intentions and the weakening of his mind, the mumbling drone of his memorizing rolled on and on every night and as often as not again in the morning. But, all things considered, this sort of life was nothing short of a disaster for Chris, for how could he preserve his popularity with his classmates, who were accustomed to getting an afternoon fretwork lesson from him— in exchange for allowing him to call them fatuous names like 'ass'—until they could do it better than he could, which they never seemed to realize? He had no more time now for popularity, then that swotting that schoolboys so despise cut more ground from under his feet, and with five more years in front of him he couldn't feel very sure of himself. He must have been desperate for months and months on end. Then, after his first report (he was third in his class), he had an idea that could have been brilliant if anyone else had thought it up. With four of his friends, one of them a not very bright boy from the second year, he launched a peppermint factory.

That wasn't as crazy as it sounds. In the first place, the peppermint factory didn't take much of his time. It was only a factory on paper, a company with shares he sold for cash, lending the money out or giving it away to other classmates he was frightened of. He babbled about statutes and regulations, schedules and graphs, some the product of his imagination, some just taken from old books of my father's on economics... From time to time he showed round a peppermint he claimed he had made in the attic. That was partly true. He bought big peppermints, filed them into another shape with regular notches around the edge. When he had a good supply he exhibited them on his desk at school, and then more money flowed in. The victims were presented with ridiculously worded receipts. I saw one of them after the crash. He hadn't even taken the trouble to formulate it grammatically. It was a document reflecting the mind of a hopelessly muddled, incredibly naïve would-be man of affairs: 'I, Christiaan Karl Rieske, hereby declare receiving money for a share in the CKR, the finest peppermint in Holland, guaranteed and with prices and by appointment supplied to the Royal family for the sum of fifty cents (50 cents) (preference share).

If he'd been smart he could have kept his little racket going for at least six months. Had his shareholders got suspicious he could have let them sniff a lump of loaf sugar sprinkled with peppermint oil, and if he couldn't bluff any more there were all sorts of infallible pretexts and excuses to fall back on. He could have been the first to point out the absurdity of the idea of a peppermint factory, how stupid or how childish it was. He could have unobtrusively wriggled out of it—as he always did with anything he started—by paying off the not very pressing debts bit by bit, by good marks in his next report, and the reputation he had of being a lad with energy and initiative who was, after all, the soul of honesty.

Those graphs of his, and the administration and the economics of production, proved his downfall. At first this might have served to mislead my father or any inquisitive teacher and hide the fact that the whole thing was a swindle, and, at the same time, it probably eased his conscience, for he could feel he was at least doing something for the CKR and earning the cents he was raking in. In the end it was like a drug he couldn't do without. He had rings under his eyes from sitting up, night after night, first at his homework, then, till after midnight, studying 'economics', compiling peppermint statistics, pricing shares with stock exchange quotations and all the fiendish complications of dealing in shares. He got thin and haggard, he looked as if he was bent under a heavy load. Even my parents, who knew nothing of his nightly labours, began to show the strain because he talked of nothing else at the table and persecuted my father with unanswerable questions. He always had a supply of peppermints of diverse shapes with him. Sometimes he would offer these to us after dessert. It was all treated as a joke though my parents used to look at each other with raised eyebrows and never kept the peppermint long in their mouths. I didn't like them either, and I put them in my pocket so they would get dirty. On the table in his room there were peppermints arranged in rows and in patterns. The maid was never allowed to touch them. I wouldn't go so far as to say that Chris was going off his head, but he was obviously overwrought, and this was trying to my mother, all the more because she was, despite the show of affectionate understanding, already so far apart from my father that they could not face together the responsibilities of bringing up their children. There was nothing more gruesome than Chris making fun of the whole grandiose enterprise. His eyes would fill with tears at the huge joke of it all, he laughed with an odd sound of gulping and wheezing, he jerked and shook, and then he'd offer you a peppermint. I think it would be correct to say that his mental faculties showed a distinct decline. Chris reached his highest peak of intelligence at the age of ten when he knew everything about court procedure without really being interested in the subject. This was an apogee Chris never reached again, though he did later acquire the reputation of being a reliable lawyer and a model husband and father.

One evening I heard him walking up and down in his room. His chair creaked resignedly and after that a silence. Then that walking up and down again. Mumbling. Squeaking of the floorboards. Was his homework so difficult, I wondered. Silence again. I got up, tiptoed along the passage and opened his door without making a sound. There he was, sitting at his homework, his head in his hands. But on his big table, in front of the upright row of school books, there were peppermints arranged in heaps and squares and circles like a usurer's hoard ready for counting, and sheets of paper with hideous spidery lines running triumphantly upwards to record heights of peppermint production, open notebooks with pages of figures, new share certificates. The gaslight hissed and the small gas-heater gasped and spluttered. No one would hear us. I walked over to him slowly. 'Chris,' I said softly, and my heart started thumping. I didn't feel any hate for him, but he had kicked me on my shins, under the table, the table where we sat in the protective presence of my parents, for years he'd been doing that.

When he finally looked up—his glasses were crooked, I remember, probably from leaning his head more on one hand than the other—I took a couple of steps so that I was standing to the side of his chair and a little in front of him, then I punched him on the nose, hard and high up so that his glasses fell on the floor, but without breaking, I could tell that from the sound. He bounced back in his chair, and sat there dazed. The full shock of the blow had been absorbed in his neck muscles, for he'd been sitting hunched and tense. He wasn't any paler than he usually was. Then he put his hand to his nose, slowly and thoughtfully, and all of a sudden his nose started bleeding. In a few seconds he had a thin red moustache, and the blood trickled over his lips, then in two lines from the corners of his mouth down his chin like grotesque wrinkles. Rubbing absentmindedly, he smeared it all over his face. But the moustache, that thin, running blob, kept renewing itself through the mess, a gleaming ribbon between his nose and his lips. I watched it, hypnotized. First he sat bent forward a little, but soon he slumped back in his chair, sniffling, looking at me sideways. In the meantime I had picked up his spectacles and put them on the table.

'What did you do that for, Nol?' he asked in a dull, tired voice. I said nothing, and he repeated the question, again calling me by my name.

'Oh, I wanted to,' I said, and suddenly I remembered 'Blue', who had told me that I would have to wait for the right moment when no one could say I was in the wrong. 'Because of those peppermints of yours, that you're always going on about. You'd better stop it. Does your nose hurt?'

'Yes, it hurts a lot,' he said emphatically, then listlessly: 'No, it doesn't hurt, but I can't stop the bleeding.'

He squinted at me, sniffing, he licked the blood off his lips and almost put his red-streaked tongue in one of his nostrils.

'If you don't stop that nonsense I'll hit you again,' I said.

He closed his eyes and gave a resigned sigh. 'I can't stop now, it's too involved. You don't understand.'

'If you give them their money back. . .' Chris had once taken me into his confidence, only because he could never let a chance go to boast about anything he did. 'I can give you some if you need it. We can't stand any more of your silly peppermints, Mother can't either. We don't want to see another peppermint. We're starting to look like peppermints.' I'd heard my mother saying that. 'You have to promise.'

'Promise what?'

'That you'll stop that peppermint nonsense.'

'Promise you? Did Mother say anything to you about it?'

I shook my head. I stepped over to the table and swept all the peppermints on to the floor. Then I took the graphs and the shares and the notes and ripped the lot to bits. He didn't try to stop me. The one peppermint that lay gleaming in his wastepaper basket was soon covered with scraps of paper. He sat there not saying a word, his nose had almost stopped bleeding. When I handed him his spectacles he cleared his throat and gulped a few times. The blood must be running back into his throat, I was thinking, it would end up in his stomach. I'd had a bleeding nose once and I knew it didn't hurt at all.

'Do you want me to put a cold key on the back of your neck?'

'If I tell Father in the morning,' he blubbered.

'Then I'll hit you again tomorrow night, and you'll get your glasses in your eye. You see if I won't,' I shouted, stamping my foot, and my face felt as if it was burning, just like when I had watched Trix Cuperus fighting that night outside the school.

'I'm not going to tell anyone,' he said with a sullen laugh.

As I walked to the door, the peppermints crunching under my feet, I watched him out of the corner of my eye. He could easily jump on me from behind. But he wasn't intending to do anything of the sort. That was obvious from the way he acted the next day, when the peppermint factory seemed to belong to the far-distant past. He had put his blood-stained shirt in the washing basket and, just to be sure no one would suspect anything, he said that his nose had bled a little the night before, it must have been from staying so late at his homework. This led my father to observe that moderation in all things . . . with which Chris agreed.

That evening I gave him ten cents out of my week's pocket money. He treated me with a distinct coolness. I didn't realize that I had, in fact, saved him, but I could hardly be blind to the change that came over him in the days, and weeks and years that followed. He was so well-behaved, so subdued, and so unimaginative. He never interrupted my parents any more at the meal-table. He was going to study law, that had been definitively decided. Once I heard him sobbing during the night.

But to finish the tale of that evening I punched his nose. Back in my own room I undressed quickly, I was so tired. Before I crept into bed I locked my door. Chris might come in and bend over me and let the blood drip out of his nose over my face. I knew he wouldn't, but I knew that I would think he had if I woke up suddenly in the middle of the night. I fell asleep straight away and soon afterwards I must have started dreaming.

I was lying in the pond in the Garden, and beside me there was a big crocodile, so long that its snout was almost touching the bandstand. The pond was dirty and shallow. The bridge was gone. I was doing nothing, but the crocodile was breathing blasts of flame and sparks against the bandstand, and every time a glow of flame rose upward the music of brass instruments rang out in a solemn fanfare and flutes played. Every now and then I caught a glimpse of gleaming brass instruments, but not a single musician. I lay pressed close against the crocodile. It had no scales. It did nothing else but blow fire and smoke, with all its might, but almost without a movement of that long, slippery body.

Then I was sitting next to Cuperus on the grass under the rocks. He was speaking to me in a high-pitched, quivering voice that sounded like young Tjallingii's. His arms waved about as he spoke, and he had rolled up his morning coat because of the wet grass. He pointed to the trees, to the muddy pond, and to the bandstand where flame turned into sound, and brass came forth from fire. On the other side of the pond, just behind the crocodile's tail, Trix Cuperus was standing with one foot in the mud and tilting the knee of her other leg just as she had done that afternoon when she flung her arms round her father's neck. Cuperus stretched out his arms, raising his hands imploringly, and mumbled strange words. As the crocodile sank deeper and deeper into the mud Trix imitated her father's gesture, it was obviously a sign to exorcise the beast. Now there was not so much flame pouring out with the fiery breath. Cuperus turned away from me, leaning down as if he was going to pluck a blade of grass, but his daughter was still waving her outstretched arms, standing like a ballerina with one knee raised high. The further the crocodile sank into the mud, and the softer the music, the wilder were the movements she made. With her arms flying she bent far over the simmering morass. I felt frightened, I wanted to scream. She was all in white. . . . The crocodile was lying next to me again, but now the sky was dark, and I could feel how quickly that immense body was sinking, and I could sense the torment of sorrow the beast suffered knowing its striving had been in vain. Even when I woke shouting I still didn't realize that I was sinking down with it into death by suffocation. I stared at my watch that was hanging on the wall, half visible in the light of the gas lamp in the street. My school books were lying on the table.

After I had wiped the sweat off my forehead with the edge of the sheet I heard the sound of a piano somewhere. I had to think for a long time before I could be sure where it came from. Not from downstairs, from one of my mother's musical evenings. No, it was from the lame girl two houses away, a sad creature about thirty, who lived in seclusion with her grand piano and a rich mother. Her music was discreetly accompanied by the late tinkling of a bell from the canal and once or twice a ptt–ptt that didn't intrude. It was only years later, when I was a student, that I found out what piece she was playing—a sonata in D major by Haydn, the ninth in the first volume, acording to some critics the best, and as good as anything by Beethoven. I lay listening, scarcely breathing. In one of the rooms a clock chimed ten. There's nothing more wonderful than listening to piano music from two houses away, and this music was sweeping and stately, almost menacing in an intensity of genuine emotion, for all its seeming playfulness. A motif of thirds with a staccato accompaniment sounded so tenderly mysterious that I could have listened to it forever. Even if you forgot it after you'd heard it, it would come back again; that was the wonderful structure of those sonatas. The slow second part emerged with an almost uncanny simplicity from one single bass note. The bass note and the melody were worlds apart, and went on and on with an infinite patience, two voices with no other link between them than the distance that separated them, forever changing, enlarging and shrinking but remaining always the same. I don't know if she added variations of her own, I tried to keep awake by pinching my arm, but I was asleep before the end of the adagio.

Two days later I told my mother that I wanted to learn the piano.

[5]

I told Chris myself, just to enjoy the suspicious, reproachful look he gave me. He didn't know that I knew he had long since betrayed our anti-music alliance by giving my father moral support, sitting next to him when Brahms was being played (an early piece before 1860), and by shaking hands with young Tjallingii's poodle —once he had been allowed to let it outside, but he wasn't quick enough, it left a pool on the hall carpet. My mother was doubtful whether I was serious about learning the piano, this decision was so sudden, and besides, I had shown a dislike for music ever since I was three. But that was the music I heard Chris playing, I explained. In the Garden I had liked Cuperus's music, I had even danced to it. I had hoped she would tell me more about Trix and her father, but she didn't, she was offended perhaps because I hadn't said I liked hearing her play. Instead she started off about how strict Mijnheer Talsma was, how Chris hadn't been able to keep it up, and Mijnheer Talsma was so terribly exact and so dull. We put our arms round each other—two red cheeks close together and a hasty kiss on the corner of her mouth—then I assured her that I hadn't even thought of Mijnheer Talsma. There were other music teachers besides Mijnheer Talsma in W...

'None of them is any good. Mijnheer Talsma is the best.'

'Mijnheer Cuperus,' I said looking at the floor.

She kissed me on the forehead, a kiss that was, under the circumstances, rather discouraging, and she began to laugh with short rasping sounds in her throat. She seemed to think this was all the comment she needed to give. She was very obviously relying on the unspoken understanding between mother and child.

'What's wrong with Mijnheer Cuperus? I've heard from other boys that he is cleverer than Mijnheer Talsma.'

'Oh, he's such a strange man,' my mother said. This sounded promising, the objection showed that she was at least considering my suggestion. But I wasn't altogether sure from the tone of her voice. It was just as likely that she wasn't taking any notice of what I said and she only wanted to make me realize something I hadn't been aware of. I gave a derisive hoot of laughter.

'Oh, I know you mean Chris's silly stories. He's mad. All that talk about Cuperus getting drunk, Chris is crazy. How could a pianist get drunk, he'd be hitting the wrong notes all the time!'

We both burst out laughing, we yelled with laughter, and calculatingly I kept this exuberance going as long as I could, till there was no room in our bobbing heads for any thought but the absurd and romantic possibility of a staggering music teacher who would roll in and vomit over the piano. I knew my mother was thinking of something like that or worse, but I didn't put these thoughts into words. I had to keep her laughing, laughing with her eyes getting smaller and smaller and her cheeks flushed and purple. That would stop any discussion. When I ran out of the room without a word she was still sitting on the stool by the piano, rocking from side to side. In those years laughing was her greatest pleasure. Sometimes I felt a little anxious about her when she was in one of these endless bouts.

Thirteen years older than my mother, set in his ways and the routine of his work which he performed efficiently but without enthusiasm, my father had dealt out punishments for so many far more serious offences that he considered the only sort of drunkenness that could be held against artists, all of them temperamental and unstable, was drunkenness and disorderliness in public. My mother had told him about Cuperus's latest performance in the Garden, which was at least halfway within the scope of this norm, but he had forgotten it, just as he forgot almost everything she told him. He wasn't really concerned whether I learnt the piano or not. In any case, he had heard from Mijnheer Vellinga that Cuperus had more talent than he got credit for in W . . . (it seemed that Vellinga had heard this from Caspers). We could give it a trial. If the man didn't conduct himself respectably or if he was no good as a teacher, we could easily stop the lessons. It would be better if he came to our house so my mother could keep an eye on him.

The day he was to come I was shaking with nervousness. I wondered if he would wear his morning coat, and if I ought to tell him that I had danced with Trix three years ago when he had conducted one of those noisy marches by Sousa (I had learnt by now that those marches were nothing, nothing at all, a mockery of real music). We had had a letter from him too, with a list of the lesson times. A jagged script, a careful choice of words, without mistakes and without any servility. A man's letter. I treasured it for a long while.

As soon as I heard the bell ring I ran to the room where the old piano was. Standing in a corner I listened to the firm, regular footsteps and the deep voice when he thanked the maid who had opened the door of the drawing-room for him. The second door was half-open, I didn't dare to raise my eyes until after he came in and stood by the doorway looking round the room, his hands behind his back. His black, curly hair was a little thinner, his face was red in patches, his moustache was still as imposing as Leoncavallo's. He wasn't wearing his morning coat and so he seemed bigger, sturdier, more like a country gentleman than I remembered him. It was only as he approached me with something of a resoluteness in his movements that I noticed again that unusual squint of his that wasn't really a squint at all, it was only that he screwed his eyes up playfully when he was in a friendly mood. He shook my hand and I said: 'Good afternoon, Mijnheer,'—a warmth seemed to radiate from him, a heavy, implacable warmth that stopped me saying anything more. He didn't say anything either. After he had looked around he plopped down in the only armchair with his back to the door. It must have been a minute before he broke the silence. Then he said quietly and a little hoarsely: 'Maybe someone will show up to do the honours. . .'

As though summoned by a magic incantation, my mother came flouncing into the room, small and slender in a close-fitting green dress with puffed sleeves that were going out of fashion. Her face was redder than usual, and she stared with elaborately feigned surprise at the curly hair sticking up behind the velvet back of the armchair. Cuperus just sat in the chair gazing at his hands. When my mother said all too sweetly: 'Mijnheer Cuperus?' he got up slowly and made a brief bow sideways, for my mother hadn't bothered to stand in front of him. Then he turned so that he was facing her and stood looking at her intently, endlessly, it seemed to me. He wasn't just looking at her, he stared, he sucked her up into those black eyes of his that didn't squint any more now. Finally he turned his eyes away from her.

'Mevrouw . . . What do you want me to call my new pupil, Master Rieske or. .?'

'Nol,' I said helpfully, and got a strange glance from my mother, who wasn't so red in the face now as she had been. But I blushed crimson. Of course I was Nol for Mijnheer Cuperus. I shuddered at the thought that he might call me 'Master Rieske'. Not even the tradesmen did that, nor the maids either.

'Whatever you prefer,' my mother said indifferently, at the same time walking quickly over to the piano. But she did this in the oddest way. Instead of walking in a straight line that wouldn't have brought her within three or four feet of him, she passed close to him, stepping in the direction of the music stand to the right of the piano. I had the impression, too, that at the moment she was nearest to him she bowed her head ever so slightly. After she reached the piano by this crazy detour, she stood between the two chairs that had been put there ready for the lesson, letting her right hand run over the keyboard, effortlessly playing the notes of a scale. She turned round, but he spole first: 'You play very well, Mevrouw.'

She looked at him with her eyes unnaturally wide open: 'Oh, I take lessons from Mijnheer Talsma.'

'I see,' Cuperus said.

'Would you care to give me a lesson now and then?' she asked with concealed irony, blinking as if the sun was in her eyes.

'Certainly, Mevrouw, but not if you are taking lessons from Mijnheer Talsma.'

'But why not? Do you think he has spoilt my touch?'

The expression on his face didn't change, he didn't move except to look downwards and raise his hand an inch or so, the thumb and index finger pressed together. He seemed to be thinking quickly and carefully.

'I said that you played well, Mevrouw. But I never take pupils from someone else unless they ask me to.'

'But I asked you.'

'Excuse me, Mevrouw,' he said softly, 'you weren't asking me that at all, you were trying to catch me out.'

For a moment my mother's eyes blazed, but she kept control of herself just as I had learnt, thanks to Chris, to keep control of myself, and with a distant friendliness, in the tone she would use to a maid, she said quickly, walking to the door: 'You'll have to make the best of this old piano, Mijnheer Cuperus. Once . . . Nol has made a little progress we'll let him try the grand piano. This one has just been tuned. How do you want to be paid, for each lesson or by the quarter?'

'By the quarter, Mevrouw,' Cuperus said, with a slight bow at my mother's back.

I could have run after her and kicked her. What a beginning! How could I expect him to stay and teach me, a little dilettante, to play the piano! She had never been like that to anyone, not even to the most miserable beggar. . .

I walked over to him, and he put his hand on my head and said something like we must get down to work. We were standing just behind the two chairs.

'I hope you'll call me Nol, Mijnheer.'

'No,' he said with a pretended gruffness.

'Why not?'

'Master Rieske sounds much better.' He tweaked my ear

57

playfully. 'Maybe I'll call you Nol when you've learnt to play as well as your mother.'

'Oh,' I said, disappointed, and I wanted to tell him about the lame girl who played so much better than the woman who had just been so ill-mannered to him, but he had already sat himself down on one of the stools. I sat down beside him, and he gave me my first lesson, a whole hour without a flicker of boredom on his face and never more than five words at a time. He laid my stiff, unpractised fingers delicately on the ivory keys, and he pressed a little under my wrist so that my hand hung loosely, the fingers dangling like little asparagus stalks. He played a few scales for me, slowly and exactly. His fingers were thick and reddish, and he smelt of tobacco. When the hour was up he said it was a good start. He played the scales again, only once or twice, and ever so quickly—different from the tuner who spent a good five minutes, after he had finished, improvising on the 'Blumenlied' or 'Fremersberg'—then he jumped up and strode across the room without saying good-bye, his head high. He pushed the door to the drawing-room open as if he was storming a building to force his way inside.

Like a faithful dog I ran after him. I'd guessed right. My mother was in the drawing-room with a book on her knees. She couldn't have read very much, what with listening to us all the time, but as she was far more agreeable now, saying something about the beginning was always difficult and perhaps mightn't I be too old to learn the technique, I felt less hostile to her, and I even felt annoyed at Cuperus for saying nothing. He should, I considered, have seized the outstretched hand. But he didn't take his eyes off her for a single second. I escorted him downstairs, handed him his coat and bowler hat, and he said something friendly to me. I raced back upstairs to enjoy hearing my mother's impressions. She must think he was wonderful, in spite of everything.

All I could get out of her was that she thought he was 'provincial'. The word didn't convey anything to me. Even later I never understood what she meant, for, although there certainly was a provincial side to Cuperus, he never let it show in front of her. There was no reason to say he was 'provincial' just because his coat was rather the worse for wear or because his hair wasn't trimmed and his neck clean-shaven—that was the barber's fault—and that northern accent of his, after all, wasn't nearly as noticeable as Mijnheer Vellinga's or young Tjallingii's. But I could see that my mother's defeat had prejudiced her against my hero. She didn't think he looked like an artist either, with 'that coarse frizzy hair of his. . .'. I let her go on talking. For me, Cuperus could only be compared to Napoleon or Alexander the Great—though his appearance reminded me rather of Admiral de Ruyter —or perhaps some very famous composer. Anyway, Mijnheer Talsma had long hair and young Tjallingii let his hair grow long to hide his baldness, but that didn't make them artists.

'You can tell Chris that he wasn't drunk,' I said.

She wouldn't look me straight in the eye. 'No, he certainly wasn't drunk.'

'Why didn't you shake hands with him?'

'Next time I will. I wanted to see first. . .'

'Why did you walk so close to him?'

'You want to know everything, don't you?' my mother said, and the conversation went no farther. It might be hard to believe of a perhaps dreamy but certainly not weak-minded young boy, but it was years before I knew what answer she should have given to this last question of mine.

Cuperus hadn't let himself be discouraged by the breath-testing he had been subjected to, and the next time, and many times after that, he strode into our house like a prince, saluted my mother, who still came to take up her sentry-post in the drawing-room, with a courtly greeting, shook hands with her, and, if he got the chance, stared at her with his imposing black eyes until she blushed and looked away. Sometimes she came in during a lesson and started talking away, or she would suddenly discover she had something to do in the room that couldn't wait. If she looked back too long, then he lowered his head, not embarrassed, but just as he might do if he wanted to think deeply. Fascinated by this duel, I had the impression that he still wanted to punish her for her uncouthness that first afternoon. Maybe he exaggerated it all, maybe he did have a vindictive streak, but that's what he was like. For months the lessons continued, right into the spring, and nothing spectacular happened.

Not that I made much progress. I didn't consider the exercises I had to play were real music, and Chris pointed out, not without reason, that I played my scales even more carelessly than he had. The 'homework' that Cuperus gave me was often puzzling, and sometimes annoying, like the time he handed me a sheet of music that he had written out himself and scrawled across the top in that autocratic script of his: 'Watch out for the trebles, Master Rieske.' He didn't react to my reproachful look, but all through that lesson he was more cheerful than usual and he pinched my left ear so hard that if my mother hadn't been in the drawing-room next to us I would have yelled with the pain.

Soon after that she gave up this malicious habit of keeping watch and only appeared when he was about to leave. She had almost to force him to accept the first payment for the lessons. He insisted that he never sent bills and that his wife didn't know how to. When my mother laughed at this he stared at her, his head a little on one side as if he felt sorry for her, and with a bow and a deep sigh he went out of the room. She had heard that he'd been through a difficult time in his youth, and that later he'd had one disappointment after the other. That was partly because he wasn't easy to get on with. She must have got this information from Mijnheer Vellinga.

A few weeks later I found out that Vellinga did in fact know him personally. The journalistic ex-lawyer often turned up at the musical evenings, he liked to listen, he said, and upstairs the blare of his voice was more penetrating than the music. He was certainly not musical, I had sensed that when I saw him on the windy football field. After I had met him two or three times I didn't look up to him any more. His eyes, behind his pince-nez, were too small and too blue in the midst of that mass of pink, sometimes brick-red flesh, and his bulldog smirk was a sort of undisguised deceit, the treachery of a vicious but faithful dog. He had bad teeth from smoking a pipe, at least that was what I heard from Chris, who had admired him for a long time as the only man-sized lawyer he had seen at close quarters. He was always friendly enough with me, he didn't thump me on the shoulder, a habit I hated, and in his glib journalist's mouth the inevitable remark that my cheeks were just as red as my mother's sounded original and intelligent. That powerful skull, long exercised in 'heading', could stand up to the hardest knock, and he could listen to others too, even to that little, stuttering Mijnheer van Son, who detested him—there was quite a bit of smouldering antipathy amongst the male members of that small group. He would get his own back, and at the top of his voice, in his newspaper office and in the company of his cronies when there were no ladies around. But there was a softness in him that I couldn't understand. From what I'd seen of him that day at the football match I knew he was hard and heartless.

One Saturday afternoon when he had come to see my father with some or other subscription list I was seeing Cuperus out just as he was leaving. From the top of the stairs Vellinga shouted out: 'Another day's work done, hey?' Cuperus turned round, squinting, and answered him: 'So there you are, Vellinga, doing the rounds too?' I thought this all rather strange. I couldn't imagine him calling my father (who never bothered to look in when he was there) 'Rieske', though they were both lawyers, and high up the social scale, the noisy Vellinga by birth, and my very respectable father by reason of the persevering diligence of two or three generations. In the hallway, by the coat-rack, there was a lot of clapping of shoulders. I kept in the background, and neither of them took any notice of me. The jovial conversation was brief and inconsequential, and I had the impression that they would go their separate ways once they were outside the door. I felt that Cuperus had at the same time fallen and risen in prestige.

Shortly afterwards his prestige dropped much more but that was, in a way, my own fault. Not that it mattered, his prestige could have sunk to nothing as far as I was concerned and he would still be the man I admired most of all in the world. Sooner than might have been expected I was playing Clementi, and I confided to him that this music depressed me, and couldn't he pick out something else for me. There were tears in my voice, for I thought he would refuse, just as he had refused to call me 'Nol'. But this was the first real talk we had with each other, it lasted at least a quarter of an hour. That was possible, now that my mother didn't sit listening in the drawing room. I told him about Chris, what I'd had to put up with, that sonatina I couldn't bear listening to, and I even told him about punching Chris on the nose and about the crippled girl playing that sonata of Haydn's. He listened patiently. At the end of my tale I laughed through my tears and said I would play whatever he thought I ought to play.

'I'm not going to force any music down your throat. But in this book'—he brought his open hand down on it sharply—'there are other pieces besides Clementi's. Sonatinas by Beethoven, and he is the greatest composer of them all, so they say. Pieces by Haydn, too. You'll see there's a lot more of Clementi than you ever heard your brother playing. Marvellous, some of them, often better than anything by Beethoven, who wasn't always the greatest composer, not that Beethoven cared about that. We'll do it like this: I'll play a piece and you can say whether you want to practise it. Then you can forget about Chris . . . your brother. Will we try that?'

Of course we'd try it. With his foot he pulled his stool over to the middle, pushing mine out of the way and knocking me against the piano. He sat down and played a sonatina that I didn't remember ever hearing Chris trying to play. But he made the most shocking mistakes—if I had made mistakes like that in the much easier pieces I struggled through he would have twisted my ear. This was the first time I had heard him play more than a few bars. Up till then he could just as well have been a flautist who happened to give piano lessons to small boys to earn some extra money. Every now and then he seemed to hit two keys together with one of those fat red fingers. After he had played it through, he openly admitted he had made a mess of it, but he always played these easy pieces badly, his eyes weren't so good these days, and if he wore glasses his pupils would be frightened of him. These excuses were meant as a joke, but the fact remained that he had made a lot of mistakes and, as he had spoken about it first himself, I didn't see any harm in talking it over with my mother, not as a criticism of my teacher, but as a problem. Fortunately she surpassed herself by confiding that Mijnheer Talsma made mistakes too. Maybe they got bored teaching, or maybe they didn't want to discourage their pupils. Her answer to my question whether Cuperus played better than Talsma if he was playing just for himself on a grand piano was that Cuperus, good musician as he might be, had never given a public performance as a pianist, not in W . . . anyway, so perhaps he didn't feel so sure of himself on a platform. I asked her: 'Why aren't you nicer to him, at least you could talk to him about music?' She promised she would.

She did, and the conversation was anything but a success. Not only because Cuperus, who was allowed the privilege of sitting behind a cup of tea in the drawing-room, was more interested in intently watching my mother's face than in listening to what she said, but the difference in taste seemed to me, in my youthful absolutism, quite irreconcilable. As a true disciple of the Talsma school, my mother raved about Beethoven and one or two modern composers, while Cuperus made it unmistakeably clear that he didn't think any of those old dodderers was worth anything, except perhaps Haydn and one of Bach's sons (Philipp Emanuel, I think it was), and, of course, Bach himself, who was also one of Talsma's idols, and then the romantics, Liszt, certainly, and Chopin. My mother almost visibly turned her nose up at these preferences, not so much because of Talsma's influence as from a distaste for mixing emotional abandon with her domestic duties, and perhaps she had other reasons as well. When the weather got warmer she often went out in the afternoon. My lesson was from half past three till half past four, and she hardly ever came back before five. She seemed to have got over her suspicions.

Cuperus took to extending the lesson beyond the hour. He rarely played a piece through, but he was stricter than ever, he made me play everything over and over again, and at the most unexpected moments he caught hold of my arm to see if my wrist was loose or not. Sometimes he explained the correct rendering, then the various other possible interpretations and improvisations, and this would easily take up a quarter of an hour or more. Other times he kept me practising, with ruthless discipline, and he was never satisfied with the scales in D and B flat major, the most difficult of all. My playing did gradually improve, I began to appreciate Clementi's music once it was dissociated from Chris, and I was never tired at the end of a lesson. But when he stretched the hour to almost two hours, and met my mother on the stairs, she couldn't help remembering that I had my homework and other things to do, and these extensions were also embarrassing because he ought to be paid for all that extra time. I couldn't argue against my mother's plan to stay at home for one afternoon to put an end to my music teacher's noble-mindedness. There was no reason why this should offend him.

The first time she waited ten minutes, till twenty to five, then she began singing in the drawing-room, just when Cuperus was explaining the intricacies of a new piece by Clementi. She sang Wolf's 'Der Gärtner' and played a one-finger accompaniment. Like a hound that has sniffed an exciting scent, my teacher looked up the moment he heard it and listened for a while with his head turned away from me. When he looked at me again there were deep furrows across his forehead, his eyes were screwed up as if from pain, and after mumbling something like 'a fine voice your mother has', he just stared straight in front of him, his head slightly bowed. Then he started playing the accompaniment softly, with a fuller harmony, so softly that the notes were hardly audible. When she had sung the song through twice he stood up, tweaked my ear and walked into the drawing-room. I sat there bewildered. Was he going to lose his temper and give my mother a piece of his mind for her uninvited intrusion into our world of chords? But all I could hear through the open door was the compliments he paid her, a good-bye, and his heavy step in the hall. My mother didn't say much. We agreed that next time the best thing would be for her to call out from the drawing-room at a quarter to five that I had to run off and do my homework. This couldn't be taken as an affront, no, we talked it over and we were sure he couldn't feel offended.

That was on Wednesday, and on Saturday he turned up with a big bunch of flowers wrapped in a piece of paper. As I went to meet him in the drawing-room I saw our maid's chinless face peering inquisitively round the door. He put the flowers on the sewing-table in the corner of the room we used and didn't glance at them again. I knew better than to ask who the flowers were for. I concluded that after the lesson he was going to visit some-body whose birthday it was, maybe another one of his pupils. While I played a staccato exercise I was thinking with a secret satisfaction that when my mother came home at a quarter to five she would probably find the bird had flown.

I noticed that Cuperus had closed his eyes. Was he sick? This was the first time that he hadn't followed every note. Five times I played the staccato *étude*, each time with more mistakes than the last, then I went on to another piece without saying anything. Finally he roused himself. He told me to start on Clementi and he was himself again, as exacting as ever. The spasm of absentmindedness was over. He talked about the demands and possibilities of playing *cantabile*—that was the secret of the pianist's art—then something I couldn't follow, about introducing subtle nuances that changed babbling and monotonous accompaniments, and it was this sort of sensitive rendering that composers like Clementi and Dussek and Mozart and Beethoven had to thank for their solid classical reputations. I played some more, we talked, and I asked him questions. He seemed more alert than ever, and if I didn't understand straight away what he was explaining his black eyes flashed with impatience. I didn't dare look at my watch, but I knew it wouldn't be long before my mother came home. I was waiting for her to clap her hands at the drawing-room door and call out: 'Nol, you'd better go and do your homework now.'

Cuperus defeated this little conspiracy of ours by darting over to the sewing-table immediately he heard the front door bang, grabbing the bouquet and striding aggressively in the direction of the drawing-room. He pushed the easy chair out of his way, and he flung the door open the way he had done at the end of his first lesson. I watched him step towards my mother and, bowing deeply, offer her the bouquet. She backed away without taking the flowers from him.

'Is that for me?'

'Yes, Mevrouw,' he said, 'a small tribute . . .'

'Tribute? Whatever for?'

'For . .,' he tried to find the words, 'for . . . for your exquisite voice, Mevrouw.' Probably he had intended to say something else altogether. But it was too late, he had been tactless, now she could interpret the gift as an ironic gesture to punish her for singing 'Der Gärtner' during the lesson.

'I hope you will accept these flowers.'

'No, I can't, Mijnheer Cuperus.'

They stood silently facing each other for a long time, so long that I couldn't look at them any more, and I began to feel that same tingling and weakness in my legs that I had felt that day I had heard him conducting Sousa's march. Cuperus had flushed a deep red. I saw the bouquet shaking in his hand, his heavy moustache moved nervously up and down. Something menacing had broken loose, an unknown secret, an unspoken conflict, a struggle to the death perhaps, and I could have screamed with fear. Then I realized what it was. My mother, in her light tailored costume, her blue hat in her hand so that her angry face was in the full light, was struggling, not against the flowers that were still being held out for her to take, but against something else, against his look. And in my deepest feelings I sided with that look, I took sides against my mother, I knew it and that's why I was afraid.

'I can't accept these flowers, Mijnheer Cuperus, you must understand that.'

'Perhaps I find some things difficult to understand, Mevrouw. Do you think I am presuming too much?'

'No, it isn't that,' she said quickly, with an almost pleading movement of her hand. 'But you really must. . .'

'I don't care what it is,' he snapped. 'I've known women who would have been proud of being offered these flowers. I'll leave them here, you can throw them in the dustbin if you want to. Till next week, Mevrouw, Good-bye.'

He slammed the bouquet down on the table and stepped over to the door, where he stood still for a moment. He had felt behind him the distress of someone who wanted to explain, to put everything right again. But my mother stood fumbling with a long, white glove, she didn't say a word. As he went to open the door I ran across the room to open it for him. He waved me away, for the first time looking at me with a squint that didn't convey any hint of friendliness or good humour. In a resounding voice, his moustache quivering, a sly, incredibly sly, expression spreading over his inflamed face, he said over his shoulder: 'I would prefer that Master Rieske did not see me out today. Will you be so good as to ring for the maid?'

67

Before my mother could reach out for the bell on the table I rushed past him into the hall and called the maid. She came so quickly that she must have been eavesdropping in the next room. Cuperus strode out of the drawing-room and stamped, grim-faced, down the stairs, followed by the maid to whom I had explained in a whisper that she was to open the door for him. I tried to catch his eye but he ignored me.

My mother was still standing by the table in the drawing-room, angry and unhappy.

'If you throw those flowers in the dustbin . . .' I growled—but I was interrupted by a loud scream from the hall downstairs, a howl as if someone was being murdered. There had never been a sound like that in our house since Chris's anti-musical fit when he was ten or eleven. The front door shut with a bang that echoed through the house. My mother and I rushed out to the landing and saw the maid almost flying up the stairs, holding her apron over her face and yelling: 'He kissed me, he kissed me on my mouth, that fellow. . .'

A quarter of an hour later when I came downstairs—I had lain down on my bed with a throbbing headache— the inquiry was in full swing in the dining-room, my father, who had emerged from his study at the sound of the screams, conducting the hearing. Now he could work off all the frustrations of his legal career on this chinless servant girl, this mousy creature I had always thought a bit cracked, who had been inexplicably kissed, and kissed on the mouth, by my respected music teacher. He had bitten her too, she wailed, but not even my father could believe that. He had given her such a fright. I was called on to say what I had seen when she went downstairs with Cuperus. My mother didn't mention the flowers, she didn't say much at all. After my father had heard the evidence and the whole tale had become confused and con-tradictory, he asked the still snivelling victim if she hadn't perhaps imagined it all, a rather stupid question, implying as it did that she wasn't just scatter-brained but completely off her head. Fortunately Chris wasn't at home. While my mother was declaring that in any case we would have to give the man a chance to explain himself, my father walked over to the cupboard in the corner to get a sheet of note-paper and an envelope. My father sat writing the letter, my mother seemed to be having some difficulty in keeping a straight face. The maid had finished crying and started telling her story all over again, darting reproachful glances at me every now and then as if I had kissed her as well. That man, he hadn't even spoken to her, he had just grabbed hold of her and kissed her hard on the mouth, twice he did it, maybe three times. She didn't have to put up with that sort of thing, an old horror like him with that awful moustache. I walked out of the room, infuriated by the endless wail of her stupid voice. I was angry, but I felt some doubt too. If Cuperus had really kissed that scrawny thing, well . . . Not that I held it against him—he could skin her alive for all I cared—but I realized it would only mean the end of my lessons.

My parents must have had some doubts too, for the letter wasn't ready in time for the mail collection at eight o'clock. Just before eight a letter was dropped into our box after a soft ring of the bell. It was addressed to my mother. She opened it and handed it to my father to read aloud, again, fortunately, without Chris being there to hear. He had been sent upstairs on some pretext or other by my father, an act of thoughtfulness that I still think back on with gratitude. The letter was short:

'Dear Madam: After the incident in your hall today it is obvious that I cannot continue giving Nol piano lessons. My only excuse is that I had been drinking. Even if you were so kind as to insist I should go on with the tuition, I could only enter your house with a blush of shame on my face and I am not accustomed to feeling ashamed. Please convey my greetings to Nol and tell him that he must keep on studying under a better, or at least worthier, teacher than myself.

Yours respectfully, Henri Cuperus.'

'That certainly makes a good impression,' my father said, folding the sheet of paper. 'It's a very decent letter. I'm glad we hadn't sent ours, otherwise we'd have had to write a reply. . . After all it isn't such a crime to kiss a housemaid, and she's so feather-brained, she may have encouraged him. Ah well, you see what comes of drink. . .'

'He wasn't drunk,' I broke in desperately, 'anyone could see that. That stupid girl, she's spoilt everything. Mother, you saw him, you know he wasn't drunk.' My mother said nothing.

'You know bloody well he wasn't drunk.'

'Only common boys swear,' my father said. 'You shouldn't speak to your mother like that.'

My mother began to smile, a mysterious smile it seemed to me, as if she had achieved a triumph that none of us knew about. 'No, he wasn't drunk,' she said in a clear voice.

Muttering, my father took up the letter, looking at it again— 'Then it's . . . well . . . it's even more of a riddle.'

As softly as I could, so Chris wouldn't hear, I lay in my room sobbing myself to sleep. I remembered how I used to listen to Chris crying and wailing, and that was because of piano lessons, too. . . But with him it wasn't real grief, it was just his nerves, and being set on getting his own way, and blind rage. Cuperus had called me 'Nol' twice in his letter. For the first time he had called me 'Nol', and that was what drew the bitterest tears. That was the cruellest thing he could have written. If he'd wanted to say good-bye forever he couldn't have picked a better way of saying it.

[6]

Cuperus's self-contrived effacement had a whole train of consequences. I can hardly attempt to describe how the whole situation
appeared to me at that time. Once or twice I tried to sort it all
out, but I wasn't really interested. Now that I had lost him as a
teacher I felt I shouldn't bother about him any more. By kissing
that maid of ours he invited contempt and he had fallen in my
esteem, too. I noticed this a few months later when I saw him on
the other side of the long, winding main street where the shops
were, walking along jauntily, his hands stuck in his pockets, an
ominously black, sloppy, wide-brimmed hat pushed back on his
head. I turned away the moment I caught sight of him, I didn't
even need to think what I should do.

Then the life I led, particularly after the summer holidays, was
hardly compatible with thoughts of music and respect for my
elders. Not that I neglected my piano studies completely—my
mother had taken it upon herself to give me lessons—but if you
come home with a black eye or a bleeding nose (one that hurt a
lot) you're not in the mood for Clementi, not even for Beethoven,
'the greatest composer of them all', whose sonatas my mother,
applying a watered-down Talsma method, had decided to let me
loose on. My hand would be trembling too much from fighting
to play exercises. The time was past when I could easily hold my
own by beating up smaller boys, and all through that year before
I went to the lyceum I had to wage a bitter struggle against a few
of my class-mates. They had reached the turbulent beginning of
adolescence, they wouldn't put up with anything from me, they
poked fun at my girlish face and my rosy cheeks—'Nola' was the
new name they had given me—and when I punched them it
sometimes turned out that they were stronger than I was, in any
case more belligerent. I decided I'd have to be thorough about it,
so every time a finger was pointed at me I attacked. This was
exhausting, but in the end it put me in a better position. From

an older boy I knew, who had already left school, I learnt some dirty fighting tricks, and my skill made my opponents in turn my irreconcilable enemies and then my friends again.

It was a wild time, anything but conducive to the strengthening of family bonds, but certainly facilitating a tolerable relationship with Chris (much as he disapproved of my fighting). The wildness included excursions into the unsophisticated night life in the streets of W..., for, if I had been successful in the afternoon with my fists or my feet, I felt obliged to wander out after seven with a cigarette between my lips to do justice to the silent instruction I'd had from 'Blue' and 'Brown'. Slouching past the lighted shop-windows, I was, in my imagination, a notorious figure, and I lost count of the girls I spoke to, walked a little way with, and then tried to push into one of those alleys I have since forgotten, never very far, so that it was always as if we were standing in a doorway. Usually these encounters ended with a bit of tussling and a quarrel. I never managed to get as far as kissing any of them. After a while I got tired of these forays, especially after a couple of girls identified me as 'the judge's son' and made a lot of nasty remarks about judges. After that I went out in the evening with a few friends, at least they passed for friends.

Halfway through the winter I saw Trix Cuperus fighting again, not with girls this time, but with a group of young boys, smaller than she was, whose heads didn't reach to her shoulder. Her technique was to kick them in the stomach or a little lower down. This was a form of attack that not even the heroes of antiquity could withstand, and so she was soon alone, looking down from her enraged tomboy tallness. Turning her head every few steps to watch the gang of them in full flight, she passed close to us. Her face was thinner and there were blue shadows under her eyes. I wasn't very moved by the sight of her. When one of my companions said: 'She's an odd one, that girl, better to have nothing to do with her', I just shrugged. I felt an admiration for her—quite impersonally, as if she had become something impersonal, almost symbolic—but I wouldn't have liked to have had to tell the others that I knew her from a long while ago, and that I had once danced with her.

The next time I went to the Garden that winter I took a few other boys with me just for safety. Previously, my occasional visits in spring or in summer (but never on Sunday afternoons) had always given me a feeling of solemnity, and when I was having piano lessons I used to go there like a pilgrim. I would walk past the cages with the golden birds and the waddling goose, then, clambering up the slope, always with the impression that there were children behind me, till I reached the top of the rocky ridge, I would look down, with still something of the wonderment of that first time, over the miniature valley, to the pond and the bandstand and the few people sitting on the chairs. In the autumn these chairs were covered with fallen leaves. But with my friends there too it was a rowdy expedition through a leafless garden without flowers and without birds. The half-frozen goose had escaped being eaten for Christmas dinner. Though we had intended to drink a glass of milk in the restaurant, we didn't get further than the rock wall, where the noise we were making got us chased away by one of the waiters. We ran off shouting names at him. At the entrance gate we stopped to throw stones on to the thin ice over the moat, they sunk like frogs diving into a weed-covered ditch.

Cuperus had to bear the full burden of his conduct in our hallway. Not that my parents deliberately spread the tale around, but at those musical evenings some reason had to be given why 'that man' wasn't coming to our house any more, because some of the guests were rather interested in him, not only Vellinga and young Tjallingii, but even more so Caspers, a smooth young banker with cultural leanings, who had had lessons from him for about six months and considered him a remarkable personality, a man with character.

Naturally, the maid talked about the incident too, in her own circle, just as Chris did at school. It was only reasonable to explain the whole affair to a few close friends to avoid any exaggerations getting around. Besides, it was an amusing story and I have the impression that in the pauses during those musical evenings my parents would be, as often as not, at a loss for conversation material and that my father did not want to leave all the talking to the 'young people' without giving some display of initiative of his own. I do know that my father, more than my mother, found excuses for Cuperus, but perhaps they would have done better to wait till they had a more suitable audience.

Vellinga, whose journalistic indiscretion could hardly be regarded as a vice, wasn't there, and neither van Son nor young Tjallingii, in spite of his delicate mannerisms, nor Caspers, the carefully groomed and widely-travelled banker, was given to gossiping, even though they were all bachelors. The coteries they belonged to weren't of any importance for Cuperus, who, like all the music teachers in W..., was dependent on the favours of less exalted social strata. But Dijkhuizen happened to be there. He was older than the others, a bachelor too, fat and round, satisfied with life and with himself, a good drinker, and a passionate lover of music. Chris and I couldn't stand the sight of him, but not because he made a show of being religious. He did this for business reasons that I won't go into. The church choir Cuperus conducted was one of the things he meddled in with his fat fingers. That was only to be expected, for, as it turned out later, he was no stranger to the red light district in the big towns and so he had to do something to ease his conscience occasionally.

The loss of the church choir led to the loss of one of the others as well. Only the 'socialist' choir—the name was an exaggeration —remained true to the sinner. The number of his pupils shrunk daily. The ladies and young girls of W... did not want to or were not allowed to go near him. Whether there were some ladies and young girls who would have liked to take lessons from him now I was never able to find out. All these details barely interested me. I heard them, I scarcely took any notice, I didn't feel any responsibility, and I had finally come to accept as a fact the inexplicable convention that my mother, who was probably the only guilty one in the whole business, could not accept a bouquet of flowers from 'a man like that'. According to the tales that were going round, Cuperus was on the bottle all the time, his daughter would come to a bad end the way she was growing up, they had to use chicory because they couldn't afford coffee, his sick wife had to go out washing, the daughter had been begging on the streets, a policeman had caught her at it once and when he was marching her off she started struggling and fighting and a little boy got a kick between the legs from her.

It was difficult for me now to deny that my former music teacher did drink and that he always had, but I tried to put it in a less serious light, which could be convincing if only my account of personal observation was accepted. I said that I had seen him at least three times walking down the street, maybe not briskly and smartly, but he was as sober as Mijnheer van Son himself, who was a teetotaller. I knew how a man walked if he was drunk, swaying and shouting and vomiting. It couldn't be as bad as they said, my mother thought, and anyway, he didn't have that much money to spend on drink. Then there was a lot of talk about 'that girl', 'that Trixie', I said, but if she fought in the street— and she could fight better than I could—it was because her father had been insulted.

This conversation ended with the question that had long since become a stereotyped formula: Why, why did he kiss Joukje in the passage?—a riddle that even lawyers couldn't solve. Maybe it's a habit of his, my mother said, with such a far-off look in her eyes that I went back to my homework. I heard from Chris, who had conscientiously avoided taunting me over the Cuperus affair, that he had been caught at the same sort of thing before, kissing girls in corners, and worse than that, during lessons. I should point out that all this was just so much invention like all the other tales, except about the money difficulties—it appeared that his wife was jealous and she spread all this gossip though without any motive of malice. But at that time I believed it might be true, and obviously, kissing pupils in the middle of a piece by Clementi, or even Beethoven or Haydn, was far more improper than kissing servant girls who started screaming.

One spring afternoon of alternating sunshine and rain I was walking along the canal in the direction of the little railway bridge. With the noise of the barges and barge captains and the peat boats, the canal was the ultimate contrast with the quiet moat on the other side of the town, and as my interest had, years and years before, been transferred from the canal to the moat, my stroll that afternoon was more a question of physical exercise than recalling old memories. I saw it was going to rain again, and I decided I wouldn't go any further than the bridge, I'd watch a train going past, if there was one coming or going, and then go back home. As the first drops were falling I passed a side street, a street like ours but the houses were far less imposing, and there I saw Henri Cuperus, his collar turned up, his big black hat pulled over his eyes. It would not be quite correct to say he was on the footpath, for half the time he walked with one foot sunk in the leaves piled up in the gutter and his legs wide apart, as if he was determined to keep a hold on the footpath. These gymnastics didn't prevent him from looking in my direction. Not only that, but he must have recognized me, for he stood still, looking, though not very intently. It was like the way a cat looks at a bird it knows can't get away. That one second I stopped had delivered me into his clutches, and now the one second was suddenly ten seconds. When he was only a few yards from me he straightened up, his hand holding down his hat, that now was pushed a little back on his head and threatened by a gust of wind. His face was thinner, too, so that he didn't resemble Admiral de Ruyter any more. His eyes weren't watery or bloodshot as they used to be, only squinting with delight, and this reassured me, while at the same time heightening the feeling of guilt I had towards my parents and the town of W... How could anyone in his position glow with happiness? However, there was no one in the street or along the side of the canal who could see us. After he had ceremoniously cleared his throat, he shook my hand warmly. The rain had formed a silver curtain.

'How are you, Nol? Fine that you still recognize me after all these months.'

'Of course I'd recognize you, Mijnheer,' I said in a firm voice, and while the rain splashed on both our hands I let him keep his grip on mine.

'We'd better find some shelter, you haven't got an overcoat on,' he mumbled, turning round to the two rows of porchless houses. He cleared his throat again. 'No, it's not like that, it's not just to be taken for granted, and even if you'd kept on walking you would still have been one of my favourite ex-pupils. The others are a miserable lot, it wasn't any of their business, and it must have given you a shock, that noise in the hallway and everything. I've got a lot of ex-pupils these days, you know,' he went on in a cheerful tone. 'Some of them have started to say good-day to me. That's fine. Soon they'll all be back again, the little rascals, and then we'll go and have a meal, the three of us together, at home...' He let my hand drop, squeezed his moustache dry, and looked around. He was humming softly to himself. Just as suddenly as it had begun the rain stopped again. There were still a few fleeting silvery streaks that blew away as if a hand was whirling them out of sight, and at the end of the street a hopeful shaft of blue pierced the grey clouds. Cuperus had taken his hat off. A thin red line ran across his forehead. He looked at the palm of his hand: 'Cheap dye they sell now. I'm only forty-three, but this moustache of mine was getting greyer and greyer, but not my hair. And that at the beginning of the new century, the twentieth century. Oh, well! Will you walk a bit with me? Ten houses more, that's all.'

I walked along with him, on his left side. He fanned himself with his big hat, that gave off the aroma of a barber's shop. Now and then he mumbled something, or started humming again. Once he looked round at a stone that he had probably wanted to avoid stepping on and by some miracle had managed to miss. His voice boomed over my head like the sound of a gong.

'We're damned poor now.' I didn't know what to say, I only knew that I wouldn't walk off and leave him after the tenth house. 'Don't worry, I'm not going to ask you for ten cents.' He gave a laugh and coughed. 'Don't take any notice of what I say, young fellow, I was just teasing you. You'll know soon enough that you can run into a rough patch. It's just temporary in my case.'

I would have liked to say: 'If I had a hundred guilders, Mijnheer...' But a hundred guilders was a lot of money for a young boy to have, and if it was a thousand he wouldn't have believed it. When we reached the twelfth or thirteenth house he stopped: 'Do you want to hear really good music, for the first time in your life? My wife is fortunately a little deaf.'

The connection wasn't clear, but I quickly said I would, for I felt that the slightest hesitation would have been an irreparable insult. He nodded, strode on, and didn't say a word until we were at his door. The house was rather squat with a ridged roof. It would have been as high as the neighbouring houses if the rooms hadn't had such low ceilings. This made the front room with the grand piano, where I found myself when he pushed me through a quickly opened door, seem to have much less space than an ordinary room of the same length and breadth. The street was quiet and respectable. Opposite, there was a blacksmith's forge, silent and deserted, with the name of the smith on a big white board across the whole façade, the letters faded in patches. 'G. J. Douwes' looked like 'G. J. Doodis' or 'Doodvis'. The last letters could be anything at all.

I heard him muttering and mumbling in the passage, and the clatter of a coathanger indicated that he was having some difficulty in hanging up his coat, maybe the tag on the collar was torn. The piano keys were a dirty yellow. There was a notebook with a red pencil at the end of the keyboard. I didn't see any music scores, probably they were in the bookcase. On top of the piano there was a cup of tea, no longer warm. The musty smell in the room would, I assumed, come from the numerous dried-up laurel wreaths on the wall, with ribbons that looked as if they had been gnawed at by rats and mice. But no, it was the smell of tobacco smoke. The mustiness was in the passage, a dusty smell that didn't come from food or cooking. A big portrait of Liszt was hanging on the wall, the same one as my mother had in an album. As a girl she had idolized Liszt, all the more because she had never heard him play, and she learnt from my grandmother, who had heard him play, that that name was the magic word for all musical young ladies. The rest of the things in the room testified to a gruesome lack of taste. There was a hideous pipe-rack, imitation handicraft, without a single pipe in it. From this I concluded that Cuperus smoked nothing but cigars, and probably the cheapest sort for the last few months. An assortment of books was stacked on a little table, and on top of the books was a diary, probably without a single appointment in it for weeks and weeks.

He was, in fact, puffing at a just-lighted cigar when he came in dressed in an old velvet house-jacket. He had straightened the ends of his rain-drenched moustache and while he was speaking he blew big puffs of smoke.

'Take a seat, Nol, you're soaking wet, but never mind, it's a mess here anyway. Oh damn, that tea's still there.'

Hitching up his trousers, he walked over to the piano, took the teacup and went over to the window. Seeing the faces he pulled I wasn't surprised when he poured more than half of the tea over a wilting potplant. I was almost sure he swayed as he walked, but I promptly dismissed the thought that he might have taken a quick swig out in the hallway.

'That's for the mistress of the house'—as though the tea was an offering of precious wine. 'The ladies are fortunately out. If they noticed you were here they'd think, "Ah, a new pupil", and they musn't get ideas like that.' He winked at me slyly and walked back to the piano, ruffling his black curly hair. 'What will we play? You've never heard *really* good playing, have you, now?'

'No, Mijnheer. Only my mother, and Mijnheer van Son...'

Just for a second he looked up, as if the name of a formidable rival had echoed through his room. Then, shrugging, he sat down on the piano stool, half facing me.

'And the lady two houses away from us, she plays very well, too...'

He didn't seem to be listening. His head sank lower and lower on his chest. His eyes were shut, but his face wasn't relaxed, and when he put his right hand up to his chin I realized that he wasn't dozing but thinking. With his head bent down like that his red neck and the roughly trimmed edges of hair were plainly visible. I looked at the neck with a twinge of affection. Suddenly he stood up to push the teacup, which was back again on the piano, to one side... In case it rattles when he starts playing, I thought to myself. Then he laid his cigar in the saucer and sat down again on the stool facing me.

'Nol', a deep sigh stopped him from going on. 'Nol, you're still young, but you saw what happened, and you must have thought too that I was drunk...'

'No, Mijnheer, I swear I didn't, I never thought that at all. My mother didn't either. When my father asked her she said: 'He wasn't drunk...'

'Your mother didn't think so either,' he repeated hoarsely and put his hands over his eyes. His broad shoulders were shaking.

'My father and mother hoped you would come back,' I lied, 'and my mother told me herself that she appreciated those flowers, and they were in a bowl for three days.' (That, at least, was true— the flowers were considered too good to throw away.)

His shoulders were shaking again, he was holding his face in both hands. He had done everything that should lead to an outburst of sobbing. But even though, as I calculated later, he must have had at least eight good nips of gin, his eyes, when he lifted up his face, were dry and fiery, drawn a little with sadness, but certainly defiant.

'Do you know why I did it?'

I shook my head. None of us had ever been able to make out why he had done it.

'Because I was in love with your mother,' he said solemnly, looking up, 'was, but not any more. She didn't deserve the love I felt for her. She looked down on me. I was just a hired performer, a servant, and when I saw that I decided to behave like a servant and so I kissed that girl in the passage.'

A whirl of confused thoughts prevented me from doing anything more than staring at him with an expression of mistrust. I couldn't very well believe him, especially as he was really drunk now or, at least, he had been just a little while ago.

'You're not shocked, are you?... No, of course you're not, you're still young and innocent. This was a pure love, as pure as Lohengrin's love for Elsa or Parsifal's love for Kundry, and there are others, too, you haven't heard of. I never expected any encouragement. But those flowers were ... Still, it's over and done with now. Since then I've fallen in love with two other women. The first one was taking lessons, then she decided to stop, but she'll be back again in six months or so. I know she will. When she told me she wouldn't be taking any more lessons, here in this room it was, I suddenly fell in love with her, and she could sense that. They always sense it, these women, and your mother too, that was why she acted the way she did. I've been to a fortune-teller—not that I believe any of that nonsense, I only went because my wife wanted me to—and she said that everything will be fine again in two months. I'm on the rocks at the moment, but in two months' time ... and there's a dark-haired woman somewhere, that's the second one, you see. Oh well, maybe by that time it'll be a blonde,' he grinned, the ends of his moustache sticking up uncouthly at odd angles. A moment later he was serious again.

'You can explain all that to your mother.'

'About the blonde... ?'

'Don't be bloody silly, of course not,' he said, annoyed, and I felt as if his eyes were knives cutting me to bits. 'Only that I ... You don't have to explain anything to her, Nol, but you can if you want to. You can say I fell in love with her, or, if you like, that I thought a lot of her, or that I liked her, and that was why I cuddled the maid, and that I've got over it. Now I'll play something for you. We haven't got much time, they'll be back any minute, those women of mine.'

He got up and swinging his arm towards the wall he shouted: 'Liszt!' Then he sat down again without bothering to get the score and rattled off a few introductory bars. After a minute or so of rippling arpeggios—I didn't know whether they were part of the piece or not—he nodded to me to shift up next to him, and I had scarcely shoved my chair nearer to his stool when it began in earnest. A fascinating melody welled up over those arpeggios, it rose and fell and spoke and sung, and then came a wild ferment from which, after a crescendo of thunder and lightning, the melody was distilled anew, but this time in a lower key. Suddenly the melody rang out in a powerful bass with dizzying, breath-taking embellishments, the arpeggios swirling higher and higher, and now he played a few false notes. It was obvious, even to my untrained ear, that he was disregarding every convention, but never clumsily or crudely, and never in the deep, resonant bass tones, and his touch, his rendering, his mastery over the spirit of the music were a magnificent display that made of me his humble admirer, a slave, an insignificant nobody. If only my mother could hear him playing like that. What was this Liszt, with his disagreeable face who, so my father had once told me, turned Catholic—what was Liszt compared to an artist like Cuperus?

Admittedly, while I listened my attention was distracted by the way he twisted and turned. He blew immense clouds of smoke from the cigar that was back in his mouth, clenched between his teeth, and sometimes he turned and nodded at me, squinting with that squint of his and an enraptured expression on his face. After he began on a second piece—it was Chopin's study in A flat major but I thought then that it was another of Liszt's compositions—I could tell when he was going to turn round and nod. It was always at the most exciting passages, where the music took an unexpected turn. Then he nodded quickly and emphatically, and his face, framed in a happy smile, was engrossed and guileless, despite that squint which probably wasn't a squint but only seemed so because one eye was closed and the other gleamed in a setting of playful wrinkles. I bent forward so I could watch every change of his expression. Halfway through the nineteenth bar, the receding counterpart, he shut his eyes, puckered his forehead and rocked from side to side with his whole body, once, twice, an irresistible swaying that seemed to be part of the music. A lot of the high notes were wrong. But with the pedals or by some other trick he managed each time to preserve the rich, full flow of sound. Those wrong notes weren't due to drunkenness, he knew he always made the same mistakes and he could always cover them up. I didn't realize that at the time, but later I often heard him play this *étude* and he even taught me to play it in my own halting way.

Right in the middle of that ecstatic pedal bass in E flat, just after the indication '*appassionato*', he suddenly stopped, and hissing: 'There they are back again, those damned women', he pulled me up out of the chair. I hadn't heard the front door being opened or shut. The voices in the hall died away, one, sharp and shrill, the other listless, larded with provincial accents. Cuperus stood listening, then, when it was silent again, he hustled me out of the house, not forgetting to tweak my ear. Now I could smell the drink on his breath. He didn't ask me to come and see him again.

7

My first impulse was to ask my parents if I could have lessons from him again, at his place. When I thought it over, I felt it would be imprudent to announce my intention all at once, without first making some effort to rehabilitate Cuperus in my mother's eyes. I wasn't worried about that tale of Cuperus's that he was or had been in love with my mother. Anyway, as I had never associated my father with the idea of being in love, it was hardly a surprise to me that other men could fall under her spell. The only disturbing aspect was the implication that the others who came to the house must be or had been in love with her as well, that little, musically-minded van Son no less than that hulking, unmusical Vellinga. After all, none of them was married, while Cuperus had a wife of his own. It was only when I thought of young Tjallingii, more womanish than his own poodle that licked everyone's hand, that I ran into difficulties, but there probably weren't any rules that prevented simpering, hip-wiggling males from losing their hearts to pretty, lively, smiling and blushing females. I got over the problem of a possible reciprocity, not so much by keeping in mind her determined reaction to Cuperus, the most irresistible of them all, as by giving due consideration to her married state. Besides, I didn't know for sure whether or not my father mightn't be or mightn't have been in love with her. He could hide his feelings, and perhaps he just mightn't think about it for months on end. There were endless possibilities.

My disclosures of how love and deep respect and feeling slighted had led to that kissing episode didn't raise the slightest blush on my mother's cheek. She had guessed it, almost from the beginning, she said. She thought he was crazy, now she felt sorry for him, and she could believe his explanation about kissing the maid, she'd heard of a young man who had been courting a cousin of hers and he did almost the same thing when she broke it off. These disappointed men tried to take advantage of young housemaids.

The maid at her cousin's had hit back, and the man stood there cursing and swearing, not in a hallway, but outside in the vegetable garden. It wasn't only her intuition. Mijnheer Vellinga had told her, only two weeks after the first lesson, that one evening he had met Cuperus, all excited, and he had confided his feelings to him. She said the word 'excited' so emphatically that she obviously meant he was drunk or 'ebullient', a favourite word of my father's. But at least, so Mijnheer Vellinga, who had told her this when no one else was there, had assured her, 'the man' hadn't said a single disrespectful word about her. They'd laughed about the whole business, Vellinga and her, it was so absurd. Vellinga had been drinking with him at the bar in the Garden restaurant and I was really too young to hear about things like this, and she didn't think it was very nice of Cuperus to try and use me as a go-between. As a final move I remarked that Cuperus certainly did drink but he never drank much, and it was only sorrow that made him drink now. However, this didn't make any impression on my mother's conscience.

For a few days I mulled over the idea of bribing Joukje. If she said that Cuperus hadn't kissed her at all, had given her a little peck, or that she had said to him: 'You never give me a kiss' or something like that, then my father, who hadn't sided against him and wasn't likely to appreciate the love aspect, would be favourably impressed. But Joukje, the chinless skivvy, wasn't with us any more, and she hadn't gone to work anywhere else. I knew where she lived, I knew what her parents were like, and I knew I'd have to bribe the rest of her family as well. Or maybe Joukje, once she had the money, would rather be kissed by Cuperus again than come and face my father with a brazen lie on her lips.

The thought of bribery gave me another idea, for a scheme that assumed gigantic proportions when it was put into effect. The project grew and grew just like Chris's peppermint factory. I started by asking my mother for twenty guilders to help Cuperus.

I didn't need to point out that it was her haughty attitude that had as good as ruined him. She gave me the money, and I assured her that even if I couldn't give it to him at once it was quite safe with me. When she said she didn't doubt it, I was sorry I hadn't asked for more. I didn't know what else I was going to do. I still had a feeling that even a hundred guilders, the limit of my youthful imagination, could be taken as an insult, but maybe only if it was offered as a bundle of notes, not if it was handed over in a sealed envelope. An envelope was essential. I certainly couldn't go to him with less than a hundred guilders.

I thought I'd try Chris. I asked him if he wanted to earn five guilders. Chris could do with five guilders, for going round with rich friends was a weakness of his, and his years at the university would cost my father a fortune even though his personal inclination was more for library and lecture-room than for bar and brothel. Chris's eyes gleamed behind his glasses. But what did he have to do? Not much, I explained. It was just to help that poor devil, Cuperus, who'd given me piano lessons. I'd been to see him, he didn't drink any more, his wife was sick and she didn't have enough to eat. If I couldn't give him a hundred guilders I was going to leave school and work to get some money for him. This, Chris thought, was a little too drastic and he promised to see what he could do.

If he could pry the money loose from his friends—and that meant his friends' parents—it would be good publicity at the same time. The publicity would make up for whatever Chris might keep for extra commission. There was no way of checking this, and I decided I wouldn't give him the five guilders until he had handed over a reasonable amount. He should ask the lecturers too, I suggested.

A week later he brought me forty guilders and I promised him ten guilders instead of five if he could make it up to eighty. I'm sure he did his best. From what I could find out later he didn't keep back more than ten per cent. and that his method of approach was highminded, cunningly invoking feelings of social duty and charity. But he never got it higher than seventy guilders, and since he was stupid enough to hand the money over before I paid the commission, there was a violent quarrel, because I gave him seven and a half guilders for his trouble and he insisted that this wasn't the agreed percentage. Frantic from pent-up greed, he accused me of every sin and crime he could think of. I shook my fist in his face, and strangely enough he quietened down. In the end I did give him another two and a half guilders in exchange for an old watch-chain I had wanted for a long time. I was still seventeen and a half guilders short.

Now I would have to see what I could do with my own friends. There was another reason for that, too. If I went to Cuperus by myself with all that money he might think it was from my parents —conscience money, or a sort of bribe to keep quiet about being in love with my mother—and refuse it. But if I turned up with a crowd of others, preferably including a few old pupils, that would make an altogether different impression. The seventeen and a half guilders—it was actually twenty-one guilders and some small change, and we divided the surplus amongst ourselves—was soon collected, largely due to my own powers of persuasion. At every chance I had I gathered a small group together, and painted in the blackest colours the same picture that I had inspired Chris with, and I elaborated it with details Chris had invented himself. Cents and guilders trickled in and I didn't rest until the parents of about forty pupils, boys and girls, had been moved to pity. Some of my schoolmates even put forward absurd suggestions like going round from house to house, or standing singing in the rain with a collection box or an old hat. I said that Cuperus was the best pianist in Holland and we couldn't let him die of hunger just because a couple of idiots in W... had it in for him. I assured them, I swore, that he *didn't* get drunk, that he never had been drunk, that he didn't even like strong drink, that it made him sick. Had anyone ever seen him staggering along the street?

Besides an unmusical group of twelve boys and a few girls (selected by reason of contributions exceeding two guilders) I now had three former pupils who wanted to and had permission to take piano lessons from the outcast, and four others with older brothers or sisters or cousins or mothers or aunst similarly disposed. It was remarkable how soon the kissing incident seemed to have been forgotten, for not once was there any comment from the contributing families about sins of the past. After the first excitement at school the interest died down, so there were only eight supporters with me, two of them old pupils, the day I set out with the envelope in my pocket. After long reflection I had decided not to take any girls along with us. I had a vague suspicion that their presence might have the wrong effect.

It was raining again that afternoon when we turned into the quiet side-street where the signboard with the name of G. J. Douwes in faded letters looked as if it was shedding new tears. The faded letters were more ominous than ever. I didn't know whether he would be at home or what sort of reception we would get, still, I was calm and sure of myself, with a slight feeling of being virtuously noble, like Johan de Witt who never took money for himself no matter how much he was urged to. There wasn't any sound of music from his room. I had arranged with my friends that I would go in first, alone, and then call them inside at the right moment. I found myself face to face with a woman who couldn't be anyone else but Cuperus's wife. My companions were standing at the side of the house so she couldn't see them. She was fairly tall and thin as a rake, with pale blinking eyes that had the wateriness of frequent weeping, and she had an air of scruffy poverty that was both contradicted and confirmed by a long, neatly ironed apron she had on. Anyone who took so much trouble to look clean and tidy must have a lot to hide. She held her head pushed forward, listening. She put a hand up to her ear.

'Can I speak to Mijnheer Cuperus? Or isn't he at home?'

'Oh yes, he's at home,' she answered, and she made coughing

noises, rubbing her hand against her hip while she peered with a worried look at the pouring rain that was falling in a slant away from the house. She hesitated, perhaps she didn't know what to say, but suddenly she shut her eyes, as if an idea was forming in her mind. She took a step backwards and called out with a forced shrillness in her voice: 'Hendrik, there's a boy here to see you', then she said to me: 'Come in, young man', making a half-hearted attempt to smile. She went back to the end of the hall, standing there expectantly. In the room something scraped along the floor, I heard him stumbling and muttering, and I was thinking to myself, but without anxiety, 'How drunk will he be this time?'

There he was standing in the doorway of his room, in his shirtsleeves, blinking at me. Perhaps it was because of the envelope I was holding in my hand that he didn't recognize me. In the half darkness he looked like a negro, with that ruffled frizzy hair and those bloodshot eyes, a negro with a moustache, and out of that bushy moustache the smoke from a nearly finished cigar streamed upwards. At that moment my only thought was why hadn't I put a single hundred-guilder note in the envelope instead of a bundle of smaller notes that he might want to count. If he didn't count them he wouldn't believe us, he wouldn't believe that it was really a hundred guilders. At last he recognized me.

'Nol,' he growled, his face dark with irritation, 'a surprise visit, heh?'

'Yes, Mijnheer,' I said, involuntarily flicking the envelope enticingly from side to side. 'I came ... you said ... told me you ... you were having a hard time ... and we thought, myself and a lot of my friends at school, two of them used to be pupils of yours ... no, three of them ... we thought ... we'd like to give you this. As a token of appreciation,' I added hastily, for I had learnt this expression by heart. He didn't seem to understand.

His wife had edged hesitantly nearer. 'Give it to me, young man, thank you very much.'

'We've collected some money,' I said. This statement made

89

it clear to his wife that our initiative didn't directly concern her. But she became more insistent and grabbed at the envelope.

'Keep your paws off,' he snarled, and stepped protectively in front of me, tossing his smouldering cigar butt past me out on to the porch. 'Is this money?'

'Yes, Mijnheer,' I said, looking him straight in the eye though I was trembling all over, 'My parents don't know anything about it, we collected it at school, just amongst ourselves, nobody else knows ...'

'Let me have it, young man,' his wife broke in, a whine in her voice.

Obviously it would have been crazy to let her have her way in defiance of my old teacher's command. At the same time I felt it would be inadvisable to hand him the envelope before I had some assurance that it wouldn't be torn in four pieces and thrown after the cigar butt. Cuperus turned round and bellowed, immediately lowering his voice (the bellowing was evidently to pierce a wall of deafness): 'Get out of here, you don't understand anything. This is a great moment for me, a moment I'll never forget ... all those young lads ... and all you think of is food. Get back to your kitchen.'

She must have heard the last bit as well. 'Yes, if there only was some food there to eat,' she jeered and walked a few steps down the hall, stopping to listen with her back to us. A vague smell of cooking implied some exaggeration on her part. While Cuperus and I went on talking, I heard her whisper: 'Hendrik', pleadingly, but without turning round.

'Why don't you say I spend everything on drink?' he hissed at her, but she couldn't have heard it. To get his thoughts off her I resumed my little speech.

'We all want to take lessons from you again, Mijnheer, because we think you're the best teacher in the town. But if that money ... if you feel offended about it ... well, when we've started having lessons again ...'

90

'Offended?' A youthful gaiety lit up his face, his eyes squinted, his moustache, with magic puffs of smoke still floating up out of it, shook from the lilting curve of his full red lips, and his chin, a conqueror's chin, had a dimple.

'Give me that envelope.' He took the envelope, his wife turned round, leaning towards us. He shoved the envelope inside his waistcoat, pushing his tie out, then he flung his arms wide apart.

'Nol, if that's all true, from now on I'll treat you as I would my own son. You'd still be the same as a son to me even if it wasn't all true. You're a damned fine lad, and if you want lessons from me again it won't cost your parents a cent.' Beaming with happiness he stood looking at me but he didn't put his arms around me as I had more or less expected.

'The others are outside,' I said, a little embarrased.

'We'll have to have them all inside. If they all want lessons from me I want to shake their hands. This is the most wonderful day of my life. My God, if I had only known that the Philistines had sons like this. Ah yes, what's that line from Hans Sachs . . .' He thought a minute, trying to remember, shook his head sadly and then sang in a soft, slightly hoarse bass: '*Dem Vogel, der heut' sang, dem war der Schnabel hold gewachsen* . . .' An abrupt movement of an imaginary conductor's baton ended the singing. Tears were glistening in his eyes. 'Where are they, the other lads? . . . Tell me, Nol,' he whispered, bending down over me, and now I sniffed the drink through the tobacco mustiness, I smelt the drink on his breath but I didn't flinch, 'you won't get into trouble at home for all this, will you?'

'No, Mijnheer,' I whispered back. 'I'll talk to my parents this evening, and if my mother says I can't—my father doesn't bother, you see—but she'll let me . . . But if she says I can't . . . then . . . I would have added triumphantly: 'I'll run away' if the dignity of his presence, even though he was a little drunk, had not forbidden this excess of bravado.

He thumped me on the shoulder, and then I went and called the others—some of them were already putting their heads round the front door—and he shook hands with them all, not making the slightest distinction between old pupils and the unmusical ones. They laughed with him and they said afterwards that he was a wonderful chap, full of fun. Then his wife had to come and shake hands with us all. When the noise in the hallway was at its loudest Trix appeared in the background. I noticed her at once, and Cuperus, who stood out between those two tall blonde creatures like an Italian organ-grinder, must have felt she was there, for he turned round and bellowed: 'Your born enemies, Trix. Come here and shake hands with them,' and he sang gaily in German: '*Die jüngste Gevatterin spricht den Spruch! Selig, wie die Sonne meines Glückes lacht, Morgen voller Wonne selig mir erwacht: Traum der hochsten ...*', but the invitation didn't entice her any more than the song. After a contemptuous stare at us, she disappeared as silently as she had come, like a shadow in that long hallway where the now stronger smell of cooking rose and fell with the draught that brushed past our legs.

A week later I started having lessons from him, and that lasted until I went to the university. I came almost completely under his spell. I walked the way he did, with something of a military step, I tried to squint without squinting, I tried to smoke cigars, with disastrous results. As I was his benefactor I felt myself all the more obliged to submit to him spiritually. Actually, it was far from negligible what I had done for him. He got his choir back, and a lot of pupils (not the two who had given money and now, probably after further parental reflection, found him a 'big fool', so provoking the last fight I had at the elementary school), and my, mother held it against Dijkhuizen personally that the church choir wasn't returned to him as well. She did a lot for him too, and in the end she must have been just as sick as I was of the account of the 'spontaneous action of those lads' that she always opened her intercession with. As she had given up her music lessons shortly before that, she didn't have to consider Talsma's feelings any more, though Talsma himself, strict and honest as he was, seemed to have spoken up for Cuperus too. There was certainly a favourable wind blowing for the sinner, and I don't think that, for the next year at least, he drank much, though Mijnheer Vellinga talked about evenings at the Garden bar where Cuperus 'was always really priceless', but never making a fool of himself. According to Vellinga he kept his dignity no matter how much he'd drunk, and if he wanted to go home, he went. Once Dijkhuizen had tried to be clever at his expense, and Cuperus lifted him up, chair and all. But Cuperus knew how far he could go, he just held the chair above the floor with Dijkhuizen trying not to show how frightened he was by blowing kisses to the girls behind the buffet. By then Vellinga wasn't a frequent visitor at our house. Whatever his reason had been for coming often he seemed to have got over it.

I could fill volumes with all that Cuperus taught me. He brought me to a certain point and I never managed to get beyond that point, partly because I was more interested in music as such than in the perfect rendering of a score, partly because he himself didn't bother overmuch with technique, though he must have mastered it thoroughly when he was younger. Whenever he made a mistake he gave an amused smile. Each time he played a piece the mistakes would be different, it must have been a surprise for him to hear which notes he went wrong with. I have since heard Chopin's 'Barcarolle' played better (quicker too, but that isn't any advantage) than he played it, but never with the same inspiring passion which, towards the end, soared higher and higher to a sort of monumental yet serene frenzy, as he pounded the bass notes exultantly and unleashed the melody with its harmonic variations and the swirl of chromatically ascending trills, a cry of desperation and pathos. He played the dreamy middle passage in A major with a disregard for tempo that no concert pianist of the time would have dared.

He was without equal in the way he could explain a piece after he had played it through, or even when he was playing it, and, in simple terms, impart an understanding of the beauty or the originality or the warmth of certain passages. He accompanied the famous, dissonant pedal point in the 'Barcarolle', which he placed on the same level as Bach's immortal pedal points, with the oddest grimaces and shouts. He bit through his cigar, he seethed, his moustache gleamed, and then he would play the whole piece over again, slowly, tracing for me, in simple wording that I could understand, the outline of a harmonious framework, an anatomic miracle of co-ordinated sounds, seven or eight bars high, a symmetric with arms and legs, standing strong and dynamic on the solid basis of a deep unending F sharp. The discords that arose from the inherent impulse of this living organism to retrieve, again and again, an even balance surprised me far more than I could ever say, but he maintained that these were not the most important feature, merely a device for the transposition from the first F sharp major (after the prolonged *ritenuto*) back to the F sharp major in *calando* at the beginning of the coda. But the melody shouldn't be forgotten in admiration of those incredible harmonies. Once he sang it in a soft tenor—he could do that too—with a subdued accompaniment, and it sounded like the voice of a lover from far across the water. We could never reconcile our opinions. I listened most for the unusual details, unexpected chords, contrapuntal discords, but, after all, I had learnt that from him, and I don't really think the difference was as great as he made it seem. I have never blushed so much as when he told me I listened with a more expert ear than he did himself.

His preference for Liszt, which he so loudly proclaimed, wasn't so deep any more. It was rather a lingering memory of his wild long-haired student years that he wanted to stay true to. But he often used to play for me a brilliant rhapsody, far more exciting than the better known ones, never once making a single mistake. He must have studied it thoroughly when he was younger. He hardly ever spoke of his past. He had never composed anything, which rather disappointed me, but it was in keeping with his character. I could never imagine him scribbling notes on a piece of paper, and sitting for hours biting his pencil if his inspiration failed him. He was too constantly inspired for the discipline of composing.

He was fond of relating stories about Liszt and the other Romantics, and then he would fetch books and photos and newspaper cuttings. But even so, he was reticent on some points. I never heard from him that Chopin knew a certain George Sand, or that Liszt ... well ... He seemed inclined to desexualize the lives of musical celebrities, and he would rather hold forth on Schumann and Clara, who remained true to each other on every concert platform in Europe, than rake up the murky episodes of Wagner's private life, most of which he wouldn't have known anyway. Besides, I was now his 'son'—although he never uttered the word again to me—and perhaps he felt he was under some obligation to my mother, seeing that he had so brazenly kissed her maid.

His real favourite, not as a person but as a composer, was Wagner. But he never admitted this openly. At the time Wagner was regarded in W... as a noisy upstart, though a few adventurous spirits were expressing admiration for Richard Strauss—and it was months before he stopped smiling ironically whenever he played passages that were meant to suggest an orchestral rendering. He even sang as he played, all parts, and he would comment on the chromatic ecstasy of Tristan's love, the exalted ocean of sound, the counterpoint and the ninth chords of the *Meistersinger*, the leitmotif of the *Ring*, and talk about the problems of stage presentation. He picked out the best passages and he conveyed Hagen's treachery just as faultlessly as the trickery of Mime, the surly manner of Klingsor or the naive folly of Gunther. He told me that the Mark motif from *Tristan* was far better music than the famous love motif, and he played it and I still think he was right. He would play the finest passages and for days I walked around dizzy with happiness over the *Meistersinger* overture, evening after evening I was stunned by the final scene from *Siegfried*, and Siegfried's 'Rheinfahrt' from the *Götterdämmerung* was for me the ultimate in the musical depiction of nature. The piano rocked, the teacup, which he seemed to accept as an incidental percussion, tinkled and rattled, the windows shook a little as well, and the sky, like a pale spectator clinging to the housetops, peeped in. In these grandiose renditions he didn't make any more mistakes that the most accomplished player might have done. But there was no doubt that by nature he wasn't a pianist, his talent was the interpretation of colourful orchestral music whether it was with a conductor's baton or those hammering fingers. He thought and felt in the sounds of instruments, and in his versatile homage to Wagner's genius he wouldn't hesitate to imitate the fagot or the tuba.

Although I used to see Cuperus's wife regularly—she brought the tea in—I rarely caught sight of Trix. If I came face to face with her in the hallway or at the door, she didn't seem to recognize me. That was not so surprising. During the last few years the only times I had seen her was when she was fighting in the street. Even if she remembered me bringing the envelope, her pride would certainly not allow her to make a closer acquaintance on that account. Her face was strongly featured, with something of defiance and despair in her expression. But she still had that proud walk and that habit of half shutting her pallid, but still exciting, eyes when she smiled. She didn't smile at me. If Cuperus mentioned his wife he spoke with a sort of rough tenderness, and, perhaps to erase the bad impression of the envelope scene, he made a point of going to the door and carrying the tea-tray into the room himself, talking to her with affected cheeriness—'Now, Mother, you poor old soul, there you are, slaving for us again', and other inanities that no woman over forty can bear hearing from her lawful wedded husband.

If he ever spoke about Trix he was vague, even when I told him about Sousa's march and how we had danced. 'Trix, ah yes, it's a pity she won't take up singing seriously. She'd rather fight, though she seems to be getting a little tamer these days ... Yes, it's a pity ... she's got a good voice.' When I countered these disparagements by pointing out that if she fought it was to defend him, and telling him that I had seen her myself and admired her for it, he flashed a quick glance at me. 'But not always. When things were going badly, you know how it was, then those two thought I was cheating them with the housekeeping money. Ah well, it's better not to think about it any more. But once she punched me in the face, you see. Just imagine that, a father, and you're set about by your daughter ...' He shook his head, then he said: 'An awkward one she is, Nol, but she thinks the world of me, even if she is still a little angry with me.' After another pause he said: 'She's going away soon, she's got to get away from here for a while.' I wondered if she had maybe fallen in love, or whether Cuperus wasn't trying to prevent anything like that happening.

It wasn't until just before or just after the next summer holidays that I had a chance to talk to her. In October of that year she went to stay with a spinster aunt in a smaller town quite a way from W... The idea was that this aunt, who had been a nurse or something like that and held a domestic science teacher's diploma, would teach her housekeeping and good manners, 'tame' her a little as my teacher put it, and he insisted that she should keep up her singing lessons. But it was only later that I heard all this, and when I found myself standing in front of her one afternoon I didn't know that in another month (or it might have been three months) she would be going away. I was alone in the music-room. Cuperus always took an afternoon nap and sometimes I had to sit there waiting for him. But we always did 'overtime' that more than made up for the minutes he was late. With a look of surprise when she saw her father wasn't in the room she came in with the tea. I stood up at once and walked to meet her with an outstretched hand. Without looking at the hand I held out to her, she put the teapot and the cups on the piano. I put my hand in my trouser pocket and said: 'I'm Nol Rieske. We danced together once, but you won't remember that. It was when I was only little.'

'Danced?' she asked, without interest, 'where?'

I didn't think she was pretty. Her lips were too thin, on her face there was a criss-cross of tiny wrinkles each telling a tale of unhappiness, and her ash-blond hair was scraggy and greasy. She was still almost a head taller than I was, and her willowy figure, and the way she carried herself, erect and defiant, made a deep impression on me. I felt strangely weak, but at the same time I felt free to do just as I wanted, all the more because I had never been shy with girls, at least not after I managed to get talking to them. Her watery eyes were expressionless, her mouth was slightly open, without making her look foolish, and she had the same curved nose as Cuperus. In answer to her question I said we had danced in the Garden when her father was conducting the band.

'Oh, then,' she said with a glimmer of recollection in her eyes, and looked round a moment at the door. I was determined to make those eyes smile, somehow or other.

'When we were dancing you said I had rosy cheeks.' She just stared at me as if she expected to hear that she had said I had nice bare legs as well. I added hastily: 'I still have. Or don't you think they're quite so rosy now?'

Finally she seemed to realize that she should show some politeness to one of her father's pupils, particularly one she could thank for a good part of her daily bread.

'They're still rosy,' she said, very seriously, 'but you mustn't go looking in the mirror too often.'

It didn't worry me at all that she spoke to me the way she might speak to a child. I would have let her cradle me in her arms like a baby, this tall, slender girl, this amazon. With a smile I said: 'You look pale. It's not pretty, really. Once I saw

98

you fighting, with some girls. That was ... that was wonderful.'

The hint of a sneer around her mouth, the eyes cooler than ever... but what beautiful eyelashes she had—I hadn't noticed till that moment.

'Do you stick your nose into everything?'

'No, Trix,' I said teasingly. For a few seconds neither of us spoke. 'I hope you'll call me Nol, not Master Rieske.'

'I certainly won't call you that,' she said decidedly and looked through the window to the opposite side of the street where 'G. J. Douwes' was blistering in the boiling sun.

'Do you like music?'

'No, not at all,' she said quickly as she walked towards the window. Over her shoulder she added: 'Music bores me, but it usen't to.'

After she had pushed the window open she called out loudly: 'Wait a minute, I won't be long.' I saw two girls coming towards the house from the other side of the street. She seemed to be pleased about this visit, for as she walked past me with a mumbled 'Bye, Nol', her eyes were smiling, not at me, not because of anything I had said. Nevertheless, I felt pleased with myself.

This smile wasn't like the sunlight breaking through the clouds. It was something altogether different, it must have been the lines around the eyes that lit up again with their natural mischievousness, the eyelids, and those lashes ... I don't know how to describe it exactly. I don't know either how soon I forgot her again during those summer holidays, or how long, how many months, years even, I let pass by and scarcely gave her a thought. I don't know how that was ever possible.

8

While ice sports, ice-skating and such, were the main winter
diversions in W..., the local Opera Society, founded by Mijnheer
Vellinga and a few well-to-do music-lovers, came to be a modest
rival of these outdoor activities. The most important soloists were
brought from Amsterdam or The Hague, the other roles were,
as far as possible, filled by local talent. In a matter of a week or so,
Cuperus, the unanimous choice even of the other musicians in
W... for conductor, transformed the choir that had remained
faithful to him into an opera chorus, subsequently joined by a few
members of the church choir, more or less with the encouragement of Dijkhuizen who didn't want to be thought a spoilsport
now that the prestige of W... had to be maintained against the
pretensions of the neighbouring university town with its population twice as big as W... and much better known, yet every
whit as provincial. It was bad enough that some of the musicians
had to be borrowed from that high-handed crowd.

Now that Chris was living there as a student, distinguishing
himself in economics and commercial law, probably the result of
his peppermint factory experiment, I could enjoy the preparations
and the discussions at home unhindered by his presence. The
aggressive assertions of manhood that I had so diligently cultivated
became unimportant, I was just a sensitive register, absorbing
everything that had to do with the stage, oblivious to everything
else, and when Cuperus shook hands again with my mother I
didn't consider it a great moment in my life. I was allowed to
watch rehearsals, and to enjoy hearing a real orchestra—not just
an imitation on a piano—the deep and savage blare of the brass,
the woodwind, refined and primitive, and if the violins were
faultless that was wonderful too, though string instruments, even
played by a Kreisler, have always been somehow suspect for me.
Apart from local professionals and more talented amateurs, the
orchestra was made up of veterans from the university town with

whom Cuperus was constantly at loggerheads, just as he was with the stage manager from Amsterdam who wouldn't come back a second time and was replaced by a more submissive fellow, half dilettante, but resourceful and conscientious, and without all Wagner's operas in his head. The first time—I was in the third year at the lyceum then—the Opera Society hadn't aspired higher than von Flotow's *Martha*, a chunk of sentimental lightheartedness that Cuperus conducted with verve and with disgust in his heart, unfortunately without me there to see it for I was in bed with influenza and I hadn't been able to go to the dress rehearsal either.

To avoid aggravating a tender issue it had been decided that only one of the Amsterdam professionals, the far from unknown tenor, Wessel Stegeman, would perform as a soloist, while the title role would be played by a local beauty, Jantje de Ridder, a brunette with a trained soprano voice and a good measure of theatrical temperament. She had other inclinations too, for she had taken lessons from Cuperus, and for years I suspected that she must have been the 'dark lady' who would, according to his fortune-teller, bring him renewed fame and fortune. She flirted with everyone, not just casually or frivolously—she was well over thirty—but with the calculated determination of a full-blooded woman who wanted to keep on enjoying life as long as she could without attracting too much attention. Her smouldering eyes made me think of dark-brown egg-yolks. She had very high cheek-bones that I found attractive, and her figure and her walk could only be called seductive, with those broad, swaying hips that had to cope on the stage with so much passion and pathos. Her voice was low, with a knowing, amorous undertone. I never understood how that voice could suddenly become a high-pitched soprano. Bold enough by nature for the role of Martha, she had a certain provincialism that excluded any successs with, say, Vellinga, Caspers, and their sort. It was mostly obscure youths with musical aspirations that she lured on and then discarded, having, as everyone knew without holding it against her, treated them to an adequate initiation. The moment she set eyes on Stegeman she rushed at him, not to flirt this time, but to conquer him.

I admired Wessel Stegeman myself, an authentic opera singer who came bearing high the light of culture from the city and— what was for me a personal honour—stayed at our house. If he hadn't been so thin and elegant and slightly tubercular, with such surprised, grey, wide eyes in a long oval face peering at a no doubt hostile world, he would have replaced Cuperus as my hero. But, on reflection, I was glad that Jantje de Ridder appropriated him, and during the following weeks I observed with an affectionate tenderness how they studied their parts by scarcely noticing any-thing but each other's nearness. Stegeman was, at heart, just as much the respectable, middle-class citizen as she was, and it would have been a good match if they had got married, which, despite the good intentions of all concerned, never happened. He was always friendly to me, he took me with him on long walks, and discoursed from behind his scarf on the character of French and German girls, all of whom were, according to him, deceitful hussies. Dutch girls were the only ones who could be trusted, and so much the better, because they were the ones 'we' (he and I, that is) were interested in most.

That scarf was the most important medium through which the singing couple expressed their affection. Never have I seen a woman run around so devotedly with an article of clothing as Jantje de Ridder did with Wessel Stegman's scarf. Once when they were at our house for supper and someone said there was a draught, she went and fetched it from the coat-stand in the hall. On such occasions they sat gaping at each other, swallowing each other with their eyes, each pair so different in colour and expression, and Jantje, languishing and bullying, mothered him in the hallway, in the street, in the snow, probably in her own apartment, and even at Cuperus's house, where I met them once when I came for my lesson. They had just been rehearsing, they were still filled with music, trilling and cooing, serious and playful, and they were busy for at least five minutes with that scarf, though they both found a chance to stroke my head, while Cuperus, standing in the doorway of his room watching, amused at their antics, did his best to set his moustache on fire with his cigar. When they had gone he said to me: 'We'll have to see that they don't make a mess of it, my boy. We'll have to keep chasing them on to the stage, I can see that.'

After he had been staying with us for a week Stegeman was so communicative that more than once my mother hurried out of the room hiding her mouth with her hand so she wouldn't burst out laughing in the middle of one of his tales. I felt some doubt myself about his truthfulness, but he went on and on so impassively and with so little humour that, even allowing for his extravagant criticism of foreign girls, I considered deliberate falsehood unlikely. He had the habit of reducing every word that had even the slightest offensive connotation to an indistinct whisper. I remember the long reminiscence he entertained us with after he came back from one of the last rehearsals: 'Oh yes, jealousy in our profession, it's all too common. You can expect it all the time, I'm sorry to say. Take Ordelio, the baritone, a great singer, a marvellous actor. I do take my hat off to him. But, you know, for some reason or other he simply detests me.' (Stegeman said 'dee-tests', and the 'dee' sounded like a gasp of despair.) 'And it's such a pity the man boo ... he drinks like a fish, and that has often got him into no end of bother... Imagine, if you have to work with someone like that. I've told Jeanne' (He always referred to Jantje as Jeanne, perhaps because she insisted he should.) 'The most unbelievable things about him. Besides his bre ... has such a sm ... so dreadful that when we did d'Albert's *Lowland* and he was playing Pedro—I had to throw him on to a table, hopeless it was because he wouldn't help at all—I simply couldn't go near him, it was poisonous, especially when he was singing the high notes. After the performance I said to him: "D ... it all, Ordelio, keep off the b . . . a little, and think of the rest of the cast." And didn't he fly off the handle, calling me a d . . . busybody, and a lot more too. Six months later we were doing *Carmen* in Rotterdam. I was José and he was Escamillo, he is wonderful in that role, I will say that, but, you know, just before the curtain went up he was st . . . dr . . . Mevrouw, my heart was in my mouth.' (At this point my mother got up and went out, almost tripping over in her haste.) 'But, would you believe it, Mijnheer, that afternoon he went and bought a real Spanish knife, a *navada*, no *navaja*, that's the word, *navaja*. He showed it to everyone and when we stood facing each other in the big scene in the third act, the man was completely under the wea . . . bli . . . dr . . . he was, he pulled that sharp knife out, then he came and stood right next to me, blowing his rot . . . bre . . . all over me and while we were singing he said: "I'll slash your belly open." What a situation! But I didn't get frightened, I said,—and this was while we were singing, don't forget — "And I'll batter your head in." And he kept toying with that knife, it was a genuine Spanish knife, engraved. . .'

My father liked him well enough, but he decided this was the moment to interrupt with an observation that had just as much a professional ring as Stegeman's story, but, to my ears, was far less interesting and enjoyable, disappointingly realistic. My father said that great actors often did things like that as a stimulus, so they could play their part with a feeling that it was true to life. In Germany, in Dortmund if he wasn't mistaken, it had gone too far once, and an actress had been killed on the stage. Quite unintentionally and without malice he had suggested that the colourful, individualistic, alcoholic chaos of the theatre was nothing more than a commonplace, easily explained phenomenon, but Stegeman took it as a veiled indictment of his indiscreetness. He didn't go on with the story, he looked at each of us, one after the other, with his surprised eyes, said something about having heard that such things did happen in southern countries, where the people were a wild lot, then he stood up and went up to his room after a friendly and polite 'Good-night'. There couldn't be another tenor as good-natured as he was.

Unlike Ordelio, Stegeman was fond of playing innocent jokes on the stage, much appreciated by the women and rather in the nature of harmless party games. He told us beforehand, opening his babyish eyes wide, that in one of the tearful arias in *Martha* he was going to sing 'May the devil forgive you for the pain you made me bear', instead of 'May Heaven forgive you', and you'll see, no one in the audience will even notice. It was certainly no predilection for blasphemy that inspired this absurd word change, which he did sing, as he said he would—my mother told me when she came home at half past twelve—on the night of the performance, quite clearly and quite unnoticed, but a little, sharp-featured second-rate soloist, whom Tjalingii, himself a sort of infantile monster, had once dubbed the 'Devil', heard it and thought it no end of a joke. Stegeman departed in an aura of good will and anticipation of next year's performance. Jantje de Ridder wept for a couple of days, got a letter from him, waited two months for the next letter, and after that went off somewhere, but not alone, for a holiday. My mother got roses, and two days later we all received a signed photograph of Stegeman as Tannhäuser, pilgrim's staff in his hand, the bearded, or rather hair-ringed, face in the final, almost fluid, stage of remorse and devout despair.

At first I thought that we (*we*, of course) were going to try out, or put on, or, better still, present *Tannhäuser* for next year's programme. But quite apart from the fact that Cuperus had unpleasant memories of the music of this opera, he didn't intend to overreach himself after a success, to our not so discerning ears, with a mere trifle like *Martha*. Stegeman and Jeannetje (that was what Cuperus always called her) had, he confided to me, sung well, but there was nothing good about the rest of them, especially the hotchpotch orchestra, a lot of conceited clods who would never learn to play unless a bit of musical feeling was knocked

105

into their thick heads with a hammer. I remember him during the rehearsals shaking with indignation, banging with his baton for them to stop, his face red and bursting, his shirt grey with sweat, letting loose an unrestrained vocabulary: 'What a bloody mess! Keep time, you idiots. Is the clarinet listening? Well, is the clarinet ready to try again?' Wagner's operas, even the less difficult ones, would have to be put aside for all time. Maybe an unambitious production of *Faust* could have been considered, but then Cuperus couldn't stand the music, it made him dizzy, except the Mephisto serenade, one or two duets, and parts of the waltz. He was on the whole not so enthusiastic about French musicians. He regarded Chopin as a full-blooded Pole who had to put a revolutionary fire into every noise he made on the piano, a talented musician whose talents were destroyed by a certain George Sand, just as Berlioz, who was less brilliant and not very important, had been ruined by that slut of an actress he gadded about with.

When I came for my lesson one afternoon some nine months later he was sitting at the piano in his shirt-sleeves, his eyes fixed on a dog-eared music book, staring at a passage he had just been playing. His cigar was lying in the saucer slowly going out in the spilt tea. I still have that music book, but the first thing I saw— Cuperus hardly looked up as I came in and just went on looking at the score and sighing—were the words *Chor der Zigarettenarbeiterinnen*, and a few staves lower *Chor der jungen Leute*. The music had been arranged for the piano by Otto Singer, the score was published by N. J. Servaas, The Hague, and on nearly every page there are unreadable jottings by the former owner, whose signature on the flyleaf looked like 'J. Models', or perhaps 'W. Toddels'. Other jottings, by Cuperus himself, are still as readable as the music itself. The book was smudged and thumb-marked, he had bought it years before at a stall in the market. This was one of the first things he told me about it.

'But I've never played a note of it,' he added, darting a distrustful glance at the cigarette girls' chorus, 'and now they've decided they want to play this, instead of *Faust*. At least, Caspers wants this and he forks out most of the money. I'd feel the same if I'd seen it six months ago in Amsterdam with a prima donna'—he brought his finger and thumb to his mouth and made the noise of a discreet kiss—'a woman you could go down on your knees for. Caspers didn't do that of course, but I'll let you see a photo of her, Nol. My God. . .' With a deep sigh, he stood up, his joints creaking, but before he had reached the bookcase he had to turn to answer my bewildered question: 'Which opera is it, Mijnheer?'

'*Carmen*, of course. I'll have the complete score and all the parts in a day or so. I've never seen it on the stage. I only know that toreador piece that you hear every butcher's boy whistling. Still, I can leave that out, or make it shorter in any case. . .'

While he was speaking he had opened the glass door of the bookcase, the interior of which was hidden by a puffy, pleated drape of threadbare yellow silk, and from a box he lifted out a pile of photos and other papers, and laid them on the table. I went and stood next to him. As far as I could make out the photos were mostly of charming, elaborately gowned females, the papers were newspaper clippings, apparently review notices, all creased and torn, only the photos mattered. I could see clippings from Dutch papers, German clippings, Italian clippings. There were a few photos of men as well, plump tenors, doll-like baritones, staring basses, but my teacher swept these all aside with most of the female singers, who were apparently not suitable for my young eyes, until there were only two women left, a heavyweight blonde in a long robe and a simmering brunette wrapped elegantly in what I later found out was called a mantilla.

'That's her,' Cuperus said, pointing to the brunette, 'I wanted to show you the other one because she was the famous Wagner prima donna, Wilhelmina Brustknappe. When I was young, I heard her once in Hanover playing Isolde. But the brunette, that's the one we're interested in. Alice de Rato—but that's not her real name, of course. Caspers wants to have her here, he's paying the extra expense, and he wants Ordelio for Escamillo, the toreador fellow, and he'll pay half of what that costs. He's an idealist, that Caspers, there's not many bankers like him. So you see, Nol, what I'm in for. It wouldn't be so bad if it was just conducting an opera I don't know, but to have a woman like Alice de Rato up on the stage in front of you all the time . . . Well, it's true that our dear little Jeannetje couldn't sing the part. So there we are. . . Now we'd better put these photos back again, some of them are pictures of dancers, and my wife doesn't approve of that sort of thing. . . No, no, what am I saying, it's a mezzo part, anyway. Jeannetje could play some other role, there's a sweet and gentle Spanish girl in it, maybe that would do for her. No lesson today, I'll let you hear some of the music and next week you'll get an hour extra, if I have time, that is . . .'

'Is Mijnheer Stegeman going to be in it too?'

Sitting in front of the piano, he turned back three or four pages—'Don't know. That's for Caspers to decide. He isn't so expensive, his voice is on the thin side, but he can act . . . Look, this isn't bad, this piece. . .' *Chor der Dragoner*, I read, *Diese Menge, im Gedränge*. Cuperus played a gay and lively march tune, here and there furtive, and sometimes reckless. It certainly didn't sound like Wagner, but it was much more exciting than anything in *Martha*. He kept nodding at me as he played, one eye shut. 'That's good, that chromatically rising bass there, but that flourish in C flat is weak, yes . . . still . . .' He stopped playing. 'It's good opera, much better than *Faust*, more modern, he must have learned from Wagner's early pieces. Around page 120 I spotted something, no, it was further on, near the end where Carmen gets finished off. I can see our Werner, or Werther was it, doing that and then sing opposite a female like de Rato . . .'

He turned over the pages, stopping at page 131. Page 130 was headed: *Duett und Schlusschor*—'Here's José pleading with Carmen to let him come back to her, the fool . . . *tempo primo*. . . Good,

good . . . very ordinary accompaniment, but you don't hear that with the orchestra—but that's not the piece I was telling you about . . . here it is, from the ninth bar . . . just listen to it, it's pure Wagner . . . marvellous! But not at the end, still, that's damned good too, that E flat-A flat-F chord, but I was thinking of the counterpoint just before it, with those damned clever imitations.' He played the passage through again, more slowly—'That's *Tristan*, that's *Parsifal* or whatever you like, but Bizet never heard or read a note of either of them. He might have heard bits of *Lohengrin* and he would have heard *Tannhäuser*, that's certain . . . Clever, damned clever.'

For me it wasn't clever, but exciting to hear, and, of course, obedient to my teacher's guidance, I found it Wagnerian. After all, he must have played half of *Tristan* for me, and the best-known pieces from *Parsifal*. I understood what he meant. It was amazing that the Frenchman Bizet had written Wagnerian music without having heard Wagner's music. But with all Wagner's works in thick red volumes in our bookcases it hardly seemed anything to get excited about.

'*Carmen, nur ein Wort noch höre!*' Cuperus sang the last line from the previous page. 'Yes, yes, that'll be a mess if the fellow starts whining. . . A little further on we have Carmen going up and down the scale. . . old-fashioned tricks . . . Let's find something Spanish, not that tin-can rattle for the toreador and the red flags for Mr. Bull . . . Just look at this, *Kinder kommen gelaufen*, yes, yes, sixteen beats to the bar, yes, that's it, and then higher and higher like soap bubbles. Here's the 'Habanera'. I'll leave that damned thing out, Caspers can whistle it if he wants to. But on the next page, there it's good again, with that jingle pianissimo over the dominant and that canon too, did you notice it, didn't he know how to write music! Oh, my God, what is this rubbish now?' Grinning like a fiend he started singing an uninspired *andantino* affectedly and deliberately out of tune. 'But what have we got now? Wonderful! Wonderful! The Muses will forgive

Bizet for that *andantino*. That descending motif back on the same dominant . . . I don't know exactly what happens here, Carmen'll be up to something again, but I can get that sorted out later. . . Here we've got the senorita Micaëla, the sweet little girl. Jeannetje'll have to change her character if she wants to play that part, she'll have to learn a bit of humility and virtue. It's not an easy scene this, you know, she comes on the stage like a little bird caught in a net with all those dragoons round her. I was playing that piece before you came. But Jeannetje isn't a little bird, and she wouldn't get caught in a cage.'

'Why not?'

'She's the one who does the catching,' he said. 'But we still haven't found anything really Spanish. You'll have to hear something genuinely Spanish before you go home.'

I'd never heard him talk so much. He couldn't have had much to drink, it was simply his enthusiasm for the music, for *Carmen* and the woman who would make *Carmen* a triumph. After flicking over the pages for a while, still with a flow of alternately derisive and admiring comment, he looked at me intently: 'No, I'm not in a Spanish mood. But what would you say if I gave Trix a part?'

I blushed, but I don't think he noticed. If he had noticed it, he would probably have thought it was from embarrassment at being asked for my opinion.

'Is she still taking singing lessons, Mijnheer?'

'Yes and no. I'm not quite sure. But I found her voice had improved the last time she was here for a couple of days and condescended to sing for her papa, the little bitch. I could give her a small part, Frasquita, or Branguita, or Brangäne or whatever her name is. It would be a good thing to let them see here that she can do something else besides fight with boys and drag her father out of the gutter. I'll play a really good piece for you now, Nol, and then you'll have to go, I want to spend the rest of the afternoon and tonight going through it a couple of times. Even then I still won't be sure of the orchestration . . . One of the intermezzos, maybe. I played the first one, simple . . . the second . . . conventional accompaniment, but it looks not too bad. The third? Ah yes, that's Spanish. Tom de-de-dom tom tom tom, tom de-de-dom tom tom tom, pluk pluk, pluk pluk. . . Well, let's try the second one then. You'll just have to imagine a pizzicato accompaniment for a cello. Are you ready, Nol? Just clench your teeth and off we go . . . Maybe it's for the harp, yes, of course, harp, and a flute for the melody . . . first, the violins, but never mind, just imagine a flute . . . What was happening just before this? Oh yes, I see it now. Carmen and José are running off. . .'

He played the second intermezzo from *Carmen* and after a few moments every glint of irony had disappeared from those squinting pirate's eyes. He played a couple of wrong notes. Then he played it all over right from the beginning, emphasizing the counterpart from the thirteenth bar onwards. The piano sang, he was using the pedal less than the first time, the tinkling of the accompaniment sounded precise and delicate and though he gave a discouraged shake of his head near the end I knew that once again a miracle had happened and it was not Wagner this time. Listening with his ears I was enchanted by this vigorous yet haunting music, even though I wasn't sure what his final opinion would be (and that would, of course, be mine). After playing a few bars over again quickly he sat with his hands on his knees.

'I don't think that the strings come in there, except in the middle. You were right, Nol. I knew that piece, I must have heard it at a concert some time, a potpourri probably. . . It's . . . yes, it's good, perfectly balanced. I'll lend you the score one of these days to take home and read right through, then you can pick out the finest pieces.'

We didn't say anything for a minute or so, the music was still in the air, and I gazed at the curved lines over the notes which were for me the only visible indication of the coherent unity of the song. He cleared his throat, reached for his cigar that was no longer alight, and managed to light it again at a third try.

'The beginning's been taken from the slow part of Liszt's piano concerto, but the melody is better, purer, more balanced, and he does a lot with that counterpoint. Liszt breaks it off too soon. . . It'll be woodwind here, I'm sure of it . . . flute, clarinet, oboe, perhaps. You got the feel of it right away, Nol. I'm proud of you. . . The end with that cheap bass could be better, but then those last six bars, wonderful, magnificent, I've never heard anything like it, but I'll look through Wagner again, you can find everything there, in Bach too. . . Did you hear that E flat A flat in the accompaniment? That piece by itself is like a cat yowling, but when you hear it all together . . . incredible.'

He played the false chord a few times, loud, plaintive, then he played the whole piece, and the chord fitted into a flawless pattern, a strident contrast with the patient, irrepressible tinkling of the accompaniment. Suddenly he slapped his hand against his forehead.

'I've just remembered, I must have a book on *Carmen* somewhere, I don't know where it is now. If I can only find it again. We'll both have to take a good look at it.'

A glance over the shelves of his bookcase confirmed that it wasn't there, and then he started rummaging in a cupboard, at the same time calling out to me that there might be something in this book about the source of the second intermezzo. If it was really Spanish he'd study it again, more carefully. Grunting, he bent down, blowing heavy clouds of smoke, as if the books, music scores, papers and maybe more photos of female singers were on fire. Layers of dust swirled up and mixed with the blue smoke. There he was holding up a paper-covered book.

'. . . "comic opera" . . . "throws a flower in his face" . . . Here's something: originally composed for *The Girl from Arles*, hmm . . . flute, clarinet and harp. So, Nol, you hit the nail right on the head again . . . What's this? What's the damned fool saying here. . . "Idyllic music, . . . pastoral mood . . . evokes the image of a rugged landscape"... My God, what an idiot!' He flung the book down on the table contemptuously and stood staring at it, his forehead angrily creased. 'Could you make any mountainous landscape out of it? The fool! The blockhead, not the slightest scrap of feeling... can't he see that José and Carmen, they've just run off together... that they...? Doesn't he understand anything, this idiot with his "idyllic" and his "pastoral"? What a lot of nonsense!' And with his clenched fist close to that paper-covered book: 'Can't he see, the half-witted eunuch? He doesn't see that this is a love song. By God, it's music that goes through you...! *Tristan*, that too, yes, yes. Ah well...'

[9]

After he had got the complete score and read the music through and through, he showered me with his infectious enthusiasm. He soon adjusted himself to the 'Spanishness', he was finally, though reluctantly, resigned to the 'Habanera', he was even reconciled to the parts where Escamillo and his troops stamped around—people like that didn't deserve any better music. When he read in that despised book of his that Bizet had had to be literally forced to compose the Toreador's march and that the master himself had called it 'rubbish', his brotherly affection for the composer was unlimited. Every time I came he was at the piano with the score in front of him, the lessons were temporarily forgotten. He was more interested in the orchestral passages than in the vocal parts, most of which he sang as he played, even attempting the duets. In the piano arrangement he had added the most important orchestral parts in his autocratic hand, and with himself as orchestra he played these over and over again to us, that is, to me, and often his mostly silent, seemingly appreciative wife, and once to Caspers and young Tjallingii, who hummed the well-known tunes in a subdued and quavering voice while his poodle lay outside on the front door step opposite G. J. Douwes. The two visitors had kept their overcoats on and, installed in old armchairs hastily fetched from the back room, they puffed clouds of cigar smoke at the low ceiling. They sat there quietly, not grinning or whispering to each other about the exaggerated polyphony Cuperus indulged in—he even imitated the castanets—and without a trace of annoyance at the technical comments that were mostly addressed to me, though he kept turning round towards them, nodding excitedly.

First, it was the delicate nuances in the José-Micaëla duet, with an ecstatic tenor part in the three-four time passage that was nothing short of divine, followed by thirds that only an angel in love could have inspired Bizet with. Obviously, gentlemen, if José had

114

just stayed true to his little Micaëla everything would have been fine, even though the opera might have been a bit dull farther on. Next, it was a thrilling passage in two-four time, during the quarrel between the two rivals with dissonant sixths, that made you want to jump out of your chair and start fighting—Cuperus had played this passage at the top of page 109 twenty times or more. Then the amazing modulations in the 'Seguidilla', the genuine, unadulterated Spanish accent, and Carmen's castanet dance in the second act with those fanfares that were the conflict of José's conscience, rising and fading away, reproduced by Cuperus's tightly pressed lips, and then Carmen taunting Lieutenant Zuniga, a melodious miracle of pizzicati, trills, sequences, sixths, and slyly interpolated flats—what a hussy, that Carmen! Caspers and young Tjalingii nodded obediently. Carmen was a hussy, and when the pianist, with an undisguised enthusiasm in his voice, declared that she was a 'little slut' they accepted his harsh judgment. A common little slut, Cuperus growled with his moustache quivering, but a singer like Alice de Rato could make something of the part. It was the crowning point in his career that that woman had agreed to come and sing in W... Caspers said nothing, merely stretched out his legs, put his hands in his pockets and gazed pointedly at the ceiling. Alice de Rato was his discovery and it would cost him a pretty penny to get her here, but as a gentleman he did not wish to discuss her with anyone else.

That was brilliant too, really brilliant, Cuperus said, flicking over the pages like a madman, what a feeling for the right theatrical touch, the death blow with the knife at the end during the 'March of the Toreadors', no rumble of drums or diminished sevenths, or tricks like that. There's something menacing in all the music in the fourth act, right up to the procession. And then the last scene in the third act! A stroke of genius, gentlemen! The 'March of the Toreadors', the butcher himself singing it off stage, José jealous again—he might as well have murdered the little bitch there and then—in any case tragic, agonizingly tragic (and a dying mother into the bargain and Jeannetje de Ridder with a blond wig praying and pleading). Real tragedy. But what are we going to do with the music? There they are all standing on the stage gawking like a lot of statues, Carmen, José, Micaëla, the smugglers. No, you can't have the act finishing with just a couple of heavyweight chords after that 'Toreador, Toreador', even if it's sung ever so softly. So what does he do? A genius, that Bizet. He digs up a haunting march theme from the beginning of the act and there you have a coda... Magnificent, gentlemen, magnificent. It's only a pity that the B in the syncopated phrase is left out, I mean, we ought to have a B here, and there it's something else, the arrangement is in F, and the other, in the beginning, that's in... what is it now... in A flat, I think, yes, I think it's A flat. Caspers and young Tjallingii gave polite nods. Yes, it was a pity. But Caspers, who had, after all, arranged for the *prima donna*, wasn't going to worry about such a minor problem, and young Tjalingii could hear his poodle scratching at the front door.

Neither of them meddled with the preparations, they left everything to Vellinga, who engaged the stage manager and the wardrobe mistress and put sensational items in his newspaper about Alice de Rato, Ordelio, Stegeman, Cuperus and Bizet. Alice de Rato was willing to come to the dress rehearsal if Caspers paid, but Ordelio wouldn't, extra money or not. Stegeman was supposed to come to W... weeks before the performance, but he declined all offers of hospitality, preferring to stay at a hotel, probably at the instigation of Jantje de Ridder—with whom he was corresponding again — for she had only recently moved to new rooms and she wasn't yet sure of her landlady's attitude.

No one in W... except my parents—and they had forgotten the story, they hadn't believed it all anyway—knew that the tenor and the baritone were sworn enemies, while Jeannetje could only assume that her friend's intrepid spirit would withstand the direst threats. In fact, so she told me much later, Stegeman had implied that the incident with the *navaja* was merely one of those practical jokes that you can always expect on the stage, you needed them so you wouldn't fall asleep standing up after the fifth performance. Now that Stegeman wasn't staying at our house I became more interested in Ordelio, a real ogre according to Cuperus, but at least he wouldn't need to tell Ordelio how to sing and act.

One evening when we were alone together he advised me not to come to the rehearsals, not even the dress rehearsal. It would need a lot of self-restraint, but then I'd enjoy the performance all the more for not having had to listen to all those misplayed passages he had to break off in the middle, and besides, I knew the whole score, didn't I, better than anyone else? Hadn't I felt intuitively, that the second intermezzo, the love scene, needed woodwind, not catgut—we'll see if Ordelio understands that much. He had talked me out of my intention to put myself in the choir, though as it happened I had a voice that was fairly deep for my age. I asked him how Trix was getting on with her part. She was studying the Frasquita role (Mercedes was being played by a rather good mezzo-soprano from a place near W . . .) and every week she came home for a day to practise with her father. Three or four weeks before the big night she was coming home to stay, that was all arranged. I had never heard her sing, I hadn't even seen her for years, and I tried to imagine her as the Spanish Gipsy girl who would dance on the stage. The days she came to W . . . were never the days I had a lesson.

'Not so good,' Cuperus grunted, answering my question, 'She'll liven up when she's on the stage with Mercedes. If she's got to show she's better than someone else she can do anything. She's just obstinate. . . She was telling me that you'd danced together. When was that?'

'Oh,' I said, 'when I was little, in the Garden.'

'She said it was when I was conducting the band.'

'Yes, I think so,' I mumbled. In my imagination I could hear again the blare of the music that I had long since grown out of.

Two children dancing, a strange improvisation. The conductor strode confidently over the bridge and came back with a broken baton in his hand, defeated, proud and drunk. I would never be able to talk to him about all this, never.

'It would be a good idea if you met her one of these days,' he said hesitantly, after he had stared for a few moments at his foot on the right pedal. 'Once I called you my "son", well, you know how I feel, but in any case she's my daughter, and I feel it's a . . . a little odd that you two have never really been introduced to each other. If you don't contradict her she can be friendly enough. Then she's four years older than you, and you've lost your heart somewhere else. . .' He stroked his moustache thoughtfully. 'I don't know what goes on inside her head . . . Maybe that Frasquita never looked at a man either. . .'

The remark about myself was an allusion to one of my fleeting infatuations, which was already over and done with when I told him about it. I hadn't lost my heart, nor my head, held so high with all the cocksureness of my seventeen years, and all the higher because of my secret decision, by now a firm resolve, to go and work as a street-sweeper before I would be a lawyer, and to study medicine only to annoy Chris, and, to a lesser degree, my father. A young fellow with ideas like that could hardly feel inferior to any female, whatever she might be.

'I don't want to intrude,' I said, 'I wouldn't like her to get the impression that I'm trying to be a sort of brother to her.'

'Nonsense, nonsense. You're taking it all too seriously. Listen: You were the first to hear me play that damned *Carmen* music and you're the only one who can appreciate all those touches of finesse from the orchestra when we perform the whole thing. What do you say if we make it a sociable occasion, have a little family party? I'll get the two women, I'll fetch a bottle of wine and we'll drink to the success of *Carmen*. If you don't want to drink you don't have to, I'm not the sort of boozer who insists everyone should drink with him.'

I didn't mind watching Trix drink wine. A little later his wife came in with glasses while Cuperus was somewhere in the back of the house trying to persuade Trix to be sociable. When he came back he looked preoccupied, but he didn't say a word. Then the mother disappeared. Listening intently for the sound of a quarrel, I sat waiting with my impatient mentor for ten long minutes before we had a definite confirmation that Trix did not wish to join us. Her mother was quite distressed about it, and she offered me her apologies for the way that 'wicked girl' behaved, a rather grotesque description, I thought, for a young lady of twenty or twenty-one who was going to make her opera début. After the apologies she brought in a tin of biscuits and then withdrew again to a back room where she must have sat all by herself, for I couldn't hear any talking, only the occasional rasping of her cough, the tinkle of a coffee pot and coal being put in a stove. Where was Trix? Upstairs, in another room at the back, in the kitchen, in the cellar? Maybe she wasn't there at all, I thought, as I listened to the toreador and the cigarette girls and the fabulous dissonance of the quarrel between José and Escamillo and the duet that Escamillo and Carmen sing in the fourth act, the only genuinely passionate music in the whole opera, rather a surprise, the hulking butcher as a passionate lover, but still, they were two of a kind, that pair, poor José was far too good for that hussy, a fine fellow, but a weak character... While he was playing, Cuperus finished off most of the bottle, but except for a flushed face he didn't show the slightest effect. There was talk, I believe, that he had started drinking rather heavily again. If he did, it certainly wasn't from resentment or sorrow, it would be from happiness, or perhaps from the fear that he might lose the happiness he had regained.

One afternoon in the week before the dress rehearsal I went to the ice-rink. The sudden heavy frost hadn't given the Rink Committee time to make any preparations for competitions. It was only a few days later that a programme could be organized, because Vellinga had to do all the work and he was busy with *Carmen*. He'd been writing a biography of Bizet for his newspaper with the help of that paper-covered book of Cuperus's. Amongst the crowd—the ice on the canals wasn't thick enough yet or hadn't been declared safe, so all W . . . was there on the rink—the members of the Committee were skating with old-fashioned top-hats on their heads above their healthy, well-fed faces. My family was represented by Chris as well as myself. He had come home for a day to arrange for the payment of debts, which he contracted as a sort of professional obligation, without getting any real pleasure from his dissipations. I greeted him with a friendly salute as I would a vague acquaintance. Caspers and Dijkhuizen were also members of the Committee. That Committee had a good sprinkling of well-to-do citizens who paraded in top-hats and sashes on the rink or around the entrance.

I noticed young Tjallingii—he wasn't on the Committee this year because, so he said, he was in a muddle being on so many committees—skating round with the future Micaëla. They were in high spirits, probably only because they were skating together, knowing they were quite safe with each other. In fact, Tjallingii was completely normal, but in the company of women he just giggled or gave them silly nicknames, like 'chickie' or 'duckie' or 'Claribell', a habit that occasionally got him a rap on the knuckles. The infatuation I imagined he had for my mother, years before, was, I realized now, not to be taken seriously. He looked rather retarded, insipidly aristocratic, thin-nosed and chinless, a skinny and bloodless specimen. But on some subjects, numismatics I think, he was very well-informed, and he knew quite a lot about music though he carefully avoided any discussion with professionals. He had never gone to a university and he had no occupation. He'd figured in quite a few comical incidents. Once van Son, the stuttering little Court Recorder, whose adoration for my mother was mostly expressed in petulant jealousy, tried to discourage his visits to our house by being particularly unpleasant to him. He stayed away for two weeks, sending my mother flowers almost every day, then rang at the door on a Saturday evening with his poodle under his arm, asked could he speak to my mother, and announced that he wanted to make it up with van Son. He did really think a lot of van Son, he said, and now he had trained his poodle to wait in the hallway without scratching at the door. As it happened, van Son was there that evening and when he saw Tjallingii come into the room it was too much for him and he stuttered something spiteful. Undismayed, young Tjallingii stepped over to him with a gold pencil in his hand, then with the quickness of a conjurer pulled one of van Son's cuffs over his wrist, a liberty van Son contemptuously tolerated, scribbled a few words on it and graciously acknowledged the applause that followed. He had, so I heard later, written on van Son's cuff: 'Out of courts, out of sorts.' He must have spent the whole two weeks thinking that up.

There was such a crowd that it was almost a relief to see a top-hat bob up. Skating alone, the members of the Committee glided slowly round, casting indolent and superior glances over the crowd, but with a lady companion they moved at a brisk pace. They preferred not to circulate in groups for they didn't want to be like a herd of prize cattle with those sashes on. Hemmed in by the low dykes that were covered with straggling bushes the ice-rink didn't offer any view of the white fields beyond. At the end where the children and beginners were trying to skate, the bushes merged into willow trees. It wasn't so far from the moat and the Garden, and for me, with my complete lack of geographic and juridical precision, the Garden and the ice-rink were inseparable. The pond in front of the bandstand would be good for skating on too, round and round, first on the left side of the bridge then on the right side. There was no music that afternoon because the band was rehearsing for the *Carmen* performance, but the skaters were lively enough, and there were collisions and falls. Old friends and enemies, rivals and lovers, cuckolds and philan-

121

derers looked round at each other with surprised smiles, and nudged their wives to smile and wave too. Groups of yelling youths, hands linked, separated to streak, one by one, under helplessly protesting arms. Hunched-up veterans of all ages sped towards an invisible objective that was nothing more than speeding past everyone else over and over again. Barge captains jovially followed the pipe-smoke trail of other barge captains. Billowing females, sturdy farm-women, hands on each other's shoulders, formed sinuous rows, some grey, some colourful. Local ladies who couldn't skate were being given dangerous instruction by strong and eager gentlemen. Just in front of me I saw a top-hat. It was Vellinga skating with Trix Cuperus, their hands crossed. Following them as closely as possible I caught a glimpse every now and then of that red, smiling, bulldog face, the bald skull hidden under the top-hat. Trix was wearing a woollen bonnet, no sweater. She wasn't pale any more. Of course, they must know each other, and it was a long-established custom for the social élite to mix freely on the rink with those of lesser standing. I decided that if I did get the chance to speak to her I would adopt the student manner that I knew quite well from watching Chris and his friends who sometimes came home with him on Saturdays. The main thing was to talk with assurance, and now and then sink into a deep silence, in this way creating the illusion that you knew far more than you could say or wanted to say or were permitted to say, and never be ruffled or look surprised.

From their expressions they might have been blaming each other in turn for having forgotten how to skate, but maybe they were talking about something else altogether. Vellinga treated her rather familiarly, but not condescendingly. Trix threw her head back, laughing. I felt it was a good sign that our local editor had put her in such a good mood. Suddenly, a near collision, a flurry and swirl, yells and squeals, and, letting her hands go, Vellinga skated off at Committee-member pace with an old gentleman and his wife, both of very respectable appearance.

He waved to Trix a couple of times, and each time I saw the winter sun flash on his jaunty pince-nez. But I was already at her side, ready to take hold of her hands that were now swinging loosely. In spite of her being too tall she skated well, with smooth sure steps. I looked at her with an inquiring smile.

'Mijnheer Rieske. . .'

'So it's going to be Mijnheer after all,' I said, taking hold of her gloved hands. 'If you keep that up I'll call you Senorita Frasquita. . .'

'Mijnheer Vellinga called me Frascati,' she said drily.

'Rieske is a name I loathe. I'd rather you called me The Risk, like my mother does. Sometimes I do take risks, you know, and go a bit too far.'

'Do you, now?' she said mockingly.

But she kept on skating with me. Gradually I edged her towards the fence along the middle section of the rink, where the races were held and where a few youths and girls were seriously clawing the air as they practised. Only the stumbling beginners, the uncertain learners, the timid and physically inept floundered about on the outside near that fence. The pace was, on the whole, lamentable, but not without certain advantages.

'How do you like going on the stage?'

I spoke as impersonally as I could. I'd soon be able to judge how Vellinga had got her in such a good mood. But somehow she seemed to react even more coolly than she had to my first questions which she had at least answered. Biting my lips I thought out my next move. One setback didn't count. Keep trying, that was the only thing to do. Chris had told me a little, not much, but a little, about his own petty escapades, and he had said, or maybe he was quoting someone else, that 'you should never give up, even if you've got to try half a dozen before you find one who's willing. That doesn't matter. They mightn't want to go for a walk, or they might be going to meet someone else. It's just a matter of luck, it's not like an exam.'

'Not so exciting, I suppose, if you don't like music,' I continued edging her as far as I could towards the fence without running into the procession of dodderers. Now there was no possibility of a collision with fast skaters. 'But still, an opera is . . .'

She had held her head turned away from me for at least a minute. Now she looked at me, as pale as ever, and with a sulky wrinkle over her nose. 'Talk about something else, will you! I'm sick of being pestered about it by everyone. Everyone's crazy. Vellinga was at it too. He said I simply must go to Amsterdam and be a famous singer. . .' She gave a scornful laugh, and that was one of the times that I, young as I was, could feel the deep-rooted provincialism in her, the small-town narrow-mindedness of her mother—this delight in sneering behind his back at the fine gentleman who has just been so kind, after enjoying the favour of his compliments.

'Vellinga doesn't know anything about music,' I said, and I didn't know whether this sounded like a defence or a criticism.

I decided to say nothing for a while, just skate round along that fence, using the time to think up a supply of questions, maybe I'd ask why she didn't come in that evening for a glass of wine. But no, that would be unforgivably stupid. I had learnt, not from Chris this time, but from my own experience, that there was nothing more likely to put girls, and that included young women, in a bad mood than being reminded of embarrassing situations that had occurred more than a week ago. If it was less than a week ago, it might be mentioned, but circumspectly.

But while I was thinking, weighing up and calculating, I slowly realized that, for the first time after all those years of growing up, I was holding those two hands again—a woman's hands, a little girl's hands—those same hands that had reached out so blithely and so innocently for mine one hot summer afternoon by the pond in the Garden. I couldn't just ask her to take off her gloves for that reason, or any other reason. I couldn't talk to her about the Garden, not after our last meeting, her patronizing superiority and the conversation that had ended so ridiculously. Should I say I was a sort of brother of hers?... Oh no, no, I mustn't say that, I groaned. If I was going to be as stupid as that I'd have to kick myself... On reflection, there weren't so many subjects I could broach without the most disastrous consequences. I was holding those hands and I could feel the warmth of her gloves, and that tall slender body, so unattainable, and because of her tallness, so bewitching. That half-head of difference, that was what made the blood rush to my cheeks and my legs tingle just like that time so long ago. This untameable tallness, this untameable girl, this Trix Cuperus, who had fought with more boys than I and all my friends ever had. She had fought with them and kicked them in the stomach, and now she was singing Frasquita in *Carmen* and she didn't let a single chance go by to put me in my place... Oh yes, of course, of course I was in love with her, I'd always been in love with her, ever since that hot day when I had climbed down the side of a rocky wall like a pioneer venturing into an unknown, hostile land. I hadn't realized before, that was all. A humdrum curtain of day-to-day trivialities had kept it hidden from me.... In love with Trix Cuperus. In love with her. I repeated it to myself, distinctly, so I could be sure that these words were true.

'Why are you quiet?' In her eyes there was a tiny glimmer of the smile that I adored, that I had adored from the start, the smile in those cool, dreamy eyes of hers. Then I noticed that the wrinkles in her face had almost disappeared and that she was prettier than before. I cleared my throat several times, but I could only say in a toneless voice:

'I've noticed that I can't talk to you about anything that doesn't make you snap at me. I don't mind that really, but if I annoy you I'd rather not say anything at all. It's nice just to skate round with you.'

Although I had kept looking straight in front of me I could see that she turned her head to observe me, puzzled. Would she notice anything? She couldn't read my thoughts. At the most she would only be able to see that, in spite of the quite strong, but not vicious, winter wind, I was unusually pale, not as deathly pale as Chris it is true, but enough for it to be all too apparent to someone who had been reminded of what rosy cheeks I had.

'Well, say something,' she said, and when I looked at her, her eyes weren't smiling any more. They were alert, not so cool and dreamy now. There was a vague hint of the vertical wrinkle between the ash-blond eyebrows, and her lips were thoughtfully, perhaps a little anxiously, pressed together.

'How do you like it at your aunt's?'

'I don't like it,' she said quickly. 'I'm no good at anything. All I can do is wash up and clear the table without breaking any dishes. My aunt says I should go and work as a waitress and maybe I will too, but she only says that when she's angry. I don't do any work, you see, I only read and go for walks. I loathe cooking and I haven't any friends there. I only like being alive if there's something exciting to do.'

'Maybe the opera will help,' I interrupted, 'But is your aunt so dreadful?'

'Oh no, it's me. She is so . . . kind isn't the word, a little unusual, a little odd in her ways. Sometimes I think she's more like my father than my mother, not in looks, but she's my mother's sister.'

'Your father is certainly unusual,' I said guardedly. 'You must think a lot of him. . .'.

Whether it was to make an abrupt gesture or to push away the blond hair that was blowing in her eyes, she started to pull her right hand out of mine, but stopped when I looked at her inquiringly. We were skating so slowly now that some of the flounderers passed us, turning round timidly and inquisitively to watch us. I wondered if I should squeeze her hand. Not a callow and stealthy pinch but a gradually applied pressure, so that she would be inspired with confidence in me without exactly being aware of what was happening.

126

I thought better of it. I thought of how tall she was. She could bend right over me, and I could stand inside the arch of her body.

'I used to,' she said, turning round, probably to nod to a friend, we had been waved to a few times already. 'I still do in a way but I can't stand his drinking and the language he uses sometimes. I'd rather not talk about it.'

'But your father is a brilliant man . . . and men like that. . .'

'You see, I'm very respectable, Nol,' she said with a smile that could have been either ironic or sad. 'You must know how old I am and that I . . . well. . . But there at my aunt's, a troop of louts after you all, the time, not for me that lot. . . But there's no sense in talking about that.'

'Why not, I won't tell anyone else. If you only knew how secretive I am, just as much as you are. . .'

'Am I secretive.'

I waited a few moments, 'Have you never been in love?'

'I'm not going to answer that.'

'So you have been!' Again a silence, I enjoyed this waiting. 'I haven't.' When she didn't comment on this disclosure I added more loudly: 'But now I am.'

Three youthful skaters in the fenced-off centre were getting ready to engage in a fierce and furious race. Preoccupied, we watched this spectacle. We were in the corner where the ice was uneven. Without swaying or jumping she skated over the gaps in the ice. I squeezed her hands, half-heartedly. It was ridiculous what I had said, what I was doing, what I was hoping. Perhaps I wasn't in love with her at all. It had happened so often, and then all of a sudden it was finished, just as Cuperus had been in love or thought he was with my mother and the dark woman and who knows how many others. Even with Wessel Stegeman and Jantje de Ridder it was all over and forgotten, for the time being anyway. . .

'Now you've lost your tongue again,' she said after we had passed the second turn.

'At least you could ask who I'm in love with,' I said casually, but with a new feeling of hope, 'it isn't a secret.'

'A girl at your school.'

'Oh yes, a girl at my school,' I jeered, 'from the elementary school, you mean, or maybe the nursery.'

She was silent for a while, then she said rather primly, in a condescending, maternal tone: 'Now don't be silly, Nol. I'm four years older than you are and I can talk like that to you. How would I know what girls you're in love with?'

'So it's got to be more than one, has it? Well, I'm not going to say any more. If you can't guess . . .'

Why didn't she understand? If she could be so maternal, giving a disappointing emphasis to the difference in our ages, then, I felt, she must be stupid not to catch on, or was she only acting stupid, and in that case she was obviously only making fun of me. . .

'There's our Frasquita, there she is.'

Spinning neatly round to face us a fat man barred our way. It was Dijkhuizen. He was muffled up like an arctic explorer, he probably had layers of rubber pads wrapped round his stomach. He put his hand on my shoulder, but it was Trix he spoke to.

'I've been wanting to talk to you, my dear, we must have a chat about that music, it's made a new man of your father. Nol, you can have her back soon.'

I couldn't refuse. That was for her to do. With a contemptuous smile she took hold of the fat business-man's hand while his beady, pouched eyes ran over her body. He was as pale as he always was, white as dough. He looked so much like a lump of dough that Chris and I used to say to each other that he was still rising. The flat nose, somehow attractively boyish, was the only feature that softened the gross sensuality of his face. He had a high forehead that made him look much more trustworthy without a cap on.

I saw the two of them skate past me a couple of times. About ten minutes later when I couldn't see Trix anywhere, though I saw Dijkhuizen busily engaged in a lively conversation with other leading citizens, I went home, not a little annoyed. But I soon realized I hadn't lost anything, that Dijkhuizen, the fat slob, hadn't gained anything, and I was sure that Trix must have understood what my thoughts were, even if she would soon forget it, just as I had so often forgotten her without really forgetting her. Towards the end of the afternoon I reflected seriously on the difference in our ages. She was four years older (not quite four years—Cuperus had told me her exact age), but to some extent the difference became less with the years, just as I had caught up on her tallness by almost half a head. In a couple of years I would be at the university, really grown-up. It would be better, I concluded, to wait patiently for a second opportunity. After the opera, once she was living at home again, I could write and invite her to come for a stroll with me.

Having reassured myself with these and other practical plans, I abandoned myself to my emotions and lay in bed crying, but not like I had when Cuperus deserted me. These tears didn't cause any pain in my eyes. They welled up, streamed like spring rain over my cheeks, and drenched the white pillow that I sensed, rather than saw, as a vague, late snow on both sides of my motionless head. No sobbing, no spasms of convulsive movement. In this little room lit by the light from the street-lamp, I felt so far away from everything, far away even from the music of *Carmen* and from all other music, so far away that I seemed to be floating in a solitude that could bring me as close to Trix Cuperus as I wished, as close, I kept thinking, as I had wished for years and years. Patiently I searched back through those years for some portent of this love. There was none. Or there were portents that had to be interpreted in another idiom. It was the difference between the Sousa march I'd been so excited about as a little boy and Bizet's second intermezzo that Cuperus had not long ago threatened to acclaim as better than anything by Wagner. It had followed a meaningful, gradually unfolding pattern, conveyed in music and traced in the heart. First Clementi, a childish dance in the Garden, then the sight of a tall girl who fought and beat boys to defend her father's reputation. Then later, the fulfilment, the proof. It was love, what else could it have been, that night when I longed to creep across the snow that was marked with her footprints. Up till then, I philosophized, what I had thought was falling in love was nothing but imitating the ways of grown-ups. Growing as it had done, concealed and unsuspected, my great love hadn't seemed to be love at all.

The only immediate result of the meeting on the ice was that I decided to ignore Cuperus's advice. Another reason for this decision was that I wanted, in any case, to see the opera twice. If I could see the dress rehearsal, my aesthetic conscience wouldn't forbid me to watch from behind the stage during the performance. This new plan, to which Cuperus raised no objections, was inspired not only by my interest in stage technique, and particularly in observing Alice de Rato and Ordelio from close by, but more by the prospect of being near to Trix and being able to talk to her again on the evening that would be concluded with a grand ball.

I sat through the dress rehearsal, which I attended with about twenty others, in an almost continuous daze. I was no more able to listen for the orchestral subtleties Cuperus had explained to me, to detect the echoes of *Parsifal* in the music, or to deplore the missing B at the end of the third act, than to be critical of the touches of 'Spanishness' that permeated the opera, at least in the design of the costumes. From the very beginning of the clamorous opening fanfare, the music vibrated electrically through my legs, my neck, my stomach. I couldn't think any more. I only knew that it was over too soon, that I wanted to listen to it twenty times over without a stop even though I would be dead before the end. There were a few things I did remember. Cuperus, so tense and serious, with the orchestra firmly under his thumb, intently following the rendering of the singers but sparing Alice de Rato and, to a lesser degree, Stegeman, the lash of his sarcastic comments. Jantje de Ridder, with a desperately blond wig, but far from convincing in what should have been simple and pious pleading, wasn't shown the same mercy. I found the second intermezzo less moving now than when I had heard Cuperus play it on the piano. I leaned forward to watch Trix, but I tried to see her only as a singer on the stage. Even if she was so tall that she looked slightly ridiculous in her Spanish costume, her voice was all the more an agreeable surprise, though it still lacked a professional finish. But her acting was inadequate, understandably enough, for she was hardly the best choice for the role of a scurrying, quarrelsome and intriguing gipsy vixen, her bearing and her figure were more suited for an Elsa or Eva or Brunhilde. The inevitable criticisms—'Now, Trix, you know how to lay out cards, you've seen me dealing a hand, haven't you? Slam them down on the table. What will Mevrouw de Rato think of you?'—gave her father one of the rare opportunities he got to speak to her as to a child, and he obviously enjoyed it. According to the rules it was the director who should have corrected her and he peeped out uncertainly from behind the stage, a spruce little fellow (I'd seen him once or twice on the stage) with his hair plastered down flat, side-whiskers, and a sad, drooping moustache. It was amusing to see Stegeman, whom I had gone to visit in his hotel a few days before, fighting with an invisible Escamillo, and rather frightening to watch him kill an intimidating Carmen with all too many thrusts of his knife, indescribably touching his last lament: 'Seht mich hier blutgerötet! Ja, ich hab sie getötet! Ach Carmen! Du mein angebetet Leben', then so reassuring to see him, after the final scene, standing with Micaëla, his arm round her waist. They stood in a row, bowing to the small audience, Trix too, and even a few of the choir who hadn't been chased off in time. When Cuperus noticed that Alice de Rato stood alone, brushing her clothes—she was the only one not in costume—he climbed up on the stage, stepped towards her as if he was going to kiss her hand, but merely escorted her nearer to the footlights to bow with her and bow and bow. That was about the only chance he'd have of getting near her. All W... knew that she had arrived at 7.15 and that she was leaving the next morning at 6.46, and the resignation with which Caspers, sitting a few rows in front of me, lowered his opera-glasses reflected the intelligent restraint an experienced hunter shows towards extremely timid or extremely rare wild life.

To judge by her well-filled bosom, Mevrouw de Rato was no longer young, even allowing as I did, long-standing expert that I regarded myself in matters theatrical, for the effect make-up might have on her face. Her performance, interspersed with frequent flashing of teeth and capricious shoulder-shrugging, was frivolous rather than dramatic, a display of hip-swaying and unconcealed indifference expressed particularly in her off-handedness during the duets with an absent Escamillo and her high-handedness with Lieutenant Zuñiga in the second act. Instead of taunting and tempting she just ignored him, a snub that evoked from him after the rehearsal—he was a painter and decorator with a rough-hewn bass—a diatribe of colourfully worded scorn. She smoked cigarettes with practised aplomb, but in a way that made you expect she would spit on the floor after she had finished each cigarette. Her voice was magnificent. There was a lot of gossip about her. Loose morals. A trail of broken hearts. Wrecked romances. It was all so stereotyped.

I hurried off home. All I was waiting for now was the night of the performance and the ball. It would be interesting to see how Cuperus and Caspers, as rivals for Carmen's smile, would, if not quarrel, at least avoid and detest each other for a time. I resisted an impulse to send flowers to Trix. During the four days before the performance I went, just once, to visit Cuperus. Coughing badly, his wife opened the door. The first thing she said was that Trix had gone to her aunt's for a couple of days to fetch her things. As she had never said a word to me about her daughter before I was so surprised that I forgot to ask if Cuperus could see me. With a few friendly, loudly spoken words I walked past her to the music-room. The door was half open, in the room it was dark and silent. She came up behind me, and without saying anything she reached round the door frame and switched on the electric light, an innovation that had become general in W . . . some months before. Then she walked on down the hallway and I stepped inside.

Cuperus was sitting at the piano, his chin resting on his hands, his elbows on the keyboard. His face was almost unrecognizable. His eyes were half open, but he didn't see me or didn't recognize me. He sat without moving, his hands weren't shaking. Before I left I looked round to see if there was a bottle or a glass anywhere in the room. But I couldn't see inside the cupboards or the bookcases. I realized that he had taken to drinking alone. If his wife had known the state he was in she certainly would have said he wasn't at home. Dazed and depressed I left the house, almost wishing that the opera would be called off. That's what it was, I was sure now, I knew him, in three weeks he would have forgotten Alice de Rato but the way he felt now he was quite capable of drinking himself to death because of her. . . The thought flashed vaguely through my head that maybe I, too, would feel like drinking myself to death, in five years time, in ten years time because of Trix.

The night of the performance I was at the entrance to the little theatre at half past seven. Alice de Rato had arrived a quarter of an hour earlier. Caspers had brought her from the train in his new car, a slow drive owing to the fog. It was a thick fog, it lay like a pall over the whole town, over the roads and over the railway line as well. According to her, Ordelio must have been on the same train. She had apparently sung with him the night before in *La Traviata*. I heard all this from young Tjallingii who stood at the main door with a large official sash over his chest. He pulled a face and said: 'He's forgotten all about it, of course. He hits the bottle even more than our famous maestro. We should have had an understudy, we could have found someone here. Wessel's all upset about it, he's blaming himself for not warning us. . .' I ran round to the stage door. It occurred to me that, tonight at least, I could have brought flowers with a card with nothing on it but my name. Then she would have had to thank me.

Backstage most of the cast were scurrying round, already dressed for their parts, their faces grotesquely smeared with grease paint. The choir, all solemnly clustered in the centre of the stage, jumped and stamped, trying to keep warm. From the expressions of the Committee-members, Vellinga, Caspers and a few others, more than from the faces half-hidden under layers of make-up, it was apparent that something disquieting had happened. The only one looking lively and unconcerned was the *prima donna*, who walked past me in a cloud of heavy perfume, waving her fan as she called out to Vellinga: '*Ce cochon, il est saoul tout de même, monsieur. Mettez-le dans un bain froid, ce toréro. . .*' Caspers stood calmly looking at her, his interest had obviously waned. Shortly afterwards, I saw her sitting invitingly near a young stage-hand, talking in broken Dutch and poking him in the side with her fan. Cuperus wasn't anywhere in sight. It was some time before I finally spotted Trix with a couple of other girls, all of them caked with make-up. Then I suddenly sniffed the smell of the grease paint, it made me think of a circus, it penetrated everything, cast a spell on everything and everyone. As I walked around feeling lost, sometimes dodging sometimes hemmed in by pieces of stage scenery, I was amazed at the slap-dash crudeness and the screaming colours of what had seemed to me at the rehearsal to be a picturesque corner of some Spanish town.

Suddenly the door of one of the dressing-rooms flew open and the director came out and stepped briskly towards the stage. In the centre of the room a tall, broad-shouldered man wearing an expensive overcoat with a fur collar stood gesticulating. Opposite him, Cuperus. Behind him and a little further away Stegeman and Jeannetje, both in their Spanish costumes. When the Committee-members, strolling sedately from all directions, had formed an irregular line around the door, like mourners at a funeral parlour, I felt it would be permissible to join them. The tall man had an oily, brown complexion, a hooked nose, and a wide, sarcastic mouth. He would be about fifty. He was waving his arms, talking and arguing, but no one heard what he was saying. In all that clamour, with the musicians tuning up, the premature joy of one of them who kept tootling the Seguidilla-motif, the clatter and banging from the stage, it could have been assumed that the din was drowning his words, had Cuperus's voice not been so clearly audible.

'You should have gone to a doctor at once, Mijnheer Ordelio.'

'We have a throat specialist in town too, I heard about him the other day,' Micaëla said, while Don José toyed with her thick blond plaits. 'But it's too late now, it's five to eight. Oh, what a pity, and after all our trouble . . .'

The tall man was waving his arms again. We pushed a little nearer to him, with Vellinga, a derisive grin on his face, in the lead, and we could more or less understand what he was saying:

'. . . rotten luck. I was here at five past five and I gargled for a full hour in my hotel and I had hot towels round my neck. It's this dreadful weather you have here, I've never had anything like this before. I'm willing, I've told you already, to act and speak the part, they'll have to be satisfied with that.'

Stegeman laughed, a high-pitched neigh: 'What a . . .'

'I'm afraid I don't like your tone,' Cuperus growled, and I heard Vellinga give a guffaw at the unintentional ambiguity of this remark. 'We're not just rubbish here, you know, and we're paying, don't forget that.'

'The Great Singer temperament,' Stegeman tittered, but Ordelio had heard him and spun round like a flash of lightning: 'You keep your bloody mouth shut or I'll gag you myself.

You little runt, just keep quiet, you look like a Spanish peddler!'

Jeannetje threw her arm protectingly around Stegeman's waist. 'You should have taken aspirin, Mijnheer. A singer need never get hoarse if he doesn't want to...'

'I don't know what to do,' Cuperus said to the Committee-members, who were by now well inside the doorway.

'Listen, gentlemen,' the singer said, indicating with a sweeping gesture that he wished to address himself both to Vellinga, who was still grinning, and to Cuperus. 'Let me make it clear first that I have nothing at all against this town. I think it's a wonderful place. I didn't get hoarse on purpose from this dreadful fog of yours. If you wish I'll leave now and you only have to pay my travelling expenses and my hotel room, and Mijnheer Stegeman there can play both José and Escamillo. I'm sure Mijnheer Stege-man is equal to that, though he'd sound better on a chamber-pot than on the stage. But what I was going to say is this: If you want me, with my talent and my experience, to give your audience a far, far better, a far more enjoyable performance than you'd get from some gawking idiot who thinks he can sing, then you'll have to give me a chance. I promise you I'll keep gargling all the time I'm off the stage, maybe I'll get my voice back before the end of the last act. I can't risk straining my voice, but I'll do everything I can to help you. That's all I can say. Any singer would take the same attitude under these circumstances, except that dressed-up ape over there...'

That was, in fact, all that he could say, for his voice broke into an irritated cough, and the last words were hardly understandable. Stegeman had lit a cigarette and was blowing the smoke vigorous-ly in the direction of the coughing baritone.

'Very well, then, that's reasonable enough,' Vellinga said, shrugging. 'I'll explain to the audience. I can sympathize with you. It's not your fault.'

Ordelio gave a slight bow, breathed out heavily and sighed, and fanned himself with his two ring-laden hands.

'A doctor,' Dijkhuizen suggested.

'A doctor can't cure a sore throat in half an hour,' Caspers said, turning away with a bored look, and then politely, but without a word, moving aside for Carmen who came in fluttering her fan and shouting: '*Hé, ce monsieur-là, est-il enfin capable de remplir ses devoirs masculins?*'

'Old hag,' I heard the baritone mumble, but by then there was no thought for anything but the performance, everyone was rushing and bustling, dodging out of the way. Cuperus went to take his place in front of his orchestra. A 'first bell' rang. Alice de Rato was still keeping the young stage-hand from his work. José kissed Micaëla. I almost bumped into Trix but she didn't notice me. From behind a closed door came the sound of Ordelio gargling. Then all at once the buzz of talk from the audience stopped, and we could hear Vellinga's voice:

'Ladies and gentlemen, I have an unpleasant, but at the same time consoling, announcement to make. Our Escamillo, the celebrated baritone, or bass baritone, I believe, has arrived here this evening, ladies and gentlemen, with a sore throat from this fog, which, according to the latest reports, is thick all over the country. Mijnheer Ordelio, I regret to say, is at the moment unable to sing, indeed, he can hardly speak. We would have understood if he had gone back by the earliest train, but Mijnheer Ordelio is made of sterner stuff. He said he can't let us go home disappointed in the cold and the fog after sitting through the whole opera without Escamillo. Even though he has quite a temperature, and really ought to be in bed with a glass of hot grog and a detective-story, he has offered to act the part, reciting the lines, and meanwhile he'll do whatever he can to get his voice back—gargling and what not, and, of course, we've sent for a doctor for him. Mijnheer Ordelio is a great artist but he's not a magician, he can't cure a sore throat with a wave of a wand, and neither can we. However, we will at least be able to enjoy his acting, and that is something we don't have the chance of seeing every day. We, that is, the members of the Committee, feel that this is a very considerate gesture on the part of Mijnheer Ordelio and, knowing you, we are sure that you will think so too. I appeal to you to make allowances for the unfortunate circumstances and I know you will appreciate the sacrifice . . . Mijnheer Ordelio's self-sacrifice and determination. The performance will start in a moment or so and I can assure you that no one else has lost his voice. I thank you.'

There was a weak patter of applause, a rumble of unfriendly grunts and coughs and growls of 'money back' from the cheaper seats, and immediately after that the overture thundered forth.

Behind the stage we were standing, pressed helplessly against each other. It was impossible to run here and there to get a rear view of Alice de Rato, for example, or to watch the cigarette-girls being rounded up to go on the stage, and any intention of moving from one place to another was effectively discouraged by the director with angry whispers and by several stolid firemen and one equally stolid policeman. But it was exciting to stand there and see the stage and the orchestra pit and a section of the audience. The arc of an intimate, exclusive, personal perspective enclosed Micaëla and José, outdoing each other in the zeal of their acting, one of Cuperus's arms above a corner of the orchestra at the moment that the paperhanger was raising his clarinet to his mouth, then further back, noses being blown noiselessly, heads tilted peering to one side, bent forward to follow the text in the pro-gramme, or turning to nod at friends, and expectant, appreciative faces contemplating Wessel Stegeman and Jantje de Ridder in the reality and make-believe of their love drama.

For me the most interesting of all was Alice de Rato. Although her singing didn't rise to any spectacular new heights, she was a completely different creature from the woman at the dress rehear-sal, and Stegeman was no more a match for her than the house-painting bass, this Lieutenant Zuñiga she taunted so demonstrative-ly and flicked her fingers at and hypnotized, so that this time he had no reason to complain, and he did, in fact, say so after the performance. More like a whorehouse madame than a gipsy girl who was supposed to work in a cigarette factory, with her slightly husky but powerful voice, her hips, her swaggering, suggestive walk, she played the others off the stage. It was an odd-sounding accent she spoke and sang in. It wasn't a Flemish dialect (at least according to an expert there), it was vaguely like Dutch, it certainly wasn't French. But that didn't matter, for the audience wasn't really interested in understanding the words, neither hers nor anyone else's. The scene with the cigarette-girls rushing Carmen was something of a flop because they weren't fierce enough, and Carmen's flight across the bridge at the end of the first act almost ended in disaster, for she stumbled over a loose board, she was far too heavy anyway, but the applause was deafening. Three times she had to come out in front of the footlights hand in hand with the two other soloists. Those of us behind the stage breathed easily again. There was a lot of handshaking. Zuniga embraced his wife, who appeared from one of the dressing-rooms where she had self-effacingly hidden herself, perhaps to pray for her husband's success or perhaps, who knows, for his soul. Waiters hurried here and there with tea and other drinks. But soon we were standing pressed against the cold whitewashed walls or the dressing-room doors to escape a piece of Lillas Pastia's inn or a stream of abuse from the director. Cuperus stayed where he was.

The changing of the scenery was nearly finished when one of the doors was thrown open, sending three or four stage-hands tumbling over, and Ordelio, dressed as a toreador, stepped out singing the famous toreador's song from the second act in a hoarse, but loud voice that cracked, however, at the second A flat. With a pathetic groan of despair he closed the door again. Something went wrong with the electric light, and it was the half dark of a Spanish dusk with singing and cynicism and drum-beating. Alice de Rato swayed her hips more than she danced. The gipsy girls twirled and whirled as they had been coached to do, Trix jumping about with big steps like a tall youth in disguise. After that, a recitative interlude, then came Ordelio pushing a way for himself to the stage, where his henchmen were waiting timidly and without torches, these having been prohibited by the local fire brigade. While Escamillo was cheered and clapped far more than he deserved, I watched the faces of two of the Committee-members. I was relieved at their complete composure for I didn't want to see this performance, which meant so much to Cuperus, end in a fiasco. There was no doubt that Ordelio, hoarse or even without his voice, could captivate an audience so long as he had arms and legs. The sounds he made were something between humming and hissing, but he exaggerated every movement threefold. He leapt and strode, he bent and twisted with a speed that Carmen could never have imitated, not even when her life was in danger. He gave a fantastic show of assailing an imaginary bull, he killed three more, he jumped over the horns of yet another, he waved invisible red cloths, he flicked them low over the floor, and then he was the victorious matador making a triumphant exit. During the splendid coda, as the 'March of the Toreadors', subdued, the harmony changed, with a pizzicato accompaniment, seemed to hint at tragic events to come, a sympathetic murmur ran through the audience—the population of W . . . wasn't temper-amental enough to be wildly demonstrative. So far it hadn't been very difficult for him. The absurdity of his hoarseness would show up in the duets with Don José, with Carmen. . .

In the interval a young doctor in the audience was fetched backstage where he announced that gargling was useless. Waved away with a snarl when he tried to take Ordelio's pulse, the young doctor stood for quite a while talking to Caspers in a corner of the crowded dressing-room, absent-mindedly tapping his foot against Ordelio's suitcase that happened to be there. Wait-ers trotted in with warm drinks, all sorts of advice was proffered, including the suggestion, from someone who had had a well-known singing teacher as a lodger once, that nothing was better than camomile tea. More and more visitors came backstage, so many that when Cuperus, his hair ruffled and a scarf round his sweating neck, came to have a look, he could hardly get to the door. Caspers, apparently watching for him, put an arm round his shoulder and speaking quickly in whispers walked with him out of earshot of the other members of the Committee. Shortly after, I witnessed what must have been his first face-to-face meeting with Alice de Rato off the stage. Nothing came of it because she was amusing herself by shouting at the patient in French, a language Cuperus didn't understand. She noticed him and no more. She would certainly not have despised him as a musician, but the next moment she forgot him. There was an atmosphere of exuberance after the success of the first half of the opera. On the stage some of the gipsy girls were dancing in a ring around the fat figure of Zuñiga who clapped his hands encouragingly. Everyone was humming, shouting or whistling the 'March of the Toreadors', even the stage-hands. There were shouts of: 'No smoking, no smoking'—not because of the firemen who overlooked everything except the torches of Escamillo's admirers, but out of consideration for Ordelio's sore throat. How could a sore throat be cured in a dressing-room?

Somebody I didn't know was explaining to me that all Ordelio had to do was to fight against it, just sing as if there was nothing wrong, just sing the hoarseness away, and not worry about his throat at all, when Vellinga, laughing loudly, emerged from a small group near where Trix Cuperus stood looking at the stage. Her face was solemn. Still, Vellinga's laugh could have been meant for her too. He manoeuvred skillfully through the crowd carrying a big glass that he took to the dressing-room. I couldn't see what happened then inside the dressing-room, but to judge from the admiring exclamations, Ordelio, driven by now to a frenzy, must have drained the glass in one gulp. I could hear his voice and then others repeating what he had said, respectfully echoing his words: 'Rum, pure, hot rum.' What a man, swallowing rum like that to cure his throat! There were shouts and cheers and Alice de Rato shrieked: '*Maintenant, mon vieux, tu peux séduire ta Carmencita!*' Stage-hands staggered under the weight of mountain summits, sinister smugglers stood around in little groups, Cuperus hurried back to his orchestra.

The second intermezzo was not without blemishes, for most of the orchestra had been backstage outside the dressing-room and a breathless race back to their seats, up and down stairs and through doors, was anything but conducive to the flawless rendering of a serene ecstasy of love. The mistakes irked Cuperus, he pulled angry faces, and hissed abuse at the offenders, particularly the paperhanger who, at one point, put his clarinet down and sat gazing up at the ceiling before he picked it up again. The rendering of the ghostly music accompanying the smuggling scene, only equalled by Mahler's Seventh Symphony, wasn't much better. Wrong timing, wrong notes, trills that faded away in a splutter— the false violins were the only fault that didn't irritate me, for violins always sound false to me, and mournful as well. I didn't know then that this was as much as could be reasonably expected from such an orchestra, and I felt that the opera was being threatened from two sides. I couldn't enjoy any of it now. I was frightened, frightened how Cuperus might take it.

After Carmen's death aria—the *andante molto moderato* so highly praised by Nietzsche (I read his attacks on Wagner much later, during a sombre period of my student years)—in which Alice de Rato unexpectedly rose above her usual fishwife level, there was the gay ensemble in G flat major with an interpolation in B major (the thirds tracing delicate grooves through it were, according to Cuperus, intended only for connoisseurs), then Micaëla all alone in the mountains singing her plaintive song, and the unconvincing echoes from the orchestra pit, the crack of the shot fired at Escamillo (no one knew yet whether he had got his voice back or not,) and the stormy duet that ended with the fight between José and the toreador. I decided not to listen to anything but the music. I didn't want to miss the beginning of the two-four passage with the dissonant sixths that I knew by heart (Cuperus had let me play it a few times as an *adagio*) and that transitional E just after Escamillo's cynical jibe that 'The amours of Carmen will seldom six weeks last', an incomparable subtlety I had somehow missed at the rehearsal. The orchestral score for this scene was, as Cuperus had time and again declared, fantastic.

As Escamillo, singing in spite of his hoarseness, began his recital of confidences that were so painful for Don José to hear, Alice de Rato was standing only a few paces from me waiting to go on, and whispering with the young stage-hand, and in the half darkness of the stage Don José's face, pale and streaked with grease paint, was fleetingly visible. I couldn't see Escamillo. With a rough and ragged accompaniment Stegeman did his best, drowning the sound of the great Ordelio's voice with his own. Hardly fair to Ordelio but, out of consideration for the audience, quite justifiable. I didn't hear the transitional E this time either, maybe it had been left out at the rehearsal and tonight as well. Then came the dissonant sixths, and still the irritating, though medically explicable, contrast in the volume of the two voices. I could see both of them now, José and Escamillo, leaning forward, glaring at each other, each with a knife in his hand. The *point d'orgue* in dominant C, and the fight could begin on F. Waving their knives at each other, they moved out of my line of vision. Ten bars, then Escamillo's knife would break and Carmen would shout at José to stop. But there was Carmen calling out too soon: 'Hola, hola!' What was the matter with her? The music went on. I could feel a rustle of confusion around me. The singing had stopped, and the orchestra had almost reached the song Escamillo sings as he leaves, when Cuperus rapped on his music-stand. There were bursts of laughter from the audience, but the muted baritone and the tenor in fine form bellowing unequally against each other had already caused some amusement.

I didn't see all that happened on the stage, nor did anyone else. But soon a coherent, more or less official, version was established, thanks mainly to Don José who stayed on in W . . . for a further three days to be consoled by Micaëla. Ordelio had his genuine *navaja* with him. That needn't have meant anything, and Stegeman never implied that he was threatened with the weapon. But just after *L'Istesso Tempo*—the beginning of the passage in F major with the heavy, oppressive diminishing chords descending from tonic to dominant—Ordelio, the *navaja* between his teeth, had grabbed the younger singer by the throat. Probably too frightened to do anything else, Stegeman dropped to the floor. A moment or so later he must have fought back, then they were rolling over the stage, the two of them, silent, Ordelio still with the knife between his teeth. (It was confiscated by the police and found to be razor sharp.) The first to try and separate them was the director. A kick from Escamillo sent him reeling. The policeman didn't interfere, not because he was frightened, he thought it was all part of the opera. The firemen, somewhat more perceptive, were deterred by the flashing knife blade. The members of the Committee were also apparently averse to *navajas*, although Vellinga, the one-time footballer, was big enough and strong enough to have rushed in where the others feared to tread. Women were screaming. As the stage was in half darkness the audience couldn't see how serious it was, and there was far more hilarity than concern.

When Ordelio, blind drunk as it later appeared, rushed at Stegeman for the second time, Cuperus jumped over the footlights, strode across to them, the chorus of screams and shouting growing louder and louder, caught hold of Escamillo, who had just at that moment rolled under a desperately resisting Don José, and dragged him to his feet, at the same time snarling at the tenor to get out of his sight. He didn't know it was a real *navaja*. If the drunken bullfighter intended to use the knife he didn't get a chance. Cuperus, mad with rage, punched him three, four times in the face, stopping only when the policeman, the firemen and a few others who wanted to see what was going on, carried the now immobile toreador off the stage.

It was only as he walked slowly, brushing his coat, towards the dimly shining footlights, that I caught sight of Cuperus. His hand raised commandingly to silence the flood of noise, the shouts of excited men standing up and the Toreador's song from the cheaper seats, Cuperus squared his shoulders, breathing deeply, stroking his moustache. After giving a reassuring nod to one of the Committee-members standing hesitantly on the stage behind him, Cuperus addressed himself to the audience, who listened fairly quietly to the first few sentences.

'Ladies and gentlemen, you have just witnessed a most deplorable scene. Mijnheer Ordelio has conducted himself in such a disgraceful manner that there can be no question of allowing him to continue. It would be risking the lives of the other members of the cast. Much as we regret it, we will have to finish the performance of the opera . . .'

There was a shout of 'Money back!'

'. . . without Escamillo, but I trust that the lack will be overcome by the music and by your imagination. . .'

These last words sounded a little too pretentious. In the second row an elderly furniture manufacturer, who liked to hear himself talk, stood up:

'Excuse me, Mijnheer Cuperus, we were assured that Mijnheer Ordelio had a sore throat, and we could hear that he had lost his voice. But this sort of thing doesn't happen just from a sore throat. . .'

'It wasn't a sore throat,' Cuperus snapped and looked confused for a moment or so, not because what he had said was so patently untrue, but because he'd had been stupid enough to answer the furniture manufacturer. (When he told me this later he said that anyone who gets carried away with his feelings at crucial moments ought to be exterminated.) Then he added: 'Yes, he did have a sore throat, but besides that he was drunk, or crazy. . .'

'You're drunk yourself!!!'

There were titters, even from the more expensive seats. The furniture manufacturer sat down shrugging his shoulders, after all, he was a gentleman. The clarinettist peeped over the railing around the orchestra pit and, jerking his head derisively at the conductor, pulled faces at the audience. Cuperus chewed at his moustache and clenched his fists.

'I should like to remind you that we can express our respect for Bizet's genius in more fitting ways than in the exchange of insults. We have taken a lot of trouble to rehearse this wonderful opera . . .'

'Bravo,' an old lady with a fine alto voice called out.

'. . . and we're not going to see all our trouble go for nothing just because some buffoon from Amsterdam thinks he can come up to the North here and . . .'

This was a good move by Cuperus, for loud applause mixed with shouts of local patriotism came from every part of the hall. When the applause died down he went on:

'We will continue the performance, without, I hope, any further interruptions'—he turned a menacing look at the orchestra to quieten some of the musicians who were unconcernedly talking and laughing, but the antics of the paperhanger over on the left escaped his notice—'without Escamillo but with the spirit of Bizet. . .'

At this point he was interrupted by the paperhanger who had spotted some friends or relatives, and not in the cheapest seats either. A comedian by nature, burning with resentment at Cuperus's sarcastic criticism, he leant over the balustrade with his hand to his mouth like a trumpet and hooted:

'Toreador, what a great big bull they've brought.

Oh, what a bull.

Watch you don't get caught!'

Then he gave a long 'moo-oo-oo.' I didn't hear this or any of what followed, as I had left the stage by a back door just after the applause. In any case this diversion didn't last long. Caspers tactfully intervened, guiding Cuperus, who was panting and sobbing from helpless rage, back to his conductor's stand. The orchestra struck up and the paperhanger played obediently with the rest.

But that still wasn't the end of the evening for me. I had walked out of the theatre because I couldn't help Cuperus in any way, and I felt that it was less contemptible to make at least a negative protest than to follow the passive example of the Committee-members. But I took care to swear loudly as I passed the firemen on my way to the stairs that led to the exit. I knew what a blow this disappointment—coming on top of his failure with Alice de Rato—would be to Cuperus. I knew how proud he was, and what a point of honour it was with him that he had never been accused in public of drunkenness no matter how drunk he might have been. But there was nothing I could do.

I walked through the fog for half an hour or more. I didn't intend to go home, I was still thinking of the ball. About the time I guessed the performance would be almost finished—assuming that everything went smoothly—I took up a position by the cloak-room—I had already got my coat and hat—and waited there near the door. From the girl in charge of the cloak-room I gathered that the opera was nearly over, that nearly everyone was staying for the ball of course, but the rest would soon be going home. I could see five or six coaches waiting in front of the theatre. We both listened to the muffled sounds of the last scene, the final chords, tragic and triumphant, and, thank God, a storm of applause, even from the cheap seats nearest the double door. Long before the clapping had died down this door burst open as a group of shabbily dressed figures hurried out, shaking off the spell of the music, and disappeared like petty thieves. Soon afterwards more sedate members of the audience came strolling through into the adjoining buffet. A dignified cigar-smoker wrapped his scarf on and wended his way with his fur-coated wife towards the exit. I noticed the Burgomaster and his family, also apparently on the point of leaving.

I was just going to hand in my coat and hat again when I heard a woman calling from outside. I thought I recognized Alice de Rato's voice, and then a moment or so later I saw her with a big coat on, standing beside one of the coaches. She shouted to someone on the left, and when I looked I saw Cuperus coming round the corner of the theatre, Vellinga holding his arm, and Stegeman, Jantje de Ridder and Trix following behind, still in stage costume under their winter coats, and all three of them arm in arm. Stegeman was carrying a load of bouquets, obviously tributes to Jantje and Alice, and one of his own hung around his neck. Trix was carrying her own flowers, or maybe they were her father's. Cuperus and Trix didn't notice me, the others recognized me and stood calling out, waving their arms. I asked Cuperus how the performance had gone, but Vellinga, who seemed to have been drinking, answered me. Marvellous. Ordelio was back in his hotel, paralytic drunk with a black eye from our maestro, as our dear Tjallingii called Cuperus—and a smack in the guts from me too, Stegeman added simperingly—and was I coming with them. This generous offer was echoed by Alice de Rato, who dubbed me '*ce joli garçon*'. They were taking Cuperus and Trix home, we all need a good night's rest, Vellinga bellowed, Cuperus just glared in front of him and stepped towards the coach. The coachman took the flowers and put them up on the seat beside him. Stegeman and Jantje followed Cuperus, and I stood just to the side of Trix, who ignored me. I didn't know what to do. I didn't want to be a spoil-sport, but I didn't want to end up in Trix's company in a rowdy carousal where I would more than likely be dumped on the copious lap of this boisterous Carmen who didn't measure up to Casper's taste and would probably make Cuperus even more unhappy than he already was. Besides, I didn't like Vellinga's noisiness. He started telling me that they were going to drop in on the Italian with some aspirin and a serenade from Don José, but I had the impression he couldn't see me very well, he seemed to be speaking to someone else.

Trix climbed inside. When de Rato tried to pull me in too, I

drew back, so giving Vellinga the right to shove me absentmindedly aside. I felt it was better not to join them, seeing that Cuperus
hadn't invited me. The coachman pushed the last two of the party
into the coach, and I saw his big hands pressed in turn against the
two rumps, first de Rato's, then the journalist's, the one as bulky
as the other though of different proportions. Hunched up, they
disappeared through the door. It was surprising that they didn't
fall back on to the roadway through the floor of the coach. The
flowers on the driver's box were half-hidden in the fog, they would
soon disappear completely. There was a shout from inside the
coach. I waved to them and I thought I saw a waving hand against
the glass panel at the back.

I stayed at the ball for about an hour talking to my mother,
who told me how the show had finished. Stegeman had been
wonderful, she said, and the soloists had to take four curtain-calls
and they all got flowers, and that daughter of Cuperus's, you
know, a whole bouquet from Vellinga, Vellinga personally presented it to her on the stage, and Zuñiga got a bouquet from his
wife, he brought her on the stage too, in spite of her protests, that
was understandable because she was carrying a pair of her husband's trousers, ordinary trousers, not the military trousers he
was wearing. Then José and Micaëla had given each other flowers,
even though the marriage had been called off again, and how many
times was that now. Someone had sent flowers for Ordelio, and
Cuperus had thrown them, all crushed up, at the orchestra—a
little uncouth, because most of the musicians had really done
their best. He didn't want to accept his own bouquet and he
tossed it over to one of the singers in the choir, but they were
going to take it to his house for him. The more amused and
sarcastic my mother's remarks, the more depressed I became, all
the more because this gay mood did not seem to me to be quite
natural. All that babbling hid a tiredness, a new sort of tiredness
that she had never shown before. When I left she didn't even bother to look round to see which friends she could go and talk to.

Two days later I went to visit Cuperus. He received me rather stiffly, and I could see he'd been drinking. But the difficulty I had in making him understand why I walked out of the theatre—my protest hadn't gone unnoticed—was due rather to apathy and preoccupation. His black house-jacket was covered with cigar-ash, the stove had gone out, and he said that in another month he would be fifty, and he felt sixty, and what was the reason? It was because of that rabble. Then he started, abusing the world, lamenting his many misfortunes and he flashed angry squinting looks at me. Yet he hardly ever looked me straight in the eye. Opera, never again, and quite right too, what can you do if the conductor's a drunkard? (Vellinga did in fact give up his efforts to make W . . . a miniature Bayreuth, mainly because Caspers, who had bought a pig in a poke with Alice de Rato, wouldn't provide any more cash, and other local magnates followed his example. The enthusiasm for music in W . . . began to decline, even the musical evenings my parents gave attracted fewer visitors.) Think of it, made a fool of by an uncultured mob, him, Henri Cuperus, and with a bit more luck and a bit more appreciation he might have reached the top as an opera conductor. A decent appointment in one of the big cities—and he'd have taken good care he didn't get mixed up with rubbish like Alice de Rato (he added a few unprintable epithets) and he'd fallen in love with her, by Jesus, as if it wasn't bad enough without that. That's what came from living in a little provincial town. In the city you saw too many fine-looking women at the opera to want to fall in love with just one, and what a one this had to be. He wasn't going to play anything for me ever again. He had kicked the *Carmen* score into a corner. I could keep on having lessons from him, but I had to realize that he was a completely disillusioned man, completely disillusioned. If that had an inspiring effect on me, well, so much the better.

When I asked about Trix he began to curse and swear, never looking at me once. He sat half turned away from me, with drooping cheeks and quivering moustache. Trix was crazy. She'd got so worked up about the whole business that she'd gone back to her aunt. Didn't want to sing again, wouldn't come home more than once in the month . . . All that trouble for nothing . . . His hands slid nervously over his jacket, his voice died away. It occurred to me that he could have, like his wife had, guessed something of my feelings. He hardly looked up as I took leave of him.

At the next lesson, when he offered me his apologies, I thought twice about asking after Trix, especially as I had decided to write to her. I had already made at least ten drafts of this letter, some of them four pages long. Finally, I compressed everything into ten lines, and when no answer came I had to endure my own reproaches for being so casual and vague. There wasn't much more in the letter than that I had enjoyed hearing her sing and I hoped we would meet again soon—another meeting like that time on the ice. My reason for writing was transparent enough, but she could hardly gather from such a letter the extent, the depth, the warmth of my affection. Besides, did she have any proof that I wasn't inspired merely by an adolescent foolishness cloaked in polite phrases?

Cuperus began to suffer from the effects of his weakness. When he pointed out a note his hand shook, and he neglected his appearance, his moustache, now undyed, was grey and the stubble on his chin was white. Once when I was there he had a sudden fit of rage, he pointed sneeringly at the old faded bouquets on the wall, and at the new one with the shining red ribbon, then he announced he was going to chuck them all out the window. When I barred his way he swore at me, but seeing the determination in my face, he walked with his head bowed to the piano, then struck match after match trying to light a cigar. Without saying a word he went over to the window and threw the cigar out into the street. Then he gave me my lesson for the remaining half-hour as if nothing had happened.

It was difficult to say why he was feeling so bitter. Before the disappointment with the *Carmen* performance there had never been any talk of ambition to become a great opera conductor. Alice de Rato wasn't the reason either. It was her photo, taken maybe fifteen years ago, and her fame as a singer that he had been in love with. Trix? It would be quite natural that he missed her presence in the house with a wife who hardly spoke and was almost deaf and was getting thinner and thinner, every day nearer the hospital or sanatorium. Once he hinted at an unhappy love affair in his youth, and from the changes in his musical preferences it was obvious that he was wandering back into the past. For a time nothing but Wagner, then a sudden tirade about how impossible it was to listen to that music without the sound of voices and without a stage spectacle, and after that a belated, almost chastened, return to the arpeggio-like, undiluted triads of Liszt.

The year that followed was the most placid, and really the happiest of my whole life. I called my love for Trix my *grande passion* and I was sure I would soon see Trix again, though I didn't want to make any move until the school examinations were over. I forbade myself to take advantage of the rare occasions when she came home, I could have easily found out in advance from her father, but I had to finish with being a schoolboy first. I had grown into a fresh-cheeked, healthy young man, broad-shouldered, deeply attached to my mother, whose rosy complexion was not what it once had been, and endowed with a pronounced degree of self-control and patience. It is possible that this was only my own vision of myself, others may have seen me in a different light— but I am thinking particularly of that one happy year that ended on a mild, sunny day in late April. Three days earlier I had turned nineteen.

That evening I had a music lesson —we'd changed to the evening a long while back because the afternoon lessons didn't give enough chance for 'overtime'. A warm wind jogged me with friendly gusts towards the quiet street that always seemed to have fewer lights than anywhere else. I can remember listening to the echo of my footsteps from the row of houses on the opposite side.

There was no moon. There was scarcely a trace of that heavy warmth of early spring with its fragrance and sounds that are always different from the sounds of other seasons. Long before I reached the house I heard him playing, and when I stood at the door I recognized the music. It was the second intermezzo from *Carmen*, a piece that he had once called 'music of passion'. But he was playing it altogether differently from the way he had played it eighteen months ago. Naturally, this music moved me—even if it was only because of the thought that he was playing it again and must have got over his aversion to the opera—but it was only later that I realized what the difference was. He sarcely used the pedal and the tempo was rather faster. He skipped over almost all the second page, except for the coda. What remained was a serenely tinkling rondo-like piece, in an unchanging E flat major, without the modulations and the more flowing, more impassioned accents of the second page. This subtle transformation, distilled to an ultimate purity, had such an overwhelming effect on me that spring evening mainly, I think, because of the tempo he used for the coda, slower and fuller, it was not a contrived, sentimental languor but, from the very first note, a sublime, unearthly hymn with the minims accentuated as a *cantus firmus*, and the one harsh discord was more hauntingly terrifying than anything else in the world. He didn't play the last three bars, the ripple in E flat major quickened, and then the whole piece began all over again. I could see from the curtain that he was sitting in the dark.

I had sat down on the porch and I listened, without moving, my head against the doorway on the side nearest his room. He didn't make a single mistake, he must have practised for days, perhaps nights on end, ever so softly, like his accompaniment that time when my mother sang Wolf's 'Der Gärtner' in the next room. There was so little *legato* in his rendering that it took on a Mozart-esque quality, with an almost inhuman remoteness suggested by the obsessional repetitions. The feeling was in the notes, not in the stroking, compelling, restraining fingers. Was this his lonely adieu to *Carmen?* But he knew that he could expect me any moment, and this made his playing even more inhuman, more harrowing —it had the jagged simplicity of a crystal that rolled softly tinkling down a never-ending rocky slope without ever reaching the bottom of the chasm below, every now and then stopping, lying still on the last little ledges, before the end that is no end. As long as Cuperus lived, operas could still be staged and played. This was what brought a lump in my throat and turned my thoughts back, back to a year ago, to the warm colours, the gay chatter backstage, the desultory idyll no brazen gipsy girl was threatening, that foolish but somehow touching love affair between Micaëla and Don José, who had let six months go by again without writing, but most of all to the smell of grease paint, that divine dross of the theatre, and even the husky voice of Alice de Rato and the music and Henri Cuperus, artist and mentor, taunted by the jeering crowd his talents and his strivings had been wasted on. That was over and done with. From now on I would restrict myself to faultless performances of *Carmen*—no more paperhangers who thought they were musicians and made fun of their conductor, no more hoarse and blind-drunk bullfighters, only well-behaved players and cardboard *navajas*.

The wood my cheek pressed against wasn't cool any more. Gusts of wind that I scarcely noticed blew past me, the sound of footsteps coming nearer hardly wakened me from my sad reverie, and I wasn't startled when a long figure stopped suddenly at the door. Through a haze I saw a shopping-bag with odd things sticking out of it. It was only when she knelt down beside me that I looked at her, but I had neither the time nor the strength to explain it was because of the music, which had stopped halfway through a moment or so before, that I was sitting there like a worn-out tramp, for she put her bag down, stretched her arm round my shoulders and I heard her whisper: 'Why are you crying, Nol?'

'You can't see that,' I whispered back. No, but she could feel the tears with her hands, I hadn't thought of that, and then I threw my arms around her, and I said I hadn't been sitting there waiting for her, that I didn't even know she would be coming home, but I loved her, that was all.

With a strength that surprised me she pressed me close to her. She held me so tight that it almost hurt.

'I love you too,' she whispered passionately.

'I've always loved you.' The light went on in the room and we could hear Cuperus's footsteps. I spoke quickly: 'But I could go on living without you, if I had to. We danced together when we were children...'

'I've always loved you too.' It didn't sound like an echo, the words were warm and earnest. We kissed each other and listened to the footsteps in the room. She stood up, lifting me with her.

'Not always, not when we were little,' I whispered. I didn't want to believe in still more miracles.

'Maybe,' she said, almost too softly for me to hear, as she picked up her bag and put the key in the door, 'or maybe it was when you brought that money. Now listen, don't forget: tomorrow night, at nine o'clock sharp, wait for me outside here, in the street. Tomorrow night.'

I repeated: 'Tomorrow night, at nine.'

She wiped my face with a handkerchief and led me inside. The handkerchief smelt fresh, without a trace of perfume.

I wasn't wearing a coat or hat. Trix kept her overcoat on, she put her hat on the floor next to her shopping-bag that had a medicine bottle wrapped in silver paper sticking out of it. This was perhaps a sign of confusion, but she wasn't confused when we both went into the lighted room where Cuperus stood by the piano facing us. Trix didn't say anything, just looked at him. When I said good evening he lowered his eyes and made an awkward welcoming gesture. Even though Trix and I weren't holding hands, nor even standing very close to one another, our coming in together just when it was time for my lesson had such obvious implications, besides begin rather impertinent, that a certain re-

156

serve could be expected from any father. But Cuperus overdid it, he said nothing, his only reaction was to avoid looking at Trix, who kept her eyes unwaveringly fixed on him. I said something or other about how mild the weather was and turned to look at her. How old her face was again. But those lines traced on her forehead by all that she had been through filled me with such a tenderness, the difference in our ages gave me such a feeling of triumph, that I forgot Cuperus and his surliness or embarrassment. Finally she turned round and went out of the room saying: 'I'll go up to Mother.'

I had brought no music with me, so he knew I would rather hear him play that evening. I didn't want to talk about the intermezzo. A glance at the piano told me that the *Carmen* score wasn't there any more. When I offered him a cigarette he refused it, and he didn't take a cigar of his own either. He slouched up and down, shifted a pile of music, talked about Wagner whom he was dabbling with—on the table there were four red-bound volumes of his collected *Musikdramen*—and what did I think of Bach. Then he was silent again. He was cold sober. After a while he said:

'I forgot to tell you that Trix was coming home for a couple of days.'

'I met her at the door,' I said casually. His hesitant manner, the uncertain way he looked at me and looked away again, didn't bother me at all. I wasn't interested in the reasons for his attitude, I was living twenty-four hours ahead.

'Yes, it had to happen,' he said, as if the meeting at the doorway was a turning-point in our lives. He propped up one of the red-bound volumes on the piano without opening it. 'There's Wagner. An artist through and through, a genius. Must have got it from his father-in-law ... it's always the same, I'll end up with Bach, at least there aren't any ... That's the only music that isn't messed up with them. Brünhilde, Isolde, Carmen,' he spat out the last name as if it was something dirty, 'not to forget Kundry, a filthy lot...'

'You haven't turned into a woman-hater, have you?'

'They're never satisfied with just one man. Most of them aren't, anyway.' He peered at me for a moment from under his now bushy, grey speckled eyebrows, the curve in his back as he leaned forward was almost obsequious. 'There's always one who turns up when you least expect it. Kundry, she wasn't the worst either, she was bewitched, so there was some excuse maybe... Kundry ... what was I going to say? ... with her it was just the other way round, she was saved, as they say, but no more love affairs after that. Bitches...'

'But there's a moral in another opera that no man should ever let another man get the better of him.' I said the first thing that came into my head, but it was really my opinion that Don José ought to have killed Escamillo instead of Carmen.

'Indeed,' he said, with a hint of contempt in his voice.

'Well, that's what I think.'

'No man by himself is a match for the rest, men and women, because he is alone,' he said, and, without giving me a chance to answer, he added: 'Bach.'

He started playing odd pieces from the *English Suites*, carelessly, and using too much pedal. As an organist he must have often played Bach, more for himself than for an audience, and in my imagination I saw him sitting at the organ in a deserted village church, in a halo of chalk-white light, his head full of fame and neglect and honour and a shopkeeper's pretty daughter he thought he had fallen in love with. I had a feeling of superiority. I began to realize then, though I was only able to formulate the thought coherently much later, that men like Cuperus had to fall in love once every three months just to establish some contact with a community they were irrevocably excluded from. He had realized that himself when he said that if he'd been in Amsterdam as a conductor he wouldn't have needed these amorous excursions, at least, not so often. It wasn't a pleasant or instructive evening. He ran his fingers over the keyboard and finally, from sheer boredom, he played the dullest of all Beethoven's sonatas (Opus 31-1 that is so dreary that no self-respecting pianist ever reaches the charming *rondo*). There was no tea brought in to us. The two women seemed to have been spirited away, it was so quiet in the house.

The next evening I waited an hour in vain. There was no sense in ringing at the door. I knew she had left again. As I walked slowly back home I had a premonition that my happiness might come to an end, for years and years. The amazement I felt at the possibility was not altogether disturbing. I had the confidence of youth that I could endure any ordeal. But how long does youth last? To judge Trix's conduct I had the choice between several explanations—a capriciousness that she had never shown any trace of before, pressure from her father who didn't have any influence over her and wouldn't have any apparent reason for interfering, or the typical provincial-mindedness of girls who let admirers wait for nothing one evening and the next evening are as sweet and inviting as they should have been the night before. In some cases this sort of naïve perversity has nothing to do with 'putting to the test...'. Following this line of thought I painted Trix in the most unfavourable colours and I passed a reasonable night. The next morning there was a letter for me on the breakfast table.

'Dear Nol, You must forgive me for not turning up. It's better this way. I'm not taking back a word of what I said, but it can never come to anything between us. I can see that now. You don't know anything about me. Just forget me. When you're studying at the university that shouldn't be difficult. Yours, Trix.'

' "... it can't come to anything between us"—that's so provincial,' I mumbled to myself, as my plate and everything around it grew bigger and hazier in a circle of vague splashes of light with prismatic effects. I folded the letter and put it back into the envelope that didn't have the name of the sender on it, and glanced at my mother who hadn't noticed anything.

12

I replied by return post, politely and understandingly, concluding
with a commentary on 'not knowing anything about her', an objection that could, I insisted, be removed without difficulty. I
didn't expect an answer, I wrote, I had to do my exams and in
three months or so, once I was settled in at the university, she
would hear from me again. I didn't put in any protestations of
affection. It had, indeed, occurred to me that I might have a rival,
someone she didn't love, or loved far less than me (or perhaps
just as much, or more even—I was allowing for all the vagaries of
the female heart I had read about in novels), but someone who
wanted to and was in a position to marry her, a likelihood suggested by her letter—'it can't come to anything between us'—and
by certain remarks Cuperus had made about the impossibility of
exclusive possession. But the more I thought about our unkept
appointment the more inexplicable I found it, and the only consoling reassurance was the memory of that kiss in the quiet street,
the miracle that had happened to me at a moment when I wasn't
even thinking of her.

After a lot of reflection I told my mother the whole story, always a silly thing to do, but in this case justified, I felt, by the
hopelessness, objectively considered, of my passion. Besides, I
took the precaution of presenting it as 'calf-love', so that I wouldn't
lose face if she just laughed at me. The discussion didn't last long.
What she had to say wasn't much more than the rather astonishing,
and to my mind smug, announcement that she had known all
the time. In a year, she said, we would have another talk about
it. She seemed to expect the university would bring about a
complete change in my nature, perhaps with the help of an allowance of spending money for sexual purposes—as much as Chris
got, though he apparently didn't benefit from this expenditure.
During the months that followed she was very quiet and preoccupied, she often sat talking with my father, more than she had

ever done before, and these long, confidential talks I saw as a portent of disaster for them both. I couldn't say why.

My father was ageing quickly. Reconciled to my choice of profession, which he considered almost ungentlemanly, he was friendly enough towards me, but there was always a gulf between us that didn't exist between Chris and him. He liked discussing legal problems with Chris, chewing over every point, like a dog gnawing at the oldest, most chewed-on bones in the garden. Except for my piano-playing there was rarely any music in the house now, and when my father wanted to hear Brahms I played Brahms. After I had discovered Debussy and played a not so very difficult piece, he gave me a talking to, and it was only by assuring him that Mijnheer Cuperus also disapproved strongly of this revoltingly effete, discordant, incoherent, and no doubt degenerate Frenchman that I managed to calm him down. From then on he was friendlier, and for the first time in my life I felt that he meant well, and that perhaps he had more need of affection than my mother.

It went from bad to worse with Cuperus. Everyone said so and did nothing to help, as if it was some rather disagreeable phenomenon of nature and best avoided. It all began when he let his wife precede him to the grave. During the summer holidays, while I was away, she died from a haemorrhage. I sent a telegram, a letter, and then flowers. I didn't get any acknowledgement. A week before I was to leave for the university town where I now would be living, I visited him. It was six months since I had been having lessons, but I had still been going to see him. He had played for me a few times and I had already asked his advice on the choice of his successor. My intention was to familiarize myself thoroughly with the whole range of worthwhile music, except what was too 'out of date'—so that excluded all the seventeenth and eighteenth centuries—and not to become a piano virtuoso performing once a week for a small circle of dilettantes. Musical theory, historical development, harmony and counterpoint,

161

some score reading, and intelligent guidance for self-study—that was what I wanted. Although he rejected as an ignoramus every teacher I suggested, he finally gave me the name of one he thought I could try. We talked all this over sensibly, for he was sober and he understood quite well that I couldn't make a two- or three-hour train trip every week for a lesson from him. But I had never seen him as drunk as he was on that first visit after his wife's death. He bellowed reproaches, that I'd let him down, that I didn't give a damn, not even coming to the funeral, a bloody awful funeral it was too, he had to wear three top-hats all at once, just for the sake of the name and the honour of the family, and Trix, selfish little bitch that she is, she wouldn't even speak to anyone there, and he, yes, he, he ... Then he burst into tears and asked me to forgive him, but that didn't stop him, a few minutes later, from ranting against Trix in such offensive terms that I could hardly restrain myself from stamping out of the room. The tirade only ended when I led him upstairs to his bedroom and half undressed him. He called me his son, but the glazed eyes he goggled at me with just before he fell into a loud, snoring sleep didn't recognize me any more. He implored me not to give the money for the butcher to that other hag.

That other hag was Trix's aunt, who stood waiting for me in the hallway. The first thing she said was that Trix was still in the village fixing up the moving, she'd had to come over first because of Hendrik, well, I'd seen what a state he was in, hadn't I? He was so fond of his wife, and her death was such a blow to him. This aunt was about the same height as Trix and not much thinner. But on that rather fleshy neck there was a wobbling head that just didn't seem to belong, it was so oddly proportioned, large and round, with an intelligent forehead, very big and clear shining eyes that could slily half close with the cheeks drawn upwards, a small finely chiselled nose with prominent nostrils, wide like the nose openings in the face of a skeleton. But it wasn't one of those snub, turned-up noses, and even after I had studied anatomy I still

162

didn't understand how such a shape was possible. The head that might have had some specious charm in her youth—she was, as it happened, nine years or so younger than her dead sister—was, that afternoon anyway, constantly moving, not only when she was speaking, but of its own accord, as a head. Shaking defensively, nodding as if she knew everything there was to know, tilted twitchingly forward, prying, suddenly jerked upwards, high and flaunting, an incessant, endless variety of positions and expressions. Better dressed, so much more poised and better spoken than her sister, she could have passed for a lady of some distinction—just a little peculiar, I thought at first, but later I discovered that she knew what she was doing, and she could keep her head still for hours at a stretch if she was so inclined.

I didn't find her so very objectionable—it may have been that her build and her ash-blond hair reminded me of Trix—but I wanted to get out of the house as quickly as possible, mainly because I was anxious to avoid the role of confidant. It was, to say the least, suspect that she had mentioned Trix right at the start. I'd have to put a stop to that. If Trix found out she was being talked about behind her back there'd be more damage done than with an appointment that hadn't come off. Walking after me in the hall with long steps she kept up her flow of talk, telling me that from now on she would be keeping house for her brother-in-law, and that Trix would have to look for work because neither of them had a penny, and if Hendrik went on like this he'd soon have no more pupils and no more choir, though he always used to get his wife to tip a bucket of cold water over him before the rehearsals. Then the cupboard would be bare, oh yes, she'd been left a little money from a gentleman she had worked for once, but just fancy throwing away money on drink for Hendrik... She didn't say any more, and she didn't say good-bye, as if she expected I would be back in half an hour or so.

On the other side of the street, the board with the blacksmith's name on it had been painted, and now the letters of 'G.J. Douwes en Zoon' shone bright and new, without tear-stains or blotches.

I wrote another friendly note to Cuperus asking him to convey my greetings to his sister-in-law and his daughter, packed my things, kissed my mother, and left to join Chris, whom I had warned in a humorous letter of dire physical retribution if he should take it into his head to rag me himself. But there was no chance of that. Ragging was beneath his dignity, he'd long since grown out of such childishness. But he still had to be initiated himself into the secrets of the female form, which he regarded only as an expensive luxury he was obliged, whenever possible, to put at the temporary disposal of his friends and future fellow-lawyers, and others likely to be of some use to him at some time or other. I installed myself in rooms in another part of the town, and the only time I encountered Chris in an amatory context was in a well-known and pricey whorehouse where I aggressively defied convention by drinking a cup of tea that had been dosed with brandy anyway. But I have spoken enough ill of Chris in these memoirs, so I'll only add that if I remember rightly, when he took off some of his clothes at the insistence of a few other students the assembled company gazed at an old much-mended set of my father's underwear. Chris is now happily married, and it isn't for me to cast aspersions on his love-life. I should mention, however, that he apparently had an unhappy entanglement when he was about seventeen, it lasted for several weeks and probably left him somewhat confused. I endured the ragging with a faint smile, carefully avoiding fights. I wanted to mature, to have done with adolescence, as quickly as possible. I estimated that I could do this under the circumstances in three or four months, and I was certainly more level-headed in my first year than in my fifth or sixth, but that is another story.

Refusing to be offended at Cuperus's silence I acquainted him briefly with what I was doing, with the achievements of my new music teacher, with my growing preference for Debussy and Ravel, which he shouldn't hold against me too much, particularly as it was, in fact, merely a consequence of his own teaching,—but he would never admit that, of course—his own emphasis on detail, on unusual combinations and spectacular harmony. (My new teacher, with his unemotional erudition, strongly disapproved of this obsession with harmony. He thought in lines, not in colour, and he ranted against Wagner at every lesson. I could never make him understand that, if he was going to be consistent, he ought to reject Debussy's music as well.) I still didn't get an answer, maybe his hands shook too much to write.

When the weeks of initiation into studenthood had gone by, when all those rites of figurative circumcision, the carousals, the acceptance into clubs and societies, the visits, the tasks and ordeals by alcohol were over, my mother came to see us both. The dispute I had with Chris about how long each of us would spend alone with her, and the childishness I displayed, aren't worth the retelling. All I wanted was to have the chance to talk to her for an undisturbed hour, not in my room, with the landlady coming in and out all the time, but in a quiet, roomy café. Alone with her, perhaps for the last time. She hadn't wanted to mention in her letters that her heart had been bad for a while, maybe for a long while. When I looked at her with my untrained eyes and noticed the pounding artery in her neck I wondered who would go first, my mother or Cuperus. I can remember most of our conversation, I think, at least where it directly concerned myself.

'That sweet little Trixie of yours seems to be getting a bad name for herself,' my mother said, too casually, her head turned away from me towards the passers-by in the light shower of October rain that sprinkled the footpath without wetting the wide windows of the café. That was the way she had always spoken when the subject was painful, implying a vagueness and speaking in a tone that suggested she had heard it from someone who got everything mixed up.

I knew all that, but still I felt every nerve in my body go tense. In just another two months I was going to write to Trix,

165

and now came this attack| before I had made a single move, a well-executed flank attack.

'You're sure it's true?'

'I've heard it from quite a few people, but even if it isn't true I thought I'd better tell you ... just in case...'

'Oh yes, I might hear it from someone else. Very considerate of you, Mother. But you can't imagine how little it bothers me.'

'Well, that's good,' she said with a sigh.

'I mean,' I said sharply, leaning back stiffly and blowing out the smoke of my cigarette sideways from her—I saw myself reflected in one of the window panes, ruddy, square-shouldered, young and well-mannered—'what I mean is that things like that do not affect my feelings for Trix in any way at all. Maybe it is true, this tale of yours, but I never expected that falling in love with Trix would make me happy. I can take a knock or two.'

'There's something else,' she said with a stifled laugh. 'You probably wouldn't know that she's working at the Garden, at the restaurant, not as a waitress but as a sort of manageress. Cuperus drinks every cent and she has to earn some money, and she just can't stand music...'

'Who did you hear all this from? Was it van Son, Tjallingii or Vellinga?' I asked with just an edge of sarcasm in my voice.

'You're not far out, but not from Vellinga.'

'A pity, seeing that he's a journalist he ought to be better informed than all the others. I don't mean about working at the Garden, that could be true, but about the bad name she's supposed to be getting, that can happen anywhere, to a lady-in-waiting or the maid in some cheap hotel.'

'Wait a minute, Nol, listen to me. Vellinga couldn't tell me because ... well, you see ... it's Vellinga who's giving her a bad name.'

I was even more tense, and my expression even more distant. My head was spinning and I took a sip of tea. It's going to be a mess, a hopeless mess. But Trix is still there. Somewhere inside me

166

there was an exultant feeling that set me apart from and above everyone and everything, a feeling that made me free. This was the ordeal I had to endure. A different sort of ordeal from gulping down five glasses of gin one after the other and then bending over head down and waiting to see who would be the first to fall.

'Yes, that bouquet she got,' I said hoarsely, 'yes, it might be true...'

'I don't know any more than that,' my mother blew her nose and coughed behind the handkerchief. 'You'll have to ... the time soon passes and then it's all forgotten...'

'I think you had better realize,' I said curtly, almost condescendingly, 'that time won't make any difference in this case. Time is just nonsense, I don't believe in it, the philosophers don't even know what time is ... When I hear this tale from you or from someone else I just have to listen, I can't bolt off whenever I'm told something, that's impossible ... But surely, Mother ... you must have been in love once?'

'Not really,' she said.

I was silent for a few moments. 'How did you know that it had always been like that between Trix and me? It's probably an exaggeration to say she always felt like that or that I'd always been in love with her, but it's partly true nevertheless.'

All of a sudden she was eager and helpful, almost cheerful, as if she had before her the prospect of an exciting conversation with a few sharp-witted and sharp-tongued friends, that would range over all the heights and depths of human nature and experience, the vagaries of fate, life, death, men, their wisdom and their follies, harmless flirtations, the risks of deeper involvements, children, no children, too many children, jokes, airy dismissals, titbits of gossip, jealousies, sweetly spoken sarcasm—a savage, polite tournament that could go on for hours until a burst of laughter she had managed to evoke conferred on her an illusory triumph, then that restrained expression on her face, wordly-wise: 'Till the next time ... if we live that long.' Now she could talk about things that had happened years ago, about the past I would have to cut myself off from completely and irretrievably if I was going to face these first years of manhood sensibly.

'I could see it at once, it all started that day you danced with her.'

'Yes, that's right,' I nodded, 'it's a little far-fetched, but that's what started it of course. Otherwise I wouldn't have taken any notice of her. But how could you be so sure?'

'Perhaps a sort of second sight. That's about the only time I had any of these flashes of intuition. I suppose because it was you, I mean becasue we're so like each other ... and I know that these childhood attachments go deep. Those boy-and-girl friendships at school hardly ever last, but it's different with very young children. I know a case of a man and a woman, both of them married, who sat down opposite each other in a train. They didn't know each other, I don't think they exchanged more than a few words, but after a quarter of an hour they knew they were in love. They both got divorced and then they got married. Afterwards they discovered from what they heard from relatives, aunts or great-aunts, that they had played together when they were children of three of four at a party, just as if they were really in love, the aunts told them...'

'Coincidence,' I commented with a bravado acquired from my few weeks of scientific studies.

'Their parents hadn't seen each other for more than thirty years. I heard all the details, I could tell you the names, where they lived, which train it was. They weren't so young either when they met in the train...'

'Very interesting,' I said, blowing the smoke from my cigarette past her, 'fancy that happening in a train. I imagine they were both so unhappily married that they could have fallen in love with anyone else in the train... I'm only teasing ... maybe there's something in it after all, but can I ask you something, Mother?'

Even more eagerly, no doubt because she wanted to repair any damage she might have done, she added: 'Of course, they're rare cases like that, and then ... besides you were much older when you danced...'

'May I ask you something, Mother?' I repeated, more softly, and when she nodded, with a surprised look in her eyes, I said: 'You just told me that you hadn't really ever loved anyone. So you weren't in love with Father, and a child could see that, even Chris noticed. I remember him telling me, during one of our truces, that Father and Mother don't kiss each other much.'

'In the beginning I thought I was,' she said calmly.

'But that's not all I wanted to ask. Both of us know that Cuperus fell in love with you. But what about all the others? I'm sure they were in love with you too. Van Son, Tjallingii, and Vellinga, and Caspers, and maybe a few others as well. What I wanted to ask was whether you were ever tempted ... you mustn't be angry with me, Mother, for asking ... But Caspers and Vellinga, especially Vellinga were ... well ...'

'I never had any trouble keeping the gentlemen at a distance. It was perhaps not so easy with Cuperus, but you know yourself what happened.'

'I believe that. But ... I mean the feeling of being tempted, you see. After all ... it's so easy for women to be tempted if they aren't in love with someone. That's what I mean.'

As if she would understand what I meant by this inquisitorial conclusion of our conversation that had set Vellinga in one role against Vellinga in another role and struck a blow for 'that sweet little Trixie' to hit back just a little at the rumours, true or not, everyone, everyone including my mother, had dared to go round repeating. Though we sat staring at each other for quite a while—the conflict between mother and son that always ends in reconciliation and always leaves some lasting estrangement—I'm sure, and I've always been glad too, that her second sight wasn't sharp enough to catch the malicious implication of my question.

13

It was, of course, unthinkable that my feelings could in any way
be affected by the new role that was being ascribed to Vellinga.
That evening, after my mother had left—and Chris made everything worse by walking to the station resolutely holding her arm
so that I could hardly hang on to her other arm—I drank myself
into a complete stupor, more from rage, at first, anyway, than
from despair. I didn't, I wouldn't, give in to despair. Nothing
irrevocable had happened, it was nothing but the beginning of a
new phase of my love for Trix, a wrenching readjustment that
seemed frightening but wasn't frightening at all. Love, I had always maintained, had nothing to do with time, there was no
beginning and no end. As I poured out one glass after the other
I pondered on this and other truths. This seeming folly was partly
due to the curious doctrine one of the older students, who came
from the Indies, had tried to entertain, disturb and edify us with
during those initiation weeks. According to him, anyone who
spent an evening drinking with a crowd, then staggered outside
raving and groaning to vomit it all up, didn't get any benefit from
drink. The only way to drink was in solitude, sitting alone and as
far as possible avoiding any movement of the body, and never
speaking aloud. By concentrating thought on emotional difficulties, or problems, or high aspirations the drinker sometimes at-
tained a flash of insight that might well be of practical use the
next day. It was a sort of mysticism. He had tried it himself before
every exam, and the time he failed it was only because of the
muck they'd sold him the night before. When the mystic was
explaining this to us he was, as it happened, rolling drunk, so
contradicting if not his doctrine, at least his observance of it.

But there was certainly something in this mystic inebriation
doctrine after all, for about midnight, just before I sank away in
several directions at once, I felt I could turn into a rocket and soar
off to land at Trix's feet in an explosion of all my pent-up thoughts

and feelings. The somewhat Goethian-accented insight that came to me was that action was a necessity and, when I sat down, after eight or nine hours snoring, to write a letter, I found I had very little reason to doubt the efficacy of the mystic's theory. I was writing this letter a few months earlier than I had intended, but this impetuosity could be overlooked since it was, in fact, nothing more than a request to Trix to let me hear from her. I asked her to reply within a week, if she was going to write at all. I softened the peremptory tone by ending the letter 'forever yours'. I posted it, and my morning-after headache eased off, thanks to the herring my worried landlady had fetched specially for me (not that I had vomited, but she had noticed the empty bottle, and, as she had seen me the day before as a mother's boy, she too, apparently felt action was a necessity). Then I wrote a second letter, this time to Jantje de Ridder. I couldn't think of anyone else. The idea of soliciting information from friends or former friends of my parents—I thought of Caspers, even Tjallingii —didn't appeal to me, though, I imagine, they would be more scrupulous than Jeannetje in observing my request not to say anything. But if she did go babbling it wouldn't matter much. All I was concerned about was making sure I didn't have to endure taunts from smart-alecks I had confided to in writing.

I didn't hear anything from Trix. But Jeannetje with those big, round, adoring eyes sent me a reply, more than I had hoped for.

'Dear Nol (I can say that, can't I),' it began, 'Nice to hear from you now that you're a busy student. I often think back on that *Carmen* performance, and I can still see you walking up and down backstage, so serious in your dark suit. We did give that Ordelio what he deserved didn't we? Do you have any chance to see an opera down there? I haven't heard from Wessel recently, but he has an engagement in The Hague. It takes most of his time and it's important for him. You don't forget old friends so quickly. I've got a lot of pupils and *I hear odd rumours*. Of course I won't gossip, you can trust me completely, Nol. From experience I

171

know that landladies do sometimes read letters that aren't meant for them, so I won't say any more than this: I have heard about what you mentioned but I haven't seen anything myself, and I don't want to say anything I can't be sure of. The one is likely to do anything, the other I don't know so well. I'm not one to criticize others. It must have been going on for some time, where she used to live, too. If I hear anything else I'll write to you. But you must come and visit me, Nol, whenever you're in W... Where I live now it is very quiet, probably you don't even know this part, you were always the absent-minded scholar. Cuperus is in a bad way, he's lost his choirs and most of his pupils. He does nothing but drink. A pity. I'm giving singing-lessons so in a way I'm a competitor of his. What do you think of that! That's all for now. Don't take things too seriously. Greetings and best wishes from Jantje de Ridder.'

Absent-minded scholars ... What a distorted picture others get of us. The letter had been written in a hurry, with words scratched out and arrows here and there, but the signature, as clear as a schoolgirl's copperplate, put a stamp of order on this chaos. The note-paper and envelope were thick and heavy, certainly expensive, and probably a present from Stegeman. Before I tossed the letter into the waste-paper basket I had to laugh. It struck me that I had reached an age that could appeal to her between Stegeman's all too infrequent expressions of affection, for she was now nearer forty than thirty. Was she giving me a delicate hint? What if she was? '... where she used to live, too.' Was Trix running round with Vellinga already before that night we met in the porch? The thought tortured me. I couldn't believe it was true, but I knew it was possible. Suddenly—the letter and the envelope rolled up into a ball in the waste-paper basket crackled—I said out loud: 'Slut.' It sounded different from what I had expected, it seemed almost biblical, a title of respect that had been debased by being cried too often from the pulpit. I wasn't angry. I realized that even if Trix did write to me I couldn't treat her with the same respect as before. But she didn't write, and the moments I didn't believe it were rarer and rarer. Vellinga was an enterprising type, one of the celebrities in W..., and besides, his success would explain the inconsistency of her attitude towards me. I spent a lot of time during the next few months looking for explanations, I took to philosophizing, my contemplative nature revealed itself. This lasted till the Christmas vacation.

Chris went home before me, ostensibly so he could 'study for his exams without any distraction', but in fact only to get away to another environment where a weekly visit to a whorehouse or some similar escapade wouldn't be required of him. He was beginning to find these excursions too tiresome, and his calculating thriftiness was also a strong deterrent, that he might have even been prepared finally to endure the ridicule of his friends rather than accompany them. I had made him frightened of possible consequences by showing him a second-hand text book with coloured illustrations of symptoms of venereal disease. It was the same as when I punched him on the nose. I showed him the illustrations only to tease him, but, who knows, I might have saved him from some terrible infection. Otherwise he passed through his student years in a groove of respectability. There was a place being kept for him in a lawyer's office in the university town. Even if there was some feeling of reserve on account of his excessive conceit he would be welcomed nonetheless, not so much for the energy he would put into his work as for the goodwill that would be established with a whole chain of impressive connections linked up with my father. I told him once that if I hadn't punched him on the nose that time he would never have got so far, but he didn't understand what I meant.

When I arrived in W... the atmosphere had changed. My mother was sick in bed, but she got up after a couple of days and spoiled us as much as her condition allowed her to. On the other hand my father gave the impression of being more vigorous than he had ever been, as if he had got over the difficult years of transition to old age, or had a young mistress somewhere in the outskirts of W..., but that is not a thought to dwell on. He was more alert, he looked me straight in the eye, cheerfully and inquiringly, and whenever he got the chance he would debate points of law with Chris. But now Chris could hold his own. Armed with his graduate knowledge and the better memory of a younger man, he could cut the ground from under my father's feet. He had no use for all that my father had learned from years of experience, it could be called out-of-date or dismissed as too rigidly formal. But my father kept on being friendly, and I can still see the forced smiles on their faces as they listened to each other, rebutted and refuted each other's arguments, and went their separate ways. But the struggle would be renewed and the air was thick with quotations from enactments and verdicts, a martyring of the mind, these numbers and figures, that were without significance and existed only by reason of the fortuity of a sequence, not in accordance with the immutably regular laws of nature. I imagined to myself all the diabolic machinations that must lie behind this parade of nonsense. I resolved I would store all this up to taunt and startle law students at debating evenings, draw them out, lure them into indiscretion and then leave them to face the contempt of the audience. A futile profession, the most futile of all occupations. The knowledge of lawyers was a symbol of the things that should at all costs be left well alone.

Father and son hurled these rulings and clauses at each other, masses of words like solid lumps they had been holding terrier-like between their teeth, a barrage that prevented either of them from adding any explanatory modification to whatever point in his argument the other had snapped at and seized on and chewed to nothingness. Often my father had to spend half an hour or so looking up old law books. Once they both went off to the Court to consult some records. Probably Chris proved my father was wrong or humiliated him, for when they came back my father suggested we should have a night out. We would go and have dinner together one evening, the three of us, a real slap-up dinner, in a good restaurant, as a sort of farewell to our youth, to the parental roof, and all the rest of it. It was a rather laboured invitation, but I felt that my poor father wasn't a match for Chris any more, so I agreed at once. Chris's glasses, which had for so long made him so like my father, shone now with a new juridical fire, with the bright pretensions of the still young, and that state of mind could only be countered by fine food and drink.

My mother listened as the plan was discussed in detail. When my father suggested the restaurant at the Garden as the best choice for our 'fodder party'—he was adopting a student joviality to win Chris over—she gave me a worried look that I answered with a reassuring nod. If we did go and have dinner there, then, as likely as not, I'd see Trix in all her glory as manageress or whatever she was. But I didn't intend to be kept away from a restaurant on account of a woman who didn't answer my letters and got herself talked about, and in a way that was humiliating for me. Perhaps Vellinga would be there too, it could be a very interesting encounter. She'd see that I could be as indifferent as she was, she mustn't get the impression that I was a lovesick adolescent pouring my broken heart out in rambling letters written with a dog-like servility. It was Cuperus's embarrassment that had removed any last lingering doubt I may have had. When I saw him he looked a wreck, physically and mentally. As I had written saying I would be coming, he was sober, and his shamefaced silence when I asked after Trix was the first definite confirmation of what I had till then only half believed. He had always complained about Trix because she never bothered about him and because she wouldn't go on with her singing, he had never just hung his head when her name was mentioned.

The restaurant in the Garden (there was another one in the centre of the town, but that was considered rather dull) had, in the last couple of years, acquired a high reputation since the new proprietor, a former cook on a big passenger-liner, had taken over

175

the lease. By ordering in advance it was possible to get a first-class dinner at a very moderate price, and served in a sort of *chambre séparée* with solicitous waiters peeping round frosted-glass doors. The view from the restaurant was an added attraction, in winter as well, even though there mightn't be any snow on the ground, like that evening of the fourth of January when the three of us, buried in thick overcoats, set out, my father breathless and quibbling in the middle. As he leaned forward to go up the high stone steps, I supported him under his arm while Chris followed behind us humming to himself.

The wooden building reposed on a stone foundation from which a row of slightly curved pilasters rose upwards between the windows on the moat side, an architecturally misleading feature, for these windows belonged to the kitchens, storerooms, pantries and the apartment where the owner lived. A look through a pair of field-glasses from the other side of the moat would probably reveal at the first window a cook arguing with a waiter, at the second, a cupboard with a lot of copperware on the shelves, behind the third a teddy-bear, and on the wall beyond the fourth window the vague shape of a framed steamship. In the big room that opened on to the part near the pond with the bandstand there were two billiard tables. Ugly brown caryatids, with bunches of fruit clasped to their bosoms, served as decorations along the walls. There were none of the usual rustic frivolities, antlers and cuckoo clocks that didn't go, and the like. High above the buffet hung an ordinary railway-station clock in a narrow casing that was the only patch of black in all that brown. The floor was parquet, but always covered with a fine layer of sand. The atmosphere was quiet, unimposing, with a slight touch of the patriarchal, especially in the *chambre séparée* where we stood as close as we could to the stove, as far as possible from the table set for three. After my first gin I glanced idly at the scene outside, where everything, measured against my memories, looked so small and insignificant, and in the gloom of the falling dusk so pathetically neglected.

The restaurant was sometimes noisy. There were occasional card evenings and billiard competitions, and often during an ordinary game a player might stamp and curse at a misjudged shot even though three or four local dignitaries were there reading their evening newspapers, old stalwarts who would feel more at home with hard-drinking, merry farmers than with their own social equals. But it wasn't a restaurant for going to every night, rather for special occasions, though there were some regulars, the members of the 'club', as they were given to calling it, a vague institution concerned more with drinking than with dining. It was mostly a floating clientele, but nevertheless there was an established hierarchy. Any thick-necked, puffed-up young farmer putting on airs soon knew where he stood with old Tjallingii, ex-doyen of the legal fraternity in W..., who spent his evenings dozing in his chair, or with another, even older, retired lawyer who greeted the farmers by raising his eyebrows as if he was looking down from halfway to heaven at some miserable, misguided mortals. The staff were treated as equals, a policy that went amiss only once or twice with new waiters.

As if by mutual agreement, my father and Chris had temporarily put their juridical polemics aside and I saw no reason why it shouldn't be a tolerable evening. A waiter came in and the proprietor came to the frosted-glass door to give a smile of acknowledgment. I didn't see Trix anywhere. But when the soup was served she came in. I felt her presence behind me, her disconcerting tallness gliding over the thick carpet. She had something white in her hand. She bent over my father's shoulder with the wine list, and as it would normally be a waiter who did this, I knew for certain that she had deliberately sought out a pretext to show she wasn't frightened to face us. She kept her eyes lowered while my father ordered a Burgundy. Her face was set, her eyes expressionless as I remembered they often used to be, but so attractive now with the curving eyebrows. Her hair was done differently, a less distinctive, less individual style. She was wearing a long white

177

apron. She was halfway to the door when I called after her: 'Juffrouw!' She turned round. 'Bring me some mineral water, I'm not having any wine.' I explained to my astonished father that my stomach wasn't too good, emphasizing my words by patting my waistcoat and rolling my eyes with a macabre playfulness.

The waiter brought the wine and mineral water. Before the soup was finished I had emptied the whole bottle. After the soup the waiter brought in the meat and all that went with it, and when he was gone and my father had solemnly begun carving, I got up and pressed the bell. Before I sat down again the waiter poked his head inside, silhouetted against the frosted glass, and I said: 'No, the young lady', at the same time raising my hand as if I was drinking, while he gave a sheepish grin that meant nothing at all. He was a young and still slow-witted waiter. 'I must have worked up a thirst from those three nips of gin,' I said to Chris, who didn't comment. I asked Trix for another bottle of mineral water, and it was brought in by the waiter. I asked my father to put a dash of wine in my glass, 'for the colour, so the waiters won't laugh at me', and I gulped it down.

'I've seen that girl before,' my father said, chewing meditatively while he took off his glasses and turned his head towards the now closed sliding-door.

'That's Henri Cuperus's daughter,' Chris said, 'You must remember her.'

'Oh, yes, yes, that girl, she was in the opera that time, she sang rather well, too. Fancy her working here.'

'Her father does nothing but drink now,' I said swallowing the rest of my mineral water, 'and she has to earn money somehow. I know her.'

'But she could have found something else, surely.'

'She probably gets a lot of tips here,' I said, with an explanatory jerk of my head in the direction of the door. 'Cuperus used to come here often and he probably knows the owner. I suppose that's how she got the job. I must ask him one of these days'.

My father waved his hand, dismissing the whole matter, and Chris said: 'Of course, you still see him. You know, I can still remember how you went round with a collection for him. I've always felt sorry for him, he's had his share of bad luck. I don't pretend to know anything about music but if everything went wrong that time they played *Carmen* it certainly wasn't his fault. I've seen conductors who weren't half so good.'

'How the mighty are fallen,' my father said.

When the dessert was served I stood up with an embarrassed laugh: 'Gentlemen, I'm sorry, you must excuse me a minute...'

They didn't even look round as I walked rather awkwardly to the door. Five minutes of freedom! The mineral water I had gulped down so recklessly would account for three or four minutes, and then there was my stomach as well. I could stretch it out easily to ten minutes.

The main room was filled with cigar-smoke. The proprietor was standing behind the buffet talking to a couple of loud-voiced rustics. No Trix. On the other side of the room I could see a waiter and a short, dark-haired girl. Then I saw our waiter coming through the door and I asked him where Juffrouw Cuperus was, I wanted to order something, something special, a surprise for the others. He pointed to a narrow passage ending at a door that probably opened into the kitchens. Near that door the passage turned sharply and there, in a sort of storeroom with a sloping roof, I found Trix at a table covered with glasses of all sizes and bottles of wine and bottles of liqueur. She looked up.

'Why didn't you answer my letter?'

She looked me straight in the eye. 'Because I thought it was wiser not to.'

'Wiser, but not politer.' I said wildly, 'I want to know why you treated me like that.' (At this point a waiter called out from the passage, with an undertone of respect in his voice: 'Trix, you're wanted', and she answered: 'Yes, just a minute, I'm busy.')

'Why do you treat me like this? It doesn't matter to me if you're a waitress—even if I have to pretend in front of my father and my brother that I don't know you. I can't help it if I have a father who's a judge, I didn't suggest coming here, and they don't know there's anything between us.'

She bent her head for a moment, then straightened up again, holding herself stiff, but there was nothing taunting in her expression or the way she moved. A shadow of the smile I remembered played around her eyes. I had to grip the table so my knees wouldn't give way.

'And you don't know anything about me. My father is sick, seriously ill, you'll have to ...'

'That's not an answer,' I managed to say, I could hardly speak. 'You can say you aren't in love with me any more, that's the only answer I'll accept.'

'I'm not going to lie to you.'

'No, but you're crazy to go on the way you do.' I moved closer to the table till I stood in front of her, trembling with rage. She wasn't frightened, and when she didn't react I asked: 'What's wrong with your father?'

'Delirium tremens.'

'Can he have any visitors?'

'I suppose he could. You'll have to go now, Nol.'

'When can I talk to you? What time will you be home tonight?'

'I don't go home. I sleep here. I couldn't stand it any more there.'

I sleep here, I sleep here. The words pounded through my head in time with my footsteps after I had turned my back on her with a brusque good-bye. I stopped a moment or so in the big room to look around. Vellinga wasn't there. Trix came in with a glass of liqueur for an old gentleman who had folded his newspaper into a fly-swatter, probably to protect himself from the temptation of reading more of it. A young farmer greeted her eagerly by name. He ordered a beer.

Half an hour later I was at Cuperus's bedside. I'd been able to be fairly truthful with my father. I had met Cuperus's daughter

180

as I was going to the toilet and she had told me how sick her father was. Before we were through the brandy and coffee they let me leave without much protest, no other thought in their bristlingly bespectacled heads than to reconsider the whole Dutch law code from a completely new angle. I was, however, preoccupied with delirium tremens and what the older medical students used to tell us about this condition to scare us whenever we pushed each other aside at the wash-basins to bring up the alcohol we had consumed in the last few hours. But I couldn't remember whether it was likely to be fatal or not, and when I saw Cuperus lying in bed, quietly sweating and mischievously blinking, I wouldn't have thought for a moment that he was in any danger, though I did notice that his face, always so red, was now more of a pallid purple. A doctor would probably say he looked far from well ... I clutched at the reassurances his sister-in-law gave me. She had welcomed me with the announcement that 'the worst is over'. According to her he'd got delirious from being cold sober for four or five days—a fable I wasn't able then to refute—and 'the worst' had been the queer animals that he wasn't seeing any more, or very few of them, and he didn't hear any more music either. As we went up the stairs I asked her why Trix had gone to work at the restaurant instead of going into service somewhere. I spoke with the manner of a young doctor who has a sense of social responsibility and she turned round, laughing, that spectral nose of hers momentarily visible in profile, while the head shook and danced, vigorously and well under control, confirming, denying, or viciously sadistic. 'Just try and tell Trix what she ought to do. She wouldn't hear of anything else,' she said confidingly at the top of the stairs. With a firm grip on my arm she guided me into the bedroom.

'I saw Richard Wagner,' Cuperus said with a wink after he had answered my first questions with a good-humoured growl. 'In the beginning it was nothing but frogs and insects, all sizes they were, and there were a lot of very little ones, even the frogs. You'll never see me drinking again, Nol. It is Nol, isn't it? Not that cousin? He's at me all the time, he thinks he's an adopted son of mine, but he won't get a single cent from me. Everything is going to you. Now have a look for the photos.'

'Which photos?'

'That wife of mine used to hide them, and when I asked her where they were she used to fly off the handle and she'd say I made up to the girls I gave lessons to. Lies, nothing but lies ... But those things I saw ... awful, hideous, hideous. The drink, that's what did it,' he explained, trying to sit up in bed and shaking all over from the effort. He seemed to be in a good mood and to keep him that way I nodded amiably, not contradicting any of his delusions. Meanwhile I felt his pulse. Fast and irregular. What did I know about it anyway?

'I'm halfway to being a doctor,' I said apologetically, 'You'll soon be up and about. What was Richard Wagner doing?'

'Richard Wagner,' he repeated, surprised, and rubbed his hands across his sweating forehead. 'Hey, what was that on your hand? It's creeping up my arm...!'

'There wasn't anything on my hand.'

'If you bring any of those beasts here with you, Nol, then you better stay away,' he said, petulantly. 'They do play the meanest tricks on me. You know, that just to try me out they put a glass full of gin, fine, old gin, right in front of me, look, over there, and they think it'll be empty when they come back ... Look, there they are again.' He pointed to the table, there wasn't even a glass of water on it. It began to be a sort of game in which I had to determine exactly how far I could go without contradicting him. All of a sudden he was wide awake and forced his twitching eyelids apart till something of the gleaming black of his eyes was visible.

'I know, you've been to see Trix.'

'How did you know?' I stammered, with a feeling in my throat as if I was being throttled. Then, quickly controlling myself, I said: 'I saw Trix at the restaurant. She sends her best wishes.'

'I used to go there often,' he said, 'We had a choir and I knew how to keep them in order. In the bandstand, you know. Draughty it was, damned draughty, sometimes they'd sit shivering in the snow. I wish I had some snow on my head now.'

'Vellinga,' I said, 'did you run into Vellinga there much?'

He squinted at me just for a moment, then a crafty expression crept over his face. It reminded me of the strong, energetic Cuperus I had known. 'A smart fellow,' he said, blinking more than ever. He waited, his moustache began to flutter and jerk, he squinted like some fiend, then he said: 'And a rotter, an utter scoundrel. He was in the fight at the opera, *Carmen* ... He was the first in W ... to fight on the stage and that was the end of Henri Cuperus who was considered by some people,' and with an infinite pride and contempt in his voice he repeated: 'by some people, as a genius... It must be ten years or more since I set eyes on Vellinga. He didn't mean anything to me at all.'

'But why is he a scoundrel?' I asked as casually as I could.

'Will I tell you something about him?' He made another attempt to sit up as if he wanted to whisper in my ear, but he fell back with a grunt. I couldn't bring myself to help him. 'I kept off the drink for two whole months, for your sake. I knew you'd be back around Christmas and you're my only son ... and look what happens ... all these beasts, and frogs and big ones too. You try not sleeping a wink for a month,' he said with a bitterness in his voice, 'but then Richard Wagner couldn't sleep either, at least that's what he said... I only need to close my eyes to see him standing there in front of me, with his big nose and his beret—and he put his hand on my arm, heavy as lead his hand was, but I wasn't frightened, Nol. How could you be frightened of a man when you've played his music for so long, a lifetime of tears and blood you could say? ... I wasn't frightened, not a bit, and then ... then he said ...'

'In German?'

'Oh, I can't remember. No, Dutch. Then he said to me: "Wait

a minute, Cuperus, with those frogs and things, because there's a dragon here as well, in the Valkyrie, you remember..." '

'In *Siegfried*,' I mumbled.

'In the Valkyrie, where Wotan says good-bye to his daughter, and be careful, he said—Wagner, I mean—be careful Cuperus, he said, it's no trifle this business, a father parting from his daughter, and then that other fellow turns up ...'

'Siegfried,' I said encouragingly, 'Siegfried, it's in the next opera...'

'Yes, that's right, he turns up,' he repeated and lay back with his eyes closed.

'What was it you didn't like about Vellinga?'

When he opened his eyes again I saw tears welling up, and he began speaking quickly:

'It wasn't my fault, my boy, tell everyone it wasn't my fault. You will, won't you? I've suffered so much. I want you to look after her.'

'Yes, of course I will. Why shouldn't I?' I whispered.

'O my God... O Jesus ... don't ... ooh, don't let my daughter ... Wagner couldn't help ... liars and scoundrels ... all of them ...' he shouted, clenching his right fist. Then he went on in a feverish mumble: 'There they are again, everywhere, everywhere, all over the bloody place ... The big frog in front with that bloody umbrella again ... Do you want to sit on my lap like last time, eh, and beat time and get it all wrong, eh? If he'd just keep the insects away with that umbrella ... But he won't, you know, he won't ... Get away!' he screamed. 'I didn't do it, it was Rato.... Hullo Big Frog, how do you do, how do you do? ...' His voice faded away, and I watched the colour drain unbelievably out of his face, and over those pallid, greyish, changed and unrecognizable features the sweat ran in thick streams.

I fled out of the room. On the stairs I almost collided with the aunt who was coming up with a bottle and a spoon. I said I was going for a doctor.

'He came by earlier this evening,' she said, listening with screwed-up eyes to the noise growing louder behind the half-open door, 'and this afternoon we got some paraldehyde,'—the last syllable rang out like a shout of joy—'that puts Hendrik to sleep.'

'Isn't he a lot of trouble? Can you handle him by yourself?'

'Me?' An amused rolling of the eyes dismissed my question as youthfully naïve. 'I'm as strong as a horse, Mijnheer ... Nol—I can call you Nol, can't I? He's like a child in my hands. I did a year or two as a nurse when I was young, and whenever a patient cut up rough they always used to send for me...'

Going home I called on Cuperus's doctor—I knew him vaguely, I'd met him once at somebody's house. He didn't invite me inside. Standing in the doorway he explained that if his heart held out his chances weren't so bad, but with alcoholics the heart was never too healthy, and Cuperus had already had a couple of close shaves. When I turned my face away, embarrassed, he looked at me with mocking curiosity. Apparently it didn't make any difference that I was a first-year medical student. Before he shut the door he said that the local hospital was too small for cases like that and didn't have any facilities for treatment. Yes, it was really a pity to see a man of his ability go to pieces ... but he'd been on the booze all his life... That was true enough, he'd been on the booze all his life.

14

The next morning I telephoned the doctor. He wasn't so optimistic. He had just been to see Cuperus and had given him a camphor injection. As a gesture to make up for being so patronizing the night before he went on talking about the symptoms and the treatments, and finally terminated the conversation with an apologetic laugh, as if he had fulfilled an obligation he had imposed on himself to cover the whole subject in ten minutes. I decided I would visit Cuperus again that evening at seven. If Trix came she would most likely be there in the afternoon, and I didn't want to force myself on her, and certainly not with others present. In the morning Cuperus would probably be still drowsy, the room wouldn't have been done, and I would have to contend with a no doubt short-tempered ex-nurse.

From the footsteps I could tell that it was Trix who was coming to open the door. I was standing at the same spot where we had kissed each other, and I knew she would be even more remote if she happened to remember that too. But she wasn't unfriendly.

'Bad,' she answered when I asked after Cuperus 'You can't come in. He's not to be disturbed, the doctor said. He's just had an injection for his heart. I've a feeling that he won't last the night, no matter what the doctor says. But I've got to go now. I'll come back again in a couple of hours.'

'I'd like to see him, if it's only to say good-bye,' I said, putting my foot in the doorway.

Then I heard the aunt's voice from the other end of the hallway.

'Don't talk a lot of nonsense, Trix. He'll pull through, you'll see. I know it. Fancy, not letting Mijnheer Nol come inside.'

'You keep your dirty big nose out of it,' Trix screeched, turning round and stamping three steps back into the hall as if she wanted to frighten her aunt away. 'Snake! I won't let Nol in, and if you let him in you know what'll happen.'

'Baggage,' her aunt said icily, and stalked off.

A few moments later I heard one of the doors upstairs bang shut. 'But this is just too silly,' I said, with an edge of authority in my voice. 'You can't stop me seeing my old music teacher for the last time, the man I have so much to thank for—even for you.' I gave a sarcastic laugh, though when I said it the words were not sarcastically intended.

She came a little nearer to me. Her face was gentle in the vague light from the street, gentle and a little afraid. 'Nol, listen to me, please. You can't go in to see him, and I want you to promise you won't go in as soon as I leave. He probably wouldn't even recognize you... Promise me, you must, if you still love me.'

I took her hand. I wasn't thinking of Cuperus any more. There was nothing I wouldn't do for her. But then the aunt was back again, slinking down the hallway in her slippers, calling out that Trix's father was feeling better, and he wanted his 'adopted son' (she emphasized the designation) to come and say good-bye. I was sure she was lying, but before I could move Trix answered her aunt by turning round for the second time and this time lashing out with her fists. I pictured Cuperus in bed waiting for me and I thought I could slip upstairs unnoticed while the two fighting women rolled struggling over the hallway floor. But whether she hit back or not the aunt was no match for Trix's onslaught of blows and curses. After she had chased her aunt away for the second time Trix came and stood in front of me again, not even out of breath.

Putting her hands on my shoulders she whispered: 'I was frightened she was going to say something, if she had she wouldn't have got off alive, snake that she is. My father says things about me, not all the time, but he might start if you were there. I don't want that to happen, Nol... I'd hit him, and I'd never forgive myself... And if you saw him when I wasn't there I'd keep thinking that he'd been talking about me, even if you said he hadn't.'

'He can't say anything bad about you,' I whispered back, loosening one of her hands and kissing it. 'I wouldn't listen, Trix. You know how I feel about you. Nothing would change...'

'Do you know what I mean?' She was close to me, and throwing her arms around my neck, she bent her head. She looked weak and yielding. 'My darling, my darling...'

'I don't understand anything any more,' I said, and my voice was shaking. 'I don't understand anything. All I know is that I love you, Trix, and I'd do anything, anything at all for you. I'd kill myself if you told me to. I won't go and see your father. No... of course I won't ... I'll even write letters that don't get...'

She cautiously loosened her arms and pushed me gently outside. 'It's not my fault. No matter what you hear about me try and remember that it's not all my fault. I'll write to you, tomorrow. You better go now, and you'll keep your promise, won't you, not to go up and see him ...?'

'As long as you do write,' I mumbled, dazed, as the door closed. I don't know how long I stood staring up at the window of the dark front room. Cuperus was in a back room upstairs. I'd never see him again through a lighted window standing by his piano. When I finally brought myself to walk away I decided I wouldn't telephone the doctor again. I'd do nothing at all, if that's how it had to be.

But that night I reached the breaking-point that had probably been threatening for months. The pent-up grief rose inside me like a mass of smouldering fire, and I had to bite my pillow to stop shouting with pain. Like a thing possessed I hit and punched myself, not from rage or disappointment at what seemed to be my fate, but to keep control of myself, something I had always been able to do, an accomplishment I had always prided myself on. I might as well have tried to stop myself doubling up after a kick in the stomach. That was what it felt like, it was a physical pain. There is no such thing as purely spiritual suffering. This black, raw misery could only be quelled by pressing as hard as I could on my stomach. I lay for a time, my head hung down over the side of the bed, in the hope that vomiting might help. I thought of Trix as an innocent victim, but I didn't know what she was a victim of. I didn't hate her, I hardly felt any affection for her even though I could realize that my torment was the physical experience of love in its most sublime form. Death could come unnoticed, or the heart could stop, just as with delirium tremens. Or was it better to follow the advice of the student from the Indies and meditate as he did in his solitary drunkenness, trying to achieve a deep and full understanding, a true sense of proportion, an all-encompassing survey of time and places and events? Or was it better just to let the body have its way and weep and sob abandonedly and bite and bite on the pillow — a surrender, admittedly, but still, a relief, a relief that soothed with the consolation of self-pity? Through it all the voice of conscience from deep within the body shouting: 'Give her up! Give her up!' at once answered by another, even more insistent voice, the deepest, or perhaps not the deepest in this secret, turbulent polyphony: 'Never, never...' I was sobbing uncontrollably, and suddenly Chris was standing by my bed in his pyjamas and he said: 'What's wrong, old chap?' He helped me to sit up, supporting me with his arm behind my back. He went and fetched a glass of water, and he said again and again: '... old chap ... old chap... old chap ...' Finally I told him that I'd got upset thinking about my mother's heart complaint. After he had gone back to his own room it occurred to me that he must have always been fond of me. It probably started from the time I punched him on the nose. This was my last thought before I fell asleep.

The next morning I had a particularly clear recollection of the voice that said: 'Give her up, give her up', and I decided I would, whether she wrote or not. Her letter came at seven o'clock, probably she had delivered it herself. The maid pushed it under my door and I read it in bed, leaning on my tear-soaked pillow.

'Dear Nol, It's just half past six, and Father died at three o'clock this morning after being unconscious for three hours. His heart just wasn't strong enough. My aunt asked the doctor to give him

189

another injection but he said one was enough and he wouldn't come again. You'll be a better doctor than that, Nol, I'm sure you will. Don't write, just send a wreath if you want to. He left something to you, a trifle. I'll post it on. He told my aunt about it in one of his lucid moments. I know you will feel his death more than I will. It's just the opposite, I think, with the other matter I had wanted to write to you about. You must find someone else to fall in love with, my dearest Nol. I can easily explain why. I'm not worth your love, not in any way, Nol. That is true, so please understand and try to think of me differently. I can't tell you everything, but if you listen to the talk about me you'll have a good idea of what I am like. It isn't my fault, but that doesn't alter the facts. Perhaps, in time, I'll be able to forget you too. So don't write to me again and don't try to see me again. Yours, Trix.

P.S. Don't go and see my aunt either, you can't trust her, though I must say she did look after Father. Usually I'm not so nasty to her as I was yesterday evening.'

The words 'Perhaps, in time...' were written in a rather different hand from the rest of the letter, at if she had sat a long while thinking or had been interrupted at the end of the sentence before. I lay quietly, the letter in my hand, relieved now that there was no problem any more. I had a melancholy smile for Chris, a thought for Cuperus, a few bars of the second intermezzo in my head, a passing anxiety over my next exam, and in my ears the boats on the canal that were still the same, unchanging as the cobblestones, the trees, the children, and circumstances and situations. If there was no alternative for me but to let Trix have her way then I was ready to do as she wanted. Trix wasn't the whole world. I calculated how much I should spend on the wreath. I couldn't order the most expensive flowers or she would think half was for her.

'Aren't you going to the funeral?' my father asked at breakfast. The news had travelled, the maid had heard it too. Cuperus had departed not entirely unnoticed from this world. I said that Cuperus had expressly forbidden it, that he objected to funerals,

190

and that when his wife died he had wanted to wear three top hats to give an impression of respectability.'Hmm,' my father sniffed, 'strange ideas. But still, I found him always a decent fellow, though I never had any personal contact with him, or did I ... No, no, never. But yes, I did meet him once, when they were playing that opera, *Martha*, wasn't it, when they all came here. I shook hands with him, and I remember now I didn't think about the time he kissed our maid. That was a silly thing to do ... one of those artistic capers...'

The legacy came with the afternoon mail. It was the piano arrangement of the *Carmen* score. The name of the former owner had been neatly crossed out and under it were the words: 'For Nol Rieske, a token of deepest friendship, a memento of the most spectacularly unsuccessful performance of all time.' This dedication must have been written long before his last illness, probably just after the *Carmen* performance, before he was even thinking of death. He had never discussed the subject of death with me, and I don't think he subscribed to any religious belief, though I imagine that he had to feign a bit of piety in the organ and church choir days. Music absorbed any religious feeling he had. If he meditated on the fate of Tristan and Isolde, or Siegfried with Hagen's lance in his back, or the repining Amfortas, he saw them wafted away to a musical heaven that rang with triads in a major key or resounded with tragic funeral marches. And Carmen ... ach, Carmen was an exception, a common slut, of no importance at all.

In those first days after his death it was in this vein of macabre humour that I thought of him more often than I recalled his kindness and refinement. In spite of his undistinguished, perhaps rustic, origin—he had never told me anything of his family—he had always been a gentleman, but this was not a point to dwell on. To judge by appearances my mother was far more upset than I was, and I took a delight in teasing her about this distress at the death of someone she had once literally chased out of the house. Cuperus, I was thinking to myself, must have been near a conquest, at least a spiritual conquest. Besides, he had always shown his best qualities in her presence and kept the crude and clownish side of his character carefully concealed. Even that kiss in the hallway was, considering the real motive, the gesture of a seigneur taking revenge on a smallminded woman of lower rank.

All through the brief week before I was to return to the lecture room and the laboratory I listened with a stoic calm to the talk about Cuperus. Whether he was slandered, ridiculed, blamed for the *Carmen* failure, whether his corpse was dug up and hacked into little bits, it didn't matter to me. I met Vellinga twice, once in the street, the second time at someone's house. He had been very considerate in the obituary he had written and he went out of his way to be friendly to me. It surprised me not a little that I felt no trace of animosity or jealousy. At most I found him rather ludicrous, as an older man who was still ostentatiously devoting his energy to serving the interests of W... He was occupying himself more and more with his newspaper, delegating the leadership in the round of social pleasures to younger followers, under his supervision, of course. The ex-footballer could still attract a retinue of youthful associates, and he was always ready with a tale about his editors and reporters who learnt the tricks of the trade from him, worshipped him, licked his boots, pledged their everlasting loyalty, and gratefully and treacherously scuttled off to Amsterdam or Rotterdam. That didn't make any difference, there were always new ones to replace the ones who went, and in three days they knew the ropes. But then, they were young. If there hadn't been a law to keep them at school he would have got hold of boys of ten—they were the liveliest, the most malleable, the most obedient, and the most inquisitive. The last year or so he had been taking on farmers' sons of eighteen, fresh from the fields with the hayseeds still in their hair. The first day they could be put on the local news, they were not only inquisitive, they believed everything as well.

At home I was the young student who was kindly permitted to display his best manners, to listen to his elders, to be modestly silent. When the subject of Cuperus had been exhausted I listened to commentaries on the behaviour of his daughter who hadn't even wanted to come to his deathbed (this lie probably grew out of misunderstood babbling by the aunt), and the scandalous life she led had, no doubt, hastened his end. At first my mother tried to lead the conversation into other channels, but it was hopeless, one against those six or seven friends of hers who had come to inquire after her health, and when she saw my unruffled expression and let herself be impressed by my unobtrusive politeness she didn't object any more, she must have thought I had put Trix out of my head altogether. I don't want to indulge in abuse of these friends of my mother's. I haven't even bothered to describe them —a small gesture of revenge. After all, they were only women who didn't know what to do with their time, and perhaps their slanderous gossip—of course they weren't being malicious, my dear—had a wholesome effect on me in this new stage of my existence.

They didn't seem to know when or how it had all started, this affair with Vellinga, who was never criticized, but they were well-informed on the regular meetings, sometimes at Vellinga's apartment (he lived next to his newspaper office) or in hotels, and, even more disgraceful, at the Garden restaurant where Trix had a bedroom. The proprietor owed a lot of custom to Vellinga so he didn't interfere. It was certainly no example for the other girls, and some of them are so respectable, from all accounts. He gave her money too, everyone knew that, but he denied it.

In the three years that followed that Christmas holiday—two years and eight months it was, to be exact—I occasionally heard news of Trix. After eighteen months or so she went to live with her aunt because the owner of the Garden restaurant objected to her 'admirer's' nightly visits, at least that's what I was told. There was talk that he visited her at her aunt's, but this was never con-

193

firmed. If it had been true a lot of tongues would have been happily clucking, but it seemed all the more unlikely seeing that the aunt let rooms to no less than three bachelors, who would certainly have noticed anything like that. Dijkhuizen, who came to see us now and then, knew one of them, a young man from a very religious family, who thought Trix was quite respectable, even attractive, though she did have a temper. That could well be a ridiculous error of judgment, still it argued for Vellinga's discretion, on this point anyway. Unless, of course, the young man slept more soundly than was usual for a bachelor of his years. This remark, I'm almost sure, came from me, a frivolous interjection that brought tears to the fat businessman's eyes as he dug me in the ribs, snorting: 'Oh, these students! They know what it's all about and they don't make any secret of it either!' Every vacation I had to listen to these tales about Trix, and three times a year I forced myself to step into the train as a cynic, steeling myself against my own tender feelings and against the heartlessness of others, which wasn't really heartlessness because no one knew what I kept hidden. In all those three years I didn't see Trix once. It wasn't difficult to avoid her, as I never showed my face in the Garden and never went near her house where now a young bachelor slumbered in a bed that had taken the place of the grand piano, and I turned my head like a half-trained monk whenever I saw a tall young girl in the street.

After about six months, when I had managed to suppress, to some extent, my feelings for her, I realized that I could only put my life in some sort of order if I made the effort to find what would have been for anyone else 'successors' to supplant her in my affections. I regarded this as a duty to myself. I set about it selectively, my discrimination was as much due to a natural taste (no whorehouse sessions for me) as to the conviction that the cure must not be worse than the complaint, even if it was only a question of not interfering with my studies. I was very systematic, very careful. Sometimes I would wait for months, and I was often inclined to tell my bright-eyed comforters just how many months it could last. I avoided alcohol. These adventures, which didn't break any hearts, were, in fact, as unadventurous as they were unimportant, and if I hadn't had my music and my interest, similarly academic, purely analytical and uncreative, in poetry, as a complementary diversion, I might have degenerated to a state of conformist respectability like Chris with his legal career. I didn't see him very often. Since that tear-stained night he had adopted a rather protective attitude toward me. But he was still the Chris he had always been, even if I had misjudged him all these years.

Not long before my fourth-year exams I drank myself into a stupor in the manner recommended by the student from the Indies. The result was disappointing, nothing more than a half-repetition of the first time, at the start of my first year. At the peak of my inebriation the idea came into my head that I must write to Jantje de Ridder, and I did write, finishing the letter just before I flopped hiccuping on my bed. The next morning I tore this letter up and wrote a better one. It was so long since we had seen each other, I reminded her. If she happened to be in the neighbourhood she must come and visit me. The brevity and the transparent hint behind my invitation made it a crude enough letter. But she came within a week, and when I had swept her off her feet—or was it the other way round—after a few hasty preliminaries without even the customary gin or liqueur, I savoured a wistful satisfaction, or at least the sense of having beside me a tangible memory of that *Carmen* performance, of my youth, of my opera past, of my half-dead love that was still the only real love.

She was sweet and amusing, but in the end all too sentimental and bitter about the chances she had let go by, though I don't think she intended to catch me in her net. She admitted that Stegeman was and always would be her one true love. He was such a gentleman, Stegeman. I was too, but Stegeman was an artist. Oh yes, I was something of an artist too, but Stegeman had such wonderful big eyes, and so on and so on. I think she must have been in love with me, especially as I understood the art of listening to her without hearing what she said, and because I treated her with almost exaggerated delicacy. It was an instructive interlude, those few months. Not that there was much to learn from her. Wide as the range of her experience may have been it always followed the same pattern. She could never put up with her lovers for long because they didn't love her enough—this was apparent from all sorts of subtle indications I'm sure her office boys weren't capable of—and if they were offended by her reproaches they just stayed away. If she hadn't been so kind-hearted, I often used to think to myself, she would certainly have had a circle of admirers, like the aristocratic huntresses in *Martha*, all with the same rights, hovering attentively round her. Her cultural horizon was rather narrow, her interest in anatomy and physiology unlimited, her concern for my well-being exasperating. The second time we went out she started helping me on with my raincoat with the same slow motherly movements I remembered so well from Cuperus's hallway. I never showed myself with her in W..., but I visited her fairly often, as far as I know, unobserved. Jantje's amours didn't attract any attention, not any more, frequency dulls curiosity.

Naturally we talked a lot about Cuperus and Stegeman and the *Carmen* performance, and she was always considerate enough to avoid the subject of my first letter to her. Cuperus, she said, had been in love with her too, only for a little while. She was still frightened of him at that time, she never liked getting mixed up with married men, and when he announced in that deep voice of his, with a glitter in his eye, that he really adored her, she burst into tears. He always held this against her—it wasn't Wagnerian enough, I suppose—and every time he met her he used to say: 'Have you fallen in love again, Jeannetje?' She was sure that Cuperus had never been in love with any other woman except his wife. I thought this was absurd then, but now I think she was right.

After our first quarrel I asked her if she knew how it all started between Vellinga and Trix Cuperus. At one time, I admitted, I had been infatuated with Trix, that was why I was interested. It must have been that evening of the *Carmen* performance, she said, but she didn't know for sure. This disclosure came as a shock to me. So, even when she kissed me that night in the doorway, she was considering Vellinga's advances or, worse still, she had already 'been out' with him, an expression I detested—'a night out' meant 'a night in'. It was not only offensively crude, it was linguistically inaccurate. They had gone off in a carriage, the six of them together, you remember, don't you, and on the way home Vellinga had invited them up to his rooms to drink to the success of the evening. They agreed, they all drank a glass of whiskey and soda, all except Trix, who sat staring straight in front of her. That's all she knew, because after Stegeman discreetly pressed her foot with his they toddled off. No one minded. Cuperus was hunched up in a corner, Vellinga was flirting with Trix and with Alice de Rato, who was yawning and speaking mostly in French, but this met with no response, not even from Vellinga. She got the impression, so did Wessel, that Cuperus wouldn't be staying long, though he drank a lot in the quarter of an hour they were there. It is possible that the journalist had fallen in love with Trix and after a time he managed to make her fall in love with him, he could be so charming when he wanted to you know. This explanation sounded so pathetically significant that I asked her there and then if she knew Vellinga as well as she knew me. She told me, assuring me it was true, that years ago (I was still a little boy with rosy cheeks, she remembered me perfectly) Vellinga had spent a lot of time running after her, but she didn't like older men, he must be over forty now, she added. Wessel was just thirty-four, she confided. He hardly ever wrote any more. He was never much of a letter-writer, but he worked so very hard.

Our affair ended gracefully. When I noticed that she was mentioning Stegeman far more often than I could accept as reasonable I whisked her off to the Hague, first-class seats in the train, and the alluring prospect of expensive hotels, taxis, elaborate dinners. After only a few hours of these extravagances we had Stegeman with us, his big round eyes as wide and innocent as ever, his thinning hair, plastered over his scalp, reflecting the lights in the sitting-room I had arranged to have reserved for us in the hotel.

I had arranged by phone for Stegeman to show up too. He greeted Jeannetje with a handshake, resolutely not looking at me. He was doing quite well. All through the ridiculously expensive lunch Jeannetje and the tenor gravely raised their glasses to me. He had a show that evening, but he would join us again after eleven. Of course, if we got seats for the theatre that would be wonderful, just like old times, even though he wasn't on the stage with Jeannetje, or that Alice de Rato, the old hag! His conversation hadn't changed either, and he knew all the latest scandals in the opera world. Alice de Rato had caused so much mischief—'that woman, Mijnheer Rieske, Nol, is a fiend. She always seems to make an impression somehow, not on me, I can tell you that, but she hasn't got the looks she used to have, you notice that if you're playing opposite her. She was guest artist here once or twice, you know, and no matter what she tries for it her breath sti... pardon, smells, really dreadful, you know. But her voice is still magnificent. I take off my hat to her. She must be over fifty, probably nearer sixty. We always say de Rato puts as much make-up on her age as she does on her face, ha ha. It seems that her mother had been a singer in her time too, but afterwards she ran a very notorious house, you know, in Antwerp, I think I told Jeannetje before. All that speaking in French? Ach, just showing off, though she had had engagements in France. Paris? No, of course not, just fancy, Paris... For my taste she's too much of a schemer. Would you believe it, a couple of years ago she got hold of a letter of mine ... yes it was to you, Jeannetje, and why? Why?... Sadis? Ach, Mijnheer Rieske, sadism, sadism ... oh, you mean... yes, yes... quite possible...—that a committee was formed in Amsterdam with the sole object of ducking her in one of the dirtiest canals in the middle of the night. Not that that made any difference. But then, it's only human to want to get your own back, you see that in *Carmen*, don't you, ha ha!'

After the performance we left the theatre together, our heads filled with the music of *Aïda*, and went straight back to Jeannetje's room, the cosiest, I thought, of the three I had booked. With glasses in our hands we sat, first in the chairs then on the edge of the bed, talking, meditating, reminiscing and predicting. Pledges of everlasting friendship were repeated over and over. I was assured of a brilliant medical future. The theatre, the opera, would hold its place with science, or anything else. When Jeannetje, sitting between us listening to our every word, threw her arms around both our necks —to a naïve observer a prelude to the most un-Carmenlike scenes—I excused myself, went to my room, packed my bag, and sneaked out to another hotel nearby from where I telephoned the reception of the first hotel to ask that the bill be sent to my home address, and mentioning my father's position. I had left a note behind on the dressing table: 'Dear Jeannetje: Only Carmen can keep Micaëla and Don José apart. Nol.' She never bore me any malice, to judge by her coy and friendly handshake a few years later. When I passed my fourth-year exams Stegeman sent me a congratulatory telegram.

15

I took my fourth-year exams before the summer and in the holidays I went for a trip through Germany with my father and Chris. Our original plan was to go to the Bavarian Alps, but the other two didn't get as far as that. Their German blood seemed to flow so thick in their veins that they preferred to stay in the centre of the country where the Rieske family came from (from Halberstadt to be exact). I hadn't known a moment's boredom all the time I was with them, but when I had the snow-covered mountains to myself I began to wonder whether those friendly feelings towards two fellow creatures with whom I had so little in common mightn't be a sign of blunted sensitivity, of insidiously pervading conformism. I stood with a troubled conscience gazing at the Alps, a glistening invitation to places further south that didn't attract me. But what did I really want? What should I do? There I was, one of the ten thousand of my sort in Holland, young and unattached and ardent, for whom the brothel was a despised indignity and the eternal snows no more than a postcard decoration. Probably a week of dangerous mountain climbing would have cured me temporarily of this discontent. But I didn't risk it. I took the train back to Holland.

On my return I found that my mother, left behind in the best possible care, was managing quite well with her heart. She rested a lot, went for short walks, and smuggled friends she liked talking to into the house. However despicable she may have considered it, the spiciest gossip was still for her a part of her life. From discussions with older students I had formed an idea of heart complaints which I now tried to relate to my mother's illness. In my imagination I pictured her heart, this intricately assembled, incessantly overworked organ, as a nervous fist, clenching and unclenching a thousand, ten thousand times without stopping, *presto*, *prestissimo*, and even in the most peaceful of peaceful nights still pulsing *allegro con brio*, then suddenly loosening, unfolding to become a hand, and this hand would be reached out to the waiting spectre of death, a grandiose gesture that brooked no refusal. In her case the symptoms were those disconcerting transitions, not the finality of a severe stroke which the more informed students I had talked to considered a commonplace but enviable way of dying. Far more interesting, far more exciting and enigmatic were the subsequent relapses, as unpredictable as they were uncontrollable, when the fist unfolds to a hand and remains outstretched for weeks or months while death is kept hovering at a distance with doses of camphor, caffeïn, ether, strophanthin, digitalis—one for each finger. These palliatives were denied Cuperus, though regular doses of one of them would probably have saved his life.

The relapse came in October of that year. Both Chris and I received a telegram. Chris left straight away after trying in vain to telephone, while I waited a few hours, realizing that I had to prepare myself. A feeling of relief, almost satisfaction, followed the first reaction of shock. Not because my mother would probably be released from her suffering (so far she had hardly suffered any pain at all), and not because of the resentful but resigned attitude of a fourth-year medical student towards therapeutic medicine, the stepchild that should be the cherished favourite of his profession, but because it was the end of something that was doomed to come to an end. My mother's death would be a protest against a life that wasn't worth living any more, and she would see to it herself, without any help. Now she had the right and the authority to say: 'No', to proclaim a refusal which, for all her truculent self-assurance, she had never in all her life dared to utter. On her deathbed she would enact a decision of incalculable implications, of truly philosophic scope, though she herself wasn't aware of it, partly by reason of the consolation of religious belief, which she took for granted, partly because her mind was receptive only to positive ideas and preferably those likely to evoke laughter. I was sure she would die with a laugh when she saw everyone else expected she was going to die and that they all found it rather

201

tragic. She would be laughing, knowing that her death was near.

An oppressive feeling of dismay finally overpowered me after a quarter of an hour in the train. Assuming that she still had four days to live—the telegram had a note of urgency and she had been admitted to the local hospital—then for four whole days I would have to adopt an appropriate attitude, not towards her or myself, but towards my father and Chris, and a number of others as well, and after her death these others would be countless. I wasn't shy by nature, I could always make myself at home in any company, I was never at a loss for something to say, but this confrontation, the thought of it, simply because it centred around my mother, intimidated me. For hours we would sit by her bed, taking it in turns to hold her hand, and without the right to do so, for that hand belonged to the waiting spectre of death. Like chameleons, we would simulate, we would laugh every time she laughed, and she would stop laughing when she saw these facial contortions. We would find ourselves at certain moments making exactly the same movements, saying exactly the same words, even thinking exactly the same thoughts as she was, as if the Great Leveller was stretching out a hand to us too. After a while a doctor would chase us away, but we would come back, the sound of our hushed voices like the buzzing of flies.

Even the thought that I could perhaps have a minute alone with her didn't comfort me. But we wouldn't be alone, and not because of the prying doctors and nurses. As long as she clung to life, croaking, half conscious, gasping, ready at any moment to take up again the strands of her existence—I know I would be the same too if I was dying—ready at any moment to climb into the coach with me to drive to the Garden where the brass band played, ready at any moment to fight it out with Cuperus until he made a fool of himself with the bouquet and kissing the maid, ready at any moment to hurry out of the room hiding her mouth with her hand so she wouldn't burst out laughing when the youthful tenor, Stegeman, talked about smelling the drink-laden breath of the famous baritone, Ordelio, as long as all this was possible, all this and much more, then I wouldn't know what to do with the priceless boon of our final meeting. They would be there, every one of them, dead and living, old and young. I would just forget she was dying, I would light a cigarette and tell the latest student joke.

A little after eight I arrived in W... I went home first but there was no message. The maid said my mother was still conscious. I resisted the temptation to telephone the hospital, it would look as if I didn't intend to come unless it was absolutely necessary. In any case, turning up so long after Chris didn't give a very good impression. I asked the maid to make me a sandwich, which I ate walking along the street. I wanted a cup of coffee, or a drink, badly. I could have lain down and slept for twenty-four hours without a break.

It was very small, the hospital in W... The most pleasing feature of the building was its snow-white colour, and besides, it was by the moat, nearly opposite the Garden. A nurse took me up to my mother's room where my father and Chris were sitting in chairs on the left side of the bed. They nodded, formal but not unfriendly. My father sat with his forehead wrinkled, and he kept putting his glasses on and taking them off again. Chris did much the same. He would take his glasses off then crease his forehead. Occasionally they stared between their bony knees down at the floor. Like an actor afraid of what he will have to face on the stage, I avoided looking at my mother for as long as I could. When I did at last sit down and look at her I saw her eyes were fixed on me. She nodded weakly, without smiling. I wondered if she was angry with me for coming so late. Breathing in short gasps, only stopping as if to conserve her strength, and then, with her eyes closed, gulping another deep draught of life, she lay suffering or, rather, her body lay there suffering. The body functioned in a way it was not intended for, it acted and reacted as it had to, the body had obligations of its own to fulfil. But I should have known this.

It was her appearance that refuted all that I had too hastily imagined. She only looked tired, even when she gasped, sleepy, like a woman who had had a long busy day. I don't think I had ever seen a woman so tired, maybe I hadn't. Limp and drowsy, sinking exhausted into oblivion, a new mother emerged before us, a mother who had chosen to surrender wisely in the face of death. If she coughed Chris jumped up to do something unnecessary, and he realized this as he was making the movement. I had the disagreeable feeling that these puppet gestures were expected from me, the future doctor. Once he tiptoed round the bed to whisper medical information in my ear—my mother had œdema in the legs, she had some pain in the heart though she said it wasn't bad, the doctor gave very little hope but they'd done everything possible for her. 'Digitalis,' I mumbled to restore my prestige, and Chris nodded implying that he knew all about digitalis—later it transpired that she hadn't had digitalis at all. He said she had had morphine too, and it helped a lot. We could sit with her until half past ten. The doctor was coming at ten to give her an injection, maybe more than one. It could go on for days, he said, just before he crept back to his chair, while my mother followed him with her eyes. My father was leaning forward, his head in his hands, my mother glanced at him, then she smiled at me. I nodded encouragingly back at her and crossed my legs now with the right over the left for my left foot had gone to sleep. So, she was getting morphine. I thought I had been watching a healthy, sleepy mother, and it was morphine.

It was probably because of the doctor's instructions that not a word was said, for after the sister came, full of talk, with coffee for us and to arrange the pillows, my father and Chris began an everyday conversation, trying to draw my mother in as well. She smiled, shook her head, made an effort to shrug her shoulders, and occasionally put in a word or two in a soft, little girl's voice. On the bedside table was an untouched, perhaps unnecessary or forbidden bottle, opulently wrapped, gold at the top, the label richly coloured, one of those childish playthings for wealthy patients about to die. Just once she twisted restlessly and said: 'You can talk louder if you want to', but when Chris and my father followed this half-command she wasn't listening any more. She wasn't gasping so much now, an indulgent smile fluttered around the corners of her mouth. I stood up and kissed her on the forehead. When she opened her eyes at me I felt I ought to carry her away, hide her somewhere, leave her abandoned.

But time ticked on—nine o'clock, a quarter past nine—and nothing happened, no one came to see how she was. There was hardly a sound in the whole building. Till then it hadn't been unbearable, this waiting, even though my legs went to sleep no matter how I sat, and in a thoughtless moment I almost put my feet up on the side of the bed. Now, the torment suddenly began, the ordeal I had foreseen and shrunk from. Death and a thousand devils seared every fibre of my being, making this twelve by fifteen foot antiseptic cubicle a hell, a misery beyond all physical endurance. My mother suffered, I suffered. But she couldn't get up and run away, I could. My chest was tight with despair and grief, my head spun with boredom and guilt, my stomach throbbed from hunger, thirst, the need for alcohol, life's bitterness and sweetness, sublime wisdom, the profound insight of the intestines. Needles slowly pierced my legs. At times I thought I had wings, there were moments when I thought I should batter my father's skull in as he sat in his chair, a pitiable figure pondering and puzzling with that legal brain of his that had cost my mother her life, though he had never stood in her way in anything. My hands were trembling. I stood up, went over to my father and whispered to him that I didn't feel well, that I had to have some fresh air. This was quite true. But it was a lie nonetheless, only I didn't know how or why. I'd be back before half past ten. He gave me a surprised glance, then his face lit with understanding, and he nodded sympathetically. Chris didn't move. I didn't look round at my mother.

Once I was outside, my first thought was that I had to drink,

drink a lot. My stomach had been right again. Something had happened to me, something was going to happen to me. The worst of it all was not that my mother was dying or wasn't dying, was suffering or wasn't suffering, but that I was alive, still living. That was worse, irreparable. Suddenly—I was walking over the wooden bridge to the other side of the moat—suddenly I hated my mother and I could have cursed her for the way she had once spoken, for saying what she should never have said. From anyone else it could have been a slip of the tongue, 'that sweet little Trixie of yours', but not from her. I was going to the restaurant in the Garden. Now I knew. I wasn't what I had always seemed to be, I'd been deceiving myself ever since I went to the university, almost three years ago. I hadn't made allowance for my stomach and my intestines, I had burnt myself out, large patches were dried up and withered, so that I had been denied the enlightenment and guidance it would have given me. I hadn't even sought the solace of drink.

I'd been Chris, oh, the shame of it ... With my knees knocking I climbed the steps up the old fortress wall. In the meantime my mother could be dying.

The blue haze of tobacco-smoke had a soothing effect on me. The restaurant was almost empty and I could only see one rather worn-out waiter. As spry as ever, on his own over by the wall, old Tjallingii sat dozing, and in the smoke-filled cones of light some young farmers were playing billiards with a couple of seedy characters whom I took to be commercial travellers. The *chambre séparée* was in darkness, the frosted-glass doors closed. The proprietor was behind the buffet-counter totting up bills. He thought for a moment then nodded to me, but he didn't send the waiter to see me to a table. As I sat down near the window with my back to the bandstand I noticed that the sky beyond the roof, in the east, was becoming strangely light. It was the moon that I had seen from the station, dark red above a row of goods wagons.

I sat there for five minutes, ingored, then I became annoyed and tapped hard on the table. The waiter came running.

'Is Mejuffrouw Cuperus here tonight?'

He suppressed a good-natured smile. He looked a decent sort of waiter. I'd better handle him carefully.

'Yes, Mijnheer, do you want to speak to her?'

'Speak to her...? I want her to serve me.'

He scratched behind his ear. 'I'll go and ask, Mijnheer. But I serve these tables, you see.'

'There'll be a tip for you too, ten per cent. of all I drink. And that won't be just one or two nips,' I added threateningly, but laughing to myself, when I saw him pull a half suspicious, half admiring face. Then he was gone, disappearing into the passageway I remembered so well.

It was an eternity before Trix came out with the waiter padding furtively and servilely after her. In the middle of the room, between two occupied tables, he stopped and stood watching her cross the floor, his head a little to one side as if he expected something to happen. Still the same tall, willowy figure. The sight of her had a soothing effect on me too. She was a little thinner perhaps, but she had worked harder than I had these last three years. She stood in front of me, brushing her hands across the full-length apron she was wearing, and I looked her straight in the eye for no other reason than that I wanted to look at her. She was a lot older. I couldn't see any marked change in her face or her eyes, she was still Trix, for a few minutes at least she wouldn't be able to escape me. Then we both put out our hands at the same time, I leant forward, bowing without standing up, and we called each other by name.

'Listen, Trix,' I said, winking her nearer to me, 'my mother is dying, I've just come from the hospital, I couldn't stay any longer. I've got to have a drink. Don't worry, I can carry it all right, but I don't want that waiter's nose in front of me all the time. If you'd get it for me, three glasses of gin together, that'll be less bother for you.'

'Shouldn't you go back to the hospital?' She looked over her shoulder towards the buffet, or maybe at the billiard-players who hadn't even glanced at her.

'My mother might live for a few more days, but I couldn't stand it there. We've already said good-bye.'

'Would you rather sit in the private room?'

I toyed with the idea for a moment. But I hadn't come here to be alone with Trix. I wanted her to bring me drinks, I wanted to watch her walking towards me and away from me, in and out of that passageway.

She brought three glasses on a tray and placed them slowly, one after the other, on the table so that I was draining the first glass while the third one was floating through the air.

'My mother has something wrong with her heart, just like your father had,' I said, peering up at her confidentially. 'Now it's my turn to go on the booze.'

'Why didn't you ever write again?' she asked gruffly, then she looked over her shoulder again at the buffet.

Her inconsistency reassured me completely. I had caught her out. I felt entirely at my ease. I was sure that I could, in some ways, hold my own with her now. It was almost laughable, she had expected me to write.

'What do you mean, Trix? After that last letter you wrote? I've got my pride too, you know. But let's not call it pride. .. I was only the obedient servant of a certain Trix Cuperus ... You haven't changed, you'll never change, that's all that matters to me.'

'Everyone changes.'

Her tone had something of a sneer, but I knew her too well, there could be a meaning behind those words. As she hid the first glass in the pocket of her apron, her face came near to mine and I breathed the smell of cheap perfume. I can't say I found it offensive. It didn't make my head spin with delight either. I visualized myself at a blackboard, drawing the contours of her personality, half the old Trix, sensitive, pure, hot-tempered, and half the provincial barmaid who knew how to handle her customers, not common but nevertheless tainted with a touch of vulgarity, a vulgarity kept within certain limits, which, however carefully preserved, became each year less distinct. I couldn't be sure which half I liked most. In reality, of course, there were no halves. When I had emptied my second glass, while she was still standing there, I knew the meaning of love. It was an absoluteness that was, fortunately, fairly rare. I reached out for the third glass.

'Are you happy here?'

She shrugged her shoulders: 'I've never been happy. Have you?'

'Yes, I have,' I answered, quickly and emphatically, as though I wanted to please her, 'When your father used to play for me, especially when it was a piece from an opera, then I was often happy. These last three years I haven't been unhappy at all. It's very interesting at the university.'

'I'm glad to hear that, and I'm glad I never made you unhappy.' As she spoke she took an awkward step backwards, and then another, obviously so as to attract as little attention to herself as possible. There was only one glass on the tray.

'Three more, Trix,' I begged, irked to see her slipping gradually away from my table. She had already turned round.

'Just one to go on with,' she whispered over her shoulder in a half-questioning tone. A thoughtful precaution in case anyone had heard her. Now I had to rely on her extensive experience in this smoky restaurant. As long as she did come back. She was standing at the buffet talking to the proprietor, her head lifted authoritatively despite the imploring movement of her hands that she accompanied her words with. I could guess what she was saying: 'The poor boy's mother is dying, he needs a drink or two. I'll keep an eye on him', and I saw the proprietor's nod of agreement.

But she didn't come back. Incensed at this unexpected treachery, I considered what I could do if I still refused to accept the services of the waiter who was prowling up and down. After all, I had told him I was going to drink a lot, and besides, drinking was more important than Trix at that moment. Every moment of existence, I realized, has its own particular significance, though I had once said that time was irrelevant to love. That was quite true, but still, the moments mustn't be neglected, there's no sense in letting everything get mixed up. I heard a stamping of feet at one of the billiard tables, a white ball had just missed another white ball or a red ball, an event to stir up the wildest passions. If it came to making a choice between drinking and love there was always a way out by switching to something else altogether. I stood up and walked to the door leading to the Garden, which I knew was closed to the public at night—this was an instruction from the police, I believe. To make it easier for my pursuers I left the door ajar. There wasn't any wind, so it wouldn't bang, and that was a point in my favour. I was determined to conduct myself with the utmost correctness.

Not a breath of wind. Only the white glow of the moon above the bandstand, and the tall trees dark against this glow, and the light from the restaurant on the gravel where my footsteps would take me past a certain spot that must be quite near. The bridge was faintly visible. Feeling my way with my feet I turned to the right, beyond the rough stone steps that went up to the path with the lime trees. Though the air was still the lime trees began to rustle softly. I lay down on the sloping lawn and decided to stay there until it got too cold. The moon rose higher and higher behind the bandstand, triumphantly cascading the shimmer of its milky radiance that sharpened the black, lonely silhouettes of the trees and the ridge of the roof. The door clicked. A waiter coming to chase me inside. That was the end of this paradise. Footsteps on the gravel, a woman's voice: 'Nol.' Involuntarily I coughed. She had seen me, she was coming towards me. Leaning on my elbows looking up at her I was amazed at her tallness and at the tender longing this physical characteristic could arouse. Yet I'd walked past a hundred women and girls just as tall as she was without giving them a glance.

'Why didn't you bring some gin with you?' I asked dully.

She sat on the grass not far away from me. 'I said you didn't feel well and you needed some fresh air. Shouldn't you go back and see your mother, Nol?'

'What's the time?'

'Twenty past ten.'

'I can't get into the hospital now. It wouldn't make any difference anyway. I've learnt a lot from you. You let your father die all by himself, didn't you? We're soulmates, you and I. I used to call myself your stand-in brother. But my mother and I are soulmates, too, and it doesn't matter whether she lives or dies. That's not being callous, Trix, it's an excess of love. We can't keep running after the ones we love. They wouldn't understand if we did. Up there,' and I pointed to the lime three path behind us, 'that's where she was sitting that day when we danced, just here,' and I pointed in front of us, slightly to the side, to where the gravel, stamped flat by countless feet all through the summer, caught a dim patch of light from the smoky, not very noisy, dining-room. 'She laughed at us, not really though, her friends all laughed, she didn't, she just pulled a face as if she was laughing. You see, she knew I was dancing with my destiny, she was clever enough to see that. Now she's dying, but you've been dead for a long time already, and what's the difference? Everything is still the same here, it's just that I'd never seen the Garden by moonlight before...'

I'd been watching the moon, in a few minutes its silvery edge would rise over the bandstand and transform this corner where we were sitting in the grass with our knees drawn up.

'Will you forgive me, Nol?'

I moved over and sat next to her. I took her hand, then let it go. 'There's nothing to forgive, Trix. How can you forgive something you don't understand? Maybe I love you because I don't understand anything. But you go too far. You make a mystery out of it.'

'You don't know anything about me.'

'That's what I mean,' I said, peering at her and watching the moonlight fall on her face a little sooner than it reached mine because she was taller than I was. A face deathly pale and solemn, and so irresistibly appealing. We looked searchingly into each other's eyes, and my ears were buzzing, and in my stomach there was a sort of ecstasy, from the gin perhaps, yes, it would be from the gin...

'Trix, is it true what they're always saying about you and Vellinga?'

'Yes, it's true. But,' she added quickly, taking my hand in hers and bending near to me, 'that's something else, it has nothing to do with what we feel about each other...'

'What we feel about each other,' I repeated bitterly. She must have been expecting the question for a long time, and she'd had her answer ready, for years maybe. That meant she still loved me and she would go on playing the fool with me. 'Everyone changes.' Yes, but with me she changed far too much, that was what she had always done, and the result was that she hadn't changed at all...

'I never loved him, it was something else, and it wasn't my fault. I can explain everything....'

I jerked my hand loose. 'Yes, you can explain everything. But first you'll have to explain why you don't find the whole business diabolic. Obviously you don't. You told me you were in love with me, then you said it again when you and Vellinga were... by Jesus...'

I controlled myself. I thought of my mother keeping her feelings under control too, as she lay on her deathbed, though they'd made it easy for her with their morphine injections... Then I felt her arms around my neck and her cheek close to mine, and I smelt the cheap perfume I had surrendered to half an hour before. Everything that had happened was inevitable. We were pressed against each other, almost as much a part of this garden of gardens as the bridge or the grass or the gravel, and I looked at the gleaming surface of the moon and I heard the words she was feverishly murmuring mingle with the rustling of the lime trees and the other trees.

'I'll tell you everything later, Nol. I love you and no one else, and I love you more than ever now because you came here at a time like this, when you're so sad.'

That isn't quite right, I was thinking, she's exaggerating. I kissed her hair, that wavy barmaid hair, that dearest of all heads.

'He's nothing to me. I've finished with him, the big clown. Don't you worry about that. Let's forget it all, Nol, let me hold you, Nol, my darling, my darling...'

So Vellinga didn't mean anything to her. It was nothing, nothing at all—she had yielded, abandoned herself to a nothingness, and now she was dead and finished, no, not for me, never, no never, but in herself. As she put her arms around me, and I let her embrace me without response or resistance, and felt the kiss of her lips and her hot breath I thought of my mother under the trees high up behind me and of her father down there in front of me by the rough-hewn railing of the bridge and of the shapes in the background beyond where the moon shone brighter now and unhindered. Passive and remote, I slipped out of her arms, I wriggled loose, and I was sitting up again next to her. With her face turned away from me she smoothed her skirt maybe she wanted to see if there was anyone looking for us.

'There's one thing you mustn't forget, Trix. Don't ever forget that I love you and that I'd do anything, anything at all, for you. My mother's dying and your father's down there with a grin on his face, twirling his moustache...'

'You shut up about my father.'

'I'm not saying anything bad about him.'

'You can say whatever you like about him for all I care,' I heard her mumble.

'And the Garden. This is sacred ground here. It was always a marvellous garden for me, even before you came into my life that day we danced on the path. There were golden birds, they're still here too, and geese and peacocks, but mostly golden birds. It was a golden garden. Then I saw all those brass instruments, and I heard that march, and the sun shone on the brass, and I watched the musicians with their faces red from blowing, and then it was a brass garden and it has stayed a brass garden. Brass is prettier than gold and simpler and livelier. *Carmen* was a brass opera...'

Entranced by the moon, which was at last free of the bandstand —a silver dish with a curved piece sliced out of the edge—I was speaking now in a rapt whisper as if the spirits of the Garden were speaking with my voice. When I glanced around I saw that Trix had disappeared. But I went on talking, she was gone but I could still see her there.

'It's still a brass garden, in autumn, but no one notices, and now, for us, it's a silver garden. Silver isn't the most costly metal, but it's the finest, the noblest of them all. A token of parting and farewell, the silver ripples in a pool whipped up by the last gust of wind on a stormy evening just before the night sky darkens. Then there's the moon, it says good-bye again and again. The sun says: "I'll be back", and drops, red and round, into the sea. But the moon says: "I probably won't be back, I've so much trouble changing and changing all the time, and who knows how it will end?" I know a lot about the moon, Trix, the saddest part is just before the new moon—that always sounds so optimistic, "the new moon"—then it hangs in the sky like a crooked line, a shadowy sigh, above the early-morning sun—I've often seen this coming home from a night's drinking—and it can't come down to rest, it has to keep going on, it has to endure its misery for another three days and three nights, chased by the pitiless sun, shrinking and fading and withering. The sun blows it away, higher and higher, like a feather, and no one thinks it can ever come back again and maybe it doesn't, maybe it's a different moon each time, a new moon, as they say.'

What a strange medley of smells filled the Garden now, mould and a tangy rottenness, the endless nuances of decaying leaves. The pond would be bubbling and splashing as if all Cuperus's frogs, with and without their umbrellas, were up to their mischief again. Beyond the silvery ripples on the water I could see Trix, a little girl of twelve, running across the bridge to her father to embrace him, one knee tilted up. How horribly these two had been done to death by time, by the decay that spread its sound and its smell through the night.

The longer I sat there, half-frozen in the chilly mist the moon seemed to suck up from the pond, the more I felt the need for company, drink, conversation, the broad speech of farmers, failing anything else. I could count Trix out for the rest of this evening, I even reckoned on the possibility of never seeing her again. Not so much because I had, let us say, spurned her, but there was no relying on her, she was made of moonlight like her mother and that aunt of hers, pale northern women who should have been mermaids, their eyes showed what they were . . . I had to get back inside. My decision was also dictated by practical considerations— at that hour there was no other way out of the Garden.

I walked shivering to the door with just one thought, to drink another three glasses before I went home to face my father and Chris. I stood for a while peering through the glass door. The restaurant was fuller now, so much the better—if Trix was serving, she'd have more chance of keeping out of my way. There were more billiard-players too, and one of them, bent horizontally over the green felt in the posture of a penitent, his hands on the cue like the hands of a martyr on a cross, I recognized as Vellinga. His bowler hat was pushed back on his head. Three small figures stood watching obediently.

I opened the door and walked to the table I had been sitting at. Trix was nowhere in sight. The waiter who came over to me was one I remembered from years ago. He was well past his prime, as likely as not he had brought my mother glasses of milk and cups of tea.

'Hullo,' I said when I saw that he recognized me too, 'how are you? I want to drink something, a lot. My mother is very sick and it's got me down. I've twenty guilders or so with me...'

'Oh, Mijnheer Rieske, we know you...'

'Yes, but maybe not very well. I'd like a bite to eat, too. Are there any éclairs?'

Clusters of wrinkles formed around his eyes. 'No more, Mijnheer. The last lot of éclairs we had, let's see, it's seven or eight years back, we ate them ourselves and what we couldn't eat we gave to the ducks.'

'The geese you mean, don't you?'

'The ducks, Mijnheer, in the pond. Would you like a cheese sandwich?'

As he turned to go when I nodded, I called him back with sharp reproach in my voice.

'You didn't ask what I wanted to drink. I'm not going to be messed about, get that into your head. Now bring me five glasses of gin. You might as well pour it all into one wine-glass. I'll put the money on the table if you like.'

Offended, he hurried over to the buffet and within two minutes I had my wine-glass of gin. We looked at each other angrily. Finally I began to laugh and he laughed too.

When I had half emptied the glass, I turned my attention to Vellinga. Although he had put on weight he moved agilely enough round the billiard-table, and, from what I could see, he played skilfully, even if he never made a long bread. His glass of beer was on a small table near where they were playing. He tipped his bowler hat forwards, backwards, to the side, at every possible angle. Still, he didn't seem to be in a boisterous mood. The way he kept silent, never saying a word to the others he was playing with, was typical of him. He didn't have to make the slightest effort any more to enhance his popularity. His companions were simply sweating with joy because they could join him for a game of billiards.

After I had eaten my sandwich I finished the rest of the gin and

I felt myself getting drunk, quickly. I thought I saw Trix in the passage trying to attract my attention, and I understood then why Vellinga didn't look round at her in the restaurant with that uncouth crowd watching. They'd agreed on that years ago. Vellinga knew a lot more about love than I did, he knew it was unwise to do anything ostentatious or indiscreet. Not that I had been rash or showy, but in my case it was a natural reserve, in Vellinga's case it was calculated slyness. They'd worked it out well, the two of them, and if Trix died she'd get a free obituary notice on the fourth page of his newspaper. I called the waiter.

'This time,' I said, wrinkling my forehead, 'I'd like the same sort of glass, but full of rum.' I had spoken rather loudly, and at some of the tables nearby heads turned round.

'Hot rum and lemon, Mijnheer?'

'No, straight. Pure and unadulterated rum. Just to bring back old memories. It's good to think back over the past now and then. Are you musical?'

'I've got a fair ear, I'd say, Mijnheer.'

'Then you'll remember the opera we had here, toreador, toreador... Do you know Vellinga?'

'Mijnheer Vellinga, from the newspaper? Of course I do. There he is, playing billiards.'

'You can tell him from me to go and drop dead. He was the one who got someone else drunk on rum that time and that's what started the fight—not with Vellinga, he's too slippery, and you can tell him that too—with Cuperus it was. You wouldn't know him would you?'

The waiter's face lit up. 'Why, as if I didn't know Mijnheer Cuperus. Five glasses of gin one after the other...'

'Eight,' I said.

'... I never saw him drink rum, but nearly everything else...'

'Good, then we understand each other,' I said, 'we remember each other from years ago, and you've often served my mother. She's in the hospital now, she's dying. Just bring a glass like Vellinga gave Stegeman—he was another silly fool... a glass full of rum, that's what I want.'

The waiter scurried off and I turned my attention again to Vellinga, who was still engrossed in his game of billiards. He would play until the restaurant closed, then he had a second item on his programme. You couldn't tell from his face. But maybe his shoes gave a hint of it, or his cuffs or his stiff collar, which was starting to wilt by now. Meanwhile I waited for the flashes of insight the gin should inspire. I felt the first tremors within me. Waves of anguish and waves of rage alternated at regular intervals, but that wasn't what I was waiting for, I wanted to hear words, clear and piercing, golden words, black words, mighty oracles. My neck filled with a droning roar that was somehow linked with my stomach. 'Never lie down,' an older student had once shouted at me, 'then you're finished. Stand up, dance or jump or fight, or anything, sweat the drink out of you.' But how could I dance and sweat the drink out of me in this depraved haunt where cheap crooks played billiards and harlots served at the tables? There's a proverb that gold comes first and then the other metals, and here I was with gold right in front of my nose, precious gold in the form of rum. I swallowed a mouthful. Gold, for its own richness and brilliance, then copper for gleaming brass, then silver for the glow of moonlight. That was a better sequence than the one the Greeks had, gold, silver, copper, and iron. A full circle is more complete than a downwards slanting line. But what was that other proverb? Never bend the knee to any man, not even to God Almighty. God didn't expect it in any case, this god who created *navajas* and billiard cues. As a snotty-nosed kid I had practised on poor Chris, now I faced the real test, the inescapable hour of reckoning when all the things that had to be put right would be put right, down to the smallest, smallest details, true justice, not the laws in lawyers' books, the full, final measure of revenge.

'Hey, Nol, what are you up to, drinking all on your own?'

I took a sip of rum and looked into Vellinga's gold-rimmed

218

pince-nez. He had apparently come and sat down opposite me, he wasn't wearing his hat, he was as bald as a badger. It was going too far, he was being too presumptuous. I watched those teeth of his. His suit was expensive, well-cut.

'Mijnheer Rieske,' I said.

'What's this bloody nonsense,' Vellinga answered jovially. 'Come on now, don't look so sad, I'll have a drink too and we can talk about old times...'

'I'm not looking sad,' I said.

He was waving to the waiter—'All the more reason to be a bit more cheerful.'

'My mother's dead,' I said.

He shook his head at the waiter, and after a glance behind him he bent reprovingly towards me.

'That's not a matter to joke about, young fellow. Is your mother worse?'

I took another swig. 'She's as good as dead, I told the waiter too, he couldn't believe it either, damn fool that he is. What are you looking at me like that for?'

'Will I take you home, Nol?'

'What the hell are you looking at me like that for?'

Everything inside me was heaving and swirling, the droning roar in my neck rose into my head, my stomach sent twisting currents round my throat. If the two streams met, then I was done for, he'd have got the better of me. Never vomit. Who had said that? Another one of those clever fellows. He could just as well have said: Always vomit, an old rule handed down from Solon. Shout and swear! Maybe if I shouted a lot of swear words, maybe I would just manage ... but why was Vellinga talking so much? Why didn't I say anything? Lawyers and doctors. The animal species and the human species. Dogs and people. Yelping and talking. Cheating and helping. I took another swig, I glanced towards the passageway, then I put my hand on his arm, I pressed my fingers into his wrist and snarled at him: 'Look, over there.'

I knew that Trix hadn't been standing there, but he looked round, he'd fallen for it, the lawyer, the shifty-eyed dog. I wanted to laugh and I hiccuped. I stood up, my hands holding my stomach, a swelling harmony boomed through that smoke-filled place, waiters and diners and drinkers boldly improvising in mass choirs, ho ho, they sung, ha ha ho ho, then suddenly, from some unknown direction, Trix appeared, ominously tall and white, pale as a phantom, her eyes big and frightened, and I was still on my feet, I had to vomit, vomit over this gloating rabble, and I was still on my feet, I was still standing, and I still had the strength to shout, loud enough for all those unwashed ears to hear, 'A soul in distress!' and the soul was Trix, but maybe they thought I said 'A ship in distress' as I spun down, spreading a thick putrid torrent on the sand-strewn floor that hadn't been so well and truly filthed for many a year.

[16]

Vellinga and the friendly waiter, so I heard afterwards, took me home by car, undressed me, cleaned me up a little, and left me in a deep drunken sleep on a couch in the sitting-room. They hung my vomit-stained clothes neatly over a chair. When they carried me upstairs—Vellinga had used my key to get in—my father and Chris were already in bed. In the middle of the night I heard someone shouting, 'Nol, Nol', from far away above me. As soon as I sat up in the dark my head throbbed and my stomach started writhing and burning. Chris called out from the stairs: 'Where are you, Nol?' I heard footsteps clattering nearer, and I recognized my father's voice. They switched lights on and off, looking in all the rooms on the first floor. I lay waiting for them to come and find me. The lawyers. At last they were coming to fetch me, to interrogate me, to despise me, to condemn my anti-social attitude my callousness, and my revolting egoism. Chris, deterred by the memory of what had once happened to him, might well think better of hitting me, but my father might forget himself for the first time in his life and box my ears. Then I would have to kill them, both of them. Something clicked inside my brain and I knew I could look after myself just by talking.

Lawyers always give way in an argument with doctors, a well-known fact that I had heard confirmed by quite a number of drunkards.

The light flicked on, and there they were, in heavy overcoats, their faces drawn with tiredness and concern. I lay without moving, staring at them in turn right in the lenses of their spectacles. It was Chris who broke the silence.

'Whatever are you doing here? We thought you were in bed ages ago. My God, look at your clothes. Didn't you hear the telephone?'

'Get your things on,' my father mumbled, looking round into the dark hallway behind him. 'Your mother's very bad ... any minute they said ... The car's waiting outside.'

I tried to stand up, but I didn't get farther than the edge of the couch. Vellinga had even taken off my shoes and socks. I shook my head regretfully.

'I've been drinking. I can't. I'll come in an hour. I know I've made a rotten show of myself.'

Chris approached me with his hands outstretched: 'That's all right, old chap. Don't worry. It was too much for you. We understand. . .'

My father, haggard and distraught, made a noise that implied sympathy rather than disapproval.

'I'll help you,' Chris said, cautiously gripping my shoulder.

Quietly and quickly he helped me on with my clothes, not the stained and stinking suit I'd been wearing, but another one, dark and immaculate, that he'd run upstairs for. So there I was all decked out for a funeral. The maid stuck her head round the door and she was sent packing. Shaking from the pain that filled my body, I let my brother dress me. My father was waiting outside by the car, once he rang the bell timidly to hurry us up. Chris offered to get me a drink of water. I told him he'd have to flavour it with a stiff dash of gin. I hadn't had so much, I explained, it was only that I'd mixed the wrong sort of drinks, I'd been a fool not to stick to gin. He brought a sandwich I had asked for as well, I put it in my overcoat pocket.

In the car I leaned my head on something that felt like velvet, and then I was fast asleep. I was looking into Vellinga's eyes and I saw the car turning to follow the driveway up to the entrance to the hospital, which showed up in the light of the headlamps like a white château where a murder had just been committed. As the night nurse, warned by the soft toots of the horn, opened the door, we got out and stumbled up the steps. I felt tired and pleasantly drunk, I promised myself I would never see Trix again, I endured Chris's hand under my elbow, I said 'Good evening' to the nurse, then nodded to the doctor, and in the corridor I held on to Chris's coat, though that wasn't really necessary. In the corridor the news was broken to us that my mother had died half an hour before. She'd had a stroke at half past one and she hadn't recovered consciousness, she certainly hadn't suffered. My father and Chris stood with bowed heads, and then there was some discussion about going to look at my mother. I could have faced that. But I was so sleepy that, without even trying, I gave a fine display of swaying and toppling that landed me in the night sister's chair. I put my elbows on her table. When she came over and stood next to me I grabbed her hand and fell asleep. I don't remember anything of the ride back home. Chris brought me up to bed and took off my shoes. He kept lifting his glasses off and I knew that he was waiting for me to speak. I asked the question I was expected to ask. I could see her tomorrow morning, Chris said before he went away.

I woke at half past nine. With a throat as dry as sand, I staggered weakly to the tap in the hallway, then I lay in bed thinking, wide awake, suffused with a feeling of happiness and of impending disaster, or, at least, some sort of impending disruption. It was a surprise to me that I didn't have a headache. Maybe that came from mixing gin and rum. It might be worthwhile investigating this possibility, I could write a thesis on it later. . . Occasionally a door opened and shut somewhere in the house, and once or twice I heard the telephone. I could hardly realize that my mother was dead—she might come in at any moment with my breakfast on a little tray. But even Chris wouldn't think of a small service like that, and the maid didn't dare come into my room. Suddenly I had a vision of Trix standing in front of me just as I had last seen her when I was falling, tall and white like an angry, protecting bird of fantastic size. My eyes filled with tears. For a few minutes I stared blankly at the ceiling, then I decided what I would do, and I leapt out of bed.

I dressed hurriedly and tiptoed downstairs past the strange coats on the rack in the hallway and noiselessly out into the street. It had got colder. I made my way warily to a bar on the far

223

side of the big square, which I didn't cross, but walked round slowly, as if I suffered from agoraphobia. I was thinking I might pass out at every step I took and it was better to fall down as near as possible to the houses, then I'd have a reasonable chance of being well treated. That was safer than lying in the middle of the square like a wounded survivor of a street battle.

Only a few doors from the bar I felt sleepy, probably the tiredness that comes from a reluctance to do something that has to be done. This servile response of the body, incompatible with its usefulness and reasonableness in other respects, had to be ruthlessly suppressed. I marched briskly into the bar, the way I remembered Cuperus used to walk. Did Cuperus ever have to steady his nerves with a drink first thing in the morning? But he never sheltered behind an excuse when he wanted to drink, I admired him for that. There was no pretence with him, he never blamed the heat, or the cold, or rheumatism, or difficulties, or a good mood, or a bad mood, or any such nonsense. He was an honest, undisguised drunkard.

I reckoned that I would need two nips of gin. It would be a good idea to telephone first. If he wasn't there, or if he couldn't see me, one glass would be enough. Then I could go and have a meal somewhere. But he was there and he could see me, now if I liked, that would be better than the afternoon. Whoever it was that I spoke to seemed to find the afternoon very important, he breathed heavily when he said it. I ordered my two glasses and struck up a conversation with the barman about high rents. I don't know how we got on to this subject.

Vellinga's newspaper office occupied a building that had once been an imposing residence, over-looking the canal spanned by the arched bridge, W...'s Grand Canal. The newspaper was printed in a smaller building in the lane running along one side of the office, and Vellinga himself lived in an apartment in the adjoining house on the other side. It was obvious that the office wasn't a private dwelling, not only from the metal plate with the name of the paper on it, but more so from the door, which never shut properly during the day. Visitors, reporters, subscribers, shopkeepers with their advertisements ran in and out, pushing this heavy dull-green door that slowly sighed as it swung back and forth. This door could be approached at a gallop, for it was difficult to open as well. In any case there was no need to ring. I walked inside, went across to a counter, and when I announced myself a grubby urchin led me to the next floor rubbing his clean, probably just washed, hands over his dirty face. Every few yards he looked back encouragingly, and each time I nodded or smiled he hung his head as if he was trying to make up his mind about me, then he started rubbing his face again.

Vellinga welcomed me with a handshake and offered me a seat in front of his desk at the end of the large room. An aroma of English cigarettes drowned the smell of paper and printing ink. The ceiling was ornate, cream with trailing green garlands, but otherwise nothing in the room recalled the opulence of the past, there wasn't even a carpet on the floor. The top of his desk was as bare as his own bald head.

He followed my surprised glance. 'That's because I'm off out of W ... this afternoon,' he said, 'For the next few days there'll be the oddest things in the paper. But the joke of it is that no one notices. My system is infallible, but only for one day at a time. After all, a newspaper isn't an encyclopedia, it's read through and thrown away. Do you smoke?'

'No, thank you,' I said very formally. 'My stomach is rather upset from yesterday evening. I must apologize to you for the disgraceful way I behaved.'

He waved his hand magnanimously. 'How is your mother?'

'She died early this morning.'

He looked at the black suit I was wearing, intently, as if he needed some proof to confirm my statement. Then he stood up and pressed my hand without saying a word. When he sat down again behind his table there was a thoughtful expression on his red, well-fed face, which wasn't at all repulsive as long as he didn't show his discoloured bulldog teeth. The blue eyes, shielded by the cynical pince-nez, were somehow sad and pensive. But the eyes were too small, beady, unaccustomed, by reason of his manner of life and his occupation, to the habit of honest self-appraisal. That expression would have had to be far more intense before it could suggest any pleasing or edifying quality.

'I feel it as a personal loss, too, in a way,' he said confidentially. 'Your mother meant a lot to me. You're old enough to understand these things. That's why I've always had a weak spot for you, you know...'

I couldn't help giving a short laugh. The waving of the olive branch, I was thinking. Given a literal interpretation the words could be taken to mean: 'I'm your father, Nol ...' My laugh didn't disconcert him. He toyed with a paper-knife that had been lying on one of the small brown cupboards ranged alongside his desk like a row of miniature barracks. Then he put the paper-knife away in a drawer that he shut and locked. He rested his big, red, sinewy hands on the top of his desk.

'It wasn't because of my mother that I came to see you, but someone else.'

Immediately he was on his guard. 'Oh?' Then in a brisk, businesslike tone: 'Excuse me a moment ...' He stood up and spoke into the telephone: 'Hullo ... yes ... Nico, I don't want to be disturbed. Hang that "Engaged" notice on the door, will you? And no phone calls either,' and to me: 'I might as well lock the door. Just for today I'll stop being a journalist ... One of the characteristics of a journalist is that he never gets left in peace, day or night.'

'There's never a dull moment, then,' I said, almost involuntarily, as he went lumberingly to turn the key in the lock. Before he was back in his chair we heard Nico's quick, springy footsteps on the stairs. He put the board on the door without the slightest sound. The whole building was quiet, everything seemed to have stopped.

'Well?' Vellinga asked.

His face wasn't interesting any more. He had assumed the anonymous mask of the businessman who never gets caught out. His forehead didn't have the cruel duplicity of the hard, red features beneath it.

'I wanted to ask you if you are prepared to marry Trix Cuperus.'

I was watching him carefully, so I didn't miss the twitch of his smooth-shaven upper lip. It might have been the beginning of a smile, or the beginning of a snarl, but it didn't come to anything. He sat there motionless, and when he finally loosened the piercing stare he had fixed on me, his eyes glided smoothly away, not to seek a hiding-place, but simply because eyes are rotating organs with a specific function. A second later he was staring at me again.

'What do you mean?'

'I don't think I need to explain, do I? I would like you to answer my question. If you don't I can only conclude that you aren't disposed to entertain the idea.'

'I can give you your answer right now,' he said, irritated. 'I'm not marrying anyone.'

'Why not?'

'Because ...'—a quick, angry flash in his eyes hinted at other histrionic possibilities, the miming of the raging bull tormented by the picadors, or the bloodthirsty, dying warrior—'It's no damned business of yours, but I'm not getting married, and I never married because ... because I can't work and be married at the same time. I'm not thinking only of the work on the newspaper. Ever since I was young it's been my hobby to liven up this town. I could say I'm married to W ... I'm the life and soul of this town, even if I'm a bit gloomy sometimes. If I ever got married, then I'd be gloomy all the time. I don't know if you can follow what I mean. Is there anything else you would like to know?'

'Perhaps ... yes, there is. Don't you think that there are very good reasons why you should marry Trix Cuperus?'

'No', he snapped, and I could see his teeth. 'But why do you find it necessary to meddle in my affairs? And only a few hours after your mother has died.'

I flushed. 'Because I've always been in love with Trix.'

He gaped at me unbelievingly. My expression or my tone of voice must have kept him from bursting out laughing or shouting 'Congratulations' or something like that. He gazed at the ceiling, tapping the fingers of his left hand on the knuckles of his right hand. 'I don't see what you are getting at, Nol. If you're really in love with the girl wouldn't it be more logical to ask me not to marry her?'

'Anyone else might do that, but not me. So you aren't going to marry her. How would you like a punch on the nose?' My hands tightened on the edge of the chair.

He gave a jolt of surprise, then he stood up and said in a jovial bellow: 'Are you plain bloody crazy, Nol? That's no way to talk to an old friend of your mother's.'

'Leave my mother out of this,' I cut in, and I felt that I had weakened my position by saying that.

Waving his arms he said: 'No, we won't. If it hadn't been for your mother I'd have ...'

'Well, what are you waiting for?'

I jumped up. If I ran round the desk on the side nearest the door he couldn't call out to Nico in time. He wouldn't have a chance to reach the telephone either. But when I was going to rush at him, not berserk as I had thought I would be, but driven on by my contempt and by a sense of duty, he just stood calmly where he was, and I knew he wasn't frightened, that this wasn't a pose. It occurred to me, too, that I couldn't hit someone wearing glasses—I hadn't spared Chris that time so it was evident that I had been defeated before a blow was struck.

'Let's sit down and talk for five minutes, Nol,' he said, adopting the commanding but gently persuasive intonation that even the most effeminate aristocrat can reduce a mob to silence with. 'Then, if you still want to fight, I'll let you throw punches at me for as long as you like. I'll do that out of respect for your mother because I was in love with her for years, though I knew I would never even get a kiss from her. I can't fight with the son of a woman I thought so much of. I want to tell you two things. Firstly, if I'd known, if I'd known for sure that you were in love with that girl four years ago, I'd never have started anything with her. I'm speaking the solemn truth, Nol. Secondly, and this is more important for you, last night she told me she was finished with me. So I couldn't marry her even if I wanted to. At first I thought she was annoyed at me for letting you go on drinking. But it was more than that. It's all finished now, for good, and I can only say I'm sorry because I was fond of her too, in my own way.'

While I walked hesitantly back to my chair he cleaned his glasses on the sleeve of his tweed jacket. His eyes were weak, helplessly open, blinking, and now his face was baggier, more worn. But still he was dangerous enough. Probably because I had never been alone with him before I'd underestimated him. I don't doubt at all that he would have let me throw punches at him for as long as I liked. With my head bent, staring at the floor, I suddenly felt hungry. I couldn't start all over again. I might as well dismiss the possibility of trying another lead so as to challenge him to fight a second time.

'It doesn't surprise me, you know, Nol,' his voice drifted across the desk, 'that you fell in love with her. But that was years ago, and she was different then. You can blame me for the change in her, but there's some excuse. I was mad about her, I simply had to have her. . .'

'I suppose it started after the *Carmen* performance,' I said, without looking at him. 'It was around that time that she told me, or her father told me, how she couldn't stand the sight of men. Oh yes, I remember now, she said that she was too respectable.'

'Yes, she was,' Vellinga nodded, 'far too respectable. She didn't know anything, every man was a rotter, and all that sort of talk. You know as well as I do that girls like that are the easiest. But she wasn't that easy. She had character. But she was pig-headed, and maybe she had a kink from her drink-sodden father. And besides, the life she's led these last three years ... May I give you a bit of advice, Nol? Now, don't fly off the handle again, you won't like what I'm going to say, but I know I'm right. You'd better forget all about that girl. She's not your type. No good can come of it.'

'Do you mean that she might have been my type if you hadn't led her astray?'

There was a puckering of the brow. He shook his head, he reflected, he was giving my problem his full and undivided attention. 'It's hard to say. Perhaps, perhaps not. But I can tell you after a whole year I had no end of trouble to ... and that was after ... well, after I had led her astray, as you put it. A woman with an iron will ... a woman all the same, and with more passion in her than most. Then three years in that restaurant, with the waiters and the rest of that crowd ... no, no ...'

'Did she run around with the waiters too?' I asked ironically.

'No, of course not. Do you think I'd have stood for that? Why, I'd have set the restaurant on fire if she had. She wasn't always easy to get along with ... Oh well, it's finished now, it's all over.'

I had the feeling he was putting on something of an act to impress me, though everything he said could well be true. But I began to lose interest. It was more important than anything else that Trix had broken it off with him. I was thinking that after I'd had a bite to eat I could feel happy about it. I viewed everything now from a high, remote vantage-point.

'How did it happen ... the first time, I mean?'

He looked at me closely for a second or so, not because he felt the question was going too far but as if he realized the irony of the attitude I had now adopted, though there was no irony intended with the question. Then he shrugged his shoulders and said:

'Ach ... that's not a very romantic tale. I'll tell you the whole story but it will only make you dislike me more than you do now.

If you feel inclined to take a swing at me then try and remember that the way it happened doesn't say much for me, but the more the fault lies with me the less she is to blame. What started it ... well ... of course, in the first place, my feelings for her, and it was the drink we had that provided the opportunity, and that woman, that singer who played Carmen ...'

'Alice de Rato.'

'Yes, that's the name ... She'd had a lot to drink, so had I, but her father had had even more. It was that evening ...'

'All I know is that you and the five others drove off to celebrate at your place and that Jeannetje and Stegeman left after a quarter of an hour or so. But I think it's rather improbable that you seduced her with her father in the same room.'

Once again he sheltered himself with a pantomime grimace from the humiliation of the admission I was wringing out of him. This time he stuck out his chin. 'Quite improbable, but it's true nevertheless. That woman, Alice, or whatever her name is, was egging us on, she'd taken half her clothes off and she was shouting in French ... A dreadful female ... Cuperus didn't want anything to do with her, he'd been drinking like a fish and he just answered 'oui' or 'bonsoir'—I couldn't make him out, he'd told me he was infatuated with her. Then she got it into her head to ... to bring Trix and me closer to each other as it were. I was really drunk. I hadn't planned this, don't forget. Before that evening I'd only spoken to Trix once or twice. I deliberately didn't take any notice of her backstage that night or at the dress rehearsal ... except for the flowers, but that wasn't anything really. I didn't intend to bring them all back home with me.'

'I saw the flowers. I watched you drive off with the others, all shouting and laughing...'

'Everyone was in a good mood, that was all. I'm not a satyr. If I'd known you were standing there and ... but, damn it all, I even asked you myself to come along with us.'

'Yes, you did,' I said, 'but that proves nothing. You didn't know I was in love with Trix. For all you knew I wasn't interested in Trix any more than Stegeman was.'

'You're more of a lawyer than I am,' he grinned, but he was immediately serious again, making an effort to achieve a tone of sincerity. 'I didn't think of trying to get anywhere with Trix. But that old hag went prancing round stirring things up, and once the idea takes hold of you, you can't stop yourself. I was the only one who understood a little of what she was babbling, and it wasn't drawing-room talk. Trix ignored her. She hadn't drunk much, Trix, no more than two glasses, I think, but she'd never drunk whiskey before, and ... well ... But I'll tell you about Cuperus first. I rather liked the fellow, we often used to have a drink together at the Garden restaurant, he'd tell me all this troubles. He had every reason to be grateful to me, I'd helped him out with money now and then... That female wanted to get Trix and me in the back room together. But I just sat Trix on my knee, and she didn't protest though I could see she hadn't fallen for me. But she was in a daze from the whiskey and Cuperus was properly under the weather. He was raving and rambling, sometimes he took hold of Trix's hand and sometimes mine, and he seemed to be encouraging us. That Belgian hag kept rushing around half naked, singing, crude cabaret stuff it must have been, that was her level. ... I can still remember Cuperus saying that I was the only friend he had in the world and that here he was at the end of his tether, that he had lost everything, love and reputation and honour, and he had to abandon his most cherished possession, and he was sinking lower than any man could sink, and more in the same strain. It didn't make any sense to me. Then he started crying and talked about "the apple of his eye". Then he said something in German ... what was it now. ... "Go on, I can't bar your way." ...'

' "*Zieh hin, ich kann dich nicht halten.*" It's from *Siegfried.*'

'*Siegfried?*'

'The opera. So you concluded that Cuperus was giving you his blessing?'

232

Vellinga clamped his mouth shut and pulled a face, turning his head as if there was something on his desk that gave off a foul stench. 'I didn't conclude anything. I couldn't make head or tail of what he was saying, and not long afterwards he was snoring. ... he'd had a hell of a lot to drink. The next day I went to see him, to confess everything and ask him to forgive me. He seemed confused, he must have been thinking it was all Trix's fault. He still wasn't sober. When we managed to get the two of them into a coach it was near four o'clock. ... Just before he started snoring Trix had gone to sleep on my lap—it might have been from the drink. That Carmen woman was at it again, she said I'd have to take Trix to the back bedroom, or was I frightened or what. By then I didn't need any egging on, I'd have murdered anyone who tried to stop me. I was certainly as drunk as Cuperus but it affects me differently. I don't get sleepy, I just lose all sense of moral restraint. ... Since that night I've never drunk so much. ...That woman stayed there, talking and talking ... I can't remember what she said ... she wouldn't go away. ...'

He had told his story sitting slightly hunched up, he was obviously feeling guilty and not expecting much sympathy from me. At times there was a tremor of self-pity in his voice, almost a whine. He, Vellinga, a gentleman and a sportsman, mixed up unwittingly with that low company and compelled to play the bounder ...

'The appearances could suggest that you had put a sleeping-powder in her whiskey,' I said, looking him straight in the eye. A glint of aggressive indignation flickered behind the gold-rimmed pince-nez, a blue and noble flame, though on a modest scale. When I said it I didn't believe that my words were more than an insinuation, but it is a fascinating exercise to prove someone guilty of the intention to commit an act he hasn't committed.

There wasn't any point in going on with these taunts. Nothing could penetrate that solid bastion of thick flesh and civic duty and conjugal obligations to the fair town of W ..., commitments for which dispensation could never be granted. He'd let me say whatever I wanted to while I was in that room with him, and if I caused any bother later he'd just deny everything.

'Take it easy, Nol,' he said coaxingly. 'So far you've borne up pretty well, better than anyone else your age could. ... I told you it took me a year, at least a year, before I was able to convince her that ... that I had certain claims on her. She wouldn't believe me. At times I didn't believe it myself any more. I used to wonder if it was a drunken fantasy, or a dream, but I got more and more crazy about her. By Jesus, what a woman, as tall as I am, so cool and aloof. ... In the end she gave in, and then she went home and beat up her own father.'

'I'd like to know exactly which month that was.'

'May or June I think, it was summer anyway ... I could easily check, I still have copies of the letters I wrote her.'

'Later than April?'

'Yes, it was later than that.'

'Did she ever talk about me?' I asked, standing up.

Giving a dispirited grunt, he followed me to the door. 'I can't remember. Somehow I could never discuss things with her. If I'd only known how you felt about each other... But listen, Nol ...' He had caught up to me and he threw his left arm around my shoulder while his right hand reached out towards the key and then drew back again. 'I've been quite frank with you and if you think I'm a rotter I won't contradict you. But this talk we've had— and it's been a rather unusual conversation—has made me feel really responsible for you. After all, I'm nearly twenty years older than you, and then your mother and all that ... Believe me, Nol, that girl isn't your type. Promise me that you won't go and see her.'

I had to laugh, I was so relieved. He had actually been able to touch a responsive chord in me with his show of noble-mindedness ... no, it was genuine, he really meant it.'

'I'll promise everything, Mijnheer Vellinga, but I reserve the right to break any promise I make.'

234

He cleared his throat disapprovingly. 'That gets us nowhere. Promise me at least that you won't repeat it all to her ... what I told you about that night. ... It'll be a stone around your neck, I know, you'll never shake it off.'

'Why shouldn't I discuss it with her? She knows what happened, and wasn't that little orgy at your apartment the best argument you could find to support your claim to her?'

'Very well then, do as you like,' he mumbled.

As we shook hands I thought I detected a nervousness, a trace of disappointment in his eyes. But he could produce, within certain limits of course, the most unexpected effects with those eyes of his. He could even betray his own feelings. Obviously, I reasoned, he's trying to keep Trix and me apart. As an older lover, who wouldn't find it so easy to replace his loss, he doesn't want to compete with a younger rival. And the less said about 'that night' the better for his reputation. This aspect occured to me as I stepped into the street. All I remember about leaving the newspaper office is the dirty-faced urchin downstairs showing me to the door with the respect of his kind for someone who can take up an undisturbed half-hour of his employer's time.

17

When I got home I faced a barrage of sharp questions from Chris. As I meekly answered him, I decided I wouldn't go to the hospital and that I would telephone the matron later in the afternoon to warn her to say I had been if she was asked. The explanation for this unusual request would be that I was feeling sick, that the family didn't realize this, understandably, for they had enough to worry about at the moment. I phoned about four o'clock from the same bar, and while I was there I drank another three nips of gin. In the meantime I'd had a good meal, I'd rested for an hour, I'd shaken hands with relatives and helped Chris to make a quick list of names and addresses for the invitations to the funeral. Now and then we consulted our father, who put his hand to his head and apparently didn't know anyone now except the members of the Rieske family. He was quite friendly to me. It wasn't impossible, I reflected, that his affection for Chris might be transferred to me, now that my mother, whom I resembled so closely in appearance and temperament, wasn't there any more. I drew him aside. and told him that just now, as it happened, I was confronted with a very important personal problem that was making heavy demands on me and they mustn't be upset if I was away for a few hours.

After I had rung the hospital I rang the Garden restaurant and asked for Trix. She wasn't there. I could go home, or wait for five minutes or even wait for a quarter of an hour or half an hour. I went home and helped my father and Chris to make new lists of names, leaving a horde of relatives and friends in the sitting-room while we discussed where we should order the cards and have the printing done. Paying tribute to the dead by organizing a display of sympathy, and grieving in our hearts whenever we realized what we were doing and where we were sitting and talking, in this house, in these rooms, that were saturated still with her presence. At my insistence it was decided to have an announcement inserted in Vellinga's newspaper. There was another local paper which my father preferred because he held it against Vellinga that he had deserted the legal profession to become a common journalist. Vellinga had called during the afternoon, but I hadn't seen him or any of the other friends of my mother's who came. The only one I saw was young Tjallingii. I met him on the stairs and after shaking hands he stood looking at me, rather puzzled, as if he was surprised at my appearance or my manner. When I went on quickly up the stairs and glanced round at him he was staring at me open-mouthed he seemed gratified in some way and a little curious to know what reason there could be for the hurrying phenomenon of happiness disappearing above him.

I was indeed happy. But I hadn't got much further with my phone call at half past five. She said she was sorry to hear the news, and I asked her if I could see her in the evening, if possible, at home. That involved several minutes conversation. It was apparently difficult to fix the time. I suggested meeting her on a street-corner somewhere, but no, I could see her at home, only it would be better if I waited for her outside. I couldn't resist the temptation to remind her that I had done that once before. She gave a short laugh, then she told me to be there at half past ten. Only later, at dinner, I realized that she probably hadn't been able to speak freely, there would be others listening. All the time I was on the phone I'd heard voices and the clatter of plates.

Towards half past ten I felt jumpy and irritable. The alcoholic slumber of the night before had merely misled my body, and I didn't lie down in the early part of the evening in case I fell asleep. But I made a bigger mistake, perhaps the biggest mistake of my life, by not having a drink when it was nearing half past ten. I had meant to, but I forgot, or thought I shouldn't, or maybe I didn't see any bar I wanted to go into on my way to my late music-teacher's house. The alcohol inside me reacted by denying me any more effect at a critical moment. I should have been in good condition, but I was barely half fit, and my physical state was reflected in my hopes: a calm discussion, a prelude to blissful happiness, and, for Christ's sake, no new complications...

At twenty-five to eleven I heard her footsteps. I couldn't distinguish her face very well under the hat. When we shook hands she bent forward and kissed me with dry lips lightly on the cheek. A bad omen, I murmured to myself, and I followed her into the hallway that was lit by the bright light shining transversely from the kitchen. There was a sound of deep young voices from Cuperus's room. That would be the lodgers, or one of them.

'Don't hang your coat here,' Trix whispered, 'and step quietly on the stairs, not because of them in there, but so my aunt won't hear.'

The aunt was already standing on the stairs, strikingly tall, her head bobbing and twisting inquisitively, looming gruesomely against the feeble glimmer of the small light in the upstairs passage. As Trix passed her she moved reluctantly aside and stretched her hand down to express her condolences. Still clutching my arm in her strong nurse's grip, she pulled me up towards her and, after her words of sympathy, she said: 'And congratulations on something else ...' I mumbled some reply. The light fell on her face and I saw her eyes screwing up, the over-ripe flesh of the cheeks lifting, the lips folding into a sickly smile. Then I was upstairs following Trix to her room.

'What did she say to you?'

She stood facing me, half turning, her fingers still on the light switch, angry wrinkles across her forehead. Behind her a sparsely furnished room, a neatly made bed, a few cheap, but not inelegant, prints on the walls, and two or three photos, but, as I noticed later, none of her father.

'Nothing much,' I whispered, 'sympathy and congratulations, presumably for different reasons.'

She walked into the room and took her hat off. 'She's down in the kitchen now. I don't want to have her listening to us outside the door.'

'Does it matter?'

With complete composure I helped her get her coat off and it was put fraternally next to mine on a hanger near the door.

'No, it doesn't really matter,' she said listlessly. Then she shifted some books from a chair she pulled out for me. Her face was grey, and the watery eyes, always so proud, changed now by tiredness, seemed arrogant, rather stupidly arrogant. Yes, she's just the same as everyone else, I was thinking, with tell-tale lines on her face and sickness in her soul. No, she was no goddess. It was a reality I could accept, knowing that it didn't make the slightest difference to my love for this tormented creature in an almost shabby skirt and a blouse that was none too clean, standing there lost in thought, plucking at cake crumbs on the table. Still, I knew that the possibility of our finding happiness together was reduced to narrow limits, as if by a convulsive twist of fate.

'What would you like to drink?'

'I've had some tea and I drank enough yesterday evening, I think, to last for a long while. I'm not a drinker by nature.'

Outside there wasn't a sound. I thought I heard voices now and then in the house, upstairs and downstairs. Maybe some of the lodgers were talking to themselves or memorizing their lessons, like Chris in his worst period of decline. The religious bachelor was no doubt praying. Below us, but not directly below us, the rattle of crockery, the rush of water from a tap. That was the aunt, busy in the kitchen, making coffee for her long vigil, a libation dedicated to curiosity.

'Your aunt might bring us some coffee ...'

'She'll think twice about being so kind-hearted. I don't want to see any more of her tonight.'

She sat down opposite me and looked at me, then deliberately stared straight past me. I was wondering if Vellinga had ever been here. It wasn't very likely, I'd worked that out already. She moved, turning sideways, one arm leaning on the table, and the slight curve of her breast in the pale yellow blouse was silhouetted against her own shadow on the cheap eiderdown that constrasted with the red, new slippers under the far end of the bed.

'I just don't want to see her. You're visiting me. What has that got to do with her?'

'It's got nothing to do with her,' I admitted, looking round at the window, which for some strange reason had rattled for just a moment.

'Did you see your mother again?'

'No.'

'You should have waited a couple of days before you came here.'

'Why?'

'People talk. They know everything that goes on.'

'I can only think about you. I'm not worried what people say or think.'

'Really?' Her eyes flashed. Was it derision or anger? She made a restless movement as if she was trying to stop me from contradicting her. 'Maybe you think about me sometimes, but last night you got drunk because of your mother. Wubbo said so himself.'

'Wubbo? Who is Wubbo?'

'Vellinga, of course.'

A nasty taste in the mouth isn't just a figure of speech. The habit some women have of referring to acquaintances, even the most casual acquaintances and virtual strangers, by their first names as if everyone should know them like brothers or sisters can be engagingly naïve or irritating, and sometimes the cause of mis-understanding, but in this instance it was ill-mannered and stupid, perhaps deliberately insulting. Barmaid that she was. But I loved her, barmaid or not. I shifted in my chair and said dully: 'I had a talk with Vellinga this morning.'

She went pale as a ghost and bit her lips. 'Oh?'

'I spent half an hour with him and he told me that you had broken it off with him.' And when she didn't say anything I added: 'On account of me.'

'That's not true,' she said hoarsely and angrily, and her shoulders turned towards me threateningly. 'I didn't mention your name, except when I thought he had ordered rum for you.'

'That's not what I meant. What I'm saying is that you broke it off because of your feelings for me. Of course I don't expect you to tell Vellinga. But is it true?'

'No.'

'I don't believe you. Why did you break it off yesterday then, or had you been intending to do that anyway?'

'Yes, for a long time. You can't imagine how long.'

'Yes I can. You see, I know the whole story. How he tricked you, and how you kept him at a distance for a year, that year when you were still in love with me ... and after yesterday evening, in the Garden ... Oh no, it wasn't because of me that you broke it off with him.'

My hands were trembling. I could have hit her, hit her and then hugged her and taken her away. A savage rage burst loose inside me and that rage enveloped my love for her, and she too had been consumed by rage year after year, made old before her time by rage, wounded, so deeply hurt, yet on the surface so cool and contemptuous. Oh, how well I understood her!

'If he told you the whole story,' she spoke with much less self-assurance, her ash-blond head suddenly bowed, 'then I don't know why you came here this evening. I didn't think you would find out everything. ...'

'I'm not altogether an idiot, I know that gossip is always sixty per cent true. That's what makes gossip so nasty. All that business with Vellinga wasn't your fault. But even if you were to blame, and even if you didn't break it off with him on account of me, I still wouldn't hesitate for a single second. ...'

I wanted to look her straight in the eye. But I couldn't say:'Look me in the eye, Trix.' I wasn't a grandfather, I wasn't some noble character out of a book or a newspaper. I had to speak to that head, to that blond head, that untidy barmaid coiffure, to an outcast I didn't feel sorry for because I loved her more than heaven and earth. I had to say something, I had to say something that could be accompanied by an appropriate posture or movement, the left leg crossed over the right, or the fingers fiddling idly with a watch chain.

'But I didn't come here to talk about Vellinga. I came here to ask you to marry me.'

I didn't feel that now something momentous had happened. If I'd only had more sense I could have asked her that four years ago. Time didn't matter. The situation was clear then, and the occasion suitable. If I'd proposed to her after our first kiss she might have laughed at me, but perhaps Vellinga would have been excluded from her life. When she didn't look up I went on:

'You can refuse, but only if you think that you don't love me enough. I've only another three or four years to do at the university but I could marry you before then, a couple of months from now even. My father wouldn't try and stop me, I know that.... If you don't love me enough and you still want to marry me, that's all right as far as I'm concerned. But don't think about what people will say. They don't mean any harm and it's just as well to realize that now and then. Vellinga is a pillar of society, but a pillar that is half glass, so you can see through him, partly anyway ... A good thing too, otherwise he'd be up to even naster stunts....'

Discouraged, I stopped. What sort of claptrap was this? And wasn't it a mistake to talk too condescendingly about Vellinga? Wouldn't I humiliate her with these unnecessary comments? And why didn't she say anything? I couldn't go on talking like this, extolling the advantages of a marriage with the judge's son over the life she was leading, and perhaps pointing out to her that, quite apart from my feelings, by marrying her I would be repaying a dept of gratitude to her father, the teacher I owed so much to. In the world beyond this world of substance I saw his massive figure rear up, Henri Cuperus, in our drawing-room, facing my mother, the rejected flowers in his hands, and the tears came into my eyes.

I stood up cautiously and walked over to her. It was only then that I noticed she was whispering to herself. More than once I heard: '... how ... not love you.' When I murmured: 'Trix', and just as I was going to stroke her head, she jumped. She pushed me roughly aside, threw herself on the bed and lay there sobbing, her face pressed into her hands. I didn't panic. I was calmly and fully aware of how I must behave, that from medical considerations too, I shouldn't disturb her or try to comfort her, that it was better for her to abandon herself to an upsurge of emotion, a procedure I had myself often found beneficial and even inspiring. No protestation of affection, no consoling words. That could only be sheer hypocrisy when a woman was lying on a bed sobbing, on her own bed. I watched her with sympathy, perhaps fear too, and embarrassment at the spectacle of this collapse. She had always been able to stand up for herself and now I would, in spite of everything, probably have to help her back on her feet again. For I was and I would remain the judge's son, nothing in the world could change that, but I mustn't give the impression that it was more than a minor handicap. And what did it matter, what did it matter if I felt a sort of triumph, and even, somewhere in the dark recesses of my mind, a tinge of pleasure at her misery? There you are, my girl, you should have realized sooner that you belonged to me.... My love could withstand any trial, it would conquer every difficulty. I challenged the world to devise harsh ordeals to test it anew.

Minutes must have gone by as we each waited for the other to speak. She wasn't crying now, she lay like a child, her face in her hands. As the silence became more solemn and more menacing, I sat on the edge of the bed next to her and tried to think of what I should say, words to open the first and crucial phase of an inevitable situation that could nevertheless evolve in a thousand different ways.

'Trix, will I go? Take a day off from work tomorrow and I'll come here early. You know now what I want to do ...'

'No, don't go.' It was a choking cry and I heard and felt her turning and sitting up behind me.

'I'll tell you everything. Come here, closer to me.'

We moved over nearer to one another and she put her arms round me. When she kissed me I tasted her tears. That sobbing hadn't been just dry-eyed exhaustion. I could have shown more sympathy than I had, I thought, a little ashamed. Once again I had made a mistake... Then an infinite tranquillity. Her body against me, rapturously soothing. I kissed her passionately, pressing her lips open, and though she sighed deeply and held me tightly round my waist (but without pulling me closer to her) that feeling of infinite tranquillity remained, a synthesis of tenderness and earnestness and sorrow and the conviction, an unshakeable and perhaps coldly reasoned conviction, that I could win against the world and the vagaries of life, against the passing of time and the encroachments of decay, by playing the role I had to play. For a moment I seemed to be sinking away, dying, and my stomach was rent again by the stress of insight and oracles, and I understood everything. I would know the deepest unhappiness. I put the thought out of my mind and existed merely as this endlessly present manifestation that wasn't myself but was still more myself than my own being. Holding her head between my hands I let my cheek rest on her ash-blond hair.

'Tell me, then.'

When she looked up I was shocked by the sight of her face. It was a face stamped with defeat, the eyes were hidden under the puffed, red lids, the wrinkles were frightening. The features were unrecognizable, there wasn't a sign of grief or resentment, only tiredness, the utter tiredness of someone who has just struggled out of the depths of a swamp and doesn't know what to do next. With her arm clamped round my waist she started speaking quickly:

'I'm not sure if I can marry you, Nol. I love you, I've always loved you. Maybe that's why I can't be sure. You've heard Vellinga's story, but it's worse than that. There's a lot he didn't tell you. But that time in the porch, when we kissed each other, that was before anything had happened, at least...'

244

'Yes, I know. Nothing could have made me happier than hearing that.'

'That same evening my father had a talk with me. I was hardly on speaking terms with him because Wubbo, Vellinga, I mean, had told me what he had been like that night. Getting drunk doesn't matter, but he just let me get caught in a trap instead of seeing that nothing happened to me. The next day Vellinga told him everything, the swine, and even hinted, I think, at the possibility of marriage. As if I would have accepted ... What an idea, marrying that oaf. But my father and I had never spoken about that night, so he could act like a real father who had nothing on his conscience, and he said he'd seen that you were in love with me, and that I mustn't let it go any further, you were too young, and you would change, you belonged to another world, your parents would object. He said something too about your mother being high and mighty...'

'Once my mother pulled him up with a jerk when he tried his charms on her,' I couldn't help interrupting, 'but she wasn't really high and mighty.'

'I don't know anything about that,' she said rather impatiently. 'And he said I wasn't the sort that should ever get married, I always wanted my own way. Perhaps he was right. But I'd thought about all the rest, before that. I still saw you as a little boy, even though I'd got to be crazy about you, especially after that day on the skating-rink. I didn't feel like going begging to your parents ... In the end I had to admit my father was right, and so I thought the best thing to do was not to see you any more, never. But I quarrelled with my father, of course, and I almost told him what I thought of him for leaving me in the lurch that night they got me dead drunk.'

'I've been wondering whether Vellinga mightn't have put a sleeping-powder in your glass. Didn't you taste anything?'

'I can't remember. Someone else said that too. But I'd never drunk anything strong before, you see, nothing stronger than wine mixed with water. My father never encouraged me, though he knew I didn't drink just to annoy him, or to be a good example, if you like. But that night I didn't want to be a spoil-sport, and that French woman kept saying I must and I was excited after the opera and because everyone, and that French woman too, said I sang very well. But I didn't want to sing again. Standing up like a fool for people to look at ... not for me. Vellinga was so gay and friendly, the dashing gentleman. I remember sitting on his lap and thinking I couldn't put up with you, Mijnheer Vellinga, the airs you give yourself. I remember vaguely being lifted up and carried away.'

'But after that you must have drunk more than a couple of glasses of whiskey in an evening.'

'Yes.' She loosened her arm from round my waist. 'Oh, you mean that wasn't enough to knock me out. Maybe he did put a sleeping-powder in my glass, he's quite capable of it. But let me finish, Nol.'

The tiredness was gone from her face. She was beautiful now, bewitchingly beautiful, as if she was as drunk as she had been that night. Her eyes were shining. That couldn't be from love, not when she was telling all this. No, it was the resolve to utter her complaint that fired her, the indictment, voiced now after being suppressed for years, a tortured soul's senseless quest for justice, to which the lawyers, finding no proof, reacted by tapping the backs of their hands and silently forming their own opinions. When I kept looking at her she gave a short laugh, that bewitching laugh of hers, and turned my face sideways with her hand.

'I went back to my aunt because my father started drinking like a madman after that night of the opera. My mother couldn't do anything with him. She used to be able to keep him off the drink by coughing and crying in bed, but that didn't help any more. Besides, I was ashamed of myself for sitting on Vellinga's lap. I just had to get away. Two days later a letter from him, he couldn't forget me, he was madly in love with me and so on and would I write soon. I'd no intention of writing, but a week after that he drove up in his car. I came home and found him sitting like a lord in the front room with my aunt, and she was playing up to him and she expected me to do the same. She'd decided on the spot that he was a good match, she was always at it. She'd burst, I think, without her match-making intrigues. And soon she left us alone on some pretext or other. I couldn't ignore him. After all, I thought I'd only sat on his lap. Then he had the cheek to tell me everything that had happened that night, and he asked me to forgive him and he said that he loved me so much. He just stopped short of going down on his knees. It wasn't because I was thinking of you, but I simply didn't believe him, I thought he'd made it all up, and I told him I wouldn't be interested even if ten men had led me astray.'

'Led you astray,' I said, derisively.

'Maybe I don't express myself very well. What do you expect? I'm not a student like you.' There was an edge of irritation in her voice. 'But what happened? Of course he came back, he probably was in love with me then. He could be worse, I suppose. These men with plenty of money, they're all swine, maybe they can't be anything else.... And my aunt forever singing his praises, he'd marry me, I ought to go out with him,—she didn't know anything about that night, of course—he was rich, and did I want to sit around moping all my life, and that she'd never let chances go by and she'd never got a bad name for it. But that wasn't true, I'd heard them shouting out after her in the village—and every week letters from Vellinga, and presents and car rides. I used to go for the want of something better to do...'

'And did he propose?'

'No,' she said decidedly, 'no, not once. He never said he would marry me, but he never suggested it either. I can't say he was dishonest. But always the same argument. That I belonged to him, and what was wrong with that anyway, and we're only young once, and you know how it goes ... or maybe you don't.'

Suddenly she forced me to look into her eyes, eyes full of flame, no longer soft and watery. Irresistible, relentless, magnificent eyes.

'I'd better not tell you any more, Nol, maybe you wouldn't understand.'

'I've been a medical student for three years and I talked to Vellinga this morning, he put the finishing touches to my education. I'm not saying I know everything about everything, but I've learnt a thing or two...'

'Are you sure?'

'As a doctor I have to. You can't start practising as innocent as a baby. Like lawyers, not that I can say much in favour of lawyers, but they have to know about the seamy side of life too.' I was a little surprised that she didn't ask me about my own experience with other women.

'Well, after that talk with my father and the letter I wrote you, I just didn't care. I'd lost you anyway, and I felt that my father was right and that I could never be happy with someone who wouldn't let me have my own way ... Maybe that's not like a woman. Do you think I've got a woman's character, Nol?'

'You know how I think about you,' I said. 'I used to be puzzled why you fought such a lot. But that doesn't say you're not like a woman, and you didn't fight for the fun of it. If a woman can use her fists that doesn't mean ...'

'And Vellinga can be really good company, and my aunt had stopped nagging at me. That made a difference, you know, because if she hadn't stopped I'd never have... well, you can guess the rest.'

'You must have been in love with him in the beginning,' I said, summoning to my aid all my knowledge of the female mind, second-hand knowledge as it was, acquired from a sixth-year student who claimed that a woman would always stay in love with you for a week if you gave her a good going-over.

'No. Me fall in love with that swine? Maybe, if I hadn't been in love with you, with that cheeky mouth and those rosy cheeks and everything about you...' She pulled me fiercely against her, she kissed my face, my hair. I didn't kiss her back. If I started too I'd never hear the end of her story.

'No,' she went on contemptuously as she tidied her hair. 'I was never nice to him, and I never thanked him for the money he was always making me accept. Sometimes I'd torment him till he was livid. Just fancy, Vellinga livid. The next morning I went back home and I hit my father in the face as hard as I could, three, four times, till he started crying. I told him I was going to work as a waitress in the Garden restaurant and that I'd serve him and I'd have him thrown out if he made any trouble. Vellinga got me that job, he could always come and see me if he wanted to. He never came to my room, though everyone said he did. But in the summer we used to go into the park or that shed, the store, you know, that low building...'

'Near the path with the lime trees?'

'Yes. They always smelt so nice in June. Once he fell over the chairs on the lawn and I ran off in the dark and left him there. Nobody was supposed to go into the park at night, but the owner said nothing because Vellinga was a good customer and the waiters and the other girls kept their mouths shut, at least they did after I gave one of them a thrashing... But afterwards ...'

'A waiter?'

'Yes. He was fairly old. He said he'd call the police. When I was much younger I'd hit my father too, but that wasn't serious. I took a swing at Vellinga once, but he grabbed my wrists, he was too strong for me. It was easier to needle him than to fight him... But my father ... They say there's a heaven we all go to, but I'll tell you, Nol, if it is true and I meet my father there, then I'll kill him.' Her voice rose almost to a shout.

'I'm a doctor, not a parson. I don't know whether your father got a place in heaven or not. But you might ... oh, not now, of course ... but you might understand him better...'

'Are you taking sides with those swine? You don't know what you're saying. Do you know what it's like to feel you're a fallen

249

woman that everyone can spit on? Do you know what it's like to feel you're a slut, and wake up in the morning and feel you're rotten through and through and watch a miserable sot putting on his underpants? Oh Christ, oh Christ ... I could skin them alive, like eels... Oh Christ ...' While she hissed these curses she drummed on the bed with her fists so that I rocked softly with the bouncing of the mattress in a sort of daze of intense, almost animal delight. I was vaguely wishing she would drum her fists on my body. She controlled herself quickly and started to speak again, now in a hurried whisper that the hoarseness of her voice made disturbingly ominous. 'But that's not all, that's not the worst. The worst part is that you want to do it even though you know the next morning you'll feel like jumping into the moat. It was the only pleasure I had, and but for that I could have killed myself ... A pity I didn't...' I took her hand, but she pulled it loose. 'Just the fun of it, I don't mean lying in bed with a clammy-handed lout, but getting them worked up and knowing that if you don't give in to them they won't come back again. That used to amuse me. I suppose I am a bitch, really, Nol. And it was never boring at the restaurant, the work, I mean. There were always people around, and I could play the boss... Maybe I was in love with them for a second or so, with the ones I went to bed with... When they're begging and begging you and they're in such a state they don't know what they're doing ... What a joke. But I liked that, and at times it was the same as a drug I couldn't do without...'

'Are you saying there were ...'

'It was the only consolation I had when I felt unhappy. If you're with someone, anyone at all, it stops you being lonely...' She was silent for a while, then she said softly: 'That's not all, Nol. You see, Vellinga wasn't the only one.'

I went numb inside, just as I had years ago when my mother told me what sort of life 'that sweet little Trixie' was leading. I sat taut and motionless. My only thought was that if I twitched or shrank back everything was lost, and then we might as well both jump into the canal. Fortunately, I had been staring in front of me as she was speaking, and I only had to keep that up. And not think, not think at all. But it isn't possible to exclude all thought simply by an effort of will. I remembered another one of those university philosophers, a fifth-year pharmacy student who preoccupied himself with the art of living and modelled himself on Dorian Gray and never referred to a girl as 'a good tumble'. At one period his mistress—he could afford a mistress, he was quite well-to-do—left him to run around with various middle-aged businessmen, and when she came back grovelling to him he more or less forgave her. She was very pretty, I'd seen her once. She had acquired a veneer of culture from this disciple of Oscar Wilde's, and it would have been reasonable to expect a more violent reaction from him on her return from the businessmen who had been enjoying the charms he had endowed her with. Still, it rankled with him, for he said to some of his friends that Julie's back but I'll have to get the smell of the market place out of her and that'll take time, and he was going to inquire at the medical faculty whether it would be better to boil her in soda or apply a calcium solution to the affected part. I sat completely motionless and let the reminiscence fade away, it was nothing more than a feeble Oscar Wilde joke, the humour of a misguided dandy...

'Nol!' With her hands gripping mine she looked intently into my eyes. 'What's wrong? Are you shocked?'

'No, I'm not shocked.'

'Yes you are. I can feel it. You're shocked.' Her eyes filled with tears. 'Oh my God, Nol, if you're going to despise me ...'

What could I say? A denial would imply a self-accusation, an admission of small-minded egoism, of intolerant pettiness. At the same time I was forming the thought that of course she's a slut, I knew that, but I love her, I could even treat her as a slut and still love her, I could ill-treat her for being a slut and still love her. I began to talk without knowing what I wanted to say.

'You could have done worse things and not... But that's

something I've got to get used to. Don't be angry with me. After all, it's not the same as hearing the weather forecast on the radio... I don't mind, I can understand. I think ... I think it's probably just as well, because if Vellinga had been the only one I might have suspected you were in love with him...'

She gave me a piercing, unbelieving look. 'But aren't you jealous?'

'No.'

'I don't believe you. If you love someone you're always jealous.'

I gulped. How dogmatic she was and how right she was. 'Not me. At least ... not over something that's past and done with. I was near to giving Vellinga a black eye this morning, but not from jealousy. More because I thought he deserved it, or maybe just because he annoyed me, with that red, bulldog face of his...' A silly argument, I reflected. Not because it was all lies but because I put myself so far above Vellinga. 'But I don't want to abuse him behind his back. He hasn't been as lucky as I have, hardly anyone could be. My mother once said that a love that begins in childhood and, after it's been forgotten for a while, starts all over again is the strongest of all.'

'Did she know about me?'

'Yes.'

'What did she say?'

'She didn't object,' I lied, or maybe it wasn't a lie.

'Do you remember if you fell in love with me that day we danced in the Garden? I can still remember how I suddenly wanted to dance with you. I wouldn't have danced with anyone else...'

'No,' I said, after pondering for a moment, 'I don't think I was in love with you. But if I'd seen you more often ... I only know it was a wonderful experience and that from then on you were never altogether out of my thoughts. When I saw you fighting I worshipped you, but I was too young to recognize the feeling. Mostly nothing comes of these childhood attachments, you never see each other again. Thanks to your father that didn't happen to us.'

We sat without speaking.

'You're so sensitive, Nol,' she said, stroking my hand. 'Why do I have to upset you with all these things? You're so understanding too, you've got more sense than plenty of others much older than you are—more than my father had.'

'If I understand anything, I learnt it mostly from your father. Not from what he said or thought, but from what he was. He was wise in a foolish way...'

She shrugged her shoulders. There was a gulf between us again, but a quite explicable gulf. I had been taught to think and to express my thoughts in words, she hadn't.

'Who were the others?'

Again the suspicion in her eyes, then a reproving shake of her head. Half playfully I took her arm and ran my hand caressingly down to the wrist. Just when I was about to say she could tell me another time, she answered me.

'You're shocked. But you ought to be. What drove me to it was that Vellinga had been going round with other women. I had no claim on him, but I wasn't going to take that from him. So the first chance I had I was unfaithful to him, and I told the next day. He wasn't even angry. But he could never get the better of me.'

'Who was it?'

'Mijnheer Caspers.'

'Caspers,' I repeated slowly. 'So, Caspers ... not such a bad choice.'

'He took me out in his car. But I had to tell you I'd been with Caspers because through him I got a better idea of what did happen that night at Vellinga's. I wasn't in love with Caspers—I was even less in love with the other two, they were just dirt—but he was very good to me, much more of a gentleman than Wubbo, and he let me tell him all about myself and he told me a lot of things about my father, and how he had managed to stop my father running after Alice de Rato—during the interval he had told him she was a trollop. She was, too. He'd seen that when he was driving her from the station, and father did at least take his advice. Then I asked him just how much of a trollop he thought I was, and so we got talking about Vellinga and how it all started. When I told him what I had heard from Vellinga he pulled a face and he said something about sleeping-powders too. He thought for a long time and then he said he didn't believe a single word of it and he would see if he could get at the truth. This was going too far, he said. It was hardly likely I wouldn't have noticed something even if I was unconscious, that was impossible, he said. Vellinga would spin him a tale, of course, and Vellinga was drunk anyway, but Alice de Rato hadn't been so drunk—I'd told him that myself—and he felt it would be worthwhile going to Amsterdam to see her, even though he said she was as big a liar as Vellinga. He did go and see her too, after he broke it off with me…'

'Broke it off? Caspers?'

'Yes, after the second time I went out with him. He said he could see I was in love with someone else, not Vellinga, but someone else. Not that I'd mentioned any name, he said, but he could feel it, and he hoped I'd meet whoever it was again, because he respected me more than any other woman he had ever known, and if I wanted to go abroad he'd find something for me—and I wouldn't be under any obligation. He didn't know anything about you, unless my father babbled in his cups…

Oh well, I thought, all those fine speeches don't cost you a cent, Mijnheer Caspers. But he was a man of his word. A month later I got a letter from him, and he wrote that he had been to Amsterdam and "putting my personal dislike aside"—I remember exactly what he wrote—he had "arranged an appointment with Mevrouw de Rato, who had, surprisingly enough, refrained from obscenities, probably because the maid was listening at the door"—that didn't make sense, they'd speak French, because Caspers spoke French very well, much better than Wubbo—"Mevrouw de Rato stated.." Wait a minute, I'll get the letter. That's easier, you can read it yourself.'

254

'No, you tell me,' I said.

She jumped off the bed and skipped over to one of the cupboards, only half opening the door so I couldn't see what was inside. A crackle of paper, a box was snapped shut, the door of the cupboard locked, the key shoved into the pocket of her skirt, and she was back beside me, the letter in her hand, her lips shaped in an ironic smile. But there was a touch of reverence in the movements of her hands as she unfolded the letter.

'Here, look. "Mevrouw de Rato stated that she remembered that night very well and she swears by every saint in the calendar that you weren't subjected to anything more than a couple of kisses from Vellinga. In fact, she implied rather that Vellinga had succumbed in the back room to her Spanish-Brabant wiles, which I am inclined to doubt. But I was impressed by her insistence that she was telling the truth and by her apparently genuine indignation. She wasn't drunk and she hadn't been taking cocaine. On my return I called on Vellinga to ask him for an explanation. He said it was possible, that he had been drinking, that he didn't remember very much, he only knew that he'd been fooling about with a woman. I must excuse myself for quoting his own words. When I said that Mevrouw de Rato denied he had even touched her, and that that would have been physically impossible that evening (I took the liberty of juggling with the facts so as to confuse him), he began blustering. I called him a liar, and left. I would advise you not to trust him very far. Yours sincerely, Caspers." So Vellinga's story was just a pack of lies, a dirty trick he played on me.'

'Now I understand why he asked me not to discuss it with you. But didn't you ask him yourself, later?'

'Oh yes, when he came back grovelling. Then I told him what I thought of him. What was the use? He didn't deny anything, he didn't admit anything, he just didn't remember. It could be true.'

'Who were the two others?'

'I had nothing to do with Vellinga for months. But that was the worst year I've ever been through. I still don't know why I didn't put an end to it all then. Sometimes I simply couldn't get up in the morning and when I looked in the mirror I'd see an old hag, and I was only twenty-four... Do you know Sjoerd Stienstra?'

'Sjoerd Stienstra? Know him? No...'

Again that tense numbness swept over me, a rigid self-control, hideous flights of imagination, a flood of memories, judgments, facts and falsehoods, as if the world was thinking for me and depriving me of my right to decide and of my happiness too. This time she didn't notice the turmoil raging inside me. Amongst the upstart tradesmen in W... who had bought or pushed their way into more select social circles there were very few who were as objectionable as Sjoerd Stienstra. He was a sly haggler, he was young, good-looking, well-dressed, and he always had a lot to say for himself. He moved with an easy sleekness, but he was as bony as a farm-labourer. He was one of those specimens that should be destroyed in great numbers every year. With a heart like lead I wondered who the third would be.

'He was a low type,' Trix went on, 'but I didn't care then, the worse the better, and he used to bring me lots of things. I didn't earn much there. Even with the tips it wasn't so easy, because often they thought I didn't need the money or that I'd be offended, and the waiters used to take what had been left for me. Then I had to be better dressed than the other girls. I was supposed to be over them. They used to call me the showpiece of the restaurant, not the other girls, but some of the customers. You mustn't forget all these things, Nol, and try to understand that I can't marry you straight away. They'd just double up laughing...'

'It doesn't need to be straight away,' I said soothingly, and pressed her hand against my cheek to let her see and feel that not a drop of blood had drained from my face. 'Let's not talk any more now.'

She gave me a glance of timid gratitude. She had slid forward a little over the edge of the bed, and I sat stiffly, silently adjusting myself to this last new blow, weighing the jealousy I felt towards Sjoerd Stienstra, her lover, against the impossibility of jealousy towards the contemptible, shifty upstart that he was. But what did I know of the ways and the thoughts of slimy types like him? When it came to satisfying ambition or desire who wouldn't stoop to the lowest depths and use others unscrupulously, no matter what the consequences were for those others? This morning I had discovered another one of these slimy types, a hero of my childhood days, and he wasn't even impressively rotten, he'd excused himself to a student for improprieties which, by some standards, weren't really immoral...

Trix threw both her arms round me, playfully, sadly, indifferently, and I kissed her on the forehead long and earnestly.

'You still haven't answered my ... proposal.'

'Yes I have,' she mumbled. 'I told you I don't know.'

'Will you know in three years time?'

'No, not that long ... perhaps in a couple of days. You'll have to give me time to think it over... But listen, Nol, even if I don't accept, I'm yours, only yours, for as long as you want me to be...'

'That's not enough for me,' I smiled. 'Not because I want to have you beside me day and night or that I must live in the same house as you, but because I want to give this town a lesson in good manners. I'm no idealist but I think it's needed. The citizens of W... have to learn to have a little consideration for people like you and your father. They let your father teach their children the piano and they let him conduct their choirs and they chased him out of the Garden because of the *Tannhäuser* overture, and they shouted at him when he was drunk and they slandered him and stopped the lessons and took the choirs away from him and then they let him teach and conduct again. They spoilt the *Carmen* performance, they accepted him on sufferance and they patronized him and they called him 'that man'—that wasn't so silly, he was more of a man than the rest of them put together—and when

257

they'd broken him they raped his daughter and put her in a restaurant to serve beer, and when he had delirium tremens they didn't give him as many camphor injections as my mother, who was dying anyway, and when he died there were no wreaths or speeches for him. I was too young then to do anything, and it wouldn't have helped if I'd tried. But I think that something should be done. A little decency, a little respect for others and for the arts. I think I could teach them that. This is my chance.'

'So I'm not the reason why you want to get married?'

'I want to marry you for yourself, because I love you, but I want to marry you as soon as possible just to see their faces. Besides, what's the sense of a long engagement? You'd have to stay on at that restaurant and put up with that crowd there. If we were together in ...'

'So you don't trust me?'

'That's got nothing to do with it.'

Her voice was bitter, and I was tired. I should have had a drink, I was thinking. It was a mistake not to, I'm too tired to work things out. I'm rambling like an idiot, not like a lover. I hadn't once shown any tenderness for her ... I looked stealthily at my watch. Twenty-five to twelve. I stood up and walked over to where my coat and hat were hanging. As I put on my coat she followed all my movements. Her face was greyishly pale again, with dark blotches under the eyes. But the eyes were calm and confident, and there seemed to be a hint of the old smile in the crinkles at the corners.

'You aren't angry, Nol?'

'I'm never angry,' I said, after hesitating for a few seconds, while I looked at my hat that I had just lifted off the hook. 'I'll come and see you tomorrow morning at ten. Take a day off. You can easily give them some excuse or other. Then we can talk it over again. I'll be able to tell my father before I come, and Chris too, yes, I'll have to tell Chris. We won't rake up the past any more. It doesn't matter if our local editor dabbled with sleeping-powders. I'd like to have the announcement of our wedding in his paper. He'd have the cheek to send us a congratulatory telegram, or a present ...' I was going to add: 'a cheque, maybe', when I suddenly realized that I was not only saying things that would hurt her, but I was working myself into a rage again to the point of regretting that I hadn't battered his head against one of the corners of his neat and tidy desk... When I walked across to her to say a tender good night she came towards me and whispered with her arms round my neck:

'I'll do anything to make you happy, Nol, my darling. But it's so unexpected. I'll have to think, and that's difficult for me... I want to ask you something.' Her hands twined and twisted behind my neck. Her forehead was cool against my lips. I felt her feet scrape against my shoes. '... Could you stay here tonight? You can sleep in my bed and I'll sleep on two chairs. There isn't another room empty, not even the attic.'

I kissed her hair. 'On two chairs. Don't be silly, Trix. You don't know me. But I'm not going to ... Let's wait first. I mean it's a sort of weapon.... But first you must promise me ...'

'Why? What do you mean, a weapon?'

I was carried away again by my jealousy, but I didn't know it. I thought it was just that I was annoyed by her uncertainty, her tentative refusal, which, if I chose to be reasonable, I could interpret as a tentative acceptance ... and angry, too, because I couldn't yield to the temptation to make love to her before I had married her.

'I don't want to spend one night with you, and then be kept dangling on a string.'

'That's not fair,' she said abruptly. She loosened her arms and turned away, then faced me again, her eyes downcast. Her fingers traced aimless circles on my tie, on my overcoat. 'I'd tuck you in like a mother and pretend you were sick. I'm frightened to be alone, that's what it is. The worst time is the morning, when I wake up and you aren't here and everything I've told you comes

259

back to me... It's not now, it's the morning I'm frightened of. If you could come back at six that would be all right too. I'm not frightened of anything or anybody, but in the morning I'm a coward. It's better, too, if you see what I'm like in the morning. Maybe you won't want to marry me then...'

'If you rest for a day or so and have a good sleep at night you'll look the same as you did five years ago...' You fool, I said to myself angrily, why did I have to hurt her, talking like an idiot obsessed with time? But now I understood why she wanted me to stay and I considered the possibilities.

'Of course I'd do it for you if I could ... But my father and my brother would think it rather odd if I stayed away a whole night, especially after getting drunk yesterday. Maybe I could telephone ... but I'd have to give some explanation ... and if I went and saw my father first—and he's probably in bed by now—if I talked to him it would only be a quarrel. I can't say that I have to sit at a sick friend's bedside, he knows I have hardly any friends here in W... Last night I didn't look at my mother when I left and now all of a sudden a sick friend ...'

'You don't need to stay,' she said, her fingers still on my tie.

'And besides, if I stay here tonight the whole town will know it tomorrow, what with all the lodgers here. I don't want to start off like that.... It's not the staying I mean, but I want to show them ...'

My recollection of what happened after I had expounded this irreproachable standpoint is vague. We kissed each other. I cheered her up as best I could. She was docile and she looked sick. I remember thinking: No, not in this house, with those lodgers and the aunt with the long nose, and the memories of Cuperus and *Carmen*, and in the morning the milkman or the baker, and the lodgers again, waking up and shouting for shaving water, and one of them going out of the door at the same time as I would be leaving.... She sat on the bed, then I was kneeling in front of her, my head on her lap, dead tired.

'Another thing,' I mumbled, and I loosened her shoes, and I put her feet into the new, red slippers I had taken from under the bed. I thought I heard her sobbing. I was going to kiss the slippers, but she pulled me to my feet and led me to the door and quickly opened it. I didn't look round at her, I was sure she didn't want me to.

'Go home now, but try not to make any noise,' she whispered, 'When you've gone I'll lock the front door. Till tomorrow at ten.'

'Or earlier, nine o'clock, eight o'clock ...'

'No, no ...' She pushed me gently but firmly into the passage where the light was still on. Halfway to the landing I turned round, but she had already shut the door.

As I tiptoed down the stairs, a shadow moved in the hallway and I was looking into the aunt's pale face. She must have been standing in the kitchen on the mark like a runner to have got there so quickly.

'I'm off home now,' I said briskly. 'It's late.'

With an insistent 'No!, just a minute', she called me back from the point between her and the front door that I had managed to reach. We stood facing each other in the half darkness. She fixed her ghostly eyes on me.

'Trix never tells me anything these days,' she said, fairly loud, though there was the pious boarder in Cuperus's room where everything was quiet now, 'and I've always done everything I could for her, and I always gave her good advice. She ought to get married. There's no future for her working in that restaurant, at everyone's beck and call, and serving those coarse farmers. And in the morning she's always tired, she never has a good sleep. Sometimes I have to wake her up with a wet sponge, maybe that's why she has a grudge against me.'

'Oh, come now,' I said, 'surely that's exaggerating.... But I really have to go.'

'Yes, your mother's dead, that's dreadful. But Trix ... You get on well together, I'm sure ...'

'Yes, we do. Good night...' I started walking towards the door again.

'She has a heart of gold, and I taught her how to work,' she said, persistently following me, 'I'm not saying that to put ideas into your head. That never does any good. We just have to leave these decisions to a Higher Power, the Spirit who controls our destiny...'

At last, the porch. The hand on my arm was withdrawn only at the very last moment. She carefully shut the door behind me. The key turned twice in the lock.

18

My father was still up and I seized the opportunity to acquaint him, over a glass of wine, with my aspirations, without mentioning the name of the girl in question but intimating a difference in social standing. I could now explain my unusual behaviour during the last twenty-four hours. There were certain difficulties, I confided, or rather, the girl was placed in a difficult situation, and the worry on that account had momentarily overshadowed the grief I felt at my mother's death. This confession would also permit me to be away for most of the next day, the day before the funeral. Patiently he listened to me. I'm not sure if he understood all that I said, and later it occurred to me that he hadn't made any promise or committed himself in any way. And I hadn't even suggested the possibility of my marrying in the near future. In due time I would have to tell him about Vellinga, and probably about the others as well, at least tell him more than he knew already, for he would certainly have heard something of the local gossip. The sleeping-powder hypothesis might interest him as a lawyer, but that theory wouldn't hold good for Caspers and the other two. On the way up to my room, next to where Chris lay peacefully and loudly snoring, I speculated cynically on whether my father mightn't recommend a sleeping-powder for the bridal night.

But within five minutes I had shaken off this mood of juridical buffoonery, and for an hour or more I lay in a state of almost perfect happiness thinking of Trix. It was as good as settled. The crucial discussion was over, and tomorrow we would be happy, as happy as it was possible for us to be. A fulfilment rarely achieved. I was certain she would not refuse to marry me, unless she wanted to test me. Of course, I had made mistakes, but what were these to a woman who could be understanding and considerate and had been through the mill herself? But for the sickening prejudices imposed by a snobbish respectability, that I was apparently afflicted with too, I could have even cherished the memory of my predecessors for having treated her to experiences which don't come the way of most women but which are inseparable from life's realities. She had suffered dreadfully. With me she would feel reborn. But it was stupid to speak of predecessors, there were no predecessors in the love she had for me. Then again, in some countries, China, I think, girls who had been prostitutes made the best wives, not so much because of the money they had earned or the fine manners they had acquired—not that Trix had acquired any fine manners, though the interlude with Caspers might have fitted in with this ethnological fantasy of mine—but because they clung to the chance of loving just one man after years of enforced and loveless variety. And Trix wasn't a prostitute, or hardly.

I felt so contented that I could smile at such thoughts. I was young, I had got over my tiredness, I saw the world framed in a rosy glow. All the more because I was going to teach the world a lesson in a few weeks or a few months. No one would understand my pride in having finally won 'that girl'. Chris would argue with me for hours, happy as a lark at being obviously now the more reasonable of the two of us, and I would refer him to the whorehouses where his mind would always remain. Delegations of worthy citizens, sanctimonious hypocrites, would endeavour to persuade Judge Rieske not to extend misplaced financial support. Should he give way to these counsels, then I could give private lessons in anatomy or physiology to earn enough to live on, and there were plenty of aunts and distant female cousins who were crazy about me, or had been, I only had to use my rosy cheeks. What had Trix and I talked about in those two hours? The conversation hadn't been confused, but I could recollect no more than odd fragments. I visualized her face, now ugly, now beautiful, I felt her pressed against me, now desperate, now passionate. Maybe she could take singing lessons again, after a time....

I slept for perhaps a quarter of an hour and woke imagining that I was holding her in my arms. I took this for the beginning of another happy reverie, but soon I was in the throes of physical desire which I suppressed because it could only lead to regret that I hadn't stayed with her. But I couldn't suppress the regret, it swelled to a fear, to a sense of failure and futility. At first it was a feeling, then it formed into thoughts. What if Sjoerd Stienstra came to the Registry Office, not to taunt us but just because he thought he should be there? I would have to shake hands with him, and Trix, in her white bridal dress, would have to look at him over her bouquet. An unknown religious maniac would rush in howling: 'She shouldn't be wearing that white dress, she's a ... oh, what's the word again ... oh, yes... whore.... Thank you, I'd forgotten.' Suddenly I remembered that inspired foreboding of a couple of hours before when my head had rested on hers. *I would know the deepest unhappiness.* Unhappiness? Why should I be unhappy, and how, and who would make me unhappy? She had admitted to me that her character made her unsuitable for marriage. Perhaps that was true. Then it would be a hopeless marriage, but how could a marriage be hopeless if we were in love with each other? We would quarrel and fight and love each other. I assumed that she wouldn't be unfaithful, but she would remain the barmaid she had always been, domineering, common, adorable. She would cause trouble and get me mixed up in it. Every year there would be another child, a small tribe that she would rule with kicks and blows, and then we would grow slowly old, and we would love each other, I would start drinking a little too much because she kept me under her thumb and chased the patients away and made a fool of me, and she was a long, hunched-up spectre of ugliness, with inflamed eyes full of hate, and I'd study old photographs of her and I'd wait on her hand and foot, and when everything went wrong I'd think of the golden, brass Garden, and the silver would come a little later, when we were getting near to dying and leaving behind us a flock of impossible offspring, one or two of them blessed with the divine spark of Cuperus's genius. But she'd be the first to go, of course, yes, she'd go first, so that I, a doddering old ex-doctor, long since retired after disposing of his practice for a tidy sum, could deliver the graveside speech, recalling in passing the memory of her father, who might never be spoken of in her presence, the father of a woman there had never been the like of in all the world and never would be, with those eyes of hers, that majestic tallness, that voice, that character, that hard aloofness. Those eyes, I would say, were cold and watery when they were pictured in words, but seen, they were bewitching, and the magic of those eyes wasn't a fantasy of mine or a senile illusion, for others too had succumbed, four of them, all dead now and lying in their graves still longing for her.

I slept for half an hour and woke sobbing, trembling and exhausted. It was ten past three. In seven hours I'd be with her again. My stomach was sleeping like an old faithful watchdog, but there was a pounding in my chest and so violent that my bed was shaking. Perhaps I'd had a nightmare. I was frightened, I tried to find the reason so that I could grapple with the menace that threatened me. It wasn't so hard to find. There could be only one, a single enemy that was a many-headed monster. But the difficulty was that most of this monster's many heads would refuse to proclaim or admit their enmity. I would know them for what they were, but I couldn't fight them. How naïve I had been to think I could 'teach this town a lesson'. It would be fighting an underwater jungle that offered no resistance, that let the intruder through and at the very last moment unleashed against me a gigantic spider, at my back, at my loins. I couldn't walk through the town glaring defiantly, Trix on my arm—too melodramatic —or drunk like Cuperus. I would have to be prepared for the sneering, unrecognizing stares, the exchange of glances behind my back and the shaking of heads that might, unexpectedly, years later even, be transformed into open malevolence, slander, unpardonable affronts, social or professional boycott, without any deliberate intention of malevolence, or simply as the actions of model citizens desirous of remaining unimpeachable members of the community, motivated perhaps only by a chance bout of ill-humour bearing no relation to the issue or to Trix or myself personally. Women were particularly sensitive to these monsters, imagining them as a pursuing plague of harmless but tireless spiders and mice, creatures they were also afraid of. Honour and good name suddenly taken away and dishonour made a public spectacle. Oh, what a joy for whoever could contrive this.

And then she'd take it out on me, and with reason. After all, why hadn't I saved her when I was eighteen instead of waiting till I was twenty-two? And I would feel that the spiders were waiting to pounce on me too. I knew my fellow-men, I could read their thoughts, I felt them inside my heart, my stomach was attuned to their stomachs, and when their bile flowed over so did mine. This situation was all the more diabolical because I could always get on well with people, individually and in groups. Everyone thought I was pleasant, well-mannered, friendly, good-looking, and rosy-cheeked. Each of them individually would disarm me to make it easier for them all to attack me together and destroy me. They weren't spiders, they were ants. Watch one of them running over your hand. A tiny little thing, but don't go and spend a night on an antheap. That's what they were like. A theatre full of them jeering at Cuperus as he faced them weeping with rage, the lot of them against him, though no one except an infantile painter and decorator had any reason to be. A gang of schoolboys against Trix, all so brave until she kicked them. A troop of yelling seven-year-olds against a little 'rotten Nol' up on a balcony. And was I any different from the others?

Hadn't I, as a small boy, developed my fighting skill at the expense of weaker schoolmates? But no personal animosity, gentlemen, that would never do. Always be polite to each other, The farce of make-believe and pretence, the open-hearted greeting. smiles and flattery, the gold-rimmed pince-nez removed when the eyes moistened, the honest glance into honest blue eyes, goodness and uprightness in the repulsive eyes, a friendly chat over a drink to cook up some scheme against some or other easy victim.

And the university—none of that personal animosity there either.

The university, the students, the professors ... that was something I'd overlooked. The news that I'd got married at the age of twenty-two would, of course, modify the image of Nol Rieske projected into those minds which were merged to become one single super-mind. A normal, quiet, healthy, rosy-cheeked, rather retiring but certainly not uninteresting young man couldn't go and marry a waitress, or worse, without being obliged to compensate his fellow students in some way for the slight change in the image they were familiar with. He was required to display, in greater measure than formerly, originality, picturesqueness, imperturbability, masculine maturity, imperviousness to practical jokes, generosity, high-spiritedness, eccentricity, and he was expected to parade the waitress in public, to give reasons and refute innuendoes. I would be talked about, and the new light in which I appeared would attract the attention of the professors, who, although—especially from the fourth year onward—less given to formalities than lawyers were, would still want to know what this married student was up to. We would have to live in a university town that was in many respects nothing more than a village. A married student could choose between two alternatives. He could do better at his exams than the average unmarried student (because he had to think of the upkeep of his new acquisition, and perhaps he even had children already, so he would want to finish his studies as quickly as possible), or he could be less successful due to the distracting influence of his wife, and to being disturbed by his wife's family—not always all that could be desired—by other students, and by sarcastic remarks, that no professor is above indulging in, in the course of lectures. I knew of such cases. One medical student who wrote poems and had had some published, and later achieved a certain literary fame, was baited by the professors right till the end of his last year. Of course, I could work harder than I had been doing. But I couldn't escape an undue

268

interest on the part of the examiners, an irritated inquisitiveness expressed in strictness and unreasonableness.

'You'll have to come back and try again in three months time, Mijnheer Rieske.' (that, when I'd coaxed my father into giving his permission and help by promising to sail through) 'You shouldn't have any difficulty, you know the gist of it, only you need to brush up on the theory... and I haven't seen you at lectures very often' (a lie, of course) ...' perhaps you have other things on your mind?' 'What do you mean, professor?' 'Well... (a smile behind the beard covered with the hand) well... your circumstances... or should I say... your social position ...' 'You mean my being married, professor?' 'Yes, yes, precisely.... May I ask you a question, Mijnheer Rieske? (so confidential, paternal, a drop or two of spittle on my tie) Did you by any chance have to get married?' 'Yes and no, professor, but what do you mean exactly?' 'Hm... (amused, but discreet, sniffing the scent of true-life drama) Is it true that your wife worked in a restaurant, Mijnheer Rieske?' 'Yes, professor.' 'Hmm, hmm ... I have personally no objection, Mijnheer Rieske, but perhaps ... it's perhaps possible that you might find it difficult to study in the atmosphere a waitress is used to ... noise... all that clatter and banging...'

I leapt out of bed. Somehow or other I'd have to stop this. I was just raving, as if professors were sadists and my *alma mater* a madhouse. Conversations like that simply didn't happen. Even so, while I half-dressed myself and looked for a text-book in my suitcase, I was wondering whether I could put off getting married until my final exams, or at least until I was through some of them. What would happen? It would be disastrous. I knew I wouldn't have a moment's peace, that I would want to be with her all the time. I wouldn't be able to study. No matter where she lived, no matter what she was doing, I couldn't bear to let her out of my sight for an hour, not even for a minute. I could trust her, I trusted her completely, but there was no cure for jealousy. And I was jealous. I'd been jealous of Chris when I was still too young to walk. I'd plumb the depths of unhappiness. Maybe I'd take to drink. Alcoholics are always jealous, it's a symptom of their weakness...

After half an hour, spent reading a chapter on cholera, a disease I would never have to treat, I felt tired. I switched off the light and slept till a quarter past nine. I was so dazed when I woke that I couldn't remember immediately where I had to be at ten o'clock. After plunging my head in the wash-basin I began to function, grateful for those four or five hours' sleep. I didn't need to worry myself over morbid thoughts. I wasn't able to think at all, and only my arms and legs followed the rhythm of the passing seconds and minutes and hours, for time has a rhythm of its own, even though our philosophers choose to think otherwise. I was curious to see what Trix would look like in the morning. As I sat alone at the breakfast table, trying unsuccessfully to swallow a slice of toast, my love for her grew more and more intense, and so did my fear that she might yet escape me. That was the sort of thing she would do. Make an appointment and not be there. Hide herself in the restaurant and leave a note for me. I spat out my last mouthful of bread and hurried out. I didn't see Chris anywhere. My father had had to go to the court on some urgent case.

The clear blue sky that morning, and the sun climbing carefully over the scurrying mist, that left a layer of dampness on the ground, seemed to promise the finest October day of the whole century. The fresh, effervescent air quenched any thirst for gin. I wouldn't have had time anyway. Striding along the quiet street I decided not to drink any more. This wasn't an extravagant decision, for during the last two years I had hardly touched any liquor and I hadn't felt any urge to drink. As I was drawing near to Cuperus's street (it was still Cuperus's street to me), I began to realize the absurdity of my fears of the night before at what I might have to endure at the university. I had never been troubled by the occasional taunts my moderation evoked in a university where moderation was not appreciated, and the absence of any reaction on my part had ensured that I was soon left in peace. We weren't living in the Middle Ages. But who knew how many medieval students had married in the course of their studies? Getting married was just as natural as eating and drinking, ever since time began, everywhere, and even idiots married if they got the chance....

As I rang, with the prospect before me of the most wonderful day of my life, I was wondering whether Trix's aunt mightn't want to get married. She gave the impression she would. And now, how strange the workings of fate, she would be my aunt too. Walking along I had been silently humming a melody from the third act of *Carmen*, the charming *terzetto*, 'Mische, Mische', sung by Carmen, Frasquita, and Mercedes. It didn't quite match my mood. My feelings as I stood on the porch would have been more truly echoed by the second intermezzo, which I had last heard at this same spot. It was a lively, frivolous tune that came into my head by chance, and at the same time it was a memory, less frivolous, tinged with sadness. The melody lingered with me all that day.

The aunt opened the door. Her appearance, her build reminded me more than ever of Trix, but a very slovenly Trix this time, for the white apron was dirty and marked here and there with pale green stains. When I asked for Trix I avoided looking her in the face. Her tone as she said: 'Yes, Nol, come in', was so odd that I glanced at her, puzzled. Her eyes were screwed up, with the inevitable effect this had on her cheeks. I hadn't noticed before that this grimace caused the sagging flesh of her cheeks to quiver. I turned my eyes away, I didn't want to waste time.

'She's up, isn't she?' I stepped inside and started taking off my coat.

At that moment the door of Cuperus's room opened. A young man in a threadbare raincoat emerged and immediately shut the door after him. He blinked inquiringly at the aunt. Giving a quick nod in my direction, she put her finger to her lips. He stared, grunted 'Morning', and went out. The aunt took me by the arm and led me further along the hallway, away from the coat-rack. At the bottom of the stairs I asked:

'Isn't Trix in? Tell me, quickly.'

'Come and sit down in the kitchen first, I'll explain everything to you,' she said in a clear and affected voice while she gave a piercing look upstairs. There was a sound of hammering from one of the rooms on the first floor. Another one of those bachelors, I said to myself as I followed her, with growing anxiety, to the kitchen at the end of the hallway. Trix has run off after Vellinga, I was thinking. I should have stayed with her, we should have tied our feet together, like convicts....

It was cold and lifeless in the kitchen. There was very little light from outside, as the glass of the back door was almost completely pasted over with red-and-green patterned paper. The table was covered with a dark-blue cloth. The dresser was untidy. And not a pot of tea or coffee ready, no stove burning, nothing simmering or boiling. Hardly realizing what I was doing I sat down on one of the chairs at the table. The aunt came and stood next to me. She threw an arm round my neck and kissed me on the forehead. I felt a solid breast on my shoulder. I shook myself loose.

'What's wrong with Trix?'

Holding one of the pleats of her apron she walked round to the other side of the table and stood staring at the door, her eyes wide open and filling with tears. Despite her plumpness there were deep grooves in the flesh at the back of her neck.

'What's wrong with Trix?' I repeated and stood up. 'Say it then, she's gone, hasn't she?'

Then we were sitting at the table facing each other. The aunt kept her brimming eyes turned upwards, imploringly, as if she was praying.

'Trix is very sick, Nol.'

I nodded. That was one way of putting it. My right hand started shaking. I ignored it. What was a right hand anyway? The aunt looked at the back door again.

'She went out at half past one this morning. I heard her, at least I heard the door close, I was in bed by then. I thought to myself if I run after her I'll only be putting my foot in it again, she's just going for a walk after that long, long talk with Nol. I went to sleep, and much later I heard her come in. I don't know what time it was, but the doctor said . . .'

'The doctor? What has the doctor got to do with it?'

I was sure that Trix had gone to spend the rest of the night with a man because she was frightened of waking up alone in the morning.

'The doctor said she must have been back at least two hours before I went to wake her at half past seven. That was later than usual. I went into her room and she was lying there, Nol, very sick. . . .'

My right hand started shaking again. The back of my throat was burning. There was a tightness in my chest—that was something new, perhaps I had pre-exam sickness, every day something different. I didn't feel my heart beating. When I looked at her, her expression was pleading and cowed. The bulging eyes were full of glistening deceit. She was half way through her scheme to destroy me. The small nose sniffled.

'She's dead,' I said, but I didn't believe it.

Slowly, hopelessly, she shook her head. 'I can't remember everything, but I fetched the doctor at once. That I'll swear to you by the Lord above, and he came straight away, he was here before eight. If I could have called him half an hour sooner, he said, maybe . . .'

'You don't mean . . . you don't mean she's really dead? . . . She can't be! By Jesus, no! No, that's not possible! . . .' My voice was shrill and hysterical like a woman's, outside my consciousness, the same as that right hand. I knew I had to stop this wailing, it would become something apart from me and leave me behind, limp and useless, without the will or the strength to reject, to confute, to drive away the spectre of death. I glanced at the back door. Sun-

273

light slanted across a high red roof, and on another roof there was a strip of blue shadow.

'It was poison,' the aunt said faintly.

I was thinking quickly. If the sun was shining outside there must still be some hope here within these walls. The human body was resilient, capable of endless resistance, that's what I'd been taught. Poison. Maybe the aunt had poisoned her. I could go to another doctor, but I'd have to be careful, not arouse any suspicion....

'What sort of poison?'

'Arsenic, the doctor said. A half-hour sooner and they might have saved her. They have good antidotes, I remember that from when I worked in the hospital …. She must have suffered dread-fully, but no one heard a sound. The lodgers don't pay any attention to noises, they're all young, and they sleep like logs.'

Trix had poisoned herself. I realized that. Not so much as a fact, but rather as a reasonable course of action that could be explained and envisaged within the range of probability. But that didn't mean to say she was dead.... I couldn't think any further, and deep inside myself I heard that hysterical wail trying to force its abject shrillness up into my throat, and then a voice within me was saying: 'She's dead, it doesn't matter who killed her, she's dead!' I didn't believe it, but the voice spoke with calm assurance, and that voice brought with it the indifference of the world outside where so many believed it already, and soon there would be many more.

'She was cold when the doctor came,' the aunt went on in a more lively tone. 'Such a shock it gave him, he could hardly stand up—and so young, he kept saying, she was so young, and I didn't have any coffee to offer him, not a thing. And she'll have to be buried tomorrow, he said. Oh God, why did she do it? You two were in love with each other, weren't you, Nol? For years, I know that … and she never looked at another man.'

As if I had been waiting for a signal I jerked my head up and stared at her, motionless, expressionless. She squeezed her eyes

274

shut and the tears rolled down her cheeks. When she opened her eyes all she saw was my stare. 'What's wrong?'

'Nothing,' I said and kept staring at her.

'Oh, you mean ... That was nothing, Nol, really....'

'Of course, that was nothing,' I repeated, and released her from her ordeal by bowing my head.

'At heart she was very respectable. I'm the same, it's a family trait.'

'Yes, that can happen,' I murmured.

'But to make such a nice, good, young lad suffer ... Oh God, I can't understand it.... No, Trixie, that was very wrong of you,' she said in the manner of a prim schoolmistress, 'and to think how often I've prayed, no, that's not the word.... I mean I've tried to commune with the Spirit, to help you to find happiness. We didn't get on, but we were fond of each other.'

'Why would she do it?' I asked. Maybe the aunt had really poisoned her, and I might be able to make her admit it.

'I don't know ... but ...' Then she pulled a crumpled letter out of her blouse. 'A note she left. It was on the table in her room... You don't have to show it to me if you'd rather not.'

She turned and walked away to stand with her back to me by the door that opened on to a small courtyard. Pigeons belonging to one of the neighbours used to strut around there sometimes, I remembered Cuperus telling me once, very dirty pigeons, really dirty, but not altogether unworthy of Lohengrin and Parsifal.... My legs were cold and numb. I couldn't sit up straight, I was slumped in the chair as if paralysed, and every now and then my heart fluttered—my mother's heart, I thought vaguely, Cuperus's heart. I read the letter.

'Dearest Nol, When you read this I won't be here any more. Life has become unbearable for me. Not all the time, but at odd moments, and then it's worse than hell. You know why. Perhaps I shouldn't have told you everything last night. I know you'll be sad, just as much as I am now, because this love of ours

275

is something I can't think about without feeling so helpless and so small. But I would never be able to make you happy, Nol. Not that I wouldn't do everything for you, but because you (this word was underlined twice) are jealous and always will be, and that's only natural. Probably I wouldn't love you if you weren't. I noticed it last night, though you tried to hide it because you are so kind and always thinking of others. But it would be a torment for you, and you would feel that I was thinking about all that too. That would never work out. But I can't live without either. Forgive me, Nol, my darling, and try to forget me, or, if you can't, then try to see me as I am—half good, half bad. I don't want to hurt you, Nol, again in this last letter, but I must tell you who the third one was. Perhaps that will make it easier for you to forget me, but you don't need to start despising me straight away, even though this was my fault, and the other times too, one thing led to another, and then I didn't care what happened to me. I thought you had forgotten me. It was Dijkhuizen, you remember, we met him on the ice-rink that day. I won't write any more about it. I have too much pride, that's my biggest fault. I tramped round for hours before I decided to do this. I got the poison a long while ago from a chemist I knew, but there was nothing between us. If there's a hell I'll go there, but you won't. But I'll always think of you, I don't suppose they could stop me doing that. Don't come to my funeral, Nol, my darling, I'd rather you didn't. I'm not frightened of the pain, so don't worry. My last thoughts will be of you. Good-bye, Trix.'

Why did that hammering upstairs keep on and on? With the letter in my hand I looked at the low ceiling, annoyed, impatient. Could I hear pigeons somewhere? Pigeons. The word even was enough to put me in a rage. The sun was rising higher, a fine time the sun was having today, like a happy imbecile.... The aunt, her eyes red from crying, stood next to me. I had put the letter in my coat-pocket. I looked up at the ceiling again, creasing my forehead, and then at her for an explanation.

276

'That's one of the gentlemen; he's always doing odd jobs. He doesn't have to go to work today. I'll have to ask him to stop it. They're a bit frightened of me... Do you want a drink, Nol? You look like a ghost.'

'Yes, pour me a drop. Gin if you have it. I'd better have a drink or I won't be able to go out in that sun. I don't know what I'll do now.... I can't very well finish myself off too...'

She gave me a worried glance, then she produced a bottle of gin from behind a pile of coffee tins and we both drank a cupful, sitting at the table opposite each other. When I asked her for a second cup she shook her head and pursed her lips. After a minute or so she said: 'Do you want to see her, Nol?'

'No. But I'd like a photo of her.' I knew a little about the effects of arsenic poisoning. My thoughts began to wander aimlessly. The worst of my grief was over, for the time being. Now it was in my stomach where the warm, comforting gin drowned it. 'Did he try a stomach pump? Of course, he wouldn't think of that. He let her father die too...'

'She was dead when he came,' the aunt said reprovingly. 'That wouldn't have helped. The doctor knew what it was as soon as he saw her. Arsenic, he said, probably rat poison, and he said she must have taken enough to kill a horse—that gave me a turn too, him saying that, because I think animals have a soul just like people. Don't you? Yes, I thought you would—otherwise she wouldn't have been out of her misery so quickly... it can last for days sometimes....'

'Suicide is always wrong,' I said, relaxing a little and putting my elbow on the table, 'I'm studying medicine, and it's better not to think about those things. But Trix was desperate...'

'Really?'

She was just aching to read that letter. I'd caught her out now, I'd toy with her and ferret out some admission of guilt. Then, with my eyes boring into hers, I continued:

'The protoplasm must be kept alive as long as possible. It's a precious substance, it's the result of a long process of biological development, or geological or climatological development or something, and we're working day and night so the protoplasm... But Trix was desperate. I was too, but not so much and I didn't notice it. With me it began when we couldn't dance any more to the music her father used to conduct—he was my teacher, you know. So it could have turned out worse than it did. But how could you understand? You don't understand anything about love.'

'Don't I?' she said, and she was getting redder and redder in the face. 'People who talk a lot should know what they're talking about.'

'I didn't really mean it,' I said, waving my hand airily.

'I've lived and loved and many things will be forgiven me,' she said, straightening and smoothing the top of her apron. Then, pointing to the wall, to a small photograph of a man with a big moustache and a peaked forehead and wearing a high stiff collar, a man well past middle age, 'He left me all his money, he was a building contractor. But love? No, no. Loyalty and kindness, that's all.'

'Thank God I had that gin,' I said, 'I'll probably go on drinking all day... Can't you guess why she did it?'

'No. Why?' the aunt asked eagerly, and she went even redder when she realized how she was giving herself away.

'Because of those admirers of hers,' I said brutally, 'and you know about them as well as I do, though I don't believe you arranged things with all four of them, only with Vellinga. You must have enjoyed that, eh? So romantic, and he was so rich too, and you could watch it all from close by. But I'm a bit to blame, too, because I was jealous and I showed how jealous I was... We're both to blame, you talked her into it and I talked her out of it, and then she was dead. But what's your name?'

'Lutske,' the aunt said, having answered my accusations with a resigned shake of her head, 'but you can call me Lottie. That's what Mijnheer always called me.'

'Well, Lottie, I'll tell you something. Those three fine gentlemen, you know them, I'm going to cut their throats today.'

'Now, Nol, you get those ideas right out of your head,' she said sternly.

I pulled a face at her, her eyes were so foolishly big, and then that domineering swaying of her head. If she kept her head still that was a sign of grief. But she meant well, she was as tall as Trix, and she was like Trix with that domineering way of hers, or Trix was like her, but she didn't have that same proud independence that Trix had written about in her letter with the last breath of her love—as if suicide was the penalty for pride.

'Nol will think twice before he goes that far,' I said. 'Nol's to blame too. I should have stayed with her, by Christ. She asked me to stay with her because she was frightened of the morning. She asked me to do that, and you start thinking filth—it isn't really filth, but let's just say filth—that's what you're thinking, but she only asked me to stay with her for an hour, and I left her, I went back to the lawyers, to the scribes and pharisees... I shouldn't have let her out of my sight for a single second. I committed the greatest crime of my life, only for the good name of your boarding-house... Aren't you pleased?' I bent forward accusingly. 'I'll have that to reproach myself with for the rest of my days, and it was all for your sake. But then I'll say to myself: It's only Lottie, she can't help it... I can never be angry with a woman for very long, you see.'

'I'm glad to hear that,' the aunt said, red as a beetroot. 'I'm used to being misunderstood. But I can put up with a lot from you....'

'Where are the photos?'

She stood up with difficulty, she had to hold on to the back of the chair. 'In a cupboard in her room... The cellar-door key fits the lock ... I've got it here... I'm not afraid, I've never been afraid of corpses... I'll go and get them...'

'No, no,' I shouted, really concerned. 'My God, I've lost the

279

three of them, Cuperus, my mother, and Trix, and I don't want you upsetting yourself too, Lottie. No, you mustn't...'

Her eyes rolling, and that nose snivelling again, she looked aggressively at the door, swaying on her feet and trying to tilt her head defiantly. 'I'm not afraid.'

'You're not going!'

Suddenly it seemed as if the demon of arsenic poisoning had risen up between us in all its chemical and physiological grandeur. The two of us alone wouldn't have the strength to subdue it, and raging fiends would run amok in this kitchen, green fiends and grey fiends and the yellow mist of the arsenic fumes. I jumped up and rushed at her.

'You're not going! If I say you're not going, then you're not going!' I grabbed her arm and the firmness of her flesh somehow reassured me. She resisted and still tried to get to the door, furious, but in a way like a mischievous child. When I looked into her eyes, she reeled back and sank heavily onto the chair, sighing: 'Very well. Perhaps if you come some other time.'

Reeling as much as she had, I staggered to my chair. After a while I said:

'The trouble with the photos is that maybe they're not just of her. I'm keeping myself under control, Lottie, don't worry, and you don't need to walk down the street with me, but there's a limit you know.'

'I'll get a photo of her for you. I'll give you all the photos of her by herself.'

'Afterwards I'll be able to stand seeing the other photos. I'm not afraid either.'

'But you'll have to come and fetch those photos. I'm sure we could get along well together, Nol, and you said I didn't understand anything about love, but I can tell you,' she went on prophetically, with energetic jerks of her head, 'that my mother-love for you is just as deep as Trix's love for you, and that was real love. You mustn't give up hope, Nol, never. I know more than you, my dear. Trix is being well looked after where she is now. She's thinking of you and you'll meet again.'

'Yes,' I stammered, and the tears came into my eyes.

'I know that because the Spirit reveals these things to me and to everyone who's willing to listen. I've got books about it, I'll lend them to you when you come again. The Spirit is the only truth, the only reality, our life here is just an illusion, all lies and deceit. Trix isn't really dead.'

'No, of course not,' I said, and I stood up to walk round the table to her. 'She's still living in my thoughts. I'll come and see you again. You've been damned nice to me, Lottie, or Lutske, whichever you prefer, and this house and everything in it and everything that's been in it...'

'That's not according to Christianity. It's a new doctrine...'

When she saw that I was standing in front of her ready to say goodbye, she threw her arms around me and clutched me tight. Sobbing, both of us, kissing each other, repeating each other's name, we stood for minutes pressed against each other. I sank into a sort of coma, into a darkness where the very essence of my being was soothed and aroused and wafted away and caressed and calmed. The more I cried the happier I was. I stroked her hair and I touched her face, her eyes, her nose, feeling that she was alive, that she lived and breathed and saw. I don't know how I came to be standing by the hall door.

The hammering must have stopped long before that. But there was someone coming down the stairs in heavy shoes. One of the bachelors. An ordinary, uncouth lodger who didn't know he had been sleeping next to the room of a saint. We stood by the door listening, I was boiling with anger, the aunt was breathing heavily and smoothing her apron. When I opened the door and flashed a malicious, triumphant glance at her she put her finger to her lips, a sign that she couldn't come into the hall to see me out.

19

I walked quickly down the hall and flung open the front door that had swung shut only a moment before. My head was buzzing but the buzzing didn't intrude in the least on the gay music from the third act of *Carmen*. Even in the kitchen it must have still been running through my head. As I stepped into the street I saw the bachelor walking in the direction of the arched bridge. He was strolling along, probably whistling, like an office clerk on Sunday, with padded shoulders, tight trousers, an awkward, slightly waddling gait, his hands in his pockets indecently scratching, and displaying other characteristics, some of which I might have imagined. He was wearing a rather small dark-grey hat, no overcoat. Soon he took off his hat, it was such a magnificent summer's day in October, so dazzling, so sadly beautiful. The bachelor's hair was wet and shiny, combed flat over his skull. It was an inconsequential head, offering little scope for a phrenologist. Suddenly I thought I saw Chris on the other side of the street, riding a bicycle. The thought, rather than what I saw—the man was nothing like Chris—was so irresistibly funny that my face swelled up from my efforts to suppress my laughter. Carmen and Frasquita and Mercedes singing: '*Mische! Mische!* ... Shuffle! Cut then! ... Three cards put down there, four down there... Now, pretty cards ... our future fate come tell us... I a youthful lover behold ...' Now I had the same droning roar in my neck as I'd had thirty-six hours before, but so much more pleasant, more restrained, more stimulating. Champagne in the veins in the neck. Even so I kept an eye on the bachelor and when he turned left at the canal I hurried on twice as quickly after him. '*Mische! Mische!*'

At the corner I found that I had almost caught him up, he had stopped to pass a few minutes of his free day gazing at the window of a tobacconist's shop. He looked round at me, a sixth sense was it, in that nondescript skull or perhaps he'd heard the quick patter of my footsteps, or maybe he'd stolen something and he was looking round at everyone. I went on uncertainly towards him. He looked round for the second time and I thought I saw him laughing. He had rather impish eyes (naturally impish, not just from the laughing) in a red, freckled face. I noticed these details a little later when I barred his way, near the bridge. There weren't many others walking along the street at that hour. On the canal two skippers were standing on their barges, only their heads visible above the stone embankment—it was a very low tide. On the other side of the canal everything was white and warm yellow from the strong sunlight. But we were in a blue shadow.

'Why are you laughing at me?'

He took a startled step backwards. 'I'm not laughing at you.'

'Yes you did, you looked round and laughed at me.'

'You're making a mistake.' Under the impish eyes a chin was thrust forward. 'I'd take it easy if I were you.' As a measure of preparedness he put on his hat, but low on his forehead, hiding the impish eyes. When I saw them they weren't impish any more. My first punch missed for some reason or other. I would have done better with the next one if a blue figure hadn't emerged from a shop doorway somewhere behind me.

'Now then, gentlemen.'

With a wave of his hand the policeman signalled the small crowd of inquisitive passers-by to move on. The bachelor took off his hat again. I said:

'This fellow was laughing at me, officer. I don't have to take that from anyone.'

'That's not true,' the bachelor said, 'I didn't even see him, and if I want to, I can laugh wherever I like. Maybe I thought of something funny. This man's off his head, or there's something wrong with him. Look at him, his eyes are all red.'

'I'm not going to be laughed at,' I said in the playfully pompous tone students adopt to intimidate members of the police force. 'My name is Rieske, I'm judge Rieske's son, I'm not going to be laughed at by some...'

283

'Have you been drinking?' the policeman asked, standing in front of me and laying his hand politely on my shoulder. With the other hand he discreetly directed my opponent to leave us. When I shook my head, the policeman said sharply:

'You have been drinking, I can smell it. You had better keep walking, or perhaps I ought to take you home.'

'I'm not going to be laughed at by anyone, not even by a judge,' I said peevishly, and I turned round to go after the bachelor. As I turned I happened to glance at the policeman's face, which I had avoided looking at up till then with the instinctive cunning drunks have in not exposing themselves to too many impressions at the same time. He had Trix's eyes. His eyes were as like Trix's eyes as a man's eyes can be like a woman's. He could have been her brother or a cousin. He was about forty, but his thin face was young and smooth-skinned. I put out my hand, stuttering:

'What ... what's your name?'

'Now, Mijnheer, you just go home, that's enough,' he said good-humouredly, again casually waving on a small group of spectators.

'Yes, I have been drinking,' I said, 'I don't want to tell lies, I'm not like that. But something dreadful has happened to me, and I don't understand it...'

I was talking to myself. The policeman walked off briskly, leaving me there, though he must have looked back once or twice. I went on towards the broad curved surface of the bridge. '*Mische! Mische! ... Wie schön das ist die Karten zu fragen*', with that delightful double accent, or whatever it's called, at '*fragen*', the same as the opening of the minuet by Boccherini that my mother used to play ... 'and I don't understand it', and no one could understand it, but not because death was beyond understanding. It was this particular death and what it meant to me. Between me and this death there was a gaping emptiness and this emptiness was filled with the unreasonable sunlight of a late summer's day. The night would be worse, I was sure of that. But I could worry about the night later. How much fiercer this sunlight was than could be reasonably expected of sunlight. That damned ball up in the sky acted as if nothing at all had happened, didn't give a sign, it was just as carefree and gay as that tune in my head, that was occasionally interrupted by Carmen's premonition.

In the middle of the bridge, all alone in the world, like a statue, I asked myself what should I do, what could I do. I realized I was confused and hopeless, but I couldn't do what my confusion and hopelessness demanded of me, I couldn't sink into the cobblestones I was standing on, or dissolve into the air around me. Eat. The warm glow of the gin was wearing off, but one thought of Trix, or a bachelor, could get me into another fight. In my overcoat pocket I found a stale sandwich that I chewed on as I went back and forward over the arched bridge. I was greeted a few times, a policeman with a moustache observed me briefly and strode on, children stopped to watch me. Yes. I did it. *'Ja, ich hab sie getötet! Ach, Carmen! Du mein angebetet Leben!'* Yes, children, look at me, I'm the guilty one, I'm the murderer because I should have stayed with her, I should have been kind to her as if she was a little child.

At the corner of one of the streets leading on to the wide, square-like expanse of the bridge, three men were standing by a kerbstone post that slanted sideways. They were talking earnestly, cheerfully, with only a partial regard for logic. They were peacefully enjoying the sunshine. Except one of them, who kept walking away, laughing and gesturing. He was the humorist of the three. His companions knew he would come back, and he did, each time, until finally he left them and went off down the side street, his head bowed as if an unpleasant thought had occurred to him. After that a scruffy little girl came and stared at me. Her nose was running and she had a red rash on her face. I smiled at her and said: 'I've eaten up all my bread', then she frowned thoughtfully but tearfully and ran away . . . There was once a brown ball that I gave back against all dictates of honour and conscience, and now

285

it was lying somewhere in the gutter, torn into four or five pieces, and you could see all the inside of it, even the hard rubber nipple, the plug where it was welded, the navel...

If I went back to see the aunt—and I would, after the two funerals—other bachelors would cross my path and I would probably end up in gaol. Nevertheless, I began to regard the aunt more and more as the only means that would make it possible for me to go on living. To start with, I would make her tell me everything about Trix, all the details that only women know. I'd be able to touch and hold the photos, souvenirs, letters, everything, and in exchange I would believe in the Spirit and let her embrace me or whatever else she might want to do. She was the only living reminder I had of Trix. The two of us together would get the better of the bachelors. I'd go and see her, I'd imagine to myself that Trix was still alive, and then I'd make her tell me all over again, just as she had an hour ago, she'd have to repeat it every time, like a ritual, with a cup of gin to dull the pain. That was something to live for, not a very noble aspiration, not an example likely to be widely followed, but still, genuine and significant, and perhaps the only chance of gradually coming to realize not why she was dead—I knew why, I could almost approve of the reasons—but that she had died, that she was dead. Suddenly I became aware that while I had been thinking of the aunt, a new practical plan had taken shape in my mind. I walked off the bridge, past the two men engrossed in their discussion, past the kerbside post that slanted sideways, and into the street the discouraged humorist had taken.

This street led to a rather exclusive part of the town extending to the square with the gothic building I had ridden past with my mother the day my life began, sitting proudly next to the coachman who couldn't hit any flies with his whip. I took long strides, marching the way Cuperus used to. Mirrored in the high, lifeless window panes, my face was pale as a corpse, haggard, like the face of a tramp resolutely on his way to fulfil the one obligation he had to fulfil every year, perhaps to put his signature on some stupid document. Now and then my right hand started to tremble again. In a short street that ended in a mass of golden foliage I read the names on the doorways until I stopped at the one inscribed 'Caspers'. No initials, only the name. It betokened a certain austerity which I found not unpleasing.

A dried-up, old manservant answered my knock, tilting his head doubtfully when I asked whether his master was at home, but he appeared willing to take my card, carrying it in the palm of his hand as if weighing it. In two minutes he returned and requested me to follow him upstairs. One of the doors was wide open, and Mijnheer Caspers was in that room. To gloss over the informality of the occasion he let a good-natured expression spread over his wrinkled face.

Coatless, wearing a Norfolk jacket and slippers and sitting in a deep armchair, he didn't give the impression that my visit mightn't be convenient for him. As soon as he saw me at the doorway, he got up to shake hands. He conveyed his condolences and invited me to sit down in a chair opposite and a little higher than his own. I noticed at the side of his chair a heap of obviously read-through newspapers, representing, no doubt, part of his day's work. The room was fairly simply furnished. This youthful, not so young, banker was too often away on business to be bothered with interior decoration. I had once summed him up as 'slick', and that may have been a correct description of him as director of an old-established banking institution, but the only outward indication of this quality was in the shrewd, steady, dull-brown eyes. The sharp lines by the mouth suggested refinement and sincerity and indolence and the wisdom of much experience, characteristics often displayed by burgomasters of provincial towns. He carried himself youthfully. I imagine that his infatuation with my mother had not lasted as long as the romantic devotion of any of the five or six others I remembered from my childhood. But they had always remained on the best of terms.

He stretched out his legs and looked at me expectantly: 'And what can I do for you, Nol?'

'No, Mijnheer Caspers, it's not a matter of help. I only came to ...'

'You don't mind me calling you "Nol"?' he asked with an amiable glint in his eyes.

'Not a bit... I only came ... I only wanted to tell you that Trix Cuperus committed suicide this morning.'

For a second or so he looked at me intently, apparently not very affected by the sudden news, and then there was a complete change in him. Slowly he closed his eyes, he sank back into the deep, comfortable armchair. His face was calm and relaxed. The distinguished, sympathetic lines around the mouth were more pronounced now. He reclined as if absorbed in solitary meditation, contemplating an agonizing tragedy. His calmness had a wholesome effect on me. I leant back in my chair too, and sat watching his face, my attention divided between him, the buzzing in my head, and a succession of not very profound reflections, including the thought that he was conducting himself with far more dignity than I had shown in the kitchen with the aunt when she broke the news to me. But it was the calm, relaxed atmosphere that I was aware of more than anything else. This was the first relief I had felt since the blow of how many hours ago. If he stayed sitting like that I could get up after a while and tiptoe away. Finally, he looked up, straight into my eyes, immediately, unhesitatingly, as if he had known, without seeing, where my eyes were.

'So it was you,' he said quietly, 'and there was nothing I could do to help.'

It sounded like a Delphic oracle. It sounded far more solemn than the words the howling Pythias on their tripods must have shrieked. I felt slightly irritated.

'If you mean that I was the one Trix Cuperus was in love with and that I loved her, then, yes. But what could you have done?'

'Everything,' he said, and sat up with a jerk, bending sideways to the left to straighten the pile of newspapers next to his chair, his last movement for a long while, for he spoke without gestures. 'I did do something ... Do you know the whole story?'

'Yes, I know that you... that you saw she was in love with someone else.'

'Intuition.'

'Then you found out the truth about Vellinga, but that didn't make any difference, and you offered to get her work abroad, but that wouldn't have been any use because she didn't speak any other language.... I don't know ...'

'Besides, I told Vellinga the truth to his face. She knew that, and it could have given her a reason to finish with him. But it didn't help. Then I managed to make it impossible for her to sleep at the restaurant, to protect her from...'

'From Sjoerd Stienstra and others like him. Only it was too late.'

'Not only that. I had to be a little underhand about it,' Caspers said musingly. 'I'm certainly not praising myself. All I could do was to warn the owner of the restaurant that the police could take action. Not that I believed she was having men up to her room, but everyone assumed she was, and, of course, it was difficult to prove she wasn't. If Vellinga, as her friend, to put it like that, was the only one, that wasn't so bad, it could be overlooked. But if there were others as well, then it was a different matter altogether. But she didn't know all this. At my suggestion the owner told her there was a new labour regulation and only girls who hadn't any accommodation locally were allowed to sleep in the restaurant. So she couldn't be offended. As it happened, the other girls—there were only two or three of them, it was in the winter—came from quite a distance away ... outside the town.'

'I can't really admire what you did for her, Mijnheer Caspers. In your place I would feel myself rather guilty. You took advantage of the situation, yourself.' I had intended to say that in any case.

'Guilty?' He shook his head slowly. 'I was in love with her, or, more exactly, I would have loved her more than I could ever have loved any other woman if I hadn't felt that coolness that could only mean there was someone else. I knew she despised Vellinga. It never occurred to me that it might be you, or I'd have left no stone unturned until I had brought you two together. I'd have done anything for her, she deserved it. She had character, so damned proud, but modest too. None of that female vanity. My God, what a woman! ... She would have got on all right in England, even though she didn't speak a word of the language. They appreciate that sort of temperament there. She was crude and common at times, and she didn't always express herself well, but given a chance she'd have soon learnt all the social graces. Any other girl in those circumstances would have been much worse. In spite of everything she kept her independence. But Vellinga managed to kill her.'

'Vellinga said he loved her, too.'

Caspers coughed behind his hand. 'The difference is that I didn't stoop to the same low methods, if that's what is at the back of your mind. But let's not start abusing each other, Nol. When I saw Vellinga was running after her again I talked it over with a couple of friends to see if we could do anything. Going about with Vellinga wasn't really so serious, but with her working at the restaurant it caused a hell of a lot of talk. Quite apart from my affection for her, I felt an obligation to her father's memory. I'd never been a personal friend of his, as Vellinga was in a way, but he was someone out of the ordinary, and so was she. These friends of mine I spoke to felt the same as I did, but they were not so inclined to do anything. The Stienstra episode didn't make a very good impression either—I had to be honest and tell them that too, though I swore them to secrecy. Nothing ever leaked out, they're completely trustworthy, from very old local families. They wouldn't talk, in fact they don't talk about anything much. What could we do? Approach Vellinga, that was all, and he's a rotter even if he has one or two good points.... Do you know about the whole business, and that I went to see Alice de Rato, our divine *prima donna?'*

'Yes. As I understand it there were three possibilities: Vellinga's own version, and that more or less excuses him for anything that happened later. Then Alice de Rato's opinion that it was a bluff. Finally, the sleeping-powder theory. What do you think yourself?'

'In a court of law I'd say I didn't know. Between you and me, the sleeping-powder. That's the sort of thing he would do. That idea of de Rato's is far too subtle.'

'Perhaps you're saying that because you dislike him?'

Caspers had to smile. 'I certainly dislike him. But he isn't really so intelligent. You can be fairly sure it was a sleeping-powder. He must have read something like that in a cheap novel or in his own newspaper.... Once I spent an evening drinking with her, and she wasn't the slightest bit sleepy.... Or we could have found her work in another town. But would that have helped? We couldn't have her put under care of a guardian or have the police keep an eye on her, that would just go all wrong. I thought for a while of trying to arrange for her to have a small income, not enough to live on, but enough so she could be in a more independent position as far as men were concerned. We could have managed a thousand guilders a year for two or three years. But I gave up the idea. She would have refused it, and if she hadn't, she would have felt she was being kept, and that would only have pulled her farther down than she was already. And as for Vellinga, there was no definite proof that he'd doped her or deceived her. A couple of my friends were lawyers ... '

'Lawyers, aha,' I said, smiling for the first time in that sunny room.

'We decided to wait and see what sort of a show she put up over the next few months. But tell me, Nol, how did it all happen that she killed herself? Wasn't there any way of stopping it? You must have seen her in the last few days, though ... of course, your mother's death ... '

'I saw her for the last time at half past eleven yesterday evening. If I'd stayed with her she would still alive. I was stupid enough not to follow the example of Vellinga and Stienstra and yourself. I'm not saying that to be sarcastic.'

He closed his eyes again and shook his head. 'Yes, she'd been through so much. Will I go on, or is it embarrassing or too painful?'

'No, go on. I want to hear everything. But I would like to say that in my opinion you shouldn't feel too guilty, even though you were a link in the chain that dragged her ...'

He opened his eyes and looked at me as if he wanted to reassure himself that I wasn't going to continue my remarks. 'So we waited ... till we heard the latest rumours. She was so open and indifferent about everything, regal almost, if it hadn't been for the bitterness behind it all, and so the news soon got around. Her new consort was far from regal. That loud-mouthed Stienstra wasn't either, but at least he was young. You remember our friend Dijkhuizen, don't you?'

'Yes, I know about that too,' I said, shrivelling up inside, for now I felt the impact of that passage in her letter that I hadn't grasped the full meaning of when I read it in the kitchen, dazed and sick with grief, 'but not the details.'

'Can I offer you a cup of coffee, or a drink?'

'No thanks.'

'Well, there isn't much to tell,' he said, and he glanced quickly at my face. 'Dijkhuizen is an old roué, though he seems to have reformed again. It comes and goes with him, he won't change probably till he's sixty, then he'll crack up. He used to come to the Garden restaurant quite often and he'd spend the evening drinking with a few others and they'd invite Trix to join them. There was never anything improper, as far as I know she never let them take any liberties. But apparently a couple of nights Dijkhuizen managed to ... My God, Nol, you look ill. I won't say any more.'

'No, don't stop,' I said hoarsely. I thought of telling him I was going to call on Dijkhuizen too, but realized he would try and persuade me not to.

'He babbled about it himself when he was drunk. He said she was a cat, she'd teased him and made him jump through hoops. What he meant by that I don't know, maybe something to do with his religious convictions.'

'You aren't religious yourself?'

'Only in public. But don't go saying that to anyone else. If my accountant hears that he'll have a stroke.... I find it anything but pleasant to have to associate with men like that and accept them as equals. There aren't many here you really could call gentlemen. Frankly that's one of the reasons why I'm so often away. In England you meet them everywhere. On the Continent you hear these sneers about hypocrisy, but they don't understand anything on the Continent, or maybe they understand too much.... It's rather strange that so many older men played a part in Trix's life. Dijkhuizen could have easily been her father, and Wubbo and myself ... well, nearly ...'

'Yes, it is strange.'

When I stood up, he jumped out of his chair and walked with me to the door where he reached out a long arm to press the bell set in the wall next to it. Standing in the doorway he shook my hand, and the distinguished lines at the sides of his mouth again took precedence over the shrewd thoughtful eyes.

'What I said about Vellinga won't go any farther, will it? I mean you won't say you heard it from me? I've told him enough unpleasant truths to his face, and if we were living in another age or in another country probably I'd have challenged him to a duel.... But behind his back ...'

I promised, I nodded when he invited me to drop in whenever I wanted to see him, and then I was shown out by the old man-servant.

In the street I felt sober and clear-headed. The roaring and buzzing in time with '*Mische! Mische!*' was hardly noticeable, and

I could see now how well armoured the bachelors were against any attack on their morals when they were cornered in confidential talks. Caspers might be ten times more refined and intelligent and sensitive than Vellinga, but fundamentally he was of the same slippery sort, reeling off glib excuses for what he had done, though it could be said for him that he had preserved a certain decency. As I marched back towards the bridge it occurred to me that both Vellinga and Caspers had been willing to see me and talk to me only because of their memories of my mother, and because my father was a judge and Chris was a lawyer and I was a medical student. No admissions and regrets, no high-minded sympathy if I'd been some petty clerk who would have to knock the man-servant out of the way before he could interrupt the stately banker's statistic-studded morning rest.

Near the bridge it burst loose, not inside me, not in my stomach or in my head, but outside me. I could see everything in a normal perspective, but the burning sun seemed to be conjuring up a shimmering white vacuum in front of me, a white column of fire that advanced belligerently with me, not against enemies, but onwards to the next emptiness and the next and the next. Each time a foot touched or penetrated these voids there came a small explosion and then it was the street. An approaching cyclist swayed through voids I hadn't reached yet and passed close to me, bowing his head, vaguely smiling. It was an old schoolfriend, pedalling furiously over the bridge and probably thinking of my dead mother. I was walking and I wasn't even thinking of Trix. I wasn't able any more to believe she was dead. During the talk with Caspers I hadn't believed it for a single moment. But I knew that this refusal to accept a fact wouldn't help me to confront a situation I had to contend with. For within it were these voids created by a gigantic natural catastrophe completely unrelated to the sun. To stop or to hesitate was to remain enclosed in one of these globes of emptiness and the emptiness would become despair, destroying body and soul. These terrors floating towards me were the configuration of time, time unleashed, let loose by the mighty hand of undying love that I had completely trusted in, and now I quailed at the cruel, careless revenge it was taking. I knew, in the same way as I could understand an abstract, impersonal concept, that my life was ruined, that from now on I would be able to continue to exist only by resorting to eccentric, dangerous, or grotesque expedients such as Trix's aunt, a death's-head filled with quivering flesh and flecked with green arsenic stains, but still, a source of consolation, a powerful ally to whom I would flee this evening when I couldn't stand sitting at home any longer, hurrying to her with a bottle of gin under my arm, because I didn't want to hang myself or drown myself. But for the time being it was simply a question of living from second to second, from cobblestone to cobblestone, straight through softly exploding voids, in time with the beating of my heart and always that tune, '*Mische! Mische!*'—it was work that demanded no small measure of skill. With my teeth clenched I finished my rush to the end of the harrowing bridge where couples dawdled in the evening and cigarette-ends glowed and burned out at the feet of giggling girls. On the other side of the canal, in the shadow, everything was placid and real again. I looked round and saw a tawdry tableau of streets and buildings. It was twenty to twelve.

20

There were a few people standing at the counter being attended to by an oldish man with a big green pencil behind his ear. Employees of lesser standing hurried along the corridor, workmen, a cub reporter, and the like, and in the room behind the counter others were busy with whatever they were doing. The black-faced urchin came singing down the stairs, walked with a package under his arm to the door, silently he passed his betters, then turned back, hanging his head as if he had forgotten something. For minutes his tired footsteps could be heard going up flight after flight of stairs, but then it was my turn at the counter.

'I believe,' I said to the man with the big green pencil, 'that Mijnheer Vellinga is out of town. I have some urgent news for him and I would like to have his address. Or I could give you the telegram and the money for it and a tip for the messenger to send it off. I haven't time myself to go to the post office. My name is Rieske, I'm the judge's son.'

Obviously he was debating with himself whether he should convey his condolences. But, after all, he had a green pencil behind his ear, so he restricted himself to the matter in hand.

'You can dictate telegrams over the phone now, but we'll send it for you, Mijnheer Rieske, if you wish. Mijnheer Vellinga is staying at the Victoria Hotel in Amsterdam in case you might want to get in touch with him by phone. He'll be there two or three days and then he's going on to somewhere else, but mail and telegrams will be forwarded. ... Do you want to dictate it to me ?'

The green pencil was poised over the pad and I started to dictate, slowly and as loudly as I could.

'Mijnheer Wubbo Vellinga—you have the address yourself— Trix — T. R. I. X. — Cuperus — Cuperus with a C — died this morning stop suicide stop Nol Rieske R. I. E. S. K. E. address ...'

It was much quieter now in the corridor, heads must have been turning to look at me. I heard the shuffle of footsteps and a fat girl with glasses appeared for a moment behind the counter. There was a chorus of coughing and mumbling.

'Fine,' I said, when I saw the man staring with a deeply creased forehead at the sheet of note-paper. 'But I see now that it's actually more of a personal telegram than a business telegram. Perhaps you'd rather I phoned it through myself?' In the corridor and in the office behind the counter the silence was complete.

'Just as you like,' the man said, looking at me uncertainly, then immediately lowering his eyes. 'It is more a private telegram ... but ...'

'I don't want you to get into trouble with Mijnheer Vellinga,' I said loudly. 'It's better to handle this matter discreetly, don't you agree? Well, thank you for your trouble. Good morning, gentlemen.'

I telephoned from a tobacconist's shop four doors along from the narrow lane. A female with a high-pitched, squeaking voice came on the line to take the telegram. She sounded pompous, it was probably the first time in W ... that a telegram had been phoned through.... When she had finished noting it I asked her if the wording was permissible. Yes, of course. Why did I think it wouldn't be? I said that it was a rather special telegram, and I didn't know the regulations that might apply in such cases. But no, it was quite in order. I said that some telegrams could be refused and she promptly answered: Oh yes, Mijnheer, we can't send immoral telegrams or anything criminal. Criminal, I asked, in what way? She began to giggle and tried to explain to me that telegrams with plans for a murder couldn't be accepted, of course. I said that that was understandable. I would leave it to her to decide, but I did think it was advisable that she should ask the postmaster. Yes, she would do that. While I was consulting the telephone directory again under the watchful eye of the tobacconist, who hadn't missed a word, I reflected that I'd put the journalists, the workmen, the message boys, the telephonists, the postmaster and no doubt his family, and the shopkeepers all in the picture, and that would do to begin with. Then I phoned my father to tell him that I wouldn't be home till later in the afternoon, then Sjoerd Stienstra to say I wished to have a talk with him as soon as possible (he suggested that I should come at once as he had some important business to attend to), and finally Dijkhuizen, who, so his housekeeper informed me, would be back home at any minute and would certainly be able to see me. My name worked wonders.

When I was paying the tobacconist I was suddenly frightened—frightened to leave his shop and go out into the street. I was half-way through it all, but the whole business was going too quickly. I probably should never have yielded to the temptation of the telephone that the telegram for Vellinga had exposed me to. It was so nice and warm in the shop, they had the stove on already as if there wasn't any October sun at all. I looked at the tobacconist's face, he was a quiet man, bald, and his ear-lobes were large and coarse.

'Don't you feel well, Mijnheer?'

'Not too well. Someone died, you see.'

'That's always upsetting.'

I asked for a packet of cigarettes. As he passed it to me I noticed bars of chocolate somewhere and I bought two. I lit a cigarette and chewed on one of the bars of chocolate. But I still hadn't conquered my fear. I was sweating from fear and it was unbearably hot in the shop as if the tobacconist was determined not to keep out the October chill, but to vie with the bright October sun. I took a deep draw on the cigarette while the bald tobacconist observed me approvingly. There was something wrong with Trix. By Christ, there was something wrong with Trix. I realized it now, suddenly. She was in danger, maybe she could still be saved. My legs were hollow and empty, my heart thrust itself noisily up into my throat. I'd have to do something, by God, I'd have to turn off halfway through all this into an unfamiliar by-way to go and save her. But how? ... I leaned forward, dizzy, weighed down by the merciless pressure of my jolting, throbbing heart. I prayed: 'Oh God, let me find a way to help her. If she's dead wake her up again....' My hands squeezing my stomach, and swaying and trembling, I repeated this prayer once, twice, while the tobacconist must have been waiting for the right moment to rush to my side. With insight gained from long years of shopkeeping, he wouldn't be over-hasty and he wouldn't offer glasses of water without being asked first. That might be taken for an insult. Probably he expected miracles from his cigarettes, as a palliative after a trifling emotional disturbance. Repeating my prayer with every ounce of strength, I suddenly realized I was looking at the telephone. My thoughts were channelled to a new idea.

'Would you,' I whispered to the tobacconist, 'be good enough to make a phone call for me?'

'Certainly, Mijnheer.'

'Doctor Lammers. It concerns a case of poisoning, a girl who has been very badly treated ... Yes, a girl.... Ask the doctor if she's really dead. Her name is Trix Cuperus.'

The tobacconist found the number in the directory. 'Hullo ... Doctor Lammers ... The doctor isn't there? ... A moment ... The doctor isn't there, Mijnheer,' he whispered, covering the mouthpiece with his hand.

'Well ... ask his wife then, she ... she'll know,' I stammered, crushing my cigarette in an ash-tray. I was feeling sick.

'Could I speak to Mevrouw Lammers,' then to me, 'Trix Cuperus, you said, is that right?'

'Yes, Trix Cuperus. She committed suicide. Poisoning.'

'Oh, dreadful, Mijnheer.'

'But it wasn't her fault. I know the ones who are to blame. I know them.'

'You don't say, Mijnheer.... Yes, hullo, Mevrouw Lammers? Yes, Mevrouw. There's a young man in the shop, it's Adema, the tobacconist, speaking. He's in a bad way.... No, no, the doctor doesn't need to come. He just wants to know if a certain Trix Cuperus, who committed suicide, is really dead.... You can't? ...

But, perhaps you could make an exception just this once, after all you understand the feelings ...'

'Christ Almighty,' I gasped, and when I stepped towards him the tobacconist quickly handed me the telephone. 'Hullo, Nol Rieske speaking, the judge's son. I would like to know whether Trix Cuperus is dead or not.'

'I'm not sure if I can tell you, Mijnheer,' said a nasal, rather timorous voice.

'I'm her fiancé. Her aunt told me this morning that she was dead, but I want to be sure. As far as I know there's no question here of professional secrecy. I'm a medical student myself, your husband knows me.'

'Why don't you go to Juffrouw Cuperus's house?'

'Because I have reason to be suspicious. I can't get into her room. ... For God's sake, tell me whether it's true or not.'

A long silence, and then the voice was apologetic: 'May I offer my sympathy, Mijnheer Rieske ...'

'You mean for my mother?'

'Yes ... your mother, as well as ...' The voice faded away like a sigh. She must have hung up and run off to her cosy sitting-room, to her children if she had any, because all of a sudden she couldn't understand what death meant.

'Dreadful woman,' I growled, paying the tobacconist again. I was all the more annoyed because the docter's wife could conclude from what I'd said that I suspected the aunt. I had suspected the aunt but a whining woman like her didn't have to follow my example.

'Not the sort of wife a doctor should have,' the tobacconist murmured sympathetically. He looked at me, waiting to hear what I would say next.

'Yes, she's dead,' I sighed, shrugging my shoulder. 'There's nothing we can do about it. She killed herself because she couldn't go on living. Do you know Mijnheer Vellinga ... from the newspaper?'

'No, Mijnheer,' the tobacconist said, his eyes wide open. I lit a cigarette. 'He'll have this on his conscience.'

'Really, Mijnheer ...?'

'I 'm sorry to have to say it, but it's true. Do you ever go to the restaurant in the Garden? You ask them there. You can understand that as her fiancé I feel rather badly about it.'

'Naturally, naturally.... Are you all right now, Mijnheer?'

Yes, he wanted to get rid of me as quickly as possible so he could go and tell his wife.

'Oh, I'm fine now,' I nodded, and after thanking him I left.

Now I blessed this sunny October day, this last remnant of the summer. Not for its warmth, not for its frivolous gladness, but for its coolness, where the shadows spread. The hellfire heat of the tobacconist's shop was behind me. A purgatory, perhaps, on the way to the paradise of certainty, for now at least I knew that Trix was dead. The hundred million to one chance that she wasn't had only a purely academic significance. I could resign myself to the reality of it, and I was, in fact, in a resigned, submissive mood as I hurried on to my appointment with Sjoerd Stienstra at his private address not much farther along the side of the same canal, a dozen doors past the hairdresser's with 'Koko for the hair', where one evening long ago I had watched a respectable young girl sitting rigidly in a slowly revolving chair. Actually it was Caspers I was thinking about more than Stienstra. I suddenly wanted to be sitting with him again, not because Caspers himself appealed to me but because he offered the prospect of friendly, sympathetic conversation that would be impossible with any of the others. Those others wouldn't ease my loneliness, with them it would be the same as talking to the tobacconist... I imagined a continuation of our discussion.... Caspers might say: 'These are things, Nol, beyond the grasp of the human mind. It's easy to see why people believe in God.' I: 'I believe in God, but He's left me in the lurch. She's dead, and He can bring her back to life, He has the power to do that.' Caspers: 'That's relatively true, but you mustn't take it all

too literally. He can bring her to life again in your imagination.'
I: 'That's deceit, a cheap swindle. By living in my imagination she
would only prove she was dead. It's all the wrong way round.'
Caspers: 'On the contrary. You know, if I believed in God I'd
trust Him implicitly, exclusively. But there's another possibility,
Nol. You might meet someone who would be transformed into
Trix for you.' I: 'Someone who reminded me of her, or looked
like her.... Yes, it's a possibility, but I couldn't have danced with
anyone else in the Garden when I was a little boy, that's how
everything started.' Caspers: 'You could have danced with a
hundred other girls in the Garden. It all depends on yourself.'
I: 'You're taking a philosophic viewpoint. But if it hadn't been
for Trix, if she hadn't been there, I wouldn't have wanted to
dance. Or at least, I wouldn't have been aware of it. And I've
never had anything to do with those other girls.' Caspers: 'I was
forgetting that you're studying medicine. An empiric approach...
Well, I've nothing against that. But you have to consider possible
alternatives, and, if I may say so, that is the attitude a doctor must
always adopt. As a banker I have to do that myself, and it's simply
amazing sometimes, all those combination of figures. It could be,
perhaps, that numbers are divinely inspired.' I: 'If God has any
pity on me, He'll let me die soon, not so I can meet her again, but
so I won't have to feel this grief any more. No one could ever
suffer an agony of grief like this, not even Christ on the cross, for
His Father was waiting for him, and mourners wept at His feet.
I can't even weep for her, even that consolation is denied me,
Mijnheer Caspers.' Caspers, after a long silence: 'There are ways
of softening the pain of grief. In six months you'll find life
liveable again, with a wound that's starting to heal, or maybe not
starting to heal, and you'll have lived through those six months,
too. You're still so very young, Nol. But promise me one thing.'
I: 'Yes, what's that?' Caspers: 'Never think of her with contempt.'
I: 'Why would I do that?' Caspers, hastily, confused, and fading
away: 'Because that can be one of the ways of softening the pain.'

Striding along as I had learnt from my teacher, I had walked past Sjoerd Stienstra's house. Over on the other side of the canal Dijkhuizen would probably be waiting for me. I'd have to retrace my steps. But what for? If I did, charging along like a soldier to the attack, I'd be half an hour farther on, and then I'd be standing again at the edge of that abyss of emptiness where blinding shafts of fire, treacherous traps, blocked my way to the other side. I saw, felt, this abyss as distinctly as I had seen and felt that little crater I'd stood at years before, breathlessly looking down, holding tight to a big rock. If I walked round first for a couple of hours I'd gain time. By then the sun would have passed its zenith, and in the early evening I could perhaps call on the remaining bachelors and carry on from where I'd left off. Or I could call on them late in the evening if I didn't want to go and see the aunt.

Of course, all sorts of things could happen if I went back now to see Stienstra, who would be getting impatient to keep the business appointment he had so he could arrange some crooked deal. It was said he didn't recognize his parents any more since he had left the tumbledown house they lived in on the outskirts of the town. He'd worked himself up by his own efforts to what he was now, and he was barely thirty. He was one of the 'coming young men' of W..., he would probably take Vellinga's place as our 'master of ceremonies', though he wasn't so festively inclined as Vellinga. Every minute was money for him, and at this very moment he must be stamping up and down. I would meet him at the bottom of the stairs as he was leaving, an expression of polite haste on his sleek face, a pimp's face. I would say: 'I came to tell you that Juffrouw Cuperus has committed suicide.' 'Who? What? Committed suicide? What Juffrouw Cuperus?' And then I'd say: 'Trix Cuperus, the daughter of the late Henri Cuperus, the conductor.' Then he would say: 'Oh, her, that tart, the waitress. Did she, now?' And he would observe me suspiciously, taking a closer look at my face even though he was in a hurry. And I would say: 'What do you think about it, Mijnheer Stienstra?' And he still wouldn't understand why I had come to see him, and he would get angry and snarl that it was nothing to do with him and what the bloody hell did I think I was doing poking my nose into his private business, wasting his time when he had an appointment at the meat market. And then I would say that I was poking my nose into his private business because it was something that should never have been any business of his at all, and that I considered him ill-mannered and impertinent, a vulgar lout who spoke of a dead girl as a 'tart', and swore at other people, and I didn't like the look of him, and that he should be battered to death with a hammer. I'd keep it up until he lost his temper and threatened me with his fists. Then the decisive moment. We could fight on the stairs and I could deliver myself from my grief by the force and the fury of the blows I'd rain on him. Or I could say: 'Well, come outside', and leave the door open behind me, or I could just say nothing and shut the door behind me, and in both cases I'd stand waiting for him to come out. And he wouldn't come. For ten minutes I'd walk back and forward in front of the house while he watched me from behind the curtain of his room on the first floor. Meanwhile, at the market, fresh carcasses, great lumps of blood-red meat, and bones, and fat, and offal would be slipping through his fingers, hundreds and thousands of guilders slipping swiftly out of his reach, and when I'd finally got tired of waiting and had gone to the next corner, he still wouldn't come out because he'd arranged his deals by telephone as well as he could. But it wouldn't help, he'd be cheated or the clerk would get his message all wrong. He'd be wondering whether to call the police or not, and I would get the reputation of being a troublemaker and the whole town would know that Trix had been mixed up with him, and the gossip I'd started over Vellinga, which wasn't so pointless, would come to nothing—it would come to nothing anyway if the tobacconist circulated a too colourful description of my behaviour in his shop.

Dijkhuizen presented a rather more complicated case. I thought about him as I walked along the side of the moat, at the beginning of it, just past the reputedly historic, high, square tower and the surrounding cluster of small buildings. The moat reflected a peaceful blue sky without the glare of the sun. Shining directly above the brown-hued tree tops behind me to the left, the sun scorned these smooth, still waters. I didn't feel so very ill-disposed towards Dijkhuizen. Not only because he had been in love with my mother, who was in a coffin in the little white hospital not far ahead, but also because, apart from Vellinga, he was the last to play a role in Trix's life, and it was from his hands, as it were, that I had received Trix just before her death. Of course, I realized that the world would be a far better place if God did as I wished and exterminated the Dijkhuizens and all the others, including Caspers and his ilk, like noxious vermin. But God wouldn't do that, for He wouldn't know when to stop, and how could I be sure that at a given moment my turn wouldn't come too. There wasn't much sense in going to see Dijkhuizen. In his best church-going manner he would take refuge behind a smokescreen of piety and ask my forgiveness and suggest perhaps that we should pray together, and I would, for this prayer would mean five minutes more before I was alone again. But he'd understand no more than his predecessor. It was quite proper to pray for a whore, but it was unthinkable to become distressed about a whore, not even a 'fiancé' of one day went that far. All my contempt, all my subtle sarcasm, would be lost on him, and finally I'd burst out laughing hysterically like my mother when she couldn't stop, and Dijkhuizen, recovered from his fright and compassion, would spread it around that I was a little touched and anything but a good Christian, because I had laughed on the evening before my mother's funeral, and I spoke well of whores, and I raked up sins of the past, and I was disrespectful to my elders.

I stood still, I didn't want to go on any farther. This town, for all its faults, could boast of more pleasant parts than the street Dijkhuizen lived in and the canal Stienstra's window looked out on. I could make my way back along other streets and along the sides of other canals, till four o'clock or so, when the sun would, at last, feel sorry for me and sink down, yellow and tired. Then there was the evening with new, sly onslaughts of grief, then the anguish would become a frenzy. I'd yell and stamp, or throttle Stienstra, or go and see the aunt first because she would restrain me and talk me into believing in the Spirit and embrace me and kiss me. As long as I wasn't asleep—and when I did sleep how often would I toss and wake and what dreams would torment me? —as long as I was awake I had to devise some or other distraction every quarter of an hour so as to keep my despair at bay. A talk with my father could fill half an hour, certainly no more, unless he revealed an unexpected profundity of thought, which was, of course, always possible. But I could stop here for a few minutes. The hospital was behind me now and on the other side of the moat the shrubs and the trees on the sloping heights of the Garden draped in the colours that come with autumn each year. I could stop here for a few minutes, a last attempt to understand what no one understood.

It wasn't my own inevitable death that I couldn't understand, but the other deaths, Trix's death, my mother's death. Midway between the tiny room where the one was lying in her coffin and the place where the other had once danced water was flowing, slow and unruffled, or perhaps it wasn't even flowing, only moving imperceptibly. Anyone tall enough could wade across it. There were some ducks on the water, and falling leaves glided and spun through the air, and in the distance the figures of people walking over the wooden bridge. It was all inexplicable. There was no point of departure and no point of return and almost no point of continuity, an incoherence that passed and melted away, and it could be argued that death—I thought especially of Trix and my mother—was an impressive example of the more or less apathetic impermanence of all that exists. But this reflection was no more help than picking up one of the brass-brown leaves and

306

looking at it and then letting it flutter down to the ground again. Trix's death was altogether different. A leaf that I had been holding in my hand only a little while before, the sweetest, greenest thing I could ever hold, was now brown and withered. For a moment I thought I could fathom this out. There was a price to be paid, a pledge to be given, proof to be furnished of the ties that bound and had bound my heart, a proof demanded by harsh, inscrutable powers who were not disposed to trust tender smiles or tender words and tore love away to see whether the love was real. No, that wasn't it either, it was different again, deeper, more gentle, more cruel, and that meant I didn't understand death—almost perhaps, but not completely, and so not at all, and I never would be able to understand.

In front of me was the old park, a lonely baroque edifice, desecrated by pleasure-seekers, and yet, for years, a sacred place. I couldn't see the restaurant because the moat curved slightly. But I could see the iron railing and the weather-beaten pillars where that long narrow street ended. Once I had sat up on the driver's seat of a coach, like a little groom, listening to my mother and her friends behind me prattling and laughing and joggling their parasols. Then the entrance, and the park with its pathways rising to heights, scarcely conceivable for a child, that were reached by a climb past bird-cages and through bushes. Away up there the piled up stones formed a not very forbidding threshold to a small valley, and in that valley something happened to two children, and she was the only one to notice, and she saw it was an omen of what was to come. She couldn't warn me, for what happened there was the beginning of the incurable pain of the grief that was now all I had, the grief that I wouldn't be without, that I would cling to even if an angel, moved by some arrogant whim, thought to hack it out of me with a fiery sword. The tall trees had watched, the bandstand with the trumpeters and the other jesters had watched too, and the music had blared, and the éclairs were handed round. How many trees were there that I had never even looked at, and now in October they were black and damp and musty beneath their brass-tinted leaves, and I was sure I could smell their sickly, deathly smell from where I was standing. When the sun went down they would rustle and shake off drops of water. The birds would go to sleep, the pheasants, the peacock, and the goose. In the morning the dew would glisten on the rocks.

SIMON VESTDIJK

Simon Vestdijk was born in 1898 in the little Frisian town Harlingen. He studied medicine but only practised as a *locum tenens*
after having finished his studies. He did, however, make a trip
as a ship's surgeon to the former Dutch East Indies, but as soon
as possible he devoted himself completely to literature. He now
lives a retired life in the forest village of Doorn.

Vestdijk's exceptional and prolific talent got its chance in
the review *Forum* (1932-5). Until 1932 he had only published
some poems which did not really draw the attention: in the
Forum period, however, which was of great importance to the
whole of Dutch literature, Vestdijk soon impressed his readers
by both the high level and the quick rate at which he published
stories, essays, novels and poems.

In the thirty-odd years which have passed since his first book, a
flood of books by Vestdijk appeared and they are so many and
so varied that we must limit ourselves here to a summary survey.

The first long prose work which Vestdijk wrote has never
been published though one may consider this enormous manu-
script the basis of a great many of his so-called Dutch novels,
of which the 'Anton Wachter' series forms the bulk. This series
comprises eight volumes and was published between 1934 (the
third part, *Back to Ina Damman—Terug tot Ina Damman*, is considered by most critics as the apex of the series) and 1960 (the
eighth volume, *The Last Chance—De laatste kans*). The 'Anton
Wachter' books are strongly autobiographical, although written
in a detached tone. *Back to Ina Damman* is very important in
Vestdijk's *œuvre*, because it is based on a theme which recurs
time and again in his later work: that of the unfulfilled and un-
fulfillable love, Vestdijk's version of the '*ferne Geliebte*'.

The third 'Anton Wachter' book was the first novel published
by Vestdijk—but not the first one finished. Apart from the
unpublished giant novel, mentioned above, he had written

309

Mr Visser's Descent into Hell (Meneer Visser's Hellevaart). The 'Anton Wachter' novels are mostly marked by a serene atmosphere, or at least a detached way of writing. One could hardly say the same about *Mr Visser*. This book is a Bosch-like portrait of a domestic tyrant in a little town (easily recognized as Harlingen), and it is written in an experimental style which prompted many critics to suggest the influence of James Joyce, though nobody ever took the trouble to prove this thesis with facts. It may, in fact, very well be that the only relation to the Irish master will prove to be the fact that the whole story happens in the course of one day, and the fact that on the first page there is a quotation from *Ulysses*.

Some of the other Dutch novels we should mention are *Else Böhler, German Maid (Else Böhler, Duitsch dienstmeisje*, 1935), *The Doctor and the Little Harlot (De dokter en het lichte meisje*, 1951, a delightful piece of irony, set in an Amsterdam décor), *The Scandals (De schandalen*, 1953), *The Voyeur (De ziener*, 1959), *Miss Lot (Juffrouw Lot*, 1964), and the important *Victor Slingeland* trilogy, of which the first volume, *The Glistening Armour (Het glinsterend pantser*, 1956) marks a new stage in Vestdijk's contemporary novels, in which his writing became more relaxed though certainly not less involved.

A special position among the Dutch novels is held by *The Garden Where the Brass Band Played (De koperen tuin*, 1950), one of Vestdijk's major works.

Among the Dutch novels we could also have mentioned *Fré Bolderhey's Salvation (De redding van Fré Bolderhey*, 1948), because the setting is clearly Amsterdam. Since the background is not of any real importance, however, it would seem preferable to label this story of a schizophrenic boy as a 'fantastic novel', though this marking-off of dividing lines is not of great importance. *The Waiter and the Living (De kellner en de levenden*, 1949), however, can only be called 'fantasy', since the fact that the events which are told are *not* real is basic for the whole idea of the book.

It is the story of twelve persons who meet a symbolic personification of Christ and of the devil (in the shape of a waiter and a head-waiter) during a 'Last Judgment' at which they are present because of a mistake. In fact one might say they meet only themselves and become aware of the basic aspects of their own life.

In 1937 Vestdijk published a historical novel, *The Fifth Seal (Het vijfde zegel)*, a lucid evocation of the life and work of the painter El Greco, and in this field too he persevered. His incredible variety of historical subjects is shown in just a few of titles: Pre-homeric Greece in *Actaeon among the Stars (Aktaion onder de sterren,* 1941); early historical Greece in *The Maimed Apollo (De verminkte Apollo,* 1952); Magna Graecia in *The Hero of Temesa (De held van Temesa,* 1962). *The Latter Days of Pilate (De nadagen van Pilatus,* 1938) is mainly set in Rome, in the first century; *The Fire Worshippers (De vuuraanbidders,* 1947), has the Thirty Years' War as a background; *Rum Island (Rumeiland,* 1940) is set in eighteenth-century Jamaica. This last novel has been published in several countries, among them England (Calder, 1962). *The Philosopher and the Assassin (De filosoof en de sluipmoordenaar,* 1961) has Voltaire as a central figure. Several books deal with nineteenth-century Ireland.

The variety of subjects of Vestdijk's historical novels is not their most striking aspect, however. Even more surprising is the thorough documentation and the ability to give life to periods of history which are so basically different. It is as though Vestdijk feels a compulsive need to conquer all aspects of human life, present and past.

This compulsive need is also manifest—we must leave the subject of his novels unfinished, since we cannot even so much as mention the titles of all forty which have so far been published —in his many short stories (four volumes, all before 1947), and his essays. Apart from very important studies on literature (the volumes *Lyre and Lancet—Lier en lancet,* 1939; *The Polish Horseman —De Poolse ruiter,* 1946; *The Glossy Seed—De glanzende kiemcel,*

1950, on poetical creation), and several volumes of literary criticism, Vestdijk has published in recent years many books on music, ranging from criticism to theory. They include *The First and the Last* (*Het eerste en het laatste*, 1956), on musical aesthetics; *The Double Scales* (*De dubbele weegschaal*, 1959), on the same subject; *Gustav Mahler* (1960), on the structure of his symphonies.

Vestdijk has also written a book on the psychology of religion *The future of Religion* (*De toekomst der religie*, 1947), one on astrology *Astrology and Science* (*Astrologie en wetenschap*, 1949), and books with notes, philosophical dialogues, introductions, novels in letters with other writers, etc. etc.

One understands why Menno ter Braak, one of the most important essayists of the 'thirties in Holland, gave his essay on Vestdijk the title *The Devil's Magician* (*De duivelskunstenaar*). Readers and critics have, from the outset, been baffled by this volcanic eruption of books in all fields. Vestdijk's poetry, for instance, has not yet begun to have the serious attention of Dutch critics. And that is characteristic, since if Vestdijk had written nothing but his poetry, he should be called an important writer: almost twenty volumes in twenty-five years (from his début, *Poems—Verzen*, in 1932, until the libretto of a Pijper opera, *Merlin*, in 1957).